BOUND PATHS

COMPASS POINTS
BOOK THREE

JILLIAN WITT

BOUND PATHS

Published by Myth and Magic Book Club Publishing
Copyright © 2024 by Jillian Witt

Cover Artwork & Map by Holly Dunn
Developmental Editing by Rebecca Faith Editorial
Line Editing by Paper Poppy Editorial
Proofreading by Isla Elrick

N
W E
S
LAKE OF THE GODS
BURY
COMPASS LAKE
SANDRIN BAY
SANDRIN
MARCIL
LOCH

BOOK 2 RECAP

Bound Paths takes place after the events of *Compass Points* and *Tangled Power*. I know it's hard to remember all the details of books you may have read weeks or months ago, so I wanted to offer a summary.

Visit here for a recap of the events of *Compass Points*:
https://www.jillianwitt.com/compass-points-summary

Visit here for a recap of the events of *Tangled Power*:
https://www.jillianwitt.com/tangled-power-summary

I hope you enjoy the conclusion of Rose and Luc's story!

PROLOGUE

500 YEARS AGO

Cassandra, Lady of the Veil, greeted Zrak with teeth clenched and blade drawn. "It doesn't matter if you're a god on the continent. You can't just let yourself into my realm." He had spilled through the space between realms like he thought himself a thief in the night. Unfortunately for him, all those who ventured beyond the veil fell with an unceremonious splash into the cold and raging river.

It would have been too much to ask that he not make the crossing. Part of her wished he could be swept up by the river's current that dragged new arrivals to Veil Lake. She shook her head. Thinking of the lake only brought pain, followed quickly by anger—at the gods.

The gods of the continent traveling beyond the veil didn't have access to all of their magic, but it appeared Zrak's wind worked just well enough to shepherd him through the dangerous flow. She resented that he could make the swim across when so many spirits could not.

The unfairness of existence was something with which she was well acquainted.

Refocusing on the god before her, she took a moment to appreciate seeing him crawling from the river on hands and knees. His head tilted back to see her and the feline predators that formed a half-circle around him.

"You're unwelcome here," she continued, standing taller, her white-blonde hair falling to the middle of her back. The host of reddish brown veil cats echoed her words with a growl, baring their teeth at the intruder. The cat on her left was particularly angry—Zrak must have used Orion's latest trip to the continent to make the crossing. Cassandra's hand fell to scratch his head as another hiss tore from his throat. "Orion agrees. Justify yourself quickly, or I'll let him express his displeasure to you directly."

She'd met the gods of the continent before, and frankly, she'd been unimpressed.

This one was the worst of them. He always thought he knew best. Knees still on the ground, he sat back on his haunches to better evaluate his position. His tall and broad figure was usually so imposing. His otherworldly beauty and unshakeable confidence were annoyingly on display the few times they'd met.

They weren't now.

She appreciated that none of his poise lingered in his current predicament. His dark brown hair was plastered against his face from the swim. Something like humility smoothed the lines of his face as he met her gaze. She cursed herself for wanting to know why.

Zrak had the good grace to look sheepish, probably at being caught so quickly. He had never visited her realm. She knew it for a fact. Her magic, now so connected with the land, alerted her to any new arrivals.

Briefly, she wondered what his plan had been. Had he hoped to hide himself in her realm and never be found?

"Lady Cassandra, I..." He stumbled over the words. This inarticulate start, so different from his reputation, only further piqued her curiosity. Their interactions were limited, but she'd never heard him speak with anything less than utter confidence.

He ran his fingers nervously through his hair as he got to his feet. "Of course, I planned to present myself to you."

She wanted to laugh—his usually stoic face gave too much away. Even if she hadn't received gossip from newly arrived spirits, she never would have believed he planned to present himself.

Had he really hoped to hide himself away here?

Zrak, Arctos, Aurora, and Aterra had no right to visit her realm. The mess they'd made on the continent continued to spill onto her shores. And that didn't even consider what their selfish choices had pushed Celeste to do... Her fists clenched inadvertently at her sides. Now wasn't the time to rehash old wounds, no matter how much she still paid the price for them. She shook off the thought and unclenched her hands, running her fingers down the length of her sword as a distraction.

Her duty was to the spirits—to this realm. She'd been blinded before by hope. Betrayal wouldn't sneak up so easily on her again.

She arched an eyebrow. "Well, isn't it convenient I've come to greet you? I've made it easier for you," she said.

The gods of the continent thought she had closed the borders and, therefore, her communication channels fifty years ago. They knew nothing about her though. She'd closed the borders to protect her realm—a realm she'd failed once to protect.

Spirits still journeyed beyond the veil, but without a veil cat's help, fewer and fewer crossed the treacherous river. Those who did brought the detailed goings-on of the continent with them. The most recent additions said Zrak and the others had failed catastrophically. Not that she'd expected anything less.

"I..." The Osten God stumbled over his words again. "Lady Cassandra, I..."

She pushed her hair over her shoulder, a casual gesture contradicting everything she felt. "If you planned to present yourself to me, one would expect you to have prepared what you would say..."

The host of veil cats at her side tilted their heads. Each looked back and forth between her and the god, waiting for her signal.

Their tails flicked like a drum beat keeping time. Orion growled again, a low rumbling sound matching the gurgling of the river behind them.

Zrak coughed. "Of course." He finally seemed to collect himself. "The continent is in peril. The greed and selfishness of the gods has upset the balance and driven us to the brink of destruction."

At least he was finally being honest about who was to blame.

"While we've done what we can to rectify the situation and created a system of checks and balances to ensure it doesn't happen again...we also needed to pay a price for our mismanagement."

Cassandra knew all this, but she was glad the gods of the continent had finally figured it out—even if it was fifty years too late.

"I was chosen to sacrifice myself—for the balance of our continent."

"And yet...here you are beyond the veil." She glanced at her fingernails, feigning disinterest. He wouldn't be here without good reason, and her heart hammered in her chest to know what it was.

"Yes." He paused as if knowing his next words would be damning but realizing he had no option but to speak them. "I'm not sure a god can die, so I planned to go to the next best place." He raised his arms, gesturing to the realm around them, his gaze roaming the dense forest surrounding the river.

She schooled her features as she replied. "My realm is not your refuge."

Zrak's eyes widened as if he hadn't considered not being allowed to stay. His lips pursed. She could almost see his mind working, considering his next move. Her lip curled into a smirk as she thought of what would happen to his precious plan when she kicked him out.

His words ran through her head unbidden. *I'm not sure a god can die.* Was that true? She shook her head again. His concern was not the same as hers. All that mattered was that she protected the spirits—her promise to the land here.

As if following her thoughts, he said, "It would be beneficial for both of our realms.".

He paused momentarily as their gazes met. It seemed like he would take a step toward her. Fury must have burned as bright in her eyes as in her heart. She was sure he could see it as something stopped him in his tracks.

How dare he speak of joint benefit? When she warned them fifty years ago, none of the gods cared about their joint downfall. They didn't care what the downfall had led the humans on the continent to do. Cassandra hadn't told them everything, but she'd told them enough.

Ultimately, the four gods were to blame for Celeste's desperation.

Zrak coughed uncomfortably as he tried to continue. "Your land requires balance as much as the continent."

Orion growled at her feet, sensing her unrest.

"Choose your next words very carefully, Zrak," she said through gritted teeth. "I tried to have this conversation with you already. I'm not above reminding you that you ignored me."

"We weren't ready then. I told you when we made the peace offering—the willow tree. But we're ready to make a sacrifice now." His words were pleading. Cassandra was almost caught off guard by his tone. Planting a tree on the continent with a connection beyond the veil had been to appease her. They hadn't wanted to deal with her rage after Celeste's actions.

She steeled her spine as she thought of her own sacrifice. "You're ready now?" Her voice was so low. Orion couldn't help himself, letting another growl rumble through his body on her behalf. "You think you know sacrifice?" she hissed. "You think your actions today show your dedication to your people?" She waved her hand in dismissal. "You will never know what I have done—what I continually do—to clean up your mess." She closed her eyes and dropped her chin to breathe. "I've done what was necessary here. You pretending to care now will only ruin it."

Zrak opened his mouth to speak and then closed it. Surely, her words couldn't be a surprise to him? He had to know that his actions had consequences in her realm. Then again, it had taken them this long to admit they even had a problem with theirs. They were that self-centered.

"I could work for you. You say you no longer send your veil cats out, but given that one's latest trip"—he gestured to Orion— "you must still need to do so. Use something you can afford to lose: me—my Nebulus—to help shepherd spirits across the river."

She tried to blank her expression, but it was likely a lost cause. His point cut deep. She could no longer trust the humans on the continent with her cats. They were too desperate, doing anything to protect themselves from the catastrophe of the god's creation.

The god stepped back from whatever he saw before realizing he was still at the river's edge.

"You're right about you being something I can afford to lose at least." Her smile was all teeth. "But alternatively, we could let Orion off his metaphorical leash and test your theory about gods dying," she said as the cat growled again beside her. "If you returned in spirit form, I'd have no right to bar your entry."

The veil cat on her right rubbed against her leg, placing its head directly under where her hand hung. She scratched her absentmindedly while contemplating this god's fate.

"Surely, you see why that wouldn't be an ideal solution," Zrak said.

He didn't sound nervous. Somehow, he had found his unending confidence again. Only the shifting of his eyes gave away his nerves. He seemed to evaluate escape routes as he spoke.

With a single snap of her fingers, her veil cats could chase him back into the river, letting him find his way back to the continent. Her spirits were safe—that's what mattered. She was comfortable in the cage she'd built for herself.

His unblinking gaze followed the movement of her fingers. "I

     JILLIAN WITT

know that people let you down—even those you trust," he said carefully.

"I don't trust you—I can't imagine you would do anything but take from my realm," she replied.

Zrak's head tilted. Finally, his legendary planning was on display. He realized she held his fate.

"Another able to bond with the land will come."

His words were a whisper, but they shook her to her core. Briefly, she wondered if she'd imagined them. Then her green eyes snapped to his, and there was no mistaking his meaning.

She was too stunned to stifle her response. "You can't know that."

Zrak's soft smile was all confidence for the first time since she found him in the river. His arguments until now had been infuriating. But this, his words about another... He was sure of those—sure they would make a difference in his plea.

How did he know? He seemed so unaware of what she was.

"Explain yourself." She tapped her sword on her palm in as threatening a gesture as she could manage. She was certain the god saw through her. Somehow, he knew she needed this, no matter how much she tried to convince herself she didn't.

"Some know my element can capture secrets on the wind." He paused so long before continuing, she wondered if he would. To her dismay, she waited with bated breath.

"The whispers aren't always from the present," he said flatly.

Cassandra clenched her jaw tight, unwilling to let her mouth fall open in surprise. The information about the gods and their elements was common knowledge, as was their creation of the fae as part of Zrak's plan. But this...

"You can hear the future?"

Zrak nodded.

If this were true—if she took him at his word that he had heard secrets from the future of another—did he also know what it meant for her realm? He didn't seem to understand what she had done to preserve the balance.

"What do you know about another?" Believing his words was too easy. She dared not hope. But if there was any chance it was true...

"I know they are the only chance you have to truly restore balance here. To free yourself from this trap of your own making. I don't know what you did, but I heard the land calling for more—more than you can give."

She hated how smug the god sounded now. She gripped the sharp edge of her sword as it landed in her palm again. The bite of the blade as it dug into her flesh kept her focused as the god continued.

"One who can answer the call of the land will exist on the continent. I've heard him."

She held Zrak's stare. Her brow pinched in thought. What else had this god heard of the future? Had he passed this gift on to his fae? She shook her head. He'd played his cards well. She couldn't let her cats chase him out now.

"If I let you stay, you will tell me everything I need to know about him." It was a statement, not a question. "You will tell me when he arrives."

Zrak nodded.

"Fine." She released her grip on the blade and turned, using it to gesture to her realm. "You are welcome beyond the veil. Don't make a nuisance of yourself. We'll discuss your work for me after you've found a place in the city."

She and her pack turned their backs on the god, leaving him to his machinations.

CHAPTER ONE

Riding the switchbacks up the mountains of Compass Lake single-file left little room for conversation. Unfortunately for Rose, this left her alone with her thoughts. Her mind spun over and over again on the scene beneath Mount Bury: the surge of power when the Compass Points came together to hold Aterra, the opening of a pit in her stomach, the terror flooding her body as she realized what Luc was doing—just a few moments too late.

Not that she had another solution to their problem. Even now, days later, she couldn't think of a better way to conclude their standoff with the god. This would be Luc's saving grace when they were reunited.

He was a reckless idiot, but she could admit they needed his particular brand of recklessness.

Admitting this to herself didn't stem her worry however—it still rose like the sea's tides. Throwing himself and their enemy—his father—beyond the veil was...well, she didn't have the words for how ill-conceived, risky, and generally dangerous his actions were.

Worse still, she'd been unable to connect with him since.

Rose glanced at Carter and Juliette ahead of her. Taking

advantage of the quiet moment, she dove into the heart of her magic—again.

While hunting Aterra, the bond between Rose and Luc had evolved differently than hers with the other Compass Points. She could connect with each of them through her magic when required to hold the rogue god. But Luc's power had taken a more permanent residence—or so she'd thought. The tunnel to his magic had been visible at the bottom of the lake.

Leaving her physical body immobile astride her horse, she searched the familiar lakeshore, looking into the calm waters. That dark tunnel was no longer present. The results of her search hadn't changed, no matter how often she checked.

His final words before jumping through the hole he'd created between realms replayed in her thoughts day and night. *"Forgive me, Rose. I know you'll come for me."*

She shook her head. The words had echoed inside her. Rose was no longer sure if they were real or a figment of her imagination. Three days of riding had done nothing to calm any of these thoughts. They left her unsure whether she would strangle him or kiss him when she retrieved him.

And she would retrieve him.

The ache she felt for Luc was a physical thing. Her magic reached for him regularly, as it had on their travels together. The realm beyond the veil must be beyond the reach of even their unique bond. She hadn't felt his magic or smelled its pine and cinnamon scent since the cavern.

They finally arrived at the top of the switchbacks, where the thin trail unfolded into a sweeping mountain pass. Rose urged her horse forward to catch up with the others.

"Carter," she said as she pulled her horse into line beside his. "We need to talk."

The anxiety would continuously gnaw at her in the privacy of her mind, but now was the time to cement their plans. When they descended the other side of the mountain, they'd be returning to Compass Lake.

Carter slowed his horse to match her pace as the familiar eastern edge of the lake came into view. It was evening, but the days were long, and they still had plenty of light for the rest of their ride. Already, the magic of her seat of power tugged at her. Her limbs, weary from over two weeks on the road, felt new life breathed into them with each step of the horse's hooves toward Norden house. She still couldn't believe she'd spent ten years away from this feeling—this revitalization of her magic.

"What is it, Rose?" Carter asked.

Juliette also slowed her horse. She'd been in the lead, likely as eager as Rose to return to her seat of power. "Do we need to get our stories straight for our arrival?" she asked in jest.

"Not quite," Rose replied. She wanted to enjoy this moment. Juliette joked, but a lot was unsaid in her words. The Compass Points had left the lake, barely trusting each other. A newly minted Norden Point, a distrustful Osten, a secretive Vesten, and a Suden with unprecedented power had started a journey two weeks ago. Returning now, they had a different perspective. They'd learned to work together—to share their power to hold a rogue god upsetting the balance on the continent. It was an impressive feat. Yet, they didn't celebrate, since only three of the four cardinal directions rode together. The fourth point of their compass was noticeably absent.

No matter how much she tried to avoid it, the pit in Rose's stomach demanded acknowledgment. Even as her magic hummed in anticipation of returning to its source, the pain she'd carefully avoided deepened. There was a vast emptiness inside her where Luc's magic should be.

That wasn't quite right. The echo of his magic lingered. The spot his magic had carved out inside her was still there. She could still feel *something*, but the open tunnel beneath her lake of power —the intimate ability to reach for his magic—was gone.

Now that she knew what it was to have Luc's magic there, she'd never accept being without it. Not even the call of Norden house could distract her. She shook her head, returning her focus to the Vesten Point and the conversation he'd avoided since they'd tested his ability to share power with Arie.

"Let's align on our plan," Rose started. "We agree. We'll try the Osten portal first. It's a proven interaction point with Zrak, and we know he is beyond the veil, too." She glanced at Juliette, who nodded in confirmation. "He owes us some answers."

Juliette bit her lip as they rode. "As I told you on the ride, he's never been forthcoming with me, but I agree it is the best place to start." Bitterness hung from her words. The ritual Juliette had to perform to secure the Osten fae's magic put her in contact with Zrak regularly. He had plenty of opportunities to tell her...something. His silence on the matter was noted. "We may get more information from him if Arctos and Aurora join us—given their history," she added.

"I hope they're only a day or two behind us, but I won't wait for them," Rose replied. They'd saved the Norden goddess when they'd confronted Aterra under the mountain. Even if they needed Arie and Aurora to save the continent, Rose wouldn't begrudge them a day of privacy after hundreds of years of separation.

"I'm not sure about Zrak being more willing to share with them though," Rose said, trying to ease some of the sting Juliette must feel from the Osten god's reluctance to tell her about his plans. "Zrak hadn't told Arie or Aurora that his sacrifice was more of an exile."

Juliette's lips remained pressed together as she acknowledged Rose's words. "Do you have a second plan?" Juliette asked, returning the conversation to their next steps after arriving at Compass Lake.

"Arie would say you sound like Zrak now—with plans upon plans," Carter pointed out.

Rose's nose scrunched inadvertently. The more she learned, the less she understood the Osten god's actions. His sacrifice wasn't so much his existence as it was his place on the continent. Zrak still meddled from beyond the veil, sending soldiers made of smoke and wind, Nebulus, as harbingers of the disaster to come if Aterra wasn't stopped. The villages they visited fell to a mist plague—the villagers in a state of endless sleep.

Zrak's actions felt like random moves on a gameboard. She couldn't piece together his overarching strategy—maybe he didn't have one—but Arie said he was a planner. She shook her head again, unsure what to believe about the Lost God. The last thing she wanted to do was emulate him now, but she did have another plan, and she wanted to discuss it while they had privacy.

"We should discuss Carter's shift," Rose said. They now had his undivided attention. His shoulders tensed in a way that reminded her of hackles rising, and it told Rose all she needed to know. She was correct in her assumptions.

"Rose..." His voice held a plea, like maybe—if he asked nicely —she wouldn't utter the ensuing words, the words he believed threatened his existence, though Rose didn't understand why. She was not in the mood to dance around the topic. Every time she closed her eyes, she saw Luc throw himself through the hole between realms. She felt his presence—and his magic—leaving the continent. While she wouldn't rage at these two about the pain of his loss, neither would she shy away from uncomfortable topics that could help bring Luc back to her.

"We let you off easy at the Lake of the Gods. We had other things to do, namely, fight Aterra," Rose pressed.

Juliette's gaze slid between Rose and Carter. Maybe she hadn't realized what Carter's reaction to Arie's shift meant.

"It's dangerous to discuss," Carter pleaded again, his voice a whisper.

"Why is that?" Rose asked. She honestly hadn't recognized the animal for what it was. Juliette had been the one to whisper its name. This was further proof that those on the continent thought the animal extinct.

Carter sighed deeply, running his long fingers through his shaggy brown hair.

"What am I missing?" Juliette asked.

Carter searched the open mountain pass. No one was present for the half-mile ride across. There was arguably nowhere better to reveal his secrets.

"My shifted form is a veil cat," he said.

"But..." Juliette's eyes narrowed, and her head tilted as understanding creased her brow.

"They were extinct, yes," Carter finished the sentence she'd left hanging.

"You both seemed so sure of that," Rose said. "I didn't question it, but the stories I remember said the cats ferried the spirits of the dead beyond the veil. Why are you both so sure they're gone?"

Carter and Juliette shared a conspiratorial glance.

"Oh, great. Are there more secrets of the Compass Points?" Rose asked, rolling her eyes.

"This one wasn't our fault," Carter said quickly. He looked much more comfortable now that they were discussing something other than his shifted form. He switched effortlessly into the lecture mode from his time as a researcher. "The Compass Points have access to rare pre-Covenant histories. Veil cats went extinct before the Flood. As you can imagine, few texts from that time survived."

"Don't say it like it was a natural occurrence," Juliette added. "The Lady of the Veil killed them all. She ensured their extinction."

Carter coughed at Juliette's brutal phrasing. "Yes, that is what history says."

Rose opened and closed her mouth, unable to determine what she wanted to ask. If the Lady of the Veil ruled over the spirits in the afterlife, she must require someone or something to shepherd them from the continent.

"Why?" she asked.

"I don't think we have the full story," Carter said thoughtfully. "The texts are from a single settlement that survived the Flood. Villagers there indicate she went mad and sealed off her borders."

"Why do you think that's incorrect?" Juliette asked. Her features were relaxed, but her gaze held a glint Rose recognized. She was intrigued by Carter's consideration.

"As Rose pointed out within moments...it doesn't make sense. Spirits have to arrive for the Lady's realm to thrive. Why would she destroy the shepherds of her realm's success? The Veil requires balance, just like the continent." Carter sighed, running his hand through his hair again.

"I'm impressed," Juliette said as she reappraised the Vesten Point. "The Compass Points before you gave this story no thought. They accepted she went mad and left it at that." Juliette tilted her head again. "I've always been more curious about her story. Especially the more we learn about the gods' actions on the continent. I'm convinced something here must have threatened the spirits. That's the only logical reason for the Lady to seal off her realm. The veil cats were likely collateral damage."

Carter shivered as he nodded at Juliette's assessment.

"Look at you two, agreeing," Rose couldn't help but say. A part of her may be lost to the realm beyond the veil, but a little piece of her broken heart warmed at Juliette and Carter's cooperation. She doubted they'd ever been able to speak so freely at past Compass Point meetings.

"We agree that it's suspicious and likely doesn't tell the whole story. But we don't truly know why the veil cats no longer live," Carter said.

"Well...they do live, right?" Rose said pointedly.

Carter met her gaze. It was rare for the Vesten Point to make eye contact, but this glare felt practiced. "You know that's not what I meant." His shoulders rose again as she returned the conversation to his shifted form.

"If you're the first veil cat in"— Rose did the math—"over five hundred years, how do spirits pass beyond the veil?"

"I just assumed it took them longer to find their way across without a guide," Carter said. "I think the cats help to shepherd, but I don't think they're required for the process." He paused, deciding whether to continue. Rose was thankful when he did. "I've been curious if that's part of what the Nebulus were doing," he said. "Maybe Zrak had to serve the Lady of the Veil to reside there. That could be why the mist seems to host a tide of spirits. Maybe he helps guide the spirits beyond the veil."

"That's a lot of maybe," Juliette said.

"True." Carter shrugged. "We could ask Zrak, of course." A sly smile crossed Carter's face. Juliette's eyes narrowed at the taunt.

Rose turned the conversation back on him. "Can you speak with them? The spirits?"

"Not truly. But..." Carter hesitated, glancing back again at the wide-open expanse of the pass, as if he worried someone had snuck up on them while they spoke. "The power I gained with the Burning Coin. It helps."

Rose wasn't surprised. Arie had given Rose the Burning Coin, the Vesten artifact, to help her learn about Vesten magic while they traveled. Instead, she'd given Carter the coin to build trust between them. It had been one of her best decisions with the elusive Vesten Point.

The lake was entirely in view as they reached the other side of the pass. Three familiar manor houses were visible on the shore. The house strategically hidden in the trees—Norden house—pulled Rose's gaze. The land drew her to it both with its beauty and its power. She'd have to reckon with Norden house tonight. Her last visit to Compass Lake had been spent almost entirely at Suden house. But without Luc present—her throat tightened at the thought.

She wished she were approaching Norden house under better circumstances. How badly she wished Luc could join her at her newly claimed seat. She wanted her partner to celebrate with.

The scene of Luc throwing himself and Aterra through the hole between realms replayed in her head. It stole the air from her lungs. No conversation, not even about the continent's fate, could distract her for long.

Rose pulled herself from her thoughts. "Helps with what?"

Carter looked relieved to hear her speak again. Her anguish must have been evident on her face, though he and Juliette wisely left her to her emotions.

"I think it helps the spirits see me for what I am. Now that I've unlocked that power, they are drawn to me when I shift," he said.

She swallowed around a lump in her throat as her gaze lingered on Suden house at the lake's southern shore. They had so much to do, but she needed to see Aaron. Luc's brother deserved to hear the news from her, no matter how much she longed to avoid it.

Rose tried to rally as she looked between her fellow leaders. "I hope you can see why I bring this up..." She hesitated. This was her second option if Zrak proved unhelpful, but she needed Carter to agree. She sat up straighter in her seat. "If veil cats can ferry spirits beyond the veil, then you"—she nodded at Carter—"need to be our backup plan."

Carter sighed. "I had a feeling you'd say that."

"That's not a yes," Rose said. She swore she saw Juliette smile out of the corner of her eye as she pressed the Vesten Point for his answer.

"Of course, I'll try, Rose. But you must know I've never done it before." He scratched the side of his head. "After seeing the space Luc created to cross beyond the veil, I have some ideas, but it will be risky."

Rose nodded through the punch in the gut she felt whenever Luc's name was mentioned. Risky wasn't an issue for her. Carter's response was the best she could ask for. It was still wise to attempt to get information from Zrak before blindly crossing realms. As both Carter and Juliette said, the borders were closed. History indicated the Lady of the Veil didn't appreciate visitors. Rose's heart pounded in her chest as she wondered what it meant for Luc upon his arrival.

"Has everyone shared their secrets now? Is there anything else we need to discuss?" Rose choked out, forcing a change in her thoughts.

Carter looked sheepish, but Juliette met Rose's gaze head-on.

"You still don't seem to understand what you've done, Rose," the Osten Point said. "Some of these secrets you pull from us have been buried for hundreds of years—it's no simple feat to ask if we're done. It's as natural as breathing for me to keep things from the Compass Points. Only time and trust will reveal everything."

So, Rose thought, that was a no, then.

JILLIAN WITT

CHAPTER TWO

As much as she wanted to avoid this conversation, as much as she'd prefer to settle into Norden house, she knew she couldn't. Luc's brother deserved to know what he'd done and where he was.

Rose's face must have said more than the words she couldn't get out. Andrew opened the back door, and rather than greet Rose, he turned to yell into the house.

"Aaron, I think you have a meeting. The boys and I are going to get ready for bed." He smiled gently as he left the door open for Rose and continued. "Boys, upstairs."

"Noooo," three voices whined in chorus.

Andrew ushered them away, not letting the young fae catch sight of Rose's grief-stricken face. She was frozen in the entryway as Andrew followed his charges, leaving her alone. It had taken everything she had to knock on the door. The sun had set, making it later than socially acceptable to drop by unannounced, but she needed to talk to Aaron tonight. She tried to swallow around the emotion lodged thickly in her throat as bedtime preparation noises drifted down the stairs. She was thankful Aaron's husband had shepherded the children away. Nothing could prepare her to tell Luc's nephews that while she had returned, their uncle hadn't. She barely believed she'd be able to tell his brother.

Aaron found her standing in the open doorway, looking like she might dart away at any second. Like Andrew, he only had to see her face before leading her into his study on the first floor. He handed her a glass of water as she sat in the plush chair opposite his desk. She hadn't even realized he'd disappeared to retrieve it. Aaron walked around the large wooden desk and leaned forward, his palms resting on the surface, his head hanging, unwilling to meet her gaze as he asked the question she dreaded answering.

"Tell me," he whispered, steeling himself for the answer. "Where is he? What did he do?"

Rose's lip twitched in an attempted smile. His questions were so apt—questions only a brother would know to ask. This was hardly how she wanted to begin her relationship with Aaron. He already blamed her for Luc keeping secrets from the other Compass Points. Telling him his brother was gone wouldn't endear her to him. Still... He deserved to know.

Aaron lifted his palms from the desk, one hand poised to drag down his face, a gesture so Luc, her heart cracked again in her chest.

She couldn't do this.

She couldn't tell him his brother had sacrificed himself for the continent—that he was now beyond the veil.

"Forgive me, Rose. I know you'll come for me." Luc's words echoed through her entire being. They expressed an uncompromising faith in her as he leaped into the unknown. He didn't doubt she would come for him. She swallowed a drink of water and glanced at the fae before her. Would he believe the same? Or would Aaron think his brother was gone?

Her breaths shortened, panic taking over. She closed her eyes, trying to suck air deep into her lungs. Unable to calm herself, she reached for her magic instead.

For ten years, she'd masked her power. Since embracing it and claiming her seat as the Norden Point, it became a strength she

JILLIAN WITT

could rely on. But like her heart, her power was restless and untamed in Luc's absence. The emptiness where Luc's magic had taken up residence demanded to be felt. Rose sighed, nodding slowly to herself, acknowledging the loss.

This wasn't helping.

A tear dripped down her cheek as she met Aaron's gaze. His nostrils flared as he sniffed the air. He'd anxiously moved back around the desk, giving the appearance of patience now as he sat on the corner. The way he crossed and uncrossed his muscled arms gave away his nerves.

Where did she even start?

"Luc is a demigod," she blurted. This fact was shocking on its own. If he fought it, Rose would know how to temper the rest of the news she delivered. If he believed it? Rose hoped it would provide reassurance.

Aaron shook his head, unsure he'd heard her correctly. "Luc is…"

"A demigod. Yes." She nodded. "Aterra is his natural father."

The hand poised to drag itself down his face made its move. "What does that…"

She waited, letting him decide what to ask or what to say.

He let the sentence hang, unfinished.

Rose realized she didn't have his patience. Now that she'd started, she needed to keep going. "It's important for the rest of the story. I need you to hold on to that."

Aaron nodded slowly, in a daze. He seemed aware he had no choice but to accept the information in Rose's provided order.

"We were tracking Aterra. I don't know how much Luc told you before we left, but I'm sure it was more than he should have." Her lip tipped into a smile, knowing Luc would have told Aaron everything, even when it was confidential. It would help her now if he already had the context of what they'd been doing.

"The Compass Points knew Aterra had done something to disrupt the balance on the continent. We were unclear on *what* he had done. We've since learned that one of his sins was creating a demigod that would become the Suden Point."

Aaron nodded again. Words still failing him.

"As you know, our purpose as Compass Points is to stop a god should they upset the balance. It was what we were created for, but the ability to do so had never been tested." Rose shook her head. This missing piece of the gods' plans was still a sore subject for her—one of the many grievances she would lay at Zrak's feet if he answered their call. "We learned to work together, the four of us."

Aaron's brows raised a little at that. It was the most animated reaction she'd received from him yet. It was telling of the state of the fae courts that he could accept his half-brother was a demigod but was unsure he believed the Compass Points worked in cooperation.

She smirked at him. "I know. It's difficult to believe."

Even though he had more experience with lake politics than she did and had the right to suspect her words, he didn't call her a liar. He seemed unwilling to stop her from getting to the heart of her story.

"We could hold Aterra when our powers merged—when we could trust each other enough to let our elements blend. Unfortunately, we fought Aterra in a location filled with wild magic that strengthened him." She knotted her fingers together in her lap, providing a physical distraction as she relived her failure.

"We could hold him, but we had nowhere to put him." Rose paused and took a deep breath. "We were out of options. So Luc came up with his own."

"What does that mean, Rose?" Aaron asked. His arms were folded over his chest again as he perched on the desk's edge, but he leaned forward to catch her every word.

"He used his power." Her voice trembled as she held back tears. "He created a hole between realms. And he took Aterra into it."

"Rose..." Aaron was on his feet now.

She paused, giving him time to respond. His jaw clenched as he paced. She could only guess what was going through his mind.

"I think he knew he could do it after the hole in Loch."

Aaron stopped pacing and turned to look at her.

"In hindsight, Loch was a primer for what he did beneath the Lake of the Gods. He had a few more ways to enhance his power." Her cheeks heated as she thought of the sword she'd made him. "But the concept was the same. His element didn't just dig a hole, it tore through realms. He took Aterra beyond the veil."

Aaron slumped into the chair beside hers. She understood the sentiment.

They sat in silence. Rose continued to mentally torment herself—trying to decide how much more to say. She focused on the Luc-shaped hole in her chest—the space where his magic should be.

Aaron's nostrils flared again. Was he smelling her? She wasn't using her magic, just reassuring herself it was there. No scent should be present. She mirrored his movement, sniffing herself. Her hygiene hadn't been its best on their journey, but surely this wasn't the most appropriate time to comment on it.

"You smell like him—his magic."

Rose sucked in a breath. It wasn't possible. Luc wasn't here—he hadn't been on the continent for days. His power was no longer connected to her. She opened her mouth to say so; she didn't want Aaron to get the wrong idea.

"How are you going to get him back?" Aaron asked, cutting off the protest on her lips as he turned to face her. His stare was piercing as it met hers.

Relief that he believed it possible washed over her, followed quickly by anxiety at the expectation. She pushed down her worries. Getting Luc back was her priority, and she'd conquer every fear if it meant returning him to her side.

She met Aaron's gaze unflinchingly. "I assure you, I have multiple plans to bring him back. I just found him. I don't intend to let him go so easily."

Aaron nodded once. "Good." He stood again, moving back to his desk. When he turned, he looked like a different male than the one she'd just spoken to. The worried brother was gone. One responsible for the Suden fae in Luc's absence stood in his place. "What do we tell the court? They will have questions with the Compass Points at the lake and the Suden Point missing."

Rose was confused but not by the question about the Suden court, which was an appropriate discussion point. She was surprised they were moving on from the fact that Luc was beyond the veil. Her initial response hadn't outlined a plan. It was a statement of intention. She expected Luc's brother to press further.

"You don't have any other questions about what Luc is, where he is, or how we will get him back?" she asked in bewilderment.

"I know I haven't warmed to you yet, Rose," he replied, "but I know Luc's faith in you is absolute. He puts himself in danger—often"—a fond smile crossed his face—"but he's never blatantly reckless."

Rose begged to differ on that assessment, but she held her tongue as Aaron continued.

"He knows what losing him—really losing him—would do to his family." Aaron stretched his neck to the side. His hand rubbed the back of it as if deciding how to phrase whatever else he had to say. "As I said, you smell like him—not like you've been around him recently—but more uniquely. His pine and cinnamon scent filled the room when you started to speak. Then again, after you told me where he was"—Aaron coughed—"knowing my brother, he wouldn't have done what you say without being sure he could get back. Given the evidence, I assume he believes *you* will bring him back." He nodded, almost to himself this time. "I will believe that, too, until you tell me otherwise."

A burning flooded the back of Rose's sinuses as, again, she fought back tears. She blinked rapidly, losing the war with herself, and nodded, unable to attain the same mask on her emotion Aaron had achieved. She took another deep breath, steadying herself to respond. "For now, we tell people he is working to stop the mist plague and bring balance back to the continent. He used to do such things before, while the other Compass Points remained at the lake."

The absence of his magic's reassuring hold felt like a physical ache inside her chest. She wanted it back. "It will buy us time. I don't plan on letting him linger beyond the veil for long."

EXHAUSTION THREATENED to pull Rose under as she finally arrived at the edge of Norden property. Letting her thoughts clear on the walk around Compass Lake had been the right move. Her magic longed to dive into the water and swim to her seat of power, but if she stood any chance of rest tonight, she needed to calm her racing mind.

Aaron could smell Luc's magic on her. Both times he mentioned were when she'd acknowledged the emptiness inside her—where Luc's magic should be.

The last time they were together was a jumble of heat, skin, and magic. Her core tightened as her thoughts lingered on his power, holding her to the workshop wall while he pleasured her. Their magic had come together as much as their bodies.

She was unsure what to make of it.

The way their magics reached for each other when near brought forth fairy tale imagery—stories of bound fae partners. She shook her head again. Bound fae were incredibly rare, if they existed at all. None of the stories spoke of partners that spanned fae courts.

A Norden and Suden could never be that.

The empty place in her chest where Luc's magic used to take up space pulsed in disappointment at the thought. Before considering what it meant, her foot touched Norden soil.

It was waves crashing against rock, the ocean's roar, and a rushing river as magic rolled through her—as she returned to her seat of power.

The imposing presence of Norden house loomed ahead. Its austere stone facade demanded her attention. The breath she felt like she'd been holding since she first saw the lake from the mountain pass released.

This was where she belonged.

She was glad her magic felt so at home because her palms were sweaty, and anxious energy filled her. It would be her first night sleeping at the house. The event should have excited her more than it did. To her, the House still represented secrecy and separation among the Compass Points.

Hoping to share this night with Luc was a secret she kept tucked away in her chest. It was no surprise she wanted a life with him at Compass Lake. No, the secret was that, in a world after the mist plague, when they restored balance to the continent, she imagined them coming and going between the two houses as easily as the breeze blew across the lake. In this future, one wouldn't be hers and the other his. Instead, each house would feel equally like home to them as long as they were together. She liked the idea that such a public connection between her and Luc would allow more connections between Norden and Suden, or members of any court for that matter.

It was a beautiful dream. Yet, here she was, walking to Norden house alone.

The magic of the land rolled through her like a cresting wave with each step she took. She wasn't away for long, but as the Compass Points had learned from the Vesten journals, their magic was never stronger than at Compass Lake.

Her mood fell further as she saw figures between her and the entrance. It may be dark, but identifying them didn't take long. Meg and Catherine, the Norden elders she had dismissed after claiming her title, stood between her and the back door to the house. Samuel, the third elder, was noticeably missing.

While Samuel had proved willing to confess his wrongdoing regarding Aiden stealing the Norden Point seat, these two had been happy to remain complacent about his illegitimate reign.

     JILLIAN WITT

This was the last thing she wanted to deal with tonight.

She briefly considered going around to the front of the house to avoid them, but she shook her head and continued forward. That wasn't the kind of leader she would be. Rose would face her problems head-on.

"Meg, Catherine." She acknowledged them each with a curt nod. "Can I help you with something?" Rose let her arms hang at her sides. She didn't want to appear closed off by letting them cross her chest, no matter how she felt about these fae.

"What do you have to report?" Catherine asked. "We saw you return today with the Vesten and Osten Points. The Suden Point wasn't with you." The elder peered around Rose as if imagining Luc would pop out of the earth behind her.

Rose opened and closed her fists, giving her body something to do while she reached for the respect she would give to anyone in her court, even if Catherine's tone left something to be desired. "The Suden Point still works to stop the mist plague, but the rest of us had to return, to continue with our plan to restore balance to the continent."

Meg's face pinched as her eyes narrowed. "What does that mean?"

"We've isolated the immediate threat, and we seek a way to remove the mist plague while ensuring it doesn't happen again," Rose said. Given her current exhaustion, she was very proud of her response.

"And you're not going to tell us anything more than that? Where did you go? Did you find Aiden?" Meg asked.

Rose let her hands fall open again. She should answer the question about Aiden directly. The Norden people deserved to know what happened to him, even if this was another topic she hadn't entirely processed. "We did."

"And..."

"Aiden understood the consequences of his actions in falsely claiming the Norden seat. He supported the Compass Points in fighting against a greater power that pursued imbalance." She held

Meg's gaze as she finished. "He fell in battle." She paused, giving those words the weight they deserved. "While his past actions can't be undone, he did what he could to ensure a better future for the Norden."

"A greater power?" Catherine pressed, giving no indication she cared about Aiden's fate. "What power is greater..."

Catherine didn't have to complete the sentence. She answered her own question. The only power greater than a Compass Point...was a god.

Rose hadn't given them much, but Catherine's awed expression said she had worked out enough. Letting them walk away with this assumption might not be her best idea, but honesty and transparency had gotten her this far. She wouldn't stop now. If any of her people appeared on her doorstep asking questions, she'd do her best to answer them.

The details didn't need to be shared. She didn't tell them which god or the plan they'd hatched, but she let them correctly assume the Compass Points were dealing with a god-sized problem.

"Indeed," Rose confirmed. "Anything else? Or may I go in?" She gestured to the door behind them—just out of her reach. "I'm quite tired from our travels, and we still have a lot of work to do."

"You should tell us what is going on," Meg said. "Give us the details, and we can advise you."

Rose took another deep breath and landed on civility. The walk around the lake had done wonders for her racing mind. "I think we're past that. You've been removed from your positions. I'm only paying you the respect I would any member of my court. The Compass Points will finish this. It is our purpose and our calling."

"But you can't trust them," Catherine started. She didn't appear at all phased at the reminder she was no longer an advisor to the Norden Point.

    JILLIAN WITT

"Can't trust *them*?" Rose echoed, stunned as she tried to process the hypocrisy of the statement.

Catherine didn't see the ocean storm raging in Rose's gaze as she replied. "The other courts—"

Rose cut her off. "I can trust them more than the elders who led our court astray for a decade," Rose snapped. Catherine refused to be cowed. Her spine straightened at the accusation, but Rose pressed on. "I trust them enough to merge my magic with theirs, to learn from the Osten Point to use the wind magic that also runs through my veins."

Meg's hand covered her mouth.

"You can't..." Catherine started.

The truth of her dual lines hadn't been revealed to the Norden court before she took the seat. It was irrelevant since she'd passed the Norden test for power. Rose wanted the information out in the open nonetheless.

"I can, and I do." Rose was leagues past a civil response. She was the Norden Point, but she also wielded the Osten element. There was no way she was the only one with such a lineage. She was confident many more fae of multiple lines hid themselves in plain sight. That wasn't the kind of court she desired. If she couldn't start the future she dreamed of with Luc tonight, she'd at least start down the path toward accepting all fae—no, all those with magic—now.

The elders seemed to have finally lost their bite against her resolve. She gave them a curt nod as she walked past them into Norden house.

CHAPTER THREE

550 YEARS AGO

Nausea roiled in Andie's throat as she stared at the storm's destruction. A glance at her father and sister's horror-stricken faces told her it wasn't in her imagination. She walked to the middle of the field and knelt to pick up a stray cat chewing on one of the leaves ripped from the ground, waiting to see what her family would do.

A group of villagers stood just behind them, staring at the same ruination. Marcil was far enough inland to avoid the flooding that had been destroying cities to the north like Sandrin. But these new storms were growing in confidence.

Andie stroked the cat's fur and hugged it close to her chest. Her mind was already racing through plans her sister would make. Fruits and vegetables, ripe and ready to pick only yesterday, were smashed and tossed in all directions. Bushes and stalks were torn from the ground, roots and all. The tornado had gone right through the middle of the village's only farm field.

It had destroyed everything.

"What are we going to do?" one of the villagers asked. The gathered group looked directly at her sister, Cee. Andie recognized him. Garth helped Cee regularly, always ready to take on any new project she'd dreamed up.

Cee swallowed before replying. "We'll replant—quickly." She glanced at their father, who was still silent. "We'll rally a group to start today." Her hesitation was uncharacteristic. Maybe even Cee knew her well-organized plan wouldn't be enough this time.

"I'll help, of course," Garth said. A dozen other villagers echoed his words.

Their father was still silent. Andie was curious what he would say.

"Do you agree, Father?" Cee asked, trying to draw him into the conversation. His brow was furrowed as he ignored them.

"We have some food stores to cover the deficit," Andie added. She set the cat down and pulled the journal she and Cee kept from the inner pocket of her jacket. Flipping the pages, she found the number. It was less than she remembered.

Cee's glare was icy as her gaze roamed the ruined field. She paused, waiting for their father to respond. When he didn't, she said, "We only have stores for a month. We can't afford to lose this much."

Andie started writing in the journal. She would want a record of their decision. Cee was right. Even though they'd taken warnings from the disasters hitting neighboring villages and had started rationing early, it wouldn't be enough.

The only way to fix this would be with blood magic.

Cee stooped, picked up an ear of corn, and tossed it onto the basket they'd brought. Anything intact enough to pick up, she did. It was futile. There was no way the scraps from this field could feed their village. But Cee, Garth, and a few others started collecting them anyway. It was in their nature to try every available practicality before relying on magic.

"Marcil needs this field. We have to replant immediately," Cee said, again looking to her father for confirmation—for anything. Her ability to bear news like this and take action was part of why she was the natural successor to their father's position as village leader. "If we start in shifts today, we can—"

Their father cut Cee off. "Andie, I need you to take care of this."

The cat she'd set down wrapped its tail around Andie's leg, the soft brush pulling her back from the focus of her writing. Andie looked up and saw her father's stare, her sister's stiff posture. The words registered a few seconds too late. Then she wished she could collapse in on herself. Their father ignored Cee's solid, practical plan in favor of her blood magic.

"I can't just make the crops reappear," Andie said. "The seeds need to be planted. Cee should organize—"

"I can try it, Father," Cee said, reinserting herself into the solution.

Their father had been fixated on blood magic since the natural disasters had increased. Magic was risky, and not all villagers supported it, but eating magically grown food was better than starving. All three had attempted to learn it, but only Andie was successful at the scale they needed.

Blood magic was easy for Andie. It made sense to her—it was a simple contract. She understood it the way Cee understood villagers and could convince them to follow her plans. The first time a windstorm swept through, Andie felt the land's pain. It called out to her in anger, wanting someone—anyone—to realize the scale of what was happening and offer assistance.

Andie did so in exchange for magic.

She realized quickly that her father and Cee didn't hear it. They were too focused on their people, their own problems, and their day-to-day survival to see the bigger picture. This connection with the land fueled her magic. Her blood offerings acknowledged what no one else seemed to notice. Something big was wrong on the continent. Someone needed to do something.

The gods certainly hadn't—and wouldn't.

"I know you're nervous," their father said, ignoring Cee's

     JILLIAN WITT

offer and speaking directly to Andie. "But we know you can do this." He turned to Cee. "Don't we, darling?"

Cee finally received their father's attention, only to urge her sister to save them all. Andie winced on her behalf. Cee had no choice but to reply. "Of course, Andie can do it. Her magic has saved us more than once." She took the journal from Andie's hands and started making her own notes.

Andie caught Garth's eye as he looked away in disgust. He seemed more against the governor's use of magic than most. However, it never stopped him from eating the food it produced.

Andie held back her eye roll. She wished things were different —wished their father saw Cee's contributions, her ability to lead their people through challenging times. But now was not the time to dwell on it. If their father was set on magic solving their problem, she would need to put together a substantial offering to correct...all of this.

"I can do it, Father," Cee said again, stepping forward.

Their father shook his head. "You've tried before, Cee. We can't afford more mistakes."

Cee's head hung in shame. She could easily cut her skin and bleed, but without the connection to the land, she couldn't access the required magic. Anything more complex than growing a few flowers was beyond her capabilities.

"Cee and I will work on replanting and putting together a worthy offering to the land," Andie said. Her father nodded and put his hand on her shoulder.

"I'm counting on you," he said. His eyes never left Andie's— never acknowledging the twin daughter offering assistance beside him.

Andie sought Cee's gaze, desperate to bring her into the plan, but Cee stubbornly refused to look at Andie and their father's exchange. Andie swallowed around a lump in her throat, feeling the weight of her father's expectation in the gentle squeeze of his hand on her shoulder.

CHAPTER FOUR

Relief flooded Rose as she leaned her weight against the closed door. That wouldn't be the last she heard from the elders. She needed a way to share information with the wider court, not just those who felt too much self-import and demanded it from her as she walked home. Mentally, she added this challenge to her to-do list.

She pushed herself off the door and took in her new home. If Suden house was a sprawling manor, all wood and natural light, then Norden was a castle fortress. It had high ceilings and stone walls and generally gave a feeling of austerity. Soft chatter and banging pots emanated from the kitchen. She headed in that direction.

It was quiet as she wandered through the main level of the house. Rose remembered the house being formal as a child, but this was something else. It seemed like Aiden hadn't added any personal touches to the decor. Most of the rooms she walked through felt like a prison, no different from Aurora's cell under Mount Bury. Perhaps, for Aiden, it had been one.

She ran her hands against the walls as memories crept in—memories she'd repressed for so long. A smile threatened as she thought of Aiden chasing her out the back door toward the caretaker's cottage. Or of her sneaking into the classrooms downstairs where his parents had him hole up with tutors for hours every day. She'd try to make silly faces at him to make him laugh during his lessons.

Her words to the elders had been true. Aiden did what he could for the Norden in the end. She would no longer push away happy memories of her childhood friend—her friend with bright blue eyes, before the grey-eyed god took over.

"Hello?" she called as she neared the kitchen so as not to startle anyone.

The noises came to a halt. She stepped into the room. It was so bright and clean compared to the rest of the house she'd walked through. The staff was larger than she'd thought—ten Norden fae were gathered eating a meal.

"I'm Rose, the Norden Point," she said.

The group burst into a flurry of introductions.

"I'm Annabeth, the cook."

"Walter, the steward."

"Harriet, the housekeeper."

The others added their names and responsibilities. Rose tried to memorize each one as she shook their hands. She hadn't had time to worry what they'd think of her. Having been Norden Point for a half-day, she'd barely had time to meet them before leaving to hunt Aterra with the other Compass Points.

"We're so glad you're back," Annabeth said. "We saw the three of you arrive in the village this afternoon. Did you have a productive trip?"

"We believe we found the cause for the mist plague and have a temporary solution," Rose said. "We're still working on the longer-term impacts."

"That sounds like progress," Walter said.

"Do you want anything to eat?" Annabeth asked.

Rose's stomach rumbled.

"I'll take that as a yes." Her smile was authentic.

"I can show you a room for your things if you'd like," Harriet offered, gesturing to Rose's bag.

"Yes, please. Annabeth, do you mind sending the food up? I'm pretty tired. I'll just have a snack before going to sleep," Rose said as she followed Harriet out of the kitchen.

"It'll be wonderful to have you back at the lake." Harriet's words didn't hold the undertone of malice she felt when she talked to the elders. They seemed genuine.

"We still have a lot of work to do," Rose replied.

Harriet nodded as she led them up the stairs. Rose's gaze swept out the back window as her hand rested on the staircase railing. While she let memories of her childhood friend sweep in tonight, she had yet to do the same for her family. There was a warm glow emanating from the caretaker's cottage out back. It had been rebuilt after the fire. A family lived there now—a new caretaker for the property. She wasn't yet ready to think about the happiness she'd had there. Or the devastation.

A final glance around the first floor left her feeling maudlin, no matter how welcoming the staff. Norden house didn't feel like a home. There was nothing to be done about that tonight. Hopefully, Arie and Aurora would arrive soon enough to fill that void. She would add the rest to the list of things to worry about after she retrieved Luc and saved the continent.

Reaching the second-floor landing, Harriet led them left. Rose had never been allowed to explore the upstairs bedrooms so freely. Harriet explained some were studies, others were sitting rooms, and many were spare bedrooms for visiting Norden. She led them into a wing with its own door. This felt similar to the space Luc claimed in Suden house.

As children, she and Aiden would sneak up here when playing hide-and-seek. They gave each other extra points if they hid in this off-limits area. Not that it was off limits to Aiden—it was his home even before he stole the position of Norden Point. But his parents were never too fond of them playing in the family's private space.

   JILLIAN WITT

Finally, Harriet opened the door to a large room in what had to be the northwestern corner of the house. The room had a southern-facing window looking out over the lake. Doors opened to a balcony on the bed's left side, providing peaceful views of the still water. Rose's gaze lingered on Suden house directly in her sights as she surveyed the familiar shores of Compass Lake.

She could admit it now—she had missed this place.

"This is perfect," Rose said. Harriet excused herself quickly, promising to return with food. Rose was thankful for the private moment. Emotion overtook her as she looked out on the lake.

She may not want to face the memories of what happened to her family, but the loving home she grew up in before that fateful day didn't deserve to be forgotten. Working with her mom in the forge was a treasured part of her childhood. Her mother's instructions on weapons-making were still ones she clung to. She missed swimming in the lake instead of looking at it, as she'd had to do at the Lake of the Gods.

Her magic loved it here, and it would love it even more when Luc and his magic returned.

She folded her arms over her chest as she did a final survey of Compass Lake. The lights were already out in Suden house. Talking to Aaron tonight had been difficult, but it was a good start. She would need his help for what came next. Rose was headed beyond the veil. Whether Zrak took her or the veil-cat-shifting Vesten Point, she would get there.

Rose tossed the small bag she still carried from travel into the corner of the room. Rooting around, she pulled out a change of clothes and readied herself for sleep. She caught her reflection in the mirror in the connected washroom. It was no surprise that she looked as tired as she felt. The woman staring back at her was no longer daydreaming about what went on inside this fancy house. The Norden house and court were hers. No matter her current grief, she welcomed the responsibility of being Norden Point.

If initially reluctant, her strides with the other Compass Points proved she was right for the position. Her perspective was good for them, and she was coming to rely on the relationships she developed with the other court leaders. As she'd said to the elders, she had already learned much from Juliette and had no doubt she'd learn more. And though many underestimated Carter's strength, she valued the calm reassurance and quiet challenge he offered.

Ready for bed, she slipped under the blankets. She doubted she'd be awake when Harriet returned with the food. It was her first night on a mattress since Sandrin—with Luc. The now familiar pang in her chest, that space shaped for Luc's magic, threatened to make itself known. With it, the fears and worries she wasn't ready to confront.

If only she had as much confidence in herself as Luc did. She pulled the covers tightly around her shoulders, reminding herself that she would get Luc back—end of story. She must have convinced her body as well as her mind because she was asleep as soon as she nestled into the pillows.

"Forgive me, Rose. I know you'll come for me."

Rose fell to her knees, mouth open to scream, but no sound came out. The familiar ache in her chest throbbed, demanding her attention. She rocked forward, collapsing into herself as fear, heartbreak, and anger struggled for dominance.

Her chest pulsed.

No, not her chest. The heart of her magic.

Part of her knew she still slept, but another part pushed away the messy emotions and focused on her internal lake of power. She followed the familiar wind, this time a gentle breeze across her lake, deep in the center of her magic.

For all her emotional turmoil, this was a place of peace. The waters didn't ripple with her changing moods, and the wind didn't rage, threatening the trees along the shore. It was a place of stillness—one she desperately needed.

    JILLIAN WITT

Rose knew the other Compass Points didn't begrudge her grief, but they also needed her to push them forward. Carter wouldn't have shared his shifted form, and neither would have shared their knowledge about the Lady of the Veil without her prodding. They were making progress. She wouldn't leave them to be consumed by grief now.

She had worked too hard, and they had too much left to do. Not just saving Luc and the continent but also shaping the future she desperately wanted.

Rose stood at the lake's edge. Dreaming or awake, her magic thrummed in her chest. She was so close to that place where Luc's magic should be. Her gaze searched the water's depths again for the familiar tunnel that led to Luc's power. This was the place—the ache she constantly felt. Unsurprisingly, there was no dark pit at the bottom of her lake now.

She let out a breath. Had she expected one?

She sat down on the shore, her fingers digging into the sand. Rolling up her leggings, she dipped her bare toes into the water. Simply touching it enhanced the feeling of peace in this place. Ripples cast out from where her foot broke the surface.

It felt good. She let her head fall back as she dipped the other foot in. The hum of her magic pumped through her body as naturally as blood.

The water called to her. Placing her feet in it wasn't enough. It was a siren song she couldn't and wouldn't ignore. Before realizing what she was doing, she stood and dove in. Every inch of this place was hers. Nothing could stop her.

Easy strokes led her to the center of the lake. She couldn't keep her gaze from dropping to the lakebed below—a final check for the connection to Luc's magic. No dark shadow was waiting there, but she found herself diving below the surface anyway—just in case.

Her water magic granted the ability to breathe underwater. She could stay below as long as she desired. Diving to the bottom, her gaze raked the earthen crater base.

What was she looking for?

The water rocked with her body's disturbance of it. The sand on the lakebed shifted with her waves. Her gaze locked on a dark streak that emerged through the dirt.

She dove deeper so her hand could brush over the streak. It was smooth and solid, like a diamond pressed under hundreds of years of pressure. It hadn't been here before. She was sure of that.

Intrigued now, she created more waves with her magic and brushed the sand back to further uncover more of the new material. This had to mean something. She pushed her water magic further, removing the sand from the lakebed, fully revealing what was beneath it. The pattern of black fissures spread out in spider-like webs across the entire lake floor.

Whatever this was, it was new, and she refused to discount the fact that it was right where Luc's magic should be.

Her fingers stretched to trace another streak of the material. It was hard and unyielding, unlike the wet dirt she could usually sink her toes into. The way the material cut across the floor was like a work of art. It was all jagged edges and strong lines, much like the image of Luc's uncompromising cheekbones or the arch of his brow when she amused him.

Now, she was just seeing what she wanted to see.

Rose swam a bit higher, leaving the material uncovered so she could see the entire pattern from a single vantage point. It was so much a part of the lakebed that Rose wasn't surprised she hadn't noticed it from the surface. More lines branched out than she'd initially realized. This new solid material was wholly interwoven with her lake.

She dove back down, her hand reaching again to touch whatever it was. It may have been new, but it didn't feel unknown. It felt distinctly a part of her, like the lake itself. Examining the material, she would swear it was a smooth black... stone. It brought forth an image of the onyx gemstone in the Suden ring.

"I know you'll come for me."

Her breath caught. Her head swung around, searching for the voice she would know anywhere.

She pushed the water from her face with her magic so she could speak. "Luc?" She ran a hand through her hair as it fanned behind her in the water. Maybe she was losing it. Was Luc talking to her? She needed more rest.

Wasn't she asleep now?

Nothing made sense.

"You'll come for me." The voice echoed again, shortening its refrain.

"You're right. I'll come for you, Luc. And we will have words when I get there," she couldn't help but reply.

His soft chuckle was a physical sensation as it ran along her skin. Gooseflesh pebbled where the words caressed her. Even under the water, she felt it—felt him. She loved and loathed the sound all at once.

How dare he laugh at her—if it was even him. Was it perhaps her mind's conjuring of him?

The fact remained that no matter how much she claimed to understand his decision, his choice still gnawed at her. Why hadn't he said something about his plan? Did he know he could cut a hole through realms? Or had it all been a guess?

Luc didn't do much without careful consideration. He might not have known he could do it, but he must have suspected. And he hadn't told her.

She shook her head again.

"It had to be done, but I'll spend the rest of our existence making it up to you." As her finger caressed the smooth black stone again, a tendril of *something* wrapped around it.

"That's a start," she said for the first time, not feeling foolish. The tendril of magic worked its sway up her hand, her arm. She would know this feeling anywhere. She'd become so familiar with it before Luc had thrown himself and his magic into another realm.

His confidence in her might be so absolute as to know she

could cross realms to bring him back, but if she had a chance to evaluate the risk, to know what he was thinking... She might not have bet on it as he did—not when the cost could be his life.

"I'll always bet on you," the voice said as if reading her very thoughts.

"You left me," she whispered.

The tendril inching its way up her arm halted. She had its attention. She'd come to rely on his power's presence like she did her own magic. Then, he'd unceremoniously severed what they'd built when he went beyond the veil.

"Our connection spans realms. You know that."

Did she? The tendril retreated. The black stone—the rock floor itself—seemed to stretch upward—elongating in impossible ways. A shape pushed up from the lakebed like a hand desperately reaching for her but unable to break through.

"Acknowledge it, Rose. Let me make it up to you."

Her finger itched to touch the material as it moved. The shape stretched like a finger pointing, a mirror of her own action. Its cool, smooth surface connected with her flesh. That presence— that heavy, insistent magic—wrapped around her skin, her hand, her arm. It moved much quicker this time, as if afraid she'd stop it.

She wouldn't.

Its caress was more a presence than the chuckle that had danced across her skin. His magic had a weight all its own, one she was intimately familiar with. She needed to smell it—to prove to her mind what her body already knew. A deep inhale in the space she'd created with her magic brought the familiar pine and cinnamon to her nose, the strongest she had scented since the cavern. Her nostrils flared at the smell she thought she'd lost. She choked back a sob as a tendril of magic—his magic—circled her body.

"But...the end of the battle... You're gone... The connection was gone." She couldn't string a complete sentence together with his magic on her skin.

     JILLIAN WITT

"Let me in." His magic teased every one of her senses, alighting her power in a way she hadn't felt since they fought side by side under Mount Bury.

"How is this possible?" Whatever this was, she would wring it for every moment of Luc she could.

"You know how. You need only to accept what you've already worked out."

His magic—and it was *his* magic. She couldn't mistake it as it wrapped tighter around her, cocooning her in its presence. It held her steady and kept her safe as she let herself fall apart and pulled herself back together.

Time passed, but she knew she needed to return to reality. Their journey so far had only been their beginning. She knew that. They would have an entire existence together. She just needed to bring him back.

She knew how... Whatever that meant. She would follow his magic—this unique connection of theirs—back to her partner. They would save the continent together and have the existence they deserved. The Lady of the Veil couldn't keep her away. She nodded to herself. The tendril retreated across her skin, releasing her as if knowing she was ready to leave.

Her fingers stretched, rethinking her decision to let Luc's magic go. She threw herself forward, wanting to hold onto the connection—whatever it was. Her body flailed, and her eyes snapped open to find herself sitting in bed at Norden house.

CHAPTER FIVE

Rose was on the Osten Point's doorstep far too early for their meeting the next morning. Her mind was restless, and waiting for a polite hour was out of the question. She didn't attempt to hide the intent of her visit. The tall, sturdy boots she wore were appropriate for travel, and her sword was strapped to her back, undermining any casual appearance of her tunic and leggings.

If Norden house was a castle and Suden a sprawling manor, Osten house was a sophisticated, single-floor building with high ceilings. It still had all the space of the others, but the entryway was more disarming, appearing like an elegant home instead of the court of wind fae.

The lingering outline of where Luc's magic should be inside her was as clear as ever. She didn't know what to think of the remaining memories of her dream last night. The feel of Luc's voice—his magic— remained on her skin. It was a feeling she was too familiar with to doubt. The how of it made less sense. When she awoke with the echo of his touch as present as that of his magic—she knew she had to do something. Now.

She tried to find the tunnel to his magic in the heart of hers again. Not every detail from last night was available to her waking mind, but she knew that's where they connected. She'd tried to find the connection so many times—the tunnel simply wasn't there.

It wasn't there this morning either.

Unsure of the protocol, she raised her hand to knock. While she waited, she rubbed at the phantom feeling in her chest—the outward reflection of whatever was going on with her magic. Last night had shaken her. Already desperate to get to Luc, the dream, or connection, or whatever it was, stirred her to action. With Arie and Aurora yet to arrive at Compass Lake, Juliette seemed Rose's best bet for an uncomfortable conversation about her link with Luc's magic.

An unfamiliar female glared at Rose as she opened the door. Like Juliette, she was tall. Rose had to look up from the step to meet her eyes. She had fair skin and blonde hair that skimmed her shoulders. It was early, but her hair was already neatly styled, a striking contrast to the knot in which Rose's hair was tied. She hadn't made herself presentable, simply rolling out of bed and rushing to Osten house. Rose could sense the wind power in the fae, who looked down her long, pointed nose at her. The fae's pinched brow accused her knock of being an inexcusable offense.

"What?"

The abruptness of the greeting probably should have taken Rose aback, but she was in a state of her own. She matched the female's grumpy greeting. "I need to speak with Juliette."

"She hasn't even breakfasted yet," the fae replied with a glance over her shoulder.

Rose rolled her eyes as if she cared whether the Osten Point had eaten. They were trying to save the continent and maybe Rose's sanity.

"Lela, who's there?" The more familiar voice interrupted Rose's standoff with the female and saved her from further verbal sparring.

"It doesn't matter. I'm sending her away," Lela replied, glaring impossibly harder at Rose. Apparently, she had seen the eye-roll and wanted Rose to know she would not stand for it.

"Juliette!" Rose called over Lela's shoulder. She felt like she was tattling on the female to their wiser advisor, but she could admit she was desperate. Rose heard Juliette's deep sigh from beyond the door.

"Let her in, Lela. She has an open invitation," Juliette called from her unseen location in the house.

Even with Juliette's command, Lela's expression was dubious. She barely sidestepped, her gaze pinched, giving Rose enough room to squeeze by. Rose nodded, working to rein in her smirk, as she walked down a long entry hall to the Osten Point.

Rose was unsurprised that even the Osten hallway was lavishly decorated. Elegant tapestries hung on the wall beside portraits of the past Osten leaders. Juliette had been in her position the longest out of the current Compass Points—over a hundred years. It was clear she'd taken the time to make Osten house hers.

Lela had made it sound like Juliette was still in bed. The woman at the end of the hallway was very much ready for the day —far more so than Rose. Juliette wore a long dress with billowing sleeves, and her dark hair was knotted elegantly at her nape. Juliette's gaze lingered on the dark circles under Rose's eyes. Her eyebrow lifted as she took in the sword strapped to Rose's back. Lela followed Rose into the room, watching like a hawk circling its prey.

Rose felt out of place with these two well-put-together fae, but took the seat Juliette offered, trying to collect her thoughts before dumping all her problems at the Osten Point's doorstep.

It was her first time in Osten house, and she would savor it. Her gaze roamed the room. Juliette's refined elegance was evident in every decorative touch. The plush sitting room had velvet cushions, wooden tables, and a sizeable floor-to-ceiling set of windows that looked out over the lake. They must contain some magic

    JILLIAN WITT

because Rose couldn't say she'd ever seen into this room from the water.

Though stylish, the desk in the corner made it feel like the Osten Point's study. With the breathtaking view of the lake, Rose would spend all her time here, too. Papers were strewn across the desk, and a book was open as if Rose had interrupted Juliette's morning routine; she supposed she had.

"You're early," Juliette commented, likely urging Rose to share what brought her to Osten house in such a state.

"We need to try...to cross..." Rose spoke in stops and starts. She'd meant to discuss her connection to Luc but couldn't decide how to start. Her bias towards action had her already making plans. On her walk over, she'd concocted a new strategy to search for Luc's power. She needed to go beyond the veil and check for the tunnel in the heart of her magic there. It was a concept she struggled to put into words, but the fact that she could smell Luc's magic—that Aaron could smell it around her—made her wonder if their mental connection in her internal lake had been more physical than she realized. She would swear he spoke into her mind in the cavern below Mount Bury. And his power had a physical presence drawn to her more and more on their journey chasing Aterra. Maybe they just needed to be closer together for it to appear. Maybe she would find their connection again when they were in the same realm.

"I'd like to try to cross now," she finally got out. She wasn't sure what else to say. Lela hovered by the door, but Rose didn't know her place in the fae courts. The female appeared about Rose's age—though that meant little to the fae. It helped a little that she, too, seemed unsure if she should stay and listen.

Juliette's gaze followed Rose's, drifting to where Lela stood. "Lela is my steward and heir. You can speak freely in front of her."

Rose couldn't help but widen her eyes at the comment. She noted the surprise in the other fae's features as well. Rose was unaware Juliette had already selected an heir. It wasn't public knowledge. This might also explain Lela's surprise that Juliette shared the information.

It made sense though. Given the length of her appointment as Osten Point, she likely would have found her successor in a recent generation. Rose hoped this didn't mean Juliette was close to stepping down. She had much to learn from Juliette and hoped to have her as a fellow Compass Point a while longer.

Rose spared a moment to appreciate Juliette's directness in providing the information. She didn't dance around sharing necessary details. A small smile crossed Rose's face for the first time that morning.

"Don't overthink it," Juliette said, her answering smile cat-like. She knew how much openly sharing the information meant to Rose. "Why do we have to try now?" Juliette brought them back to the problem at hand. "I thought we would convene with Carter at a more appropriate hour."

"I know that was the plan, but..." Rose's hands clutched together in her lap, a new nervous habit she needed to wrangle.

"What happened, Rose?" Juliette asked.

Rose rubbed at her chest again. Her magic ached, and her dream hadn't felt quite like a dream. Although the details kept slipping through her fingers whenever she reached for them, the feeling of tendrils of Luc's magic wrapping around her was crystal clear.

"I don't know," Rose said honestly. "Something is going on with my magic, and I think it has to do with Luc."

Juliette's eyes lingered where Rose rubbed her chest. "You think his absence is affecting your magic? Physically?" She scratched her temple. "Rose, think about what you're saying. That's impossible."

Rose couldn't help but notice Juliette's face turning intro-spective as she made the statement. Part of her felt vindicated, as she knew Juliette was considering the same thing Rose was—the one thing she couldn't bring herself to say out loud.

Rose chose her words carefully, circling the topic. "I know it should be impossible, Juliette. I'm just telling you what I feel." She rubbed at the pain in her chest like a phantom limb, unable to dislodge the discomfort.

"You can't be bound."

There it was. Juliette stated it so boldly; Rose had barely completed the thought. She'd circled, danced around, and tripped over it but never uttered the words. The ache in Rose's chest strengthened. Juliette was stating a fact, one that Rose already knew. Rose and Luc were of different courts. Bound fae were a myth—a forgotten faerie tale. There were a hundred other reasons why this couldn't be true.

But the tightness in her chest—the Luc-shaped hole in her magic—remained.

"Believe me, I hear you. I know the facts. But this ache in the center of my magic is growing more insistent by the day. I think his magic is trying to reach mine from beyond the veil."

Juliette's face remained skeptical. "Let's say your suspicion is correct." She arched a brow. "I can take you to the caves and even try to call Zrak, but Carter is the better option for crossing beyond the veil. What would you have me do?"

Rose didn't have to answer as another knock sounded at the door. Lela's gaze flashed, giving Rose a final glare like this was her fault as she exited the room to answer it. Rose could hear a charged conversation that sounded similar to hers.

Juliette rolled her eyes. "Lela, let him in," she called.

Carter entered the room with Lela prowling after him. "Good morning," he said. "I saw Rose headed this way and didn't think you'd mind my joining you."

Lela scowled like she *did* mind, but it didn't prevent Carter from continuing. "I'd like to try to cross beyond the veil sooner rather than later," he said.

Rose grinned.

Juliette rubbed her forehead.

"Of course, it would be both of you." She looked to Carter as if grasping for reason. "What brings you here so early with this request?"

"I can feel the realm calling me," he said. He glanced at Rose. "I told you that when you gave me the Vesten coin, the power boost unlocked more of the magic that connects my shifter form with spirits traveling beyond the veil. It's almost like the coin's presence has allowed me to feel my form's true calling." He looked around them, his gaze holding on Lela. Unsurprisingly, he wasn't ready to share his secrets with her. "Running Vesten property in my shifted form here...something calls strongly. My form wants to fulfill its purpose."

Rose read between the lines. The veil cat's purpose was to ferry spirits beyond the veil. Magic was tricky though. Rose knew that more than most. Her weapons-master sense let her understand a lot about magic that most did not. Just because your magic longed for something didn't mean you were ready to handle it. She'd learned as much when she started evaluating the Compass Points' magic. She'd grown into it, but if she had treaded a little more lightly at first—if she'd taken a little more time—she might not have been so magically drained.

"You know, you might need to build your magic up to this since it's been dormant so long," she cautioned.

Carter rolled his eyes. His response was precisely what she expected. "I can handle being a little tired if it helps us fix this mess."

Rose held up her hands in a gesture of peace. If being a little magically drained was the only sacrifice, she would let Carter pay it. She had her own magical pull to the Suden Point to deal with. "I want to be honest: My motives aren't exactly pure in all of this. I want Luc back. And I'm not sure I'll be completely objective about the associated risks. While I'm willing to risk myself, you don't need to do the same."

Rose rubbed her chest again, trying to evaluate the feeling. Juliette had said, so calmly, that she and Luc couldn't be bound.

That may be technically correct, but Rose had no other explanation for the strength of this connection she felt across realms.

"I need to test this magic sooner rather than later," Carter said. "I can be convinced to start small. Let's try to cross beyond the veil and come back. If that's successful, we can explore farther on the next trip."

Rose nodded in agreement. She was sure she could find the connection to Luc again if she was beyond the veil. It would only take a few moments. Their connection had been so easily accessible when they were both on the continent.

"Are you both sure you know what you're doing?" Juliette, the voice of reason, asked.

Carter and Rose exchanged a glance and then nodded.

"Then I won't stop you. It makes no difference to me if we try now or in a few hours." Juliette stood, and before ushering them out of the room, she pulled a custom belt from her desk. With no small amount of pride, Rose realized it was made to holster the twin daggers she had made for Juliette.

"Don't overthink it," Juliette said again, catching her eye.

A smile crossed Rose's face as they ventured deeper into Osten house.

CHAPTER SIX

550 YEARS AGO

"At least, this time, he accepted my plan...no matter how reluctantly," Cee said as they walked down Marcil's main street.

It had been days since they'd replanted the field, but Cee's resentment about their father's decision hadn't abated. Usually, it was short-lived, but this felt different.

Thankfully, their father had caved to one of Cee's plans. She wanted their family to take responsibility for the villagers by caring for the ill. If their people were suffering, Cee wanted their family to experience it with them. Their father hadn't deemed it something he could contribute to personally—he didn't have any basic healing skills—however, he supported the sisters in doing so, especially now that the crops were on their way to regrowing.

Andie grunted in solidarity with Cee. Her arm still throbbed from the blood given for the field. Even a few days later, it was still tender—that's how deep she'd gone for the offering. It was more than she'd suspected. Whatever was happening, the continent was getting desperate.

"Where are we headed first?"

Cee looked down at the list in her hand. The piece of paper was tucked into the pages of their shared journal. Her face sombered. "Nona—" She cleared her throat of emotion. "Nona is first on the list."

Andie let her head fall. First on the list meant she was closest to death. Nona had helped raise them. She had looked after them as children.

Even with her head hung, Andie could feel the eyes of the villagers on her as they walked. After their father's announcement and seeing the results of her work, the villagers seemed suspicious of her. Blood magic might be what was saving them, but few were happy about it. Even Garth didn't approach as they passed on the street today. He waved at Cee while keeping his distance from Andie and the power she displayed to replant the field.

Cee tucked the journal into her jacket pocket, and the twins entered Nona's home with a soft knock. Ilena, the village healer, was already there. She shook her head solemnly. "All we can do is make her comfortable. It would help me if you could sit with her...I have other patients I could do more for."

Cee took the lead. "Of course we will."

Andie hadn't spent much time considering the afterlife. But with someone so close to death before her, it could no longer be avoided.

"Don't look away. She helped raise us," Cee chided, taking Nona's hand. "The least we can do is let her know someone is with her as she passes."

Andie nodded, immediately feeling better when a cat jumped into her lap. Nona had always kept them as pets. She scratched the cat's head, and it purred as she looked toward Nona. Andie cheated a little. Unable to look at Nona directly, she aimed her gaze just past Nona's bed. If Cee glanced at her again, she'd appear to be following directions. Andie wasn't trying to be difficult, she just didn't know how to deal with death.

Her gaze fixed on the wall, Andie heard Cee rustling with something under her skirt. Part of her wondered if this was a test, so Andie did as she'd been asked and kept staring ahead. At the moment Nona breathed her last, magic flooded the room.

Andie jostled unexpectedly at the sensation. The cat on her lap jumped off as the scent of copper prickled her nose. Blood. "What are you doing?" she hissed at her sister.

Cee didn't respond, her head swiveling, following something Andie couldn't see above the body.

"Cee..."

She didn't acknowledge Andie's plea. Cee stood and, before Andie could stop her, was rushing from the house into the street.

"What are you doing?" Andie hissed again, following.

Cee's neck tilted back, still looking at something hovering just above their regular line of vision. Blood magic didn't usually work for Cee, but Andie couldn't deny she was using it now. Realizing she wouldn't respond, Andie cleared a path as Cee followed whatever she saw.

The sun was setting, but they still had time before the light was gone. Cee led them out of the village and into the surrounding forest. They both knew better than to be in the woods after dark. Cee's speed increased like she, too, knew they only had so much time for whatever this was.

Andie chased Cee until the river was in sight. The Othlow River had a powerful current that was too dangerous for swimming. Andie came to a halt behind her sister. Though Cee still didn't speak to her, Andie no longer cared. Her gaze was fixed on an animal prowling the riverbank.

It was huge, easily chest height. The feline's fur was reddish-brown, and though it didn't bare its teeth, it had the easy confidence of a predator. Andie wasn't afraid of it, though she was sure she should be. Her draw to the animal was undeniable—a mystery she needed to unravel. Before she acted on it, Andie needed to remove her sister from danger. She tugged Cee behind a tree.

"Stop it, Andie!" Cee whisper-hissed.

"Oh, so you can speak," Andie replied. "Why are we here?"

     JILLIAN WITT

Cee spun to glare at Andie. Blood still dripped from Cee's arm —the cut she'd made in Nona's home. "We're following Nona's spirit," she said as if it were the most obvious thing in the world.

Andie shook her head, wondering if she'd heard her sister correctly. "Following…"

"Nona's spirit," Cee finished for her. "It led us here to this beast." Cee gestured across the river.

The language affronted Andie. It wasn't a beast. The animal was most certainly a giant cat. She shook her head, focusing on her twin's words. "Why are we following Nona's spirit?" Andie asked.

"If we're to comfort our people as they pass, we need to know what happens to them."

"Cee," Andie started. She didn't want to sound callous, but she wasn't sure it mattered where their people went when they died. She couldn't entirely ignore her piqued curiosity at the cat before them though. Andie wanted to learn what it was here for, how it was connected to Nona's passing.

"Andie, you have to see this," Cee whispered. She was once again staring just above the animal's head. "Here," she said, shoving a dagger into Andie's hand. "Cut yourself."

Unsure where this was going, Andie did as she was told. She made a small cut, letting a few drops of blood fall directly to the continent as she offered a little of herself. The problem was, she didn't know what she was asking for.

She focused on Cee's words, Nona's spirit. As her blood fell in gentle drops, she asked to see Nona's spirit; she hoped that was right. Before she could question herself too much, the land responded. Magic surged around her, and a sheen of magic slid over her open eyes.

Nona's spirit was exactly where Cee was staring.

More surprisingly, Nona's hand rested on the scruff of the giant cat's neck. Nona was scratching the animal even though she no longer had a physical form. With feline grace, the animal crouched back on its haunches, preparing for a leap. Spirit Nona's hand tangled further into its fur.

"Where are they—"

"Nona can't swim!" Cee yelled, cutting off her question. Andie was sure Cee would realize her error momentarily. It didn't matter if Nona could swim—she was already dead.

Instead, Cee ripped the dagger back from Andie and plunged it again into her skin. Cee seemed to dig deeper this time. She didn't communicate with the land the way Andie did. This felt like a brute-force attempt at simple magic.

Only it seemed to be working.

Andie wasn't sure what Cee was doing, but she felt the magic. Something like a golden lasso looped around Nona's spirit as the animal jumped into the air. Andie saw the jolt when the lasso drew taught. The magic tugged Nona's spirit back, separating it from the animal. The cat turned and snarled in her twin's direction, but it seemed unable to stop what had already begun—even as Cee's lasso stole its cargo. The animal disappeared with a pop beyond something fluttering in the air above the river.

Cee had a hold on Nona's spirit. The spirit struggled against the golden lasso, almost like she fought to follow the animal. A chill crept over Andie's neck as she recognized this.

What had they done?

It was too late now—the feline was gone. They couldn't send her through the fluttering veil-like space nor drop her into the cold rushing waters below. With another burst of magic, Cee tugged hard, pulling the spirit back toward the riverbank, aiming for a tangle of bushes to provide a soft landing.

"Got her," Cee said to herself, not seeming to notice the horror Andie was experiencing.

Neither was prepared for what happened next.

It could only be described as consuming: The bush consumed Nona's spirit.

No noise was heard, but the bushes rustled violently as the plants absorbed Nona's essence. Andie's hand covered her mouth.

　　　　JILLIAN WITT

The leaves swayed, and the branches rustled as if they were licking their lips after a tasty meal.

Then, the bush sprouted. Branches, leaves, and flowers shot out in all directions as the plant grew at an unnatural pace. The flowers bloomed, the leaves shed and regrew, and the bush went through multiple cycles of life in only a few moments. Finally, it stopped moving but didn't return to a more expected size.

It had grown—even faster and larger than what Andie had done to the field.

The sisters watched in silence. They stood together until they realized the sun would soon set.

"We need to get back to the village," Andie said, unsure what to say about what they'd just witnessed.

There was no denying the bush grew from magic, but it wasn't truly blood magic—or wasn't only blood magic. It was magic provided by a spirit's sacrifice to the continent. Goosebumps rose on Andie's skin as she wondered if Nona wanted to make this sacrifice.

The image of Nona struggling against Cee's magical lasso was burned into her mind. Andie feared she knew the answer.

"This is what we've been looking for!" Cee said. Her voice was excited, out of line with what they had just witnessed.

Andie stared at the bush, unable to put her thoughts into words. She reached wordlessly for the journal. Cee handed it to her without question, and Andie began to write.

"My blood offerings for growth never work. But this—" Cee was so animated. More excited than Andie had seen her in weeks. "If one spirit could grow a bush to ten times its standard size, what might we do with multiple spirits and a field sown of crops ready to grow?"

Cee was right. It had done more, faster than any blood magic Andie had seen, but she couldn't shake the feeling that it wasn't what Nona had wanted for herself.

CHAPTER SEVEN

Lela's gaze continuously bounced between Rose and Carter. The fae protected Juliette, even guarding her back as they walked through Osten house.

The first floor was a maze of hallways. They passed a kitchen, a grand formal dining room, and an endless stream of guest rooms. Osten house didn't have the large ballroom that Norden did, but it had much more charm. Rose wondered how many Osten visited regularly to use these rooms. She dreamed of using Norden house's capacity in the future.

Rose grunted, running into Carter as they stopped before a door. Rose couldn't see much difference between this door and the others they had passed, but the longer she stared at it, the more familiar it felt. Sage and citrus filled her nostrils. Rose searched the hall for attackers, thinking Juliette had readied her wind for protection. Finding no one, a soft click from the door drew her attention back. There was a momentary pause, and then the door swung open of its own accord.

"Did your wind open that?" Rose asked.

She caught Lela's brow-rise as Rose questioned Juliette.

"You can sense that little magic use from the Osten Point?" Lela asked.

Rose was a little surprised by the question. She nodded though. "Yes, I'm a weapons master. I'm well attuned to the scents of magic."

"Juliette had said, but I didn't..." Lela trailed off. Rose couldn't tell if she was impressed or horrified by Rose's talent for scents.

"Yes," Juliette cut in. "Only wind magic can open the door."

"Any wind magic?" Rose asked.

Juliette's lip quirked at the question. "The wind has to be strong and well controlled. But I'm sure you could do it."

Rose felt herself stand a little taller. She may be Norden Point, but she relished Juliette's validation. As a magic she'd long had to hide, she appreciated someone noticing the strength of her wind.

She coughed to cover her embarrassment. Carter smirked at her, indicating she'd failed at doing so. She pointedly ignored him and turned toward the open door. A gasp slipped out in recognition.

The door wasn't similar because of the repetition in the hallway. The door and the stairs she now saw were a different kind of familiar—something she'd only ever seen in the heart of her magic.

Juliette turned to Rose. "Everything okay?"

"The door. The stairs..." Rose struggled to form complete sentences. "I've seen them before."

Juliette's eyes widened. "Where?"

"When I evaluated your power, it started like this... And in the heart of my magic, I opened a door just like this to initiate the link between us." Rose peered down the stairs. They descended into darkness. "I went down these stairs when I needed to ask you for more magic—to deepen our connection."

Carter's mouth opened and closed, but no words came out. Juliette's face held a similar surprise. No one seemed willing or able to comment on what it might mean.

"What does the connection to my magic look like?" Carter asked hesitantly.

Rose thought of the tree and the odd metamorphosis it went through to allow her access to his magic. "It looks just like the willow tree on Vesten property," Rose said. "But I can't even begin describing how the tree...opens."

Carter tilted his head. He had more questions. Juliette coughed, gesturing back to the staircase. "Do you know what is required to go down the stairs then?" she asked Rose.

"What is required?" Rose echoed. What did that mean? Opening the door with magic wasn't enough?

"I'll take that as a no," Juliette said. "The portal is at the bottom, but part of what keeps it safe is what you must face to get there." Juliette laced her fingers together as she explained.

"What must we face?" Carter asked.

"I don't know," Juliette replied.

Rose was still marveling over the door and its mirror in the heart of her magic. Did the similarity mean anything? There was no way the tree on Vesten property opened like the one in the heart of her magic did—was there? Juliette's vague response brought her focus back to the conversation.

"What do you mean you don't know?" Rose cut in, narrowing her eyes at Juliette.

"What you face depends entirely on what you fear," she replied casually.

"What we fear?" Rose echoed as her mind scattered into a million directions all at once. She feared never getting Luc back. And what the Norden fae needed of her. And not knowing how she'd improve life on the continent if they could deal with their current problems.

Juliette nodded. "You have to face your fears before you can use the portal."

"Face our fears?" Carter asked a little skeptically. "How so?"

"The magic can be quite distressing. I believe Zrak himself set it up. If I understand it correctly, it takes the idea of secrets from the wind to a new level. It pulls distressing secrets from your mind and reflects them to the traveler."

"I didn't know that was possible," Rose said.

"I don't think even I know all of what can be done with the Osten wind," Juliette said with a shrug. She had a point. They probably wouldn't know all the wind could do until Zrak was back on the continent, but that didn't make Rose any more comfortable. She peered down the staircase with trepidation. Carter rocked back and forth on his heels next to her, realizing what this would mean for them.

"When we descend, the magic will come for you both. It will play back awful thoughts, fears, memories, whatever it can find. You will need to keep going."

"You do this every time you commune with Zrak?" Carter asked, bewildered.

"I do." Juliette nodded. "I'll admit, I have learned to keep my mind blank as I descend. If you give the magic nothing to work with, it has nothing to throw at you." Her gaze rested on Rose. "I know that might be incredibly difficult for you right now, but it's the only defense I know."

Rose sighed, her shoulders falling. This was going to be bad. Her mind had been working double time since returning to Compass Lake. They had so much to do and only ideas of how to start. Emptying her mind seemed so far out of reach. "What happens if I can't do that?"

"You will have to walk through the pain," Juliette said, not unkindly. "In that case, the best news I can offer is it only takes moments once you begin, though, with the attack on your mind, it will feel longer. Keep moving, keep taking steps—it's the best advice I can offer. You'll eventually hit the portal and land in the caves."

Rose looked at Carter. He shrugged. "We don't have another option."

She moved first, leading the group down the stairs. If this was going to be awful, she wanted to get it over with. Carter followed, and Juliette told Lela to stay at Osten house as she closed the door, taking the final position behind them.

Rose supposed Carter was right—they didn't have another option—and her pull to Luc was stronger than whatever fears her mind could conjure. This challenge was a small price to get him back and save the continent. Though these seemed innocent enough thoughts, the wind struck as it found its mark.

Luc was never returning.

She would find him too late.

Tara still slept beneath a mist-plague-coated Bury.

Rose realized what she'd done as the wind whipped at her mind. She took a breath, refusing to focus on what could go wrong. Another breath and an image of the future—the balanced continent she fought for.

Rose and Luc together at Compass Lake. They left Suden house hand in hand and walked through Vesten property to Norden house where Tara waited.

She would will this future into existence if she had to. She took another step. Another strong gust pushed at her mind. She shook it off.

Another step down into the darkness. She pushed her shoulders back, readying herself. The wind whooshed around her, searching for an opening in her defenses.

It was a summer day on Norden beach. Rose and Luc sprawled on the sand. Their hair was wet and disheveled from a recent swim. Laughter echoed through her mind as their limbs entangled. He rolled over, his hands propping his full weight just above her. Her fingers twined in the hair at the back of his neck as she tugged him into a scorching kiss. He pulled back as he let some of his weight settle between them, a wicked grin spreading across his features. "I'm going to take my time with you," he said as his hand roamed the curve of her hip, the swell of her breast.

"As you should," she replied, staring into Luc's dark brown eyes.

Then he was gone.

A dark, empty room was before her. It was familiar—one of the many in Norden house. It was cold—so cold—but it was hers.

This was her room. A room she'd spent hundreds, thousands of nights in just like this.

Alone.

She curled up in her bed. She tried to read, but the words were blurry, and tears rimmed her eyes. She focused again on the page. It was a letter, a report from a Norden fae. The tests hadn't worked, and the village remained asleep.

More images flooded in. She stood outside the village of Bury. Mist still hung in the air, and the villagers, in their endless sleep, lay motionless on the ground.

Tara never woke.

The continent was never restored.

Rose looked around. No one was with her as she explored the mist-taken village, her wind-wrapped weapon in her hand. Where were the other Compass Points?

As she stood there alone, a torrential downpour started. The usually peaceful water of the Lake of the Gods rocked and swirled. Waves crashed over the shores. Rose tried to hold it back with her water magic—but she wasn't enough.

When she returned to Compass Lake, a male who seemed vaguely familiar was Suden Point. Where was Luc?

The gods' temple, once atop Mount Bury, was rebuilt in a new location near Sandrin. Arie and Aurora took up duties there. Arie waved goodbye as he shifted into a black bird and flew away.

Juliette retired as Osten Point, and Lela's sneer follows Rose at the circular table in Norden library.

Carter disappeared in his veil cat form. He jumped through a crack between realms, and only a billowing fabric-like essence showed that anything had been there at all.

Rose made herself impossibly smaller in her bed. Alone.

A tug pulled her from the onslaught of images. Her eyes refocused on the present. She stood frozen on the stairs. She needed to get to the portal. How many more steps?

That tug again. This time, a familiar hand slipped into Rose's and more insistently led her forward. She stumbled but caught herself, her feet finding even ground.

Each step brought with it a little more clarity. Juliette squeezed her hand tight. They were going down the staircase.

Her fears threatened to take over again.

Juliette pulled.

A few more steps, and they'd reach the portal. Juliette wouldn't leave her here.

Rose's feet kept pace with the Osten Point. Juliette didn't let go. Carter wasn't visible. Had he made it to the portal? A few more steps. They were jogging now—then they fell, plummeting into familiar darkness.

JILLIAN WITT

CHAPTER EIGHT

Rose hit the ground hard.

She tried to suck air into her lungs, but each gulp proved useless. Panic rose, and something contracted in her stomach as she tried to force a breath. A cough erupted, finally allowing air to pass. She rested her cheek against the cool, damp ground and waited for the rapid beat of her heart to calm.

Juliette had warned them. The magic in the stairs brought forth their worst fears. But damn. That was...worse than she'd imagined. The scenes were so real, and the fears so fresh in her mind. Rose opened her eyes, trying to focus on something else to flush away the images of failure and loneliness.

Her breathing started to even out as she took in her surroundings. She could only describe her location as a cave. Technically, she wasn't sure she was underground since she'd fallen through the portal, but it was cooler than it had been at Osten house, and moist air tickled her nose. A flame lit the otherwise dark hall, and the soft smells of chocolate and sandalwood grew stronger by the minute. From what she could see, the walls were jagged rock, reminding her far too much of the large cavern under Mount Bury, where the Compass Points had made their stand against Aterra.

A pair of slippered feet appeared in her line of vision. She pushed up to her arms from her sprawled position on the ground and dared to tilt her head back, glancing at the others. Juliette stood before her.

"Alright, Rose?" Carter's voice called from somewhere else in the hall.

She shook her head. Why did he sound so chipper? Juliette was used to this. Apparently, she traveled that nightmare regularly. Carter had no such excuse.

"Why am I the only one sprawled on the floor, Carter?" Rose raised her gaze enough to see him shrug as he toed his boot at the packed dirt.

"It did get me at first," he said quietly. "But I've had some practice avoiding things I see." He shrugged again. "So, I was able to get myself out."

Rose hadn't thought about it like that. Carter had been seeing spirits his entire life—when had he realized what they were? She shook her head as she pushed herself to her feet, her eyes meeting Juliette's green ones. "You came back for me."

Juliette nodded.

"Thank you. I don't think I would have moved." Rose rolled her neck, attempting to stretch her body. It felt like she'd physically caved in on herself as the fears took over in the stairway. "Out of curiosity, what would happen if I hadn't moved...if I'd stayed there?" She wasn't sure why she asked. It likely wasn't an answer she wanted to hear.

Juliette ran her fingers through her hair. "You'd remain exactly where you were. Locked in your mind until someone pulled you out."

"And you didn't think it helpful to tell us that before we descended?" Rose asked.

"Would it have stopped you?" Juliette responded, moving her hands to her hips in challenge.

Rose laughed as she dusted herself off. "Well played, Juliette." Rose appreciated the depth of understanding Juliette's words implied. Rose had made up her mind, and nothing, not even trauma-inducing staircases, would stop her. This left Juliette to sweep in and save Rose when she got in over her head. Her relationship with Juliette had moved past colleagues with mutual respect. If Juliette's lip-twitching, dangerously close to tipping into a smile, was anything to go by, Juliette considered Rose a friend as well.

"If you two are finished..." Carter tapped his foot on the ground. The steady beat echoed in the cave tunnel. The soft lines on his face in the dim light told Rose he wasn't actually put out by their banter.

Rose rolled her eyes at him and looked at Juliette. "Alright, where to next?" The cave glowed in firelight emanating from the Vesten Point's palm. The warm yellow and orange flames made the dark cave walls appear purple. Long shadows moved with them as they filed into line behind the Osten Point, to journey through the tunnel.

"We're in a cave network on the eastern shore now. It's not a long walk to where I commune with Zrak, but it has a few obstacles."

"Worse than facing our fears as we descend the stairs?" Carter asked. Rose could have sworn she saw him shiver. Secretly, she was glad she wasn't the only one impacted by the descent.

"Less mentally taxing and slightly more physical," Juliette said as she led them on. The path split in two, and Juliette selected the one on the right without hesitation.

Rose wondered about each Osten Point learning this path. She assumed the previous leader would teach the next. Did Lela already know the sacrifice the Osten Point made for their people? Though she'd never said as much directly, Rose knew from her evaluation of Juliette's magic that communing with Zrak was a burden she did not wish to pass on.

Juliette's voice pulled Rose from her thoughts. "I've sent my wind ahead to trigger the traps. They are simple but effective ways to ensure intruders don't make it to the end." Juliette waved her hand as she continued. "Spears that shoot from the wall and a trapdoor that plummets to a hole the Suden Point would be proud of." Juliette smiled softly.

"I'm sure he'll have notes for you," Rose said as she thought of dragging Luc back through these tunnels. Even if this trip was only a test, it was the first step to reconnecting to his magic. "Are there any left for us?" she asked as the Osten Point continued to list traps. "Or is this just a walk in the dark now?"

"I resent that," Carter said.

"My apologies to the Vesten Point. A walk dimly lit by flame." Rose smirked, and the room around her flared in light, the eerie purple glow of the rock walls even more prominent as Carter showed off his magic.

"Are you two done?" Juliette asked, echoing Carter's teasing words from the start of their walk. "Your only real challenge will be the ridge," she said, her voice taking on a more serious tone.

Rose and Carter shared a concerned glance. "What is the ridge?" Rose asked when it was clear Juliette wasn't offering more information.

"A narrow section of the path that wraps around a large opening within the cave network. Rock continues to fall away from the ridge into the expanse." She reached her hand out to touch the cave wall. "Each step can be quite dangerous. There is no surviving a fall from it."

"Is that a problem when we can use our wind to hold tight to the wall?" Rose asked.

"Ah, that's the trick," Juliette added. "The real obstacle of the ridge is the wind itself. It has a single-minded focus to drive travelers from the wall, plummeting them into the expanse."

"Really?" Carter asked. "A wind that works against you? Aren't these obstacles supposed to keep other fae out—not the Osten?"

"I'm sure we have Zrak to thank for this obstacle, too," Rose commented dryly.

Juliette nodded. "I have to assume it was his doing. It's the

       JILLIAN WITT

only way to explain the strength and inconsistency of the winds. He knew how to stress test Osten magic, ensuring only the strongest wind wielders could make it through."

"Are we sure we want to bring Zrak back?" Carter asked, looking uncomfortable. As the only one without wind on this journey, Rose understood his concern. "He doesn't seem like he's necessarily on our side."

Rose laughed, though it held no real mirth. "I've decided to withhold judgment until Arie talks to him. Zrak's actions seem questionable, but Arie still trusts his motives." She sighed. "Whereas, we know everything Aterra did was in service of obliterating the balance."

"If you say so," Carter said as he took another careful step, coming face to face with one of the spears Juliette's wind had triggered.

Not much farther ahead, the ridge curved close to the wall, and the expanse unfolded to its left. The perceived safety of the tunnel's enclosed walls had to be left behind to proceed. As Juliette said, the footpath itself was narrower than the tunnel's. Pieces of it must have been sliding off into the expanse for as long as it had existed. On their right, the jagged rock wall; on the left...Rose kicked a rock, and it tumbled over the edge into the darkness. She listened for an echo as it plummeted—at first, a few clinks as it must have hit a jagged outcrop below them...then nothing.

This was not Luc's hole in Loch. It had to have a bottom. Just as the thought crossed her mind, she heard the stone hitting the base of the expanse with a resounding thud.

Carter sent balls of flame out over the space to give them more light to guide their steps. Rose wasn't sure seeing everything helped. She'd rather not know what she could fall into, and the more significant challenge seemed to be staying close to the rock wall.

She had barely stepped from the tunnel onto the narrow ridge when the wind rushed around her. Rose hurried back before it could push her away from the wall and glanced at Juliette.

The wind was completely unnatural, the way it wrapped around her. It blew from the wall, where no wind should come from, as if it were guiding her to plummet into the depths.

"Really?" Rose glared at Juliette.

"Don't look at me. I told you the wind wouldn't help you." Juliette said.

"How do we make it around the ridge?" Carter asked.

Juliette looked at Rose. "It would be easiest if Rose could merge our magic and use the combined power around all three of us to fight the unnatural wind." Juliette sighed. "But since we won't be able to access that connection with Luc gone, we'll just have to join our winds externally—the same way we used our wind together to speed up the horses on our trip."

Rose didn't need another reason to hate Luc not being here, but now she had one. Juliette was right. The two wind wielders could combine their shared element externally, but they couldn't lean on merging their magic through her without all four Compass Points activating their power.

"I have better balance as a veil cat," Carter said. For the first time, he said the name of his shifted form without whispering, undoubtedly because they were finally in a place where no one else would hear him. She turned to mock him, but he no longer stood behind her; a large cat prowled forward.

"Carter's right," Juliette said. "It should help. Not even magical wind can shake natural feline balance."

The scent of sage and citrus filled Rose's nostrils as Juliette's wind rushed around them. Rose called her magic, too, joining it with Juliette's. This wasn't as strong as when she pulled from her internal lake of power, but if Juliette could make it around the ridge herself, then Rose supposed this method should be good enough.

"It will work," Juliette said as if knowing Rose's unspoken thoughts.

"If you say so..." Rose said slowly, stepping forward as she and Juliette's wind twisted together and wrapped around them.

          JILLIAN WITT

Juliette led, the veil cat in the middle, and Rose brought up the end of the line. She wrapped the wind shield around them tightly, pushing back on any force attempting to knock them off course. The wind spiraled out from the safety of the wall, pushing them toward the depths of the expanse. It was strong as it pressed against the combined magic of both Rose and the Osten Point. Rose took another step as she focused on flexing their shield to push back the onslaught.

Rose placed her foot down, the rock cracking and slipping beneath her. More rocks careened into the expanse. The noise of falling stones was deafening. She almost preferred the whistle of the wind whipping against them. The veil cat growled in front of her at the noise. Rose glared at him—unhelpful since she knew he didn't see it, but it made her feel better.

"I know. I know. I'm not quite as light on my feet as you are," she said.

"We're almost there, Rose," Juliette said. Her voice was tight. She must be focusing more than Rose expected. "Keep going," the Osten Point called.

Rose took another step, reaching deep into her magic to support the shield. She focused on Carter—on keeping the veil cat steady—as the ridge's winds tore at them.

She knew Juliette was right. They wouldn't be able to connect their winds through the heart of her magic. But as she closed her eyes and reached for more power, she dove into her quiet center anyway. Her body froze in place on the ridge, but she couldn't help searching for the now-familiar door. Her wind led her around the lake. As expected, no door was present. Her shoulders sagged in disappointment.

Rose felt the moment Juliette cleared the ridge. The Osten Point's body no longer required the support of their joint shield, but Carter still needed her.

The wind raged against their defense as she started inching around the ridge again. Even Carter's balance couldn't stop the rock from slipping beneath him. She wasn't sure she could hold off the unruly wind. Rose paused and dug deeper to fuel Carter's last few steps on the exposed path.

The usually still water in her lake shifted violently as she dug for more strength. The rolling waves must have been enough to disrupt the sand of the lakebed. Rose's gaze caught on something dark and shiny in the movement.

The black stone.

Images from her dream—or not dream—flooded back in. This stone was some connection to Luc. She was sure of it. Zrak's wind assaulted her shields again, leaving her unable to investigate further.

The veil cat yowled, pulling her focus. A gust of wind swept from above to try to push him off course. Rose's shield was still in place, but the unnatural angle wasn't one she or Juliette adequately defended. The black stone in her lake shook like a readying earthquake, but didn't crack as she pulled more magic to support Carter. Steadied, he stalked the last few steps to safety.

She took another step on the ridge.

Another gust swept down on her, the only remaining target on the treacherous path. Juliette's sage and citrus rushed around her, but still, Rose's foot slipped as another piece of the ridge fell away. Unable to catch her balance, she dropped to her hands and knees, her left knee slipping off the side.

"Rose!" Juliette call.

The black stone in the heart of her magic shook again, a deeper rumble, growing in strength. Power flooded her, bolstering the wind she and Juliette wielded.

"I've got it," Rose said shakily. She let the power boost stabilize her. Once again, Rose and Juliette's combined wind wrapped around her body, covering every angle for the remaining distance to the tunnel. She put weight on her hands as she worked to get both feet back under her. She righted herself and stared down at the remaining steps.

Just a few left.

She took a deep breath and sprinted, not bothering to check

     JILLIAN WITT

where the other Compass Points were in the tunnel she aimed for. Rose barreled into Juliette as she left the ridge and terrifying expanse behind.

"What was that?" Juliette asked as she caught and steadied Rose in the tunnel's safety.

"What was what?" Rose asked.

Juliette's brows raised skeptically. "The flood of power? Were you holding back as we crossed?"

"No!" Rose said, shocked Juliette would ask such a thing.

Juliette held up her hands. "I didn't think so. Your wind felt at full strength as we walked. I just don't understand where the last burst of power came from."

Rose shook her head in disbelief. She hadn't imagined any of it: the smooth black stone in the heart of her magic, shaking as if trying to set something free, and the power flooding into her. "I'm not sure I could put my theory into words," Rose said. Now, more than ever, she wanted to get beyond the veil.

She wanted to get to Luc.

Juliette gave her a final, lingering glance as if sensing Rose's renewed focus on her goal and said, "We're almost there."

CHAPTER NINE

550 YEARS AGO

Andie hoped this idea of using spirits to fuel magic would disappear. She at least convinced Cee not to tell their father immediately. They should test it again themselves before getting anyone's hopes up. The feline might fight harder next time—it might not go the same way. Cee agreed to replicate it once more before sharing their solution.

Nona's spirit, desperately fighting against Cee's gold lasso, haunted Andie's dreams.

They didn't have to wait long for a second opportunity to learn what the magic of spirits could do for them. Illness was spreading, and rations were sparse. Ilena was overburdened, so the sisters continued to give care where they could. Cee's list of townspeople who needed them continued to grow. It was a stark reminder that Nona's spirit may not have wanted to be a sacrifice, but she also might not have wanted to die when she did either. The cycle of life and death continued with or without Andie's interference.

Watching more townspeople sicken was another reminder that their problems were only beginning.

A woman Andie barely knew was on their list today. She had an illness they hadn't heard of, but Ilena said it wasn't treatable. Andie was taking notes but was unsurprised to smell copper the moment the woman's breath left her body.

Cee was moving before Andie could snap the journal shut. Andie didn't want to blindly follow this time. Knowing what Cee was up to, she pricked her finger, offering her blood in exchange for the ability to see spirits.

They followed the spirit again to the edge of the woods. It was later in the evening, and darkness was falling. "We might not make it back in time," Andie cautioned.

"I'm going," Cee replied. Her tone brooked no argument.

She couldn't stop Cee or let her venture out alone. With little choice in the matter, she followed. Andie had a reasonable suspicion of where this spirit would lead them. She didn't think the feline waiting by the river was an accidental placement. The river's running water felt like a natural meeting place to journey to an afterlife—whatever that looked like.

Most humans seemed to believe there was existence beyond the veil after death. No one talked about what that meant though. Andie had asked her father again after Nona's death. He said the questions were natural, but he had no different answers from those he'd given in her childhood. When their mother died, he'd said she went to a better place.

No one seemed sure of what lay beyond the veil. Was it really a better place? What had they inadvertently robbed Nona of by pulling her back? What were they about to steal from this new spirit?

The answer felt within Andie's grasp. She would never be comfortable with Cee's plan unless she knew the spirits were willing. Nona hadn't been willing, but they also hadn't known what would happen. Andie wasn't sure what to do this time, but she knew it was her last chance. The magic of the spirits was clearly a powerful fuel for growth. It would work again. When it did, Cee would tell their father, and he would build their plans for survival around it. Andie didn't want to take that from Cee, but she also couldn't stand by while the villager's spirits were robbed of choice.

The spirit stopped at the river. The large feline was barely visible in the fading light—but it was there. Andie and Cee took their spot behind the tree and waited.

Cee was prepared for a real test this time. She brought seedlings from the field they still toiled in when they weren't helping Ilena. Cee buried them quickly—the rougher, the better—to test the theory. The best test would be to see how well the seeds would grow with magic if they were defenseless like the current crop.

The feline's purr drew Andie's attention from Cee's plants to the scene by the river. The spirit placed its hand firmly in the cat's fur. It leaned into the stroke as it had with Nona, granting the spirit comfort as its travel companion. Andie knew the moment was near as the spirit wove its fingers deeper into the feline's scruff, and the animal leaned back on its haunches—preparing to leap.

Andie waited to see what Cee would do. She couldn't bring herself to foil her attempt, but she'd take any opportunity that presented itself. Cee pulled a vial from her cloak.

"What is that?" Andie asked.

Cee didn't have to answer. It was a lot of blood.

"Where did you get that?" Andie asked.

"Some villagers gave it as an offering," Cee replied.

Andie narrowed her gaze. "I thought we didn't tell anyone about this test," she said.

"Relax, Andie. I didn't. I just told them we were testing some magic and asked if they'd like to contribute."

Andie didn't like this. It was too much blood, and the villager's generic offering wouldn't have had clear intentions. The magic would be unpredictable. Cee ignored all of these arguments as she poured the blood out onto the ground.

Even without the spirit, the magic responded immediately.

　　　　JILLIAN WITT

The offering was hefty, and the power returned more than Cee was ready for. She breathed deeply to steady herself as magic rolled through her body. She aimed the granted magic at the spirit. With a final glance at the hastily planted seedlings, Cee unleashed the magic toward the spirit as it jumped with the animal.

The gold lasso wrapped around the spirit, and Cee tugged. Hard. She pulled with everything she had. Cee gasped as the spirit and the feline tumbled back.

Panic crossed her face as she turned to stare at Andie. She didn't know how to let go.

The magic was too much, too powerful, too all-consuming. No attempt to release what she'd grasped would help her lack of control. Andie tried to think quickly. How could she intervene without Cee accusing her of ruining the test?

"Do you want me to—"

"No, don't do anything, Andie. I've got this." Cee's face once again masked her panic—though her hands still shook with nerves.

Andie bit her lip. Cee was so driven to know what the spirit could do for the village. Andie respected her determination to try and prevent others from an early death. But Cee was willfully ignoring the fact that the feline hadn't gone beyond the veil this time. She'd pulled it back along with the spirit.

The pair, lassoed by Cee's magic, careened toward them. Cee seemed entirely focused on sending the spirit toward the seedling. Andie couldn't tell if the spirit went where Cee directed it. The veil cat found them first. It was set on a collision course with Cee, but her gaze was still firmly focused on the seedlings.

"Cee!" Andie yelled, jumping between her sister and the feline.

The animal slammed into Andie. She didn't blame it. Andie suspected it was defending the spirit. The feline's magic collided with the blood magic Cee and Andie were wielding.

The animal's magic was strong. Feelings flooded Andie as

their magics collided. Andie had been right—the feline was responsible for the spirit. It wouldn't let Cee take it. Andie recognized its protectiveness, a more violent version of what Andie felt when Nona's spirit had been fed to the plant.

Similarly, Andie realized it was the same protectiveness Cee felt for their villagers. They were in a no-win situation. Andie was ready to give up. She was prepared to let the veil cat win.

"Andie, I've got you," Cee shouted, unleashing the untethered magic onto the situation. "It won't take you from me!"

The wielder's will directed blood magic, and Andie's magic still flowed from seeking the ability to see spirits. But her intention was changing. Andie knew after only moments, she was inexplicably on the veil cat's side. There were no winners here. The villagers were experiencing a plight they didn't deserve, but that didn't mean the spirits should be taken from their afterlife.

Andie wanted to help the veil cat.

Cee's cry focused solely on not letting the veil cat *take* Andie. The magic from the excess of blood spilled was still unwieldy, holding the veil cat to the continent. That left an unlikely option for Andie to guide her own magic. She wasn't sure she could explain what happened next. Something within her started to shift.

She fell to all fours, and a growl unlike any she'd ever heard ripped through her throat. Hair covered her body, and her fur stood on end as she prowled out from behind the tree. Feline Andie turned quickly, searching for Cee, or the original animal. The veil cat was no longer visible, but another new animal stalked out from behind the tree in its place.

Andie knew it was Cee.

An insistent press somewhere in the back of her mind told Andie someone wanted in. Unsure how she knew what to do, Andie opened the link with less than a thought. Cee's voice came flooding in.

"What are we?" she spoke directly into Andie's mind.

"I think we're veil cats now," Andie replied. The name sprang to her mind—Andie couldn't say where it came from—but it felt right.

"Veil cats?" Cee asked.

Ignoring her sister's question, she asked her own. *"What did you do, Cee?"*

"What do you mean? I didn't want it to take you...then I didn't want you to be stuck somewhere without me."

Andie sighed. Cee's protective instinct reared its head at the oddest times.

"So, we jump through the veiled hole above the river, now?" Cee asked. Andie could feel Cee's excitement. Her head whipped back toward the experiment. The spirit still floated above the ground. Cee must have gotten distracted by the veil cat's attack. *"We can go beyond the veil and see if more spirits exist to test with."*

That sounded like a terrible idea to Andie, but another part of her wanted desperately to go beyond the veil. This feline she'd bonded with, she felt its urge to return to its home—to fulfill its purpose. The spirit needed to be led. The veil cat could no longer complete its task because of Andie's interference.

The spirit floated over to Andie, its hand reaching for the scruff of her neck. She shivered in anticipation, realizing what would happen next as the spirit's hand settled in her fur.

She felt it.

The spirit wrapped its fingers deep in her scruff and allowed Andie to lead them back to the original position on the river bank. She was no longer sure what she was doing. Her feline body was moving of its own accord. Like a moth to a flame, she let it take her on this new adventure.

"Yes, Andie, good," Cee said. *"Do you know how to travel there?"*

Andie didn't know how to respond. She wasn't sure if she could bring Cee with her, but she knew she had to take the spirit. Her body sank onto its haunches, her gaze drawn to a brief fluttering above the river—their target. Somehow, she knew it. The spirit's grip on her fur tightened as her body readied to leap.

She sprang forward, soaring over the river and falling through the veil between realms. Darkness consumed her, but she wasn't afraid.

CHAPTER TEN

The cave didn't get any warmer as the Compass Points walked deeper into the maze of tunnels. Rose shivered, especially after the onslaught of wind on the ridge, and she wished she'd brought a cloak.

They walked for another mile. Making this maze of caves difficult—even for the Osten—was unnecessary, one more item on a long list of things to hold against Zrak when they finally spoke to him. Conceptually, Rose knew Zrak was a better option for the continent than Aterra. She couldn't help but wonder about the impacts of switching their places. If the Osten had to do this ritual to stabilize their magic with Zrak beyond the veil, would the Suden have to do something similar with Aterra there? Surely, Luc wouldn't need it with his demigod nature. She shook her head. They wanted to build a sustainable future for the continent's people though. They'd need to think about how their actions impacted Luc's successor.

She rubbed her sternum as she thought about Luc and the boost of magic she'd received when she needed it most on the ridge. The crossing, though terrifying, had unlocked more details from her dream. The black stone was the lakebed of her magic now. The earth magic she felt—Luc was trying to break through, just like he had tried... She was more certain than ever that last night's encounter wasn't just a dream.

Before, she'd felt a devastating emptiness, a gap where she knew his magic had made itself at home. Now she felt a pulsing ache like knocking against a door, trying to enter. She wanted to let him in—she just didn't know how.

"Rose," Juliette's call interrupted her thoughts. "Are you coming?"

Rose looked up. She'd been rubbing her chest and had stopped walking. Ahead, dimly lit by Carter's fire, the path ended. The tunnel opened into a large cavern. She jogged to where Juliette and Carter stood at the entryway.

It was an oddly circular room, like a half-dome. The eerie purple glow of the cave walls was even more prominent here. "This is it," Rose said, and Juliette nodded. The wild magic was alive around them. Her skin tingled as it made itself known.

"Can you feel it?" Juliette asked.

"Definitely," Rose replied. "I know you said it was present, but this feels..." Rose took a deep breath. "Stronger even than the Lake of the Gods."

Juliette nodded. "I don't know how Zrak found this location, but I realized its similarity to Mount Bury as soon as we arrived there."

"What do we do next?" Rose asked, her gaze shifting around the room before finally landing on the Osten Point. Juliette seemed to be keeping expectations of Zrak low, but it made sense to at least try to speak with him before she and Carter blindly crossed realms.

Large stalactites fanned out around the flat circular section. The rock formations seemed to guide the eye to this specific patch of wall. The jagged columns from the ceiling led directly to it. Rose swore something almost shimmered in the air. Carter's floating flames drew nearer to the area as Juliette led them in, making the purple hue of the cave even more prevalent.

"This is where he would appear," Juliette said, gesturing to the flat space on the wall. "He appears like an outline, a shadow, when present. I will perform the ritual, but I'm unsure what to expect after the brute force approach on the planes outside Sandrin."

Rose nodded. Juliette was telling her not to get her hopes up. She appreciated the practicality. As the Osten Point prepared for the ritual, Carter prowled the cave in a movement Rose could only call feline. He kept sniffing the air and folding into himself like he was struggling with something.

"You okay, Carter?" she asked. Rose could hear the strain in his voice as he spoke.

"I'm fighting the change now," he said.

Juliette glanced at Carter. "I think Zrak's continued visits here have thinned the space between the realms even more than the magic enacted under Mount Bury had," she said.

"I agree with that assessment," Carter replied through gritted teeth.

"Well, let me try this," Juliette said. "When Zrak inevitably ignores me, you can attempt the crossing yourself."

Taking a position in the center of the rock formation-laden path, facing the empty wall, Juliette breathed deeply, pulling the vial from beneath the neckline of her dress. Her hand gripped one of the daggers Rose had made from the custom holster, using the tip to gently slice the skin on her finger.

Blood welled, and as it did, she poured the droplets of Zrak's blood atop it. She clenched her hand into a tight fist, more blood rising to the surface and mixing with Zrak's. Enough of the mixture spilled between her knuckles, allowing drops to fall to the cavern floor.

This was the mixing of the Compass Point and their patron's blood. Juliette also had Zrak's artifact, the vial, used to hold his blood. And they were in a place with great magic, one the Lost God himself had found. The only thing missing now was Juliette's will.

Juliette closed her eyes and moved her lips. Rose couldn't hear the words. She wondered if it was a way to set her intention, to tell the magic she gave this freely for the Osten fae. Something caught in Rose's throat as she thought of all the times Juliette had been down here alone, doing this exact ritual, with no one knowing the burden she carried for her people. Rose kept her eyes focused on the Osten Point. Juliette may not need it, but Rose wanted to acknowledge the weight the court leader silently carried. The weight of the burden must be heavier than Rose could imagine—being the only way to sustain the Osten's magic. Her only partner in this endeavor was a mercurial god who couldn't be bothered to share his plans. Juliette's gaze connected with Rose's as if she could read her thoughts. She nodded in recognition, then turned to the wall and spoke.

"Zrak!" her voice was strong and confident as it echoed through the cave. "I call on you to complete the ritual. We must strengthen the Osten court once again."

The words hung in silence. Moments passed. Carter and Rose shared a look, unsure what to expect. Juliette squeezed her clenched fist tighter, and more drops of blood fell to the ground. "Zrak!" she called again. "It is time!"

Nothing changed on the cave wall. Somehow, Rose knew Zrak wasn't coming. Juliette waited a few more moments, and then she gave up. Turning her back to the wall, she returned to where Rose and Carter stood.

"I can't say I'm surprised."

"How much longer do you have? Before his absence will impact the Osten magic?" Carter asked gently.

"At least a few more days." She shrugged. "He's pushed the limit before but hasn't failed us yet." Her ensuing sigh was so heavy, Rose swore she felt the weight of Juliette's burden in it.

"I guess you're up," Rose said, turning to Carter.

The Vesten Point sniffed the air again. Even in his fae form, the action looked feline. It was the same way Arie's actions sometimes reflected those of his favored bird form.

"I am confident we can cross here," Carter said. His whole

body seemed to shiver. "This place calls to my veil cat. Even more so than the cavern under the Lake of the Gods did." He rolled his shoulders and stretched his neck.

Rose didn't want to admit how delighted she was to hear this. Jumping into this as they had, she wasn't sure what to expect from Carter once they arrived.

"Let's go then," she said, clapping her hands together. Rose tried to keep appropriate expectations. Yes, the magic of the cavern called Carter, but he'd never done this before. Anything could happen. His face was set as his gaze wandered the cavern's space. The balls of flame he'd sent floating around the room cast a host of shadows from the stalactites and stalagmites around them. Carter seemed more confident than she'd ever seen him as he walked to the same place Juliette had stood. He tilted his head, staring at the spot on the wall she said Zrak used when he appeared.

The pulse of magic in Rose's chest flared as if Luc's missing magic was trying to tell her something. She rubbed her sternum again. As soon as they were beyond the veil, she would check her lake of magic and see if the connection was there when they were in the same realm.

"We'll use the same location," Carter said, nodding to himself. Rose looked at the solid wall but decided not to question it.

"What do you need me to do?" she asked.

"I'm going to shift," Carter started. "And in the veil cat form, we won't be able to communicate much. I can understand anything you say, but we'll be limited to yes and no answers."

"What's the plan?" Rose asked, staring again with apprehension toward the cave wall.

"Even in my fae form, I can see the residue from the realm beyond. My powers with the veil cat are growing. They tend to increase in places like this." He scratched his head. Then, his gaze darted away from the wall. He was considering something and didn't like the result.

"What is it?" Rose asked.

"Best if I don't share this one ahead of time. It'll only make you nervous." Carter didn't look at her, but his smirk told her everything she needed to know.

Rose opened her mouth to respond, but the pulse of phantom magic in her chest distracted her. Absentmindedly rubbing at it again, she glared at Carter. As if he'd somehow made the magic flare so she wouldn't argue with him. "Fine," she conceded.

"Should I wait for you here?" Juliette asked. "Do you think you'll return to the same place?"

"If everything goes according to plan, we should," Carter said with more emphasis on the words 'according to plan' than she cared for. "We shouldn't be long though. If we take over an hour, we'll meet you back at Osten house."

Rose didn't like the sound of that, but it was her decision to run headfirst into this. She'd accept whatever Carter thought might happen.

"What now?" Rose asked. The pulsing in her chest hadn't stopped, but she was certainly distracted by the shift in magic in this place. Carter was right about the strength of it.

He didn't respond, and when Rose looked beside her, a veil cat sat where the Vesten Point had been. The animal arched its back in a way only a feline could, signaling for Rose to reach down and touch it. She kept her hand on his back, digging into the scruff on his neck as they walked forward.

They moved toward the flatter section of the cave wall that Carter had asked about, moving around the rock formations in the floor and ceiling. It was where Juliette had said Zrak usually appeared—if he appeared at all. It looked so solid. Rose suddenly got a bad feeling about the plan Carter said she wouldn't like.

The magic in the cavern was potent. Rose had to trust Carter to know what he was doing. Or at least knew what might work. She was desperate enough to go along with either option. She lifted her hand from the veil cat's back to rub her sternum again, at another throb of phantom magic.

The cat's head spun quickly, growling at Rose. Carter's feline face was all teeth. She quickly placed her hand back in the cat's fur.

"Message received," she mumbled. "I will hold on." Her fingers wove deeper into the veil cat's scruff.

Carter nodded as if mollified by her hand's return.

Rose swallowed, a little nervous that she couldn't hold on through whatever he was about to do. She tangled her fingers into the cat's fur to secure her grip without hurting him. The cat nodded at her action, so it must not be too tight. He arched his neck toward her fingers, encouraging a firmer grip.

Rose's gaze returned to the solid stone wall in front of them. They kept moving toward it. He lifted a paw and pointed toward it.

"The wall?" Rose asked.

The veil cat nodded.

"What about it?" she laughed to herself. He couldn't answer that, and she doubted he would if he could. She had a sneaking suspicion she knew what his plan was—and he was right. She didn't like it.

"Never mind," she swallowed thickly and stared at the wall—definitely solid. Even with her magic senses, she saw nothing that indicated the cave surface had any give.

He couldn't possibly be planning what she thought he was.

Her fingers loosened as she momentarily lost her nerve. Carter's warning growl was enough to remember herself. "Just do it before I think too hard about this."

The cat's tail flicked back and forth at a steady pace. Rose secured her grip. She glanced at Juliette, wondering what this scene looked like to her. The second Rose turned her head, her body lurched forward.

She held tighter, the veil cat growling at the ferocity of her grip. As she turned her head back toward the cave wall, Rose let out a growl of her own.

He had taken a running leap. They were lunging through the air directly toward the solid wall.

They were going to hit it face-first.

Saying she trusted Carter was one thing. Letting him throw them at a solid cave wall seemed something else. Cursing Carter's name as they flew through the air, Rose closed her eyes and tightened her limbs, preparing for impact.

CHAPTER ELEVEN

Seconds passed, and they hadn't collided with something solid. Her feet were moving to keep up with Carter's consistent pull. Rose peeked, slowly opening her eyes. She closed and opened them again, unsure of what happened. The world around them was so dark, she didn't know if she was blind or if there was nothing to see. Carter growled, sensing her action. She tightened her grip on him again as they ran through a space between realms.

Nothing was visible as they traveled. To her eyes, the entire place was a void. "Do you know where you're going?" she whispered, unsure what else might lurk in the darkness.

The veil cat nodded and led without a moment's hesitation. Rose closed her eyes again. Best not to examine this emptiness too closely. She felt a tug similar to Carter's initial jump. Then she was weightless, falling.

Rose landed with a splash.

The water was ice cold, and the current was quick. Rose didn't think as she pulled on her water magic. She was a strong swimmer without the magic, but the river's flow was brutal. Searching the water for Carter, she was astounded to see him licking his paw from the opposite bank.

How had he ended up there?

The river fought to pull her downstream. Ignoring Carter, she focused on getting herself across the water. The current threatened again to pull her under, and she laughed. She was the Norden Point—she could tame a river. Her magic took over, guiding the river to lift her out and drop her on the grassy bank.

"You good?" she asked Carter. His yellow-green eyes blinked in confusion like she should be asking herself that question instead of him. He gave a low, non-committal growl as he returned to licking his paws. He'd been the one to land her in the river, but somehow, he looked smug.

This was the nature of felines.

"You are going to hear about this later," Rose said with no venom. She couldn't believe they made it. The veil cat rolled its eyes at her and finally stopped licking its paw.

They were beyond the veil.

The land looked surprisingly similar to the continent. They were in a meadow, grass beneath them and trees surrounding the space. The river behind them ran in both directions, farther than the eye could see.

"Do you know where we need to go?" Rose asked.

Carter shook his head.

Rose searched the horizon, but she didn't see any settlements or spirits in view. She wasn't sure whether she could see spirits though—even here. "Are we being watched? Any spirits around?" she asked Carter.

He shook his head again.

This was as good as anywhere else for her test. "I need to check for the connection to Luc." She chanced closing her eyes to let her magic search the place. Convinced they were safe for a moment, Rose left her physical body defenseless as she dove inward—to the heart of her magic.

She went straight to her internal lake of power. The cool breeze of her wind guided her to the lake's edge. She looked into

　　　　JILLIAN WITT

the water, unsure what to expect. Would the tunnel into his power reappear now that they were in the same realm?

The tunnel still wasn't there.

Something tightened in her chest. Not phantom magic pains —but pure, simple panic. Something had to be here. He was beyond the veil—and now, so was she. This should be no different than when they were both on the continent, and his magic was ready and willing to support her whenever needed.

Where was it?

Her stomach churned, threatening unrest. Before she knew what she was doing, she dove into the lake. Maybe she couldn't see the tunnel into his power from the angle on the beach. She gave herself any and every excuse as she swam toward the bottom.

She wanted to stomp, cry, and scream when she reached the sandy floor of the lake. It wasn't there. He wasn't there. She shut her eyes tightly, trying to hold back the stream of tears.

Opening her eyes, she focused on the next steps. Though she didn't understand it, she knew the answer lay with the shiny black stone from her encounters. It had been hidden beneath the lakebed. She dove down deeper, her hand reaching out and pushing away the sand to reveal the hidden material.

The black stone was here.

She swam up a little higher and used her magic to push the sand around the lake bed, revealing more strips of the onyx. It spidered through the entirety of the lake. This was how it had been in the dream that wasn't a dream.

The onyx stone matched that of the Suden Point's artifact. It was firmly entrenched within her lake of power. The memory of Luc's voice called to her, telling her she already knew the answer to all her questions.

Her connection to Luc must have changed.

An image flashed through her mind: the shape of a hand reaching up through the stone floor, the floor stretching around it like a glove. The pulse in her magic strengthened as her mind considered how to let him in.

"Acknowledge what it means, Rose." The words echoed those she'd heard previously. What she needed to acknowledge was on the tip of her tongue—something she knew to be impossible.

A sharp nip pulled her back from the heart of her magic. She opened her eyes in the meadow. Still in veil cat form, Carter prowled protectively in front of her. She saw a tear in her leggings where he must have scratched her to get her attention. She only had to glance up to understand why.

Six veil cats stalked opposite Carter.

"Didn't you say they were extinct?" Rose asked.

The veil cat's hearing must be better than she thought as a chorus of growls echoed across the arbitrary line Carter had drawn between them.

"Not the time. I understand," Rose whispered. "What do we do?" She shook her head. Carter couldn't answer that. She needed a different question.

The pack didn't attack. Rose wasn't sure how much Carter had tested them. He paced before her, tension heavy in each step. Rose readied her magic. Even if they didn't attack—they didn't look friendly. She cursed inwardly. She needed time to figure out how to let Luc in if the black stone was a new connection point to him.

The veil cats didn't cross the line Carter's pacing defined, but they were not secure enough to continue her experimentation. What were the veil cats doing? How were they here?

The answer to why they hadn't attacked came a second too late. They were waiting for something. For someone.

Someone worse than the pack of deadly felines was coming.

As the thought clicked into place for Rose, something triggered Carter. Snapping at her hand, he signaled her to hold his fur again. He seemed loath to give the veil cats his back. Once her hand was secured in his fur, he started walking them backward towards the river.

Rose narrowed her eyes, trying to see what he saw. Something beautiful and terrible moved in the distance. The pack of veil cats

　　　JILLIAN WITT

growled again, showing their teeth. This must be the last warning. Her wind and water were ready to defend against whatever—whomever—was coming.

The figure on the horizon charged toward them. Even on horseback, at such a distance, Rose could tell she was a force to be reckoned with. The horse moved unnaturally fast—faster even than when Rose pushed her horses with her wind magic.

Power rippled from the woman as she entered the meadow. The veil cats growled again; not a warning—a call.

Rose instinctively knew who this was: their leader.

Beings with a lot of power surrounded Rose regularly. But her senses tingled as she evaluated this new threat. Her power surpassed Luc's—maybe even Arie's—but it was different, too, more connected to the magic of this place. The hair Rose clung to at Carter's scruff stood on end. His hackles rose, but she couldn't ask what he sensed.

"Let's get out of here," she whispered. Power flooded the meadow, and the woman's face did not look friendly. She could only be one person—one known not to like visitors.

Roots sprouted from the ground, wrapping around Rose's feet and Carter's paws as they took another step back. The land stretched to hold them hostage until its leader arrived.

The veil cats readied for attack.

Carter was mentally ahead of her. Fire shot from him, burning the roots away, freeing them. He turned, and Rose followed, sprinting toward the riverbank. A chorus of growls vibrated from the veil cats as they pursued. Carter urged Rose forward—her hand not giving an inch of its hold. They reached the river. Rose could see their target this time. Though there had been no sign of the veil when they'd crossed from the continent, now, above the river, something billowed—a break between realms.

"Stop!" the woman's voice called. Power thrummed through the single word. Roots pushed through the ground again, after them—but Carter's fire held them at bay. They needed to escape quickly.

They took another running start, and the Vesten Point pushed hard off the ground as they reached the river's edge. She dug her fingers tighter into his fur and closed her eyes as they careened into the unknown.

Blackness surrounded them.

Once again, Carter moved with precision through an uninhabited space. Even panicked as she was, she tried to look in all directions, her hand still tightly laced in Carter's fur as they moved through this in-between space. She saw nothing.

They were through it even faster than the first time. Landing with a thud, the ground was familiar—the cool and damp cavern floor. Rose didn't bother to push herself up. She looked to her right to ensure Carter had returned with her. Seeing his fae form sprawled beside her, she let out a breath of relief, before her head fell back to the cave floor.

"How'd it go?" Juliette's familiar voice was somehow calming, even with their failure.

Rose replied, "It definitely could have gone better."

CHAPTER TWELVE

Andie ran through darkness in feline form. She could barely see and had no idea where she was going. The veil cat—she had to believe it was still inside her—seemed to tell her the way. It wasn't a voice in her head but an inherent direction she knew to follow.

The spirit held fast to her fur, and she needed to get it to its final resting place. A distant part of her knew she should be worried about Cee. Consumed by her mission, thoughts of her sister started to fade into the surrounding darkness. There wasn't room to worry about other veil cats in the space between realms.

It felt like forever that Andie moved through the unknown. This darkness surrounded her and the spirit until she suddenly knew it was time to leave.

She jumped again.

After so much darkness, the world forming around her was a welcome sight. Andie and the spirit exited the void between realms. They plummeted before Andie's mind could catch up with her current feline form. Andie had the sense to look down, to see what they would hit—not that there was much she could do about it.

A river rushed below them.

The urgent gurgle of the water's flow told her all she needed to know—the current was strong. She didn't know how well her cat form could swim, but this would not be pleasant if it were anything like when strays were caught in the rain at home.

Andie held her breath and waited for the cold shock of rushing water to overtake her. She hit it with a splash. A second splash sounded as she burst back above the surface. It couldn't distract her from the water's icy temperature.

It wasn't just cold—this wasn't a refreshing dip on a hot day to cool off. The river was frigid; the stab of cold was bone deep. Her body, even as a feline, started to panic. She lifted a paw to paddle forward before she lost all sense of direction.

It wasn't a paw Andie lifted, but a hand. The feline was still inside of her—she could sense it. But she looked down at her body returned to human form, dressed in the tunic and leggings she'd worn in the woods. Her clothes were heavy on her body as she swam for shore. She was shaking from cold, exhaustion, and pure panic.

She'd lost track of the spirit in her progress. Leaving the river without it was not an option. She was its guide on this journey. A splash drew her attention to not only the spirit but her sister, too.

Andie raced for them both.

"Come on, Andie," Cee said as she left the spirit to fend for itself and swam toward the bank.

Knowing her sister was safe, Andie turned for the spirit. Before she could think better, she reached for it. Without her veil cat form, would she be able to touch it? The pull to shepherd the spirit was so strong. A rightness settled over Andie as her hand closed around the spirit's solid wrist.

Andie pulled hard, swimming diagonally with the current. She set them for a trajectory of the shoreline. The spirit was another weight to add to her tired swim. Andie's ability to touch the spirit left her too stunned to notice.

She let out a gasping breath as her arm made the final stretch for the shore. She pulled herself and the spirit forward, her body shaking in earnest now that they were safe. When they finally reached shore, the spirit smiled at Andie. A soft smile she wasn't quite sure she deserved. She hadn't stopped her sister's attempt to steal this spirit's essence. She hadn't prevented her sister from following her to this...realm, even though Andie knew Cee wanted to steal more spirits.

Andie rolled over onto her back, appreciating the soft grass of the meadow. Her breaths were still heaving—she couldn't rein them in.

She picked herself up momentarily to see Cee kneeling beside her. The spirit was gone.

"Are you alright?" Cee asked.

Andie didn't know how to respond. The wound on her arm must have reopened on her journey. It didn't hurt, but blood dripped from the gash she'd made to follow the spirit.

"Cee, you can't take the spirits from here," she said, her voice, trembling from the exertion, a poor reflection of her certainty.

"We can talk about it later," Cee said, "Just breathe." She patted her sister's hand and pulled her head onto her lap.

"No!" Andie shouted. "The spirits belong here. We can't take them if they want to stay."

"What's this about, Andie?" Cee asked. "You know we need more than your blood magic to save the village." Her brow furrowed in contemplation. "Oh, do you not want another magic to be able to save us? You want to be the hero?" She tilted her head.

"I don't want my blood magic to be what saves us, but I refuse to disrupt these spirits' afterlives without their consent." The blood continued to drip from Andie's arm. Each drop hit the ground like a silent promise. She would fight Cee on this. It was bigger than saving their village. This was about preserving whatever came next.

A thrum through her veins drew her gaze to the ground. As her blood dripped into the meadow, the land seemed to suck each drop beneath the soil. It differed from how the land on the continent reacted to her offering. This felt like land accepting a promise she didn't realize she'd been making.

"Afterlife?" Cee considered. "Is that where we are?"

They were the last words she heard from her sister before magic—not unlike blood magic—flooded Andie's veins, and darkness overtook her.

ANDIE BLINKED as she took in her surroundings. The ground was no longer hard and covered in grass. It was plush—soft. Her skin was warm, bundled in a pile of heavy blankets. She was inside. She searched the room to understand where she was, what had happened, and where Cee was.

"*You're awake.*" A voice spoke into her mind. Andie pushed the blankets aside and propped up on her elbows to evaluate the speaker. No one was there.

"*We're down here,*" the voice said. It was then Andie noticed the echo to it, like the voice was a chorus of many. She looked down. A host of veil cats lay by the bed. One of the cats sat up as if sensing her gaze. Its yellow-green eyes didn't blink as it stared at Andie.

"Where is my sister?" Andie asked aloud. She inherently knew the cats could hear and understand her.

"*She is safe,*" the cat said to her. "*She's in the room next door.*"

"And do veil cats sit at the foot of her bed?" Andie asked.

The feline's whisker twitched. Andie would call it an attempt at a smile if she didn't know better. "*How do you know what we are?*" it asked.

JILLIAN WITT

Andie didn't know. She said as much. She'd felt the name when she shifted into one. It felt right—she hadn't questioned it.

"*We figured as much,*" the veil cat said.

"Do you speak for all of them?" Andie asked.

"*Sometimes,*" he said. "*My name is Orion, and this is your pack.*"

"My pack?" she said, affronted. "I'm not a veil cat." She didn't like this cat telling her they knew things about her.

"*We beg to differ, but we'll give you time to sort that out.*" Orion started licking his paw and swiping the wetted fur over his ear.

"Am I a prisoner here?" Andie asked.

The veil cat stopped its cleaning. "*What makes you think that? You're in a well-appointed room; we cared for you the best we could. This should be royal treatment for a human...*" The cat had sounded sure of itself initially, but Andie could feel its doubt by the end.

She decided to ignore the nagging feeling in the back of her mind that told her to question why this cat wanted to give her royal treatment. A different question popped into her head. "We didn't die, right?"

"*Neither of you are dead,*" the cat replied, "*though we cannot guarantee your sister's safety if she tries to take a spirit from its resting place.*" Orion's voice was still smooth—elegant—but didn't hide the hint of malice.

The cat paused before proceeding. "*You feel the same...do you not?*"

How could he know that?

"*We are bound to the land...just as you now are,*" Orion spoke quietly but surely. Was that true? Andie believed the cats were bound to the land. The longing she felt when she'd transformed —the desire to return herself and the spirit she shepherded to this place—wasn't a feeling that could be mistaken.

But was she now bound as one of them?

"I'm human," she said, running her fingers through her long white blonde hair as confirmation of the form she held.

"You are, and you are not," the veil cat said, tilting its head and resuming licking its paws.

"What does that mean?"

"You perform magic even on the continent, do you not?"

"How could you know that?"

"The vow you made to the land had the ring of authority. It was a presence we've been waiting a long time for."

Authority? Not from Andie. Cee was the one who led. Cee devised plans and could get people to agree to enact them. People were too unpredictable to Andie. She was never able to read them. It's what had drawn her to magic in the first place. The expectations of magical contracts were much more straightforward.

Andie rose and placed the bed between her and the host of cats. Another veil cat sat up. Andie could see it from where she leaned over the mattress. Its golden eyes blinked. She stumbled from nerves as she took a step backward. Andie's fingers caught on the wooden bedside table. "Ouch."

She lifted it to her lips reflexively. She could see a splinter in the pad of her finger. Blood welled at the insertion point. Instead of sucking the finger into her mouth, she didn't know what overtook her. Some desire to prove she didn't belong to the land here—that this was all a big misunderstanding. The blood fell from her finger and hit the floor.

Fur coated her body, and she was on all fours before she could blink. A growl ripped through her throat at the change. Without conscious thought, she'd transformed back into a veil cat.

"Well," the cat said lazily. *"Hope that answers that question for you."*

 JILLIAN WITT

Disappointment hung heavy over every step as the Compass Points trekked back through the tunnels to Osten house. They barely spoke, leaving Rose's mind free to wander. Her magic was on edge as they inched their way around the ridge. Juliette was right—it still required all her remaining magic to fend them off, but Rose was more accustomed to the unpredictable wind currents on the return trip.

With all her energy spent, she hadn't properly prepared for what lay between the portal and safety. After her first step up the stairs, it hit her—she was too late to empty her mind. The magic was quicker this time, as if it was more familiar with her weaknesses.

Alone again—but it was different. Underwater in her lake of power, Rose touched her fingers to the onyx stone she was sure now spider-webbed through the lakebed. She touched it, rubbed it, kicked it, stomped on it, screamed into the water. All of this, and still, nothing changed. It didn't shake again. Nothing tried to break through. Luc's voice never returned.

She couldn't reach him beyond the veil.

This new, very present fear overtook her. She didn't have to wonder where it came from—she'd thought of little else on their walk back. There was no escaping it. Rose let the fear wash over her, but she refused to freeze.

The black stone in her lake of power was a new kind of connection to Luc. Something had changed when they'd declared their love for each other in her workshop—she just wasn't sure what.

Before the negativity of the day could crush her, she met it head-on. They were disappointed with the Lady of the Veil's rapid arrival. Fine. Rose didn't think they fully appreciated the fact that Carter was able to cross so quickly. They'd done something extraordinary.

One shortened attempt was not enough to dissuade her. It only gave her more questions for their research. More questions to ask Arie and Aurora when they arrived. Rose put one foot in front of the other as she climbed the stairs.

Finally—finally—she shut the door behind her. Her body sagged against it as Carter and Juliette stared at her. She took in large gulps of air and looked up at the two Compass Points.

"Are we going to talk about how there were veil cats? I thought you both said they were extinct," Rose said as she pulled herself up from the floor. The walk back had somehow helped her organize her thoughts.

"I'm going to ask for some tea," Juliette said as she led them down a hallway back to the Osten Point's sitting room. Rose wasn't surprised that the sun had set on the lake. The journey to the part of the cavern where the ritual was performed took longer than she had anticipated. It was astounding that Juliette did it so regularly.

Rose sat in one of the plush chairs and put her head in her hands. Carter sat in another seat much more cautiously, as if afraid he'd be asked to stand. "Everything okay, Carter?" Rose asked while Juliette asked her staff for tea.

"I'm glad we're here, but it feels strange to be sitting in Osten house...unsupervised."

Rose snorted.

"Did I miss something?" Juliette returned with a tray. It had a teapot, mugs, and scones. Rose hadn't realized how hungry she was. She reached for the refreshment as soon as Juliette offered.

"We're just glad we're working on this together," Rose replied, adding the berry jam to the scone and taking a large bite.

"Now, back to the veil cats," Carter said after swallowing a bite of his own. "We discussed on the ride from Bury that some of the history about the Lady of the Veil didn't make sense. I think we have further proof that our suspicions were correct."

"The proof being a pack of veil cats who greeted and chased us as soon as we arrived?" Rose asked.

"Yes," Carter said around another large bite. He must have been as hungry as Rose was. He reached immediately for another as he continued. "The stories about their extinction seem to have been exaggerated."

That seemed like an understatement, but Rose kept going. "The woman that arrived, I assume, was the Lady of the Veil?" She felt sure of the answer already, but wanted Carter's assessment.

Juliette's brows raised. They hadn't talked about this part on the walk back.

"I think it's safe to assume," Carter said. "But what did you feel at her approach?"

"You felt her magic as she arrived—even before the roots tried to hold us?" Rose asked. Her magic had been so potent, it had echoed in the realm they'd landed in. Rose was unsurprised the land had risen to her call and tried to trap them.

"I did," Carter said. "It felt...big." He scratched the back of his neck. "It felt aligned with the realm."

"What does that mean?" Juliette asked.

"It's interesting because there is a connection between Lord Arctos and Vesten land, but it's subtle and only this specific spot on the continent... The Lady's magic was too similar, too connected to the realm to mistake."

"You sensed the connection as well?" Juliette turned to Rose.

"I had a feeling that the land would do her bidding—and it did. But I'm not as in tune with the realm as Carter seems to be." Rose shook her head. "The magic that woman put out though—it was big. I agree with that."

"So...you fled without speaking with her?" Juliette asked.

"You think we should have let the roots trap us?" Rose asked sarcastically. "The Lady of the Veil is known not to appreciate guests. We were intruders and were being treated as such."

Carter shrugged and then turned to Rose. "Did you get to test the connection to Luc? I know I had to pull you back, but...anything?"

"Our connection has changed. It's not the same as it was before he left. It's almost like I have to reactivate it," she said. Based on their experience, she didn't want to think too hard about Luc's arrival. How quickly had the land trapped him and Aterra in place? She shook her head—she had to believe he was fine.

"You were able to make your initial connection with him quickly when we were testing our magic together," Juliette continued, ignoring Rose's inner turmoil.

A blush heated Rose's cheeks. "That was because his magic had so actively played with mine while we traveled. It made finding the source of the connection simple. Knowing how to let him in now is a little harder." She scratched her head and then reached for another scone. They'd eaten almost everything Juliette had provided. Rose sighed, returning to the problem of the ruler beyond the veil. "Can we review what the Compass Points think they know about the Lady of the Veil again?"

Carter and Juliette shared a look. "As we indicated on the ride, the current information leaves much to be desired." Carter licked his lips and continued. "The story takes place just before the Flood. So, the human villages on the continent faced natural disasters that led to destruction and, eventually, famine. It indicates the Lady of the Veil took a governor's daughter. The woman was human before the fae's creation but was said to have worked

   JILLIAN WITT

blood magic. No one is quite clear on why, but the village of Marcil seemed spared from the continent's devastation due to some deal with the Lady of the Veil. It wasn't a happy deal though. The villagers recorded that whatever happened caused the death of the veil cats—they were never seen again. The story of the Lady going mad and being the one to kill them came along with that."

"Anything to add, Juliette?" Rose asked.

"No, that is the story as I know it." She shrugged.

"Where does the story come from?" Rose asked.

Carter nodded. "The Suden hold the only texts that give some form of the history. From what I understand, many key magical farming techniques the Suden still use today are in villager journals from the time. I don't know where the histories are, but I know from my duties in Sandrin that the Suden still use them."

"It sounds like we need Aaron then," Rose said.

Juliette raised her brows at the casual way Rose stated including the Suden Point's brother.

"Does the Suden historian know what we are researching?" Juliette asked.

Rose scrunched her shoulders. "He knows more than he probably should." She sighed. "But he needed to know the reality of Luc's situation." Rose stood. She didn't regret what she'd told him. "I'll stop by before going back to Norden house. I'll tell him what we need and see what help he can offer."

AARON KNEW EXACTLY what Rose was looking for. He said he'd bring what he could find to Norden house tomorrow. Her task complete, Rose cleared her head of thoughts about the village Lady of the Veil on the walk home. She wanted the time alone to focus on her magic and its connection with Luc.

Something had always been unique about their bond. That was obvious. The first time they met, his otherworldly beauty had overtaken her in a way she had never experienced. She'd been equal parts excited and terrified that she'd angered the powerful earth fae, demanding to see the weapons master.

Even then, his magic called to her. As they traveled together, the feeling solidified. The way his magic opened to her and sought her in every situation. Their connection worked differently than with the other Compass Points. She may not have acknowledged it—but she knew it. It was disappointing that the connection didn't rekindle when they were in the same realm, but she had learned something: Their unique connection had changed.

Something new was in its place. Luc was responsible for the onyx at the base of her lake of power—she knew it the same way she knew the sharp lines of his face—it was him. This stone was more cemented within her very being than the tunnel had been. It felt like a foundational part of her magic.

It felt more permanent.

Rose's thoughts fixed on the last time they'd made love in her workshop before fighting Aterra. The worship from his mouth and his magic were seared into her skin. Their magic had spun together in a way she had never experienced—intertwining internally and externally, unable to get enough. There was a moment—

Something had changed.

You can't be bound. Juliette's words echoed in her head. Juliette had said it so boldly, like she knew the word was at the center of a maze in Rose's thoughts—a maze she couldn't find the right path to complete.

Juliette wasn't being harsh. She was being pragmatic. They couldn't be. Everything that was known about bound partners was against them.

But what really was known about bound partners? The thought sprung free from a hidden place within her mind, where she kept the hope for hers and Luc's future tucked away, ready to pluck out when she needed it most. Everything she knew about bound partners was from children's fairy tales. A fae's perfect match in magic and heart seemed beyond reasonable expectation.

Then again, another thought sprang from that well of hope inside her—when had she and Luc adhered to reasonable expectations? Rose was the Norden Point even though her magic was of two courts. Luc was a demigod, the most powerful Suden in generations, born of the literal god of earth. They weren't normal.

Together, they seemed to make the impossible possible. Why not this, too?

She rubbed her chest again. The place that throbbed like a knock at the door—she wanted to let him in.

Rose had seen the black stone enough times to no longer doubt it. The stone was a part of her lake of magic now. Rose suspected access to Luc—the connection to his magic—was still there.

She just needed to learn how to let him in.

Her own magic danced beneath her skin at the challenge. It was a new evaluation of her magic's favorite partner. If she figured it out, she was sure the connection would flare back to life. The strength he'd harnessed to go beyond the veil was exactly what she knew him capable of—exactly what her magic knew of the heart of him. He protected first and worried about himself second. Though the action aligned with what she knew, he'd broken her heart by leaving her.

No matter how good his reasons.

Her thoughts scattered as she entered Norden house.

"Welcome back," Walter's low voice greeted her on her path to the library.

"Hi," she said, waving awkwardly. She winced, adding learning how to engage with the staff to her mental to-do list.

"Can we prepare a meal for you?" he asked.

"Thank you, but I've eaten."

"At Osten house?" It wasn't judgment in his tone but curiosity. She knew the difference from her few conversations with the Norden elders.

"Yes, we made progress on our goal today."

He nodded. "I'm glad to hear it." He coughed like he would say something else.

"What is it? You can ask," she said. She'd much rather answer his genuine questions than deal with the hypocrisy of the elders.

"Nothing. Don't worry about it. I'll get out of your way."

She stared after him for a moment, seeing if he'd turn around. When he didn't, she entered the library. Hopefully, he'd warm to her in time. She ran her fingers along the ornate books that lined the shelves and lit a fire. The plush chair called to her. Before she could select a book, she was sinking into the cushions. With her legs tucked under her body, she sank into a quiet moment—a moment at the end of an exhausting day that she wanted to share with Luc.

She closed her eyes and dove into the heart of her power. It was so much easier to do when she was still like this. Whatever part of her was here felt like a physical thing. The wind kissed her skin as she landed in her usual spot on the edge of her lake. Peering into the bright blue waters, she still couldn't see the onyx streaks from where she stood. Now she knew what to do to find them though. She dove into the water, swimming deeper until she reached the bottom.

Her hand stretched for the sand of the lakebed. She knew— like she knew the pine and cinnamon scent of Luc's magic—the black stone would be beneath the sand. The sand shifted under the strength of her power, revealing what she knew to be there.

Her heart beat wildly in her chest as she reached for it.

It was cool and smooth as her fingers slid over it—as grounding and calming as the touch of Luc's magic.

With their original connection, she'd had to dip her hand into its depths. His magic had required her consent—her desire—her need to use his.

Nothing had changed.

That wasn't entirely true. If anything, since he'd left, she'd wanted him more. Her need for the grounding touch of his magic could be all-consuming. Maybe she just needed to tell him that.

Pushing the water from her mouth with her magic, she whispered, "Luc?"

She spoke the word softly, like a question—still unsure of herself. Her hands scratched through her hair in frustration. She felt like an idiot. Her brain and heart were not aligned. The rapid pounding in her chest as she whispered his name told her some desperate piece of her expected a response.

The memory of the final battle below the Lake of the Gods played through her mind. *"Forgive me, Rose. I know you'll come for me."* His magic had spoken to her then. She knew it. The words were spoken directly into her mind, even after Luc had gone beyond the veil—even after he'd left her.

Rose's finger grazed the black stone again. There had to be a way to reach him through it.

"You know what this means, Rose. You only need to acknowledge it." The words echoed through her very being. Through a connection even deeper than their hearts and their magic—a connection she had never opened herself enough to have—until him.

"Luc?" she whispered again, her voice steadier.

"You know what you're feeling. Trust yourself." The words simultaneously surrounded and filled her as he spoke. The soft hum of his voice was everywhere and nowhere in the heart of her magic.

Rose wanted to scream. She was so close—so close to opening whatever this was. Her hands wrapped into fists as she beat on the stone base of her lake. She knew it was him—would know the silk and sin of his voice anywhere.

She wanted him here.

She wanted to tell him how angry she was with his choice.

She wanted to tell him she loved him anyway.

She wanted them to make the impossible possible.

Everything she was—every part of her magic and herself—

longed to be bound to Luc. They would disagree, they would strengthen each other, and they would have an existence together that changed the continent.

More than the well of secret hope she kept was willing to admit it now.

The desire for it to be possible was a truth she buried from even herself—her brain's practicality at war with her heart's desire. Now, the words were on the tip of her tongue, begging to be loosed.

As with so much about her and Luc, she had to fight past what she knew to be true. She heard the arguments against them.

They were of different courts.

Bound fae were a fairytale—not reality.

She closed her eyes and shook her head. Those details didn't hold weight against what she wanted, what she felt. She and Luc's path wasn't simple—but it would be infinitely more enjoyable if they were bound in it together.

She wanted them to be bound—desperately.

It wasn't just want. The need for their connection was a physical thing. The strain in her chest where his magic should be made itself known. Each of these pieces added up to something Rose couldn't deny. No matter how much her brain told her it couldn't be.

Rose's mouth formed the words. She tasted the truth of them on her tongue as they released.

"We're bound."

The words were her wish, her truth, and her desperate plea.

She heard his chuckle, that low, rumbling laugh, just for her. It danced along her skin and set her body aflame with want. Her finger skimmed the stone, and she felt its magic pulse, its rhythm the same as the pulse she felt in her chest.

"Finally," she heard him whisper. Power flooded her, and she knew she got her wish.

CHAPTER FOURTEEN

An insistent tapping on the window pane jolted her awake.

"Rose... Rose... Are you there?"

Arie, in bird form, was at the library window. Rose stood from the unnatural curl in which she had fallen asleep in the plush chair. She stretched and went to rub her chest, out of habit, glaring at the black bird perched on the ledge.

It didn't pulse. The ache wasn't present.

There was no denying she had been fully awake last night when she went into her magic. Rose knew what she had said—what she had felt. The all-consuming power that had flooded her with Luc's laugh was even more potent than the first time she'd evaluated his magic.

As glad as she was to see Arie, she needed a moment. She slowed her steps to the window as she considered what happened. Her words—her truth—had released *something*. No matter how unlikely. Had she restored their connection? She wasn't sure what the sign would be other than the already present relief from the discomfort of their separation.

Arie's beak tapped on the window again, urging her to move

this along. She rolled her eyes. His return would lighten her spirit even while she sassed him—family did that.

"How was the trip?" Rose asked as she let him in.

"It was uneventful." Arie flew into the library, landing on the high wingback chair she had slept on, and surveyed the room. *"What were you doing in here?"*

Rose ignored his question momentarily and replied. "You mean uneventful besides the fact you and the love of your existence were reunited?" Rose leaned out the window and looked toward the front of the house. "Where is Aurora anyway?"

Arie's bird shoulders seemed to hunch. He looked sheepish, and Rose delighted in it. She crossed her arms over her chest and waited.

"She said coming to the window and waking you was rude."

Rose couldn't hold in the laugh. It was loud and raw and lifted a weight she hadn't noticed she carried. "I see she has some manners you may have missed learning. Is she in the entryway? I don't hear Walter, but we can go get her."

Arie flapped his wings. *"She's out back. That Walter character said you were still asleep, and she refused to let herself into the house when I planned to wake you."*

"Arie!" Rose chided. "You left her outside? You are the worst." Rose looked down at the mess that was her. She was still wearing the tunic and leggings she had traveled in through the Osten caves and beyond the veil. "Give me just a moment. I'm going upstairs to change. I'll meet you in the back entry. Please, go let her inside."

Rose went about a brief morning routine in the bedroom she'd claimed before returning to the main floor of Norden house. Arie had switched to his human form and convinced Aurora to enter. She stood beside him, their backs to Rose as she entered the kitchen.

"Are you cooking?" Rose asked. The smell of eggs and sausage crackling caught her attention. Annabeth stood nervously on the other side of the counter. At the surprise in Rose's tone, she couldn't help but respond.

"That's Lady Aurora…" she stuttered. Though Compass Lake didn't have any statues of the gods, many villages on the continent did. Rose wondered where Annabeth was from that she recognized the Norden goddess. "They said they needed to cook breakfast to make up for waking you. I wasn't in a position to kick two gods out of my kitchen."

Rose smiled at Annabeth. "It's fine. They're mostly harmless."

Arie shot a glare at Rose over his shoulder.

"Good morning, Rose. We're sorry to disturb you so early," Aurora said as she turned away from the food.

"Welcome. I'm more than happy to have you." Rose skillfully avoided any names or titles for her patron goddess. Honestly, she wasn't sure what to call her. She called Arie 'Arie' before she knew he was a god. By the time she found out, it was too late to change. She couldn't help but notice, though, that the others called him Lord Arctos. Aurora, being her patron, seemed to indicate she should have a level of deference.

Her thoughts must have been written across her face as Aurora said, "You can call me Aurora. No formalities are needed between us."

Rose nodded. "Thank you."

Annabeth sucked in a breath of surprise.

Aurora glanced at the cook before turning back to Rose. "Would you walk with me while Arie finishes our meal?"

Rose's gaze skimmed toward Arie. He had his back to her, but he nodded all the same as if realizing she would look to him for guidance. "Of course. Lead the way."

Aurora was unsurprisingly familiar with the house. She may not have been there in a hundred years, but it must not have changed much. She led them out the back door, away from the lake. Rose had purposefully avoided this part of the grounds so far, but she wouldn't tell the Norden goddess that. The property was large, but even a short walk would lead them past the caretaker's house.

The tension in Rose's shoulders must have given her away.

"Is this okay?" Aurora asked, her gaze searching the grounds for the problem.

"It's fine." Rose waved off the concern as they walked. She took in the workshop and caretaker's cottage. Too many emotions were competing for the top spot—thoughts of the family she lost and the new life she'd found in returning to Compass Lake. This new realization with Luc was so fresh—she would need to ask Arie if he knew anything about bound fae when they got back.

The workshop had a few burn marks but otherwise looked unharmed. Rose sucked in a breath, getting her first up-close look at the rebuilt caretaker's cottage. On the outside, it looked much the same as she remembered. Though, for her, the beauty of this cottage had nothing to do with its physical presence. Her family —the love she had grown up with. The grief that still gripped her heart so firmly. Now was not the time to face it.

"I'm sorry, Rose. Do you need a moment?" Aurora had stopped walking. It was clear she had said something before this, but Rose had been too lost in her thoughts to process whatever it was.

"My apologies, Aurora." Rose swallowed thickly. "I haven't strayed to this part of the property yet."

Aurora's eyes flashed in recognition. Arie must have told her some part of Rose's history. "I'm so sorry. I should have taken us out front. I've always found this part of the grounds very peaceful."

Rose smiled. "I agree." She took a deep breath. She would confront her grief again soon. Avoiding part of the property indefinitely was not a life plan. Facing it was on her list, but she didn't need to do it now. She turned, strategically placing her back to the cottage and her mom's workshop. "Now, I apologize. What did you say before?"

     JILLIAN WITT

"It seems trite now. I started the conversation by offering my condolences for your loss under Mount Bury."

The words didn't make sense to Rose. Her loss? Aiden's loss didn't feel like hers to claim, no matter how much she thought she'd made peace with it. Again, her confusion must have shown on her face.

"The Suden Point? Luc?" Aurora offered hesitantly. Her brows pinched. She was concerned with how this conversation was going.

"There is no need." Rose's hands tightened into fists at her side. Luc was not a loss she would grieve. "It's a temporary separation. One he will pay for when I bring him back." Rose let a smirk tug her lip, offering a confidence she wasn't quite sure she possessed this morning. Rose wanted to change the conversation. Her best defense was a good offense. "I'm sorry you were trapped under the mountain for so long."

Aurora smirked back. The goddess knew what she was doing but went along with it. "The one good thing about being a god is that a hundred years can seem like a blink. It wasn't pleasant, and I felt useless, but time passed."

Rose wasn't sure she'd ever understand these gods. Even the one she counted as family.

"That is what I wanted to talk to you about," Aurora said.

Rose stiffened. She hoped Aurora wasn't circling back to the topic of Luc. "Which part?" she asked defensively.

"Feeling useless." The goddess's perfect posture loosened a little at the words, as if she were letting Rose in to see a more authentic version of herself than initially presented. "The worst part of being trapped was that I couldn't help. I could only stew on the one stupid decision I made."

Rose understood the feeling. It was easy to let her thoughts loop on a single event—a single action she wished she could change—like Luc throwing himself in a hole between realms. But fixating on that got her nothing but more heartache. She nodded at Aurora. "What do you want to do?"

"You plan to go beyond the veil to get him back." It was a statement, not a question. And the goddess didn't even know about the Compass Points' activities yesterday. Rose was grateful for her confidence. "I want to help you."

Rose tilted her head to the side. She wasn't sure what the help of the goddess looked like. They already knew the Lady of the Veil's realm wasn't a welcoming place. Rose had planned to ask Arie and Aurora for more information since they were light on texts that could offer insight. Did Aurora have more than information in mind?

"Of course, I'll accept any help, Aurora. Are you referring to something...specific?"

Aurora's lips split into a full smile. The goddess was truly stunning. The excitement in her features added a radiance to the property around them. "I can see why you're Norden Point." Aurora coughed into her hand. "Of course, I can feel the strength of your magic." She paused. "But that has never been all it takes to hold the seat. Your heartache is raw, but your words express an unwavering determination. That resilience. That tenacity. That makes you Norden Point."

Rose wasn't sure what to say. She felt her cheeks warm at the goddess's attention. Arie had made her somewhat immune to being intimidated by a god or goddess, but this was her patron. It felt different to have the Norden goddess tell her she belonged here.

"Anyway." Aurora waved her hand, dismissing her effusive praise. "I believe you have my artifact."

"Which one?" Rose's smile was coy.

Aurora laughed. "Good point. Can I assume both?"

Rose nodded. She first reached for the compass, tugging it from the chain below her tunic. She held it in her palm. "Since Luc left, this has just been spinning in circles. It never stops, never points anywhere." She made to pull it off her neck, offering it to the goddess.

Aurora held up her hands. "You keep it. The spinning doesn't surprise me. The veil is everywhere and nowhere on the continent. You desire something the compass doesn't know how to locate."

Rose rubbed a finger over the glass as the arrow spun beneath it. She'd figured as much. All she wanted was to know where Luc was—to get to him. It was a direction the compass couldn't give her.

"The dagger is the one I think will suit you best on the next part of your journey." Aurora glanced at the dagger on Rose's belt. "From what Arie tells me of the other Compass Points, you may have multiple paths to get beyond the veil."

"So Arie knew what Carter was?" Rose's lip tipped up into a smile.

Aurora had the grace to look a little bashful. "Oh, yes. I'm sorry. He mentioned he hadn't said anything before you confronted Aterra. He seemed confident you would figure it out."

Of course, he did. "Conceptually, we have multiple paths."

"Oh?" Aurora sounded intrigued.

"We tried both yesterday. Zrak didn't come when Juliette called, but Carter shifted and took me beyond the veil. We were only there momentarily. The Lady of the Veil was instantly alerted to our presence and wasn't welcoming."

"You found the tree path already?" Aurora seemed shocked.

"The tree path?" It was Rose's turn to be surprised. Her mind conjured the giant willow tree in the Vesten garden—the one she and Arie had dug under to find the Vesten coin—but it was no path beyond the veil.

Aurora tilted her head, seeming to realize a mistake. "How did you go beyond the veil?"

"Where the Osten Point performs the power-sharing ritual with Zrak. The location proved to have enough wild magic and thinning between realms for Carter to find his way through."

Aurora's mouth opened and closed. "Arie's right. You're quite reckless when you're determined."

Rose wasn't sure what to say to that. She moved her hand to her hip.

"I told him we should have come back with you directly." The goddess now appeared to be talking to herself. She paused as if realizing Rose was still there. "Zrak didn't respond at all?" Aurora asked.

"He didn't. Juliette said she had more time..." Rose coughed, unsure how to explain it. "That he sometimes pushed the limit on the power-sharing, but he'd never missed it. I'm hoping you and Arie can try with her now that you're here."

Aurora nodded. "May I see the dagger?" She stretched her hand out to Rose.

She handed the dagger with the bright blue gem in its handle to the goddess who had made it. Rose always wondered if her weapon master magic had been stronger than others, not only due to her dual lines but due to Aurora being her patron. Aurora herself was the weapons master of the gods. Her talent knew no comparison.

"Few know the power of the Norden artifact," Aurora began.

"Doesn't it enhance Norden magic?" Rose asked.

"It does, but in the same way the Suden artifact enhances a Suden power few are aware of."

Rose smiled at that. She should have known that Aurora's artifact would have more to it. She hadn't really tried to use it yet. She'd been so focused on pulling the magic of all four Compass Points together that she hadn't spent time trying to dig deeper into her own.

"I know you're still getting reacquainted with your magic," Aurora started. "And as I saw under the mountain, you seem to have your hands full as the Compass Points' magic lead. But I want you to know"—she cleared her throat—"you don't have to be afraid to use this."

Rose tilted her head in question.

Aurora's cheeks flushed. "I-I..." she stammered. "I thought maybe you didn't use the dagger's magic because you were afraid

    JILLIAN WITT

to after learning there was a connection between Compass Point and patron. I want you to know I'm more than fine. I know I didn't look it in the cavern. But my magic wasn't depleted like with Juliette and Zrak. It was simply that the wild magic of the cavern enhanced Aterra's power. That small edge was enough to make a difference between gods."

Rose was even more confused. "I wasn't avoiding drawing power from the dagger," Rose said. "I honestly hadn't considered what the dagger could do."

Aurora laughed. "Then why did you take the time to retrieve it?"

Rose shrugged. "I was making a statement about being able to claim it, not leaning on any power it might have." Rose's lip curled into a smile. "Sometimes the symbol of power is enough." She gestured to the dagger. "So, what unknown Norden power does this enhance?"

"The dagger's primary function is to ensure the wielder can move unnoticed," Aurora replied.

That could mean a lot of things. She couldn't figure out how her water magic could help her go undetected. Not that she knew of a deep connection between the Suden earth magic and mind shadow either. The Suden ability to change or share memories was distinct from their element. She wondered more and more if the gods knew what they were doing when they created the fae courts. Rose held her onslaught of questions and focused on one. "How?"

"Your mind is a fearsome thing, Rose. I can see it working. The dagger's power does connect to water magic. I think of it like the drops of rainwater on a lake. So many fall at once, it's hard to tell which drop caused which ripple. The dagger does something similar to shield you and your magic. It ensures your presence won't be directly felt. It creates a series of interruptions to the expected—a diversion—giving the wielder the ability to move undetected. It will be exactly what you need when you go beyond the veil again."

Rose's magic had already started to hum at the thought of having something new to try in its desperate desire to retrieve Luc. "You seem so sure," Rose said.

"Isn't it though?" Aurora's face was stoic but confident. At least Rose took this to mean the gods understood something about the Lady of the Veil's dislike of visitors. Aurora wouldn't suggest she needed the ability to go undetected beyond the veil otherwise.

Rose tried another tack. "What was it used for?"

Aurora pressed her lips tighter together. Rose was sure she was fighting a grin. "Most say the concept of trading secrets only started with the second age of Compass Points. But this dagger was given to Jacob, the first Norden Point. You've learned enough to know we had suspicions about Aterra, even then. Jacob tracked him when he could. He tried to learn what Aterra was doing when he spent time with the Suden. The dagger protected him from Aterra realizing he was being followed, though Jacob never collected enough information for us to use." Aurora tilted her head. "He was also setting up a court, so I understood. I asked a lot of him. Just as a lot is being asked of you."

Interesting, but not quite the information she was looking for. It seemed too convenient that Aurora knew they needed to be undetected beyond the veil. They must know something about the Lady of the Veil's magic—how she could know when someone crossed into her realm. Rose would try again later to figure out what the gods knew. Rose switched gears to the opportunity before her. "How does it work?"

"It's activated with the blood of the Norden Point. You need only poke yourself, and you'll feel it's magic."

"Like blood magic?" Rose asked. First, Juliette used blood magic in her ritual, and now the Norden Point's blood was used to access the blade's power.

"Blood magic isn't that different from ours," Aurora said. "It wasn't the gods that looked down on it. The gods' magic is an innate balance with the continent, hence why we had to offer some of our power to create the fae to reclaim the balance we had lost." Aurora shook her head as if pushing away memories she would rather not dwell on. "Blood magic is nothing more than giving an offering to the continent and requesting something in return. The land responds."

Rose considered how the land beyond the veil had responded to the Lady when she approached. Her power seemed to do more than uphold balance with the land—it seemed a part of it. Carter had noticed the connection as well. What had led to such a union between goddess and realm, and how would it change their ability to retrieve those they needed from beyond the veil?

CHAPTER FIFTEEN

Andie shifted back to her human form. This time, it was a conscious decision. The change occurred because she willed it. Changing back into a cat again would be even easier next time.

Her thoughts had run away from her. Was this even what she wanted?

How quickly she'd grasped shifting back and forth aligned with the veil cat's assertion—that she was somehow bound to the land here.

"This is the realm the humans call 'beyond the veil'?" she asked when she'd collected her thoughts. It wasn't a question she needed answered, but she was still trying to get her feet under her. Her jacket was on the chair next to the bed. She reached for it and pulled out the journal, hoping to find clarity by writing the words.

"*It is. But why are you asking questions to which you already know the answer?*" the cat replied.

Andie rolled her eyes as the cat's tail flicked back and forth in a steady rhythm and returned to her note-taking. "Fine... What do veil cats do here?"

"You already know the answer to that, too. We are the shepherds of this land; we ferry spirits from the continent to the afterlife, as you did with our most recent arrival."

"But you're not the rulers of this land? Is there a..." She wasn't sure how to word the question. "Is there a leader here?"

Orion's tail continued to flick back and forth. Seconds felt like minutes. Another voice slipped into her mind, sounding more female than Orion's. *"Just tell her."*

"Patience, Alice," he said. The entire pack's voices were present in Andie's mind.

"Tell me what?" Andie pressed.

"The land here, the veil, has been waiting for a ruler. Someone who understands the land, protects the spirits, and will give their blood to protect it."

Andie laughed, but it rang hollow. She swallowed thickly, realizing what Alice was saying. "I can't imagine you get a lot of candidates with blood crossing into this realm."

"You would be correct," Alice said.

"So, you think it's me?" Andie asked. Again, the question was near rhetorical—Alice's intention was clear. Orion wasn't disagreeing. He just seemed to be taking a more meandering approach to springing the news on her.

"We think you know the answer to that."

She needed to find Cee. Cee was a born leader; Andie was just the one who liked to play with magic. She wasn't fit to rule the land beyond the veil.

Andie growled, sounding more like one of the felines than she meant to. She shut the journal and stood. These cats were so enigmatically frustrating! "I'm going to find my sister," she said. "You've got the wrong twin."

Storming out of the room, she turned right, the direction the cat's tail flicked when she asked about her sister. She opened the door without knocking. "Cee, we need to talk—now."

Cee was still in bed, and no cats surrounded her. The room

was as plushly appointed as Andie's. A tray of refreshments sat on the bedside table though it appeared untouched.

"Andie! What happened?" Cee sat up as Andie approached.

"I was going to ask you the same thing. Are you alright?"

"You left me!" Cee shouted. She was clambering out of bed now. More of the events preceding this must be coming back to her. "You shifted into a beast, and then you left! Taking the spirit with you!"

"They're not beasts; they're cats," Andie replied.

Cee tilted her head, confused at the correction. Andie's shoulders tensed as that calm, authoritative voice slid back into her head, even from the other room.

"See how quickly you defend us? Like a queen with her subjects."

Andie wanted to growl again but knew it was useless. Her fists clenched at her side, and she shouted loud enough for the veil cats in the neighboring room to hear. "I am not your queen!"

"What's going on, Andie? Who are you talking to?" Cee looked genuinely worried now.

Andie released a deep sigh. She handed the journal to Cee, hoping she might be able to make sense of what she'd written. "The veil cats—they're speaking to me. Directly in my head. Have they spoken to you?"

Cee shook her head, her eyes scanning the pages. The look of worry was not abating.

"We need to get out of here," Andie said.

Cee shook her head again. "I'm not leaving until I find a source of spirits. It works, Andie. We need them. It's the only way our village survives the worsening catastrophes." She folded her arms over her chest.

"You can't, Cee. That is not their fate." She didn't know how to explain what she'd felt, but knew she needed to try. "When you used the first spirit—Nona's—I felt her cry out. She didn't want to be sacrificed to fuel our magic. We didn't even give her a choice." Andie was close to breaking.

Cee's brow furrowed.

　　　　　　　JILLIAN WITT

"Nona's spirit isn't here now. Her afterlife is over. She doesn't get to exist in peace. She's just gone."

"How could you know that, Andie? Be reasonable."

"You're right, Your Majesty, but she does have you there. How can you know that if you hadn't given your blood to the land? If you don't belong here?"

Andie growled again in frustration.

"We have to save the villagers, Andie. They're counting on us. Father is counting on us. A few spirits are worth the cost! I know it's sad, but they've already lived their lives."

Andie didn't know how else to explain it. Yes, one life was over—but that didn't mean they should forfeit their existence in the afterlife. She felt in her bones that it was part of a cycle of balance for humanity.

Cee would defend their village, and Andie was glad for it. But part of her also wondered—who would defend the spirits?

An idea formed in Andie's mind. If the veil cats wanted her as ruler, they'd have to answer some questions. Andie was sure that if those more knowledgeable about the realm explained it to Cee, she wouldn't want to disrupt the balance here. She voiced her plan for Cee and the felines next door. "We'll have the veil cats give us a tour. They'll explain the process and how the spirits enter and exist. You can ask them all your questions. See what your plan will cost the spirits."

Cee was already shaking her head.

"Please, Cee. I'm asking for you to let them make their case. Please."

Cee considered her twin. Her gaze held fast to the point of Andie's discomfort. "Fine." She grabbed her jacket and slid it around her shoulders, tucking the journal into a pocket.

"We'll play along, too," the cats replied.

THE VEIL CATS insisted the explanation start at the river. Andie couldn't tell if this was the exact part of the riverbank where they'd arrived or if the entire bank looked remarkably similar.

"For this tour, it would be easiest if you were both veil cats again. Though, you will need to help her shift." Orion's tail flicked toward Cee.

"How do we do that?"

Orion let his tail sway back and forth, a clear indication he would wait as long as necessary for her to figure it out. The rest of the pack—a dozen in total—sat back on their haunches in solidarity.

"He says we both need to shift," Andie said to Cee. "Can you do it again?" she asked.

"Can you?" Cee shot back.

Andie nodded slowly. As much as she wished she couldn't, the veil cat form was just below the surface of her skin, begging to be released.

"Of course, you can," Cee huffed. "Well, you do it. Maybe I'll learn from watching you."

"That won't work," Orion said. *"You'll need to ask the realm to allow her to change."*

"She did it before," Andie pointed out.

"She used magic that wasn't hers," he replied evenly. *"The realm only gifts the change to worthy individuals."*

Andie held in another eye roll. "Fine." She sliced her arm before she could think better of it and offered her blood to the realm. She didn't state her intention aloud, but her focus was clear: Grant Cee the ability to shift—at least for this tour.

The land absorbed the blood where it fell. It was just as concerning as the first time, but she couldn't focus on the implications now. Within seconds, she and Cee fell to all fours, fur covering their bodies.

"Now that we're all settled, we can begin the tour," Orion said. Andie assumed this was spoken into both her and Cee's minds as her sister's head turned toward the pack leader.

"Do all spirits enter here?" Andie asked. As a veil cat herself now, her mouth didn't move when she spoke, but she knew the cats could hear her—Cee included.

"They do," Orion replied. *"Though not all can cross the river."*

"Why not?" Cee challenged.

"What do you know about the balance on your continent?" Orion asked.

Something prickled beneath Andie's fur at the question. It was one she'd asked herself many times. The way the land on the continent cried out to her—the way it demanded attention—something big was wrong. Andie just had no idea what.

Orion's tail flicked again like he saw more in Andie's feline reaction than she had hoped. Andie waited, wondering what Cee would say. Cee didn't hear the land's cries like she did. Did she know what the storms at home represented?

"I'll assume not much," he said when neither replied. However, his yellow-green eyes blinked directly at Andie before he continued. *"Your gods of the continent—Aterra, Arctos, Aurora, and Zrak—are responsible for maintaining the balance there. You may have noticed they are doing a terrible job."*

"What have they done?" Cee pressed.

"We're not their keepers," Orion said with another twitch of his tail. *"Though I would hazard to guess it's not so much what they've done, but what they haven't done. Balance must be proactively maintained. In their immortal existence, they've become apathetic to the needs of those to whom they're supposed to give care."*

"So, they've...ignored the humans on the continent?" Cee asked. Outrage bubbled beneath her voice. Andie could feel it even in this feline form.

"You're missing the point," Orion continued. *"The balance on the continent is dangling by a thread. We wanted to bring to your attention the lack of care for its maintenance. The balance here, though suffering impacts from the continent's unrest, is more actively preserved."*

"How is the balance here maintained?" Andie asked.

Andie wasn't sure if it was possible, but she swore the cat smiled at her. *"We're so glad you asked. The river is the first way. Those who make it across can select where on the land they want to spend their existence."*

"What about those who don't make it across?" Cee asked.

"They help to support the other's existence. Their spirits still find rest—albeit a second existence of more solitude." Orion's green-yellow eyes met Andie's like he was trying to tell her something but wouldn't voice it.

"Show us," Cee said.

THEY WALKED AS A PACK. It could have been hours, but Andie was lost in thought as Orion shared other information about the realm. Their life here seemed peaceful, and though they had responsibility, they hadn't faced destruction like the twins were seeing on the continent.

Cee was quiet for the entire walk. Andie knew she was stewing over what the cats had shared. Had she really not known something bigger was wrong?

The fact that the seemingly natural disasters resulted from the god's apathy was a blow but not entirely a surprise to Andie. She'd often wondered why the gods were silent in the face of their plight. Her real question now was—did humanity even stand a chance when these were the odds stacked against them? Combating the apathy of the gods seemed a tall order.

If Andie couldn't save the continent, maybe she could preserve some part of human existence—even if it was only the afterlife.

They followed the river as it flowed. If Andie thought the place they fell into the water was dangerous, it was nothing compared to some of the rushing rapids they passed. The entry point was giving the spirits their best chance at crossing.

Andie glanced at Cee as they reached the point where the

rushing river poured into a large lake. Her face was stubbornly resolute. The lake was surrounded by the same forest they'd walked through but abutted a prominent rock feature she couldn't completely see. It was so tall, it pushed up beyond the trees. A waterfall trickled down from the unexplored heights, its constant patter the only disturbance to the lake. It was stunningly serene, but Andie couldn't ignore the quiet gloom present.

"*What is this place?*" she asked.

"*The Lake of Spirits,*" Orion replied. "*This is where spirits go if they cannot cross.*"

Andie searched the waters. It did look calm. She wasn't sure what to ask.

"*It's not torture for the spirits—as you can see, it's quite peaceful. It's just a different kind of existence than those that continue on in the cities.*"

"*If it's not bad, why do you help the spirits cross the river?*" Andie asked.

Orion sighed in a way that only a feline could. "*The river has gotten harder to cross in recent years. And more spirits have been crossing from the continent. The mismanagement there is slipping into this realm with those who are perishing from it.*" One of the other cats growled as if urging the leader to share more information. Orion's tail twitched in response. "*Too many were ending up here. The water level is too high—near overflowing. We seek to return to the proper balance.*"

"*What happens if too many spirits end up here?*" Cee asked.

"*The spirit's energy fuels the magic of this realm. With too many, we have an excess. We don't want to benefit from spirits being sent to the wrong resting place.*"

Andie's gaze turned to Cee. She couldn't read her as well in her feline form, but she feared what was going through her mind —an excess of magic was hard to ignore. The lake was full but not overflowing. It seemed the cats had done well helping more spirits across. There may be excess, but it didn't feel extreme.

Andie knew that wasn't what Cee would see.

She remembered the original tests that got them into this situation—the spirit, the bushes. They were past wondering if the energy of the spirits could grow food for their people. As the cats had pointed out, famine was a symptom of a more significant problem. They needed to focus on the heart of it.

Cee would only see the excess as a means to protect her people from the imbalance on the continent.

CHAPTER SIXTEEN

A knock sounded on the lakeside door as Rose and Aurora returned to the house. "Go ahead, Aurora, I'll just be a moment." Aurora dipped her head and went toward the kitchen.

Rose ran into Walter as she approached the front door. A blush touched her cheeks as she realized this wasn't her responsibility here. She smiled weakly and shrugged at Walter, who carried on as if the lady of the house weren't standing in the entryway with him.

A disheveled Aaron stood at the door. His usually tidy clothes were wrinkled, and the glasses he wore sat atop his head. She had a feeling he'd be wondering where they were later. He held a stack of books in his arms and immediately glanced around Walter's shoulder to where Rose stood. "I found some helpful texts at the house, though the one we really need isn't here."

"You didn't have to stay up all night to look into it," Rose replied.

"I'll leave you to it," Walter said, welcoming Aaron in and closing the door behind him.

"Thank you, Walter," Rose said.

Aaron narrowed his eyes at her once the butler departed. "Yes, I'm sure you got a full night's rest as well," he said dryly.

Rose rolled her eyes and led him to the library. His gaze roamed the room, focusing on the blanket that still held the shape of her legs over the chair. He was right that she hadn't slept per se, but her night had been very different than his.

Familiar magic surged through her.

"You know what you're feeling. Trust in yourself." The words were Luc's. Rose knew that. She felt them inside her heart and her mind. They were dizzying as she struggled to determine if they were a present connection or an echo of their conversation in the heart of her magic.

Either way, she knew what they asked of her. She'd said the words aloud in the deepest part of her—and the relief had been immediate. Could she say them aloud in the light of day?

Luc's brother might be a good test. He hadn't questioned the last set of unique truths she'd shared.

Aaron's look of smug satisfaction proved too much for her— like he knew she was working up to some revelation that had left her as exhausted as he looked. The confession stuck on her tongue. They were bound, yes, but what did that mean? What could this connection do? The power flooding her receded as she let the moment pass. She rubbed her chest out of habit.

"I was testing something with my magic last night. I'm still trying to sort out the results."

Aaron turned to look at her. "What did you do?" He took a deep breath and added, "It smells of pine and cinnamon in here."

Rose sucked in a breath. It really shouldn't surprise her this time. Luc may not have been physically present last night, but his magic was. It had wrapped around her skin, and it flooded in with her declaration. What was surprising was that the physicality of the heart of her magic was strengthening if his scent followed her here.

Her tongue stuck to the roof of her mouth as she searched for

     JILLIAN WITT

the words again. Aaron would probably believe her. But he'd want to know what the connection meant. Rose didn't have answers about that yet. Her gaze darted to the hallway leading to the kitchen and the soft conversation emanating from there. Arie and Aurora. If anyone could tell her more about bound fae, it would be their creators.

"I wouldn't even know where to begin, Aaron. I'll tell you as soon as it proves useful in returning your brother." She didn't want to get his hopes up until she knew more about what this connection could do. She gestured to his books. "You found something on the Lady of the Veil or that period at least?"

He sighed, seeming to accept her response as he sat at the table and started unstacking and opening books to marked pages. "I can't believe no one talks about this history," he said. "You were seeking information on why the Lady of the Veil closed her borders? What magic she might have to know when one enters her realm?"

Rose nodded.

"Well, we do have texts from the period. I'm not familiar with all of these. Others, I've been through multiple times."

"Why?" Carter had told Rose that the Suden were the only court with these histories, but she hadn't pressed for details. "Why do the Suden have these texts and no one else?"

"You know what my father does?" Aaron asked. She wondered if he was evading her question, but something in his gaze was determined. Rose wondered if this was a small test of how much Luc had shared with her. She would play along to get the answer.

"He teaches magical agriculture methods and works with humans to implement them for a more stable food supply." She tilted her head. "What does that have to do with the period before the Flood?"

Aaron smiled. She must have passed. "I realize this was before the creation of the fae, but it held the most advancements in the use of magic for farming." Aaron coughed. "The humans turned to magical experimentation in their time of need."

"I see." Carter and Juliette had made the famine clear, but maybe they'd been unaware that villagers resorted to blood magic to survive. She bent over Aaron's shoulder to look at the page he'd flipped to. Focusing on their task, she asked, "What did you find?"

"From your brief explanation yesterday, I'd guess you don't quite believe that the Lady went mad." He looked up for Rose's confirmation and then continued. "You are right to suspect. This text is a journal of a villager in Marcil. It indicates the Lady of the Veil gave the governor's daughter the means to protect her village."

"What means?" Rose asked, surprised by the difference in the story Carter told about a woman being taken from her village.

"It doesn't say—just that a deal was struck. I have to believe it has some ring of truth because this journal survived. As you can imagine, most texts from the time were destroyed in the Flood." He flipped through more pages. "This journal isn't the only one that mentions something like this. I'm still searching for the journal of the governor's daughter herself. I swear we had it..." He scratched the back of his neck. "If it's the one I'm thinking of, it includes even more examples of using blood magic to grow crops."

Rose was skimming the text. It was open to an entry where the author talked about their food source being destroyed. Celeste, the governor's daughter, was referenced—a plan to experiment with magic to regrow the crops. "This is a good start." She almost shooed Aaron out of the chair so she could sit down and read from the beginning.

"Does this journal talk about the magic?" Rose wondered how much Aaron would tell her from memory versus what she would need to read for herself.

"No. This villager seemed afraid of it but willing to put their trust in Celeste's plan. We'll need Celeste's journal for details on the magic or the real exchange with the Lady of the Veil."

   JILLIAN WITT

"Did you know blood magic could do something like this?" Rose asked.

"Fae have never paid attention to blood magic. We're spoiled and, some would say, too prideful with our inherent elements. The Vesten Point will probably know the most." He shrugged. "There are scholars and practitioners of blood magic in the Sandrin library where he studied."

Rose nodded as she continued to skim the text for more details or mentions of the Lady of the Veil.

"You have some reading to do." Aaron's lips curved into a smile as his hand searched his face absently for his glasses.

"They're on top of your head," Rose pointed out without looking up.

Nonplussed, Aaron continued, pulling the glasses down to the bridge of his nose.

"I've seen the Lady of the Veil... She certainly wasn't... welcoming when we ended up in her realm. I can't imagine she would just give someone the ability to save her village out of the kindness of her heart."

Aaron's eyes widened at the confession that Rose had journeyed beyond the veil. "I'm going to pretend I didn't hear that."

Rose swatted at him. "As if you didn't expect I've already tried to get to him." There was no need to define the him of who she spoke.

"I expect nothing less, Rose. It's best I don't know the details in case the Suden ask questions. I'm a terrible liar."

Rose hmphed. "Anyway, she seems more of the 'I'll take what I want, and you can't stop me' type."

"That may be true now, but this was five or six hundred years ago. A lot could be different."

Rose nodded. He was right, and she needed to know what had changed. It likely held the key to understanding the Lady of the Veil. Even if the knife worked and Rose could enter the realm undetected, she'd still need to deal with the realm's ruler when it came to Luc and Aterra.

"I'll keep looking for other journals. I expect there is more to the story."

Rose flipped toward the end of the journal—an entry about food and shelter from the elemental storms. She would read this more later. "Thank you, Aaron."

He smiled. "Don't thank me yet. I wanted to get you these. I'll continue searching for the others." He gestured to the stack of books. "I'll leave these for you as well. I've left bookmarks on the most relevant pages. They're other villager's perspectives on the same."

"I'm glad you're not one to fold pages down as markers," Rose said.

He scoffed. "A researcher who did such a thing wouldn't deserve their name." Aaron stood, tucking in the chair and moving toward the exit.

Rose trailed behind him to the door. "You can stay," she offered hesitantly to his back. "The Compass Points value your perspective."

Aaron turned and seemed to evaluate her offer. Unsure if it was genuine. "I need to go continue my search. A big piece of this is still missing. I can return this evening, though, with any additional information I find."

"Sure. That would be great." She didn't expect Aaron to have the same trust in the Compass Points as Luc had come to. The last time he saw his brother, Luc was still contemplating what to tell the Compass Points, so Aaron's knowledge was outdated. "We came to trust each other on our journey," Rose added. "The others trusted Luc as well." She shrugged. "Well, mostly."

Aaron gave her a doubtful look. "I would challenge you on that, but the entire village is abuzz with the fact you and the Vesten Point were seen coming out of Osten house yesterday. No one can remember the last time the Compass Points conversed outside this room." He glanced around the Norden library where the Compass Points usually held meetings. He ran his fingers

　　　JILLIAN WITT

through his hair. "I know something has changed. I do hope it's for the better." He shrugged. "I'll be back later when I have more information."

Rose saw him out, hoping she could soon prove to him and the rest of Compass Lake that it was for the better.

CHAPTER SEVENTEEN

"You already tried to cross?!" Arie shouted as Rose turned the corner and was visible to him and Aurora in the dining room. Arie and Annabeth must have reached some agreement, because even as the god and goddess were seated with the food Arie had prepared before them, more plates were arriving from the kitchen.

Rose put her hand on her hip. "Don't act like you thought I would wait." She pointed to the dishes laden with eggs, bacon, fruits, and pastries. "Who is all this for?"

Arie shrugged and ran his fingers through his hair. She was still getting used to him making such a gesture. It felt too human —too common for the shapeshifting being who was her best friend. "Annabeth insisted. And I hoped you'd at least take a minute to try to research where you were going. Texts about the realm beyond the veil are few and far between. I figured you'd search for at least one, giving us time to catch up with you."

"We're doing research now!" Rose replied, gesturing back toward the library.

Arie sighed loudly and dropped his head down on the table. Rose didn't miss Aurora's sympathetic smile as she patted Arie's shoulder through his overreaction.

"Aaron brought some very specific texts. Journals from villagers in Marcil—apparently, the governor's daughter made a deal with Cassandra to protect the village."

Rose tested out the Lady of the Veil's name. The name felt powerful—as she knew the ruler to be from their brief encounter.

"Really?" Arie raised his head and tilted it with interest, and she could once more see the movements of the bird form he usually held. "What did it say?"

"I thought you guys weren't supposed to help us?" Rose tapped her chin playfully. Even though she was unsure where exactly Arie and Aurora fell on this question. "I also didn't wait for you because I figured, as with stopping Aterra, we'd have to do this ourselves."

"We were only a day behind you," Arie replied, avoiding her question. "How did you even make the crossing already? I figured it would take Carter days to come clean about his abilities."

"I was pretty proud of him as well." Rose smiled again, marveling at their progress as a team. "I may have pushed him a little, but he told us on the ride back."

"Now he decides to start sharing information," Arie mumbled as he shook his head.

"I still had to ask," Rose offered. "He was just much faster to cave than he had been about his other abilities."

"Okay, so..." Arie didn't finish the sentence, waiting for her to fill in the blanks about their attempt to cross beyond the veil.

"I'm sure Aurora already told you," Rose said with feigned exasperation. "We tried, roots shot from the ground to hold us, veil cats chased us. The Lady of the Veil was kind of scary. We didn't want to become prisoners, as I suspect Luc and Aterra are. What else do you need to know?"

"You didn't speak with her?" Arie asked, his elbow on the table; he let his hand fall, palm upward in a gesture that begged for patience.

Rose's eyes widened. "Did we speak..." That wasn't the question she'd expected. "No. She met us moments after we arrived. Her magic felt a little unhinged as roots tore through the soil to ensnare us, and a host of veil cats with very large teeth were growling angrily. We didn't have time for introductions."

"I see," Arie said.

Rose put her hands to her temples, wondering if there was another way. The roots trying to hold them had been her breaking point. They would have been at the Lady's mercy.

"How did she know we were there?" Rose looked between Aurora and Arie. By telling her about the dagger's power, Aurora had already indicated that the Gods knew something about how the Lady ruled her realm.

"Cassandra's control over her domain is very different than ours over the continent," Aurora said. She gave Rose and Arie a grace period, allowing them their usual give and take, but her calm insertion steered them back to the business at hand.

"How so?" Rose asked.

Arie sat up straighter and glanced at Aurora. He appeared unsure—like he didn't know what Aurora would say.

"Her entire purpose is to protect the spirits, shepherding them into the next phase of their existence."

Rose didn't feel like that was an answer to her question. "Are you saying the nature of her duties grants her some magical knowledge over those entering her realm?" Rose considered this. It at least explained how quickly she'd shown up. It did not explain her demeanor upon arrival. "Neither she nor her veil cats seemed very welcoming."

"Her cats would have known you were alive. They would have considered you intruders," Aurora said.

"I've always thought she had a way to communicate with her cats," Arie said, resting his chin on his hands. "I'm sure they alerted her that this was no normal crossing."

Aurora nodded. "And once she knew you were alive...well..." Aurora gestured with her hand as if to explain Cassandra's extreme reaction. "The living have no business in her domain."

Aurora and Arie shared a look that spoke of an eternity of communication.

"Don't hold back now," Rose said, finally sliding into the chair across the table from them. The food Arie and Annabeth had prepared smelled wonderful. She could still see the steam rolling off it. She began piling the plate set for her with food while she pushed on the question she again needed to ask. "Where did we land on the gods helping the Compass Points with this anyway?" She focused on her food, pretending the answer didn't matter.

She had understood the nature of Arie's inability to help with Aterra. In hindsight, she agreed with his decision to search for Zrak separately from them. The Compass Points needed to learn to work together, and no one could have helped them. Arie's presence likely would have only exacerbated the strain between herself and Carter—but this felt different.

Aurora and Arie knew the Lady of the Veil and her realm—at least more than the Compass Points did. Rose was confident their knowledge wouldn't be available in any texts. She wanted their help with this.

"That was part of what we needed to discuss before we arrived," Arie started.

"Sure. I bet that was it," Rose said wryly.

Arie coughed primly, ignoring her suggestive comment. "Anyway, we agreed." He shared another look with Aurora. She reached for his hand and squeezed it. Something in Rose's heart melted at the small gesture. Arie deserved this—no matter his answer. Rose was glad to see him reunited with his lost love.

Arie continued, pulling Rose from her warm moment. "We agreed the balance on the continent is already in shambles. The mist plague may have been tamed. But since it only paused after Juliette's brute force communication with Zrak, it's clear enough the plague is his."

"What are you saying?" Rose asked.

"We're sure that to stop Aterra's plans for good and return

balance, the Compass Points need to work together," Arie tried again, but then seemed unsure how to continue.

Aurora picked up the thread. "We're also certain the gods have meddled even more than we originally thought."

"It's one thing if the mist plague were the continent's natural response to the imbalance, it's another to have Zrak send it, masquerading it as such," Arie said. He scratched the back of his neck. It clearly still bothered him that Zrak was doing this. Rose hoped they would have answers to ease his anxiety on the matter soon. She still wanted to believe in Arie's view of Zrak—wanted to believe there was some master plan behind all that he had done.

Mostly, she was worried about what it would do to Arie if there weren't.

"We're comfortable telling you what we know," Aurora said.

"We'll give you every advantage we can in this fight," Arie said, nodding to himself.

Rose smirked, wanting desperately to pull the melancholy from Arie's face. "So, you believe we're so screwed your interference won't make anything worse?"

Arie's smile returned immediately. He perked up and rolled his shoulders back as if Rose's playful words had lifted the weight of the world from them.

"What an elegant way to sum it up, Rose, as always."

"Well then." Rose smiled. "Let's dive right in." She took a bite of the eggs on her plate, chewing as she considered her first question. "Tell me everything about the Lady of the Veil."

"Well," Aurora started, "we're embarrassed to admit we didn't know she existed until"—she glanced at Arie—"about five hundred and fifty years ago?"

"How could that be—isn't she a goddess?" Rose asked dryly, scooping another forkful of eggs.

"Isn't that the question?" Arie replied. "We don't pretend to know everything about every realm that isn't ours, but as you can imagine, the continent has a connection to the realm beyond the veil. Before Cassandra showed up, we thought the veil cats were the only shepherds of the spirits."

"So, you think she..." Rose couldn't figure out what they thought. She just appeared? She was hiding?

"My guess is that something brought her into existence," Aurora said. She shared another look with Arie. It was understandable that the gods weren't sure about Cassandra; the leader Rose had encountered didn't seem one to explain herself. Rose was sure the limited interactions between Cassandra and the gods of the continent had been prickly at best.

"Like what?" Rose asked.

"You have to understand," Arie started, "we're not the same as we were then." He sighed deeply. It was the sigh of an immortal who knew less than he liked to pretend. "We haven't discussed it much, but we were different before the Flood."

Arie was right, of course. Rose hadn't truly examined it—hadn't thought through the implications as it pertained to her friend—but she knew it. She'd started to feel it even as she read the journal entries Aaron brought. The selfish gods were just so incongruent with the Arie she knew. She wanted to think only of this Arie—only of the friend, the protector, the one who'd stuck by her side for ten years. It wasn't fair to him though. She had to see him both as he was before and as the god he'd grown to be. She nodded at Arie's words. "I know."

"I'm not sure you see it fully. I'm not sure I want you to." Aurora put her hand over Arie's again as he spoke. Rose lost her appetite and pushed her plate forward.

"I know what your selfishness caused, Arie." She scratched her temple. "Of course, I don't dwell on the apathy you must have had to let the world burn as you did, but I can see that version of you." She sighed. "I also see how much you've changed from that god."

"I will choose to believe that," Arie said.

"So, did the same behavior that affected the continent affect

Cassandra's realm? Is that it?" Rose asked, trying to make the connection.

"Cassandra, well, she never told us what happened." Aurora continued. "She confronted the gods about fifty years before the Flood. That was the first time we met her. She was upset."

"More than upset," Arie chimed in.

Aurora nodded. "She was furious, claiming our negligence of humanity on the continent nearly destroyed her realm."

Rose swallowed. "I could see why she'd be upset if that was true. Do you know what happened beyond the veil?"

"No." Arie shook his head. "She wouldn't tell us much. She and Zrak negotiated for some kind of recompense for our actions, and that was that."

"It sounds like the journals Aaron brought you might have insights we don't." Aurora gestured toward the library.

"Yes," Rose agreed. "Although, the one we need, Aaron is still looking for. He thinks the most useful journal will be that of the governor's daughter, Celeste."

Arie nodded. "She did something to Cassandra. Stole something from her?" he questioned as he ran his hand through his hair again.

"From what I skimmed in the journals, she made a deal with her," Rose said.

"Cassandra was far too angry for it to have been a deal," Aurora said. "We need to consider the perspective of who is telling the story. The villagers might think it was a deal, but as you said, the truth will probably lie with someone closer to the situation. We suspected a human stole from her out of desperation and somehow affected her realm's magic. It would explain why she blames us for it."

"As Juliette would say, it always comes back to power," Rose said.

"I would say that, but what does it apply to in this case?" Juliette drawled as she and Carter entered the dining room.

"You're just letting yourselves into Norden house now?" Rose asked, turning her head with a smile that said she was delighted by this development.

"I heard a rumor we were friends," Juliette replied, looking at her nails. "That we were inseparable in our efforts to save your lover and the continent. The least I can do is let myself in the front door."

Rose couldn't hold in her laugh. The mention of Luc didn't bring forth the familiar pulse in her chest. She needed to test her theory on her connection with this group—see if they knew what it was capable of, or if they'd doubt her.

"I'm glad you're here. Have a seat and grab some food. Arie and Aurora were giving me a history lesson about the Lady of the Veil, and Aaron brought journals that might provide helpful context. But before we go further..." Rose allowed herself to reach toward the Luc-shaped space within. Though not in the heart of her magic, she could sense where his power resided.

Acknowledging her and Luc's connection—no matter how unlikely—strengthened it. Part of her still knew it sounded ridiculous. A stronger part was sure that the more she told her friends—even ones recently added to the list—the more easily she could access this bond between them.

And she needed to know what it could do.

She took a deep breath as she looked around the table. Her silence lingered for too long. All four of her guests stopped what they were doing to stare, waiting for her words.

Either they would believe her, or they wouldn't. Rose couldn't let her truth be governed by what they would think—no matter how much she respected the opinions of everyone in the room.

"Luc and I are bound." She let the words hang there, the familiar warmth flooded her as she spoke them aloud. The more she said them, the truer they felt.

"*We're bound,*" Luc's voice echoed through her mind. She couldn't see him, but she could feel the smile on his face—one she hoped to see again soon. Was he actually speaking to her? Could he hear her words? The connection was alive between them. She had to learn the details of what it could do. They had communicated across realms last night in the heart of her magic—of that, she was sure.

"We're bound," she said again, the strength of the words growing with the echo of Luc's voice inside her.

Finally, she looked up. Her gaze met Arie's sitting directly across the table. She wasn't sure what reaction to expect from him, but his smile was broad and genuine. Warmth bubbled in her chest again. It was just as quickly doused as his smile turned to a smirk with his reply.

"I'm glad you figured that one out on your own. That's one awkward conversation I can check off my list."

CHAPTER EIGHTEEN

"Y ou already knew?" Rose asked as Arie casually brought a forkful of eggs to his mouth.

"You actually think they're bound?" Juliette asked at the same time.

Arie swallowed. "I suspected." He furrowed his brow. "Luc confirmed it before he commenced his heroics with Aterra."

"I'm going to kill him," Rose said with absolutely no heat. She crossed her arms over her chest for emphasis, but it didn't help. The empty threat made her feel better though.

"I already told you I'd spend my existence making it up to you. Did you not believe me?" His voice was decadent in her mind. She sat up straighter. Luc's words were new, not ones she'd heard before. He was responding to her now. He could hear her words. The more she leaned into their bond, the stronger it became.

"Your threat needs some work. It sounds more like fore-play...and gross. We're eating," Arie said.

Rose flushed and took a sip of water to collect herself, focusing on the voice—his voice—inside her head.

"How does this work?" Rose thought back to him. She wondered how much he understood their connection versus how much they were figuring this out together.

"I'm not sure." She could imagine his shrug. *"So far, I've been aware of your extreme emotions when they're about me. I hope the more we solidify the bond, the more we can choose."* It felt like they were choosing right now.

She had a million questions for him. *"Are you safe? Were you captured by the Lady of the Veil?"*

"We were..." Luc started. *"But I'm fine."*

She believed him—and knew she would feel if he wasn't. It would have to be good enough for now as conversation erupted at the table.

"It's impossible," Juliette said, glancing from Rose to Arie.

"I don't know if I'm quite following what you're saying," Carter started. "But if it's impossible, we should assume Rose and Luc can do it."

"Thank you, Carter. You may have the last sausage." Rose happily passed him the last piece of meat from the serving tray just as Arie reached for it. It was a double win as she also got to give Juliette an 'I told you so' smirk.

Carter immediately flushed at the attention and raised his plate to pass the meat back to his patron god. Arie swatted his hand through the air like he no longer wanted it. "I deserved that."

"How do you know you're bound?" Aurora asked, cutting through the clutter.

Juliette pointed with her fork at Aurora, emphasizing her enthusiasm that Rose and Arie answer the question while she continued chewing.

"I've...connected with him since he's gone beyond the veil," Rose said.

"Ew," Arie offered.

"Not like that," Rose said, but she felt heat rise to her cheeks as she remembered the feel of his magic against her skin. "Well, not totally like that." Now, she wondered what was possible in the heart of her magic.

"What are you even saying?" Juliette said. "Do you hear your-

　　　　　JILLIAN WITT

self?" The Osten Point waved her fork at Rose. It was the most casual Rose had ever seen her. She'd be flattered if she weren't unhappy with Juliette's position. "The Norden Point cannot be bound to the Suden Point. You cannot connect with him—whatever that means—across realms."

Aurora's presence was somehow calming amid all of these strong opinions. She asked a follow-up question softly, but everyone turned as she spoke. "What is the connection like?"

Rose smiled, and the corners of Aurora's eyes lit with understanding. Rose had said they had connected, referring to the time in the heart of her magic. Aurora had asked in the present tense what the connection is like. Maybe her ability to speak to Luc, mind to mind, was common among bound fae.

"I can speak to him in my mind," Rose said. Her eyes remained fixed on Aurora. Her announcement was met with gasps from Juliette and Carter, so she hurried to explain to the rest. "Listen, I acknowledge what Juliette is saying. I really do. I've thought it more often than you have," Rose said as she turned to the Osten Point. "You have to understand, on our journey to find Aterra—well, I guess before that—Luc's magic had...formed opinions about me. It seemed dead-set on protecting and supporting me at every opportunity."

Rose shook her head like she couldn't quite believe what she was saying. But that wasn't right. She did believe it. She knew what this was. Luc's magic pulsed inside her. Juliette's words reflected her self-doubt about its authenticity and what it meant. She had to confront the perspective—one that had so recently been her own. She had to acknowledge the truth of her experience. Juliette and Aurora were giving her a path to do so in their own ways.

"His magic was very active on our trip," Juliette acknowledged. Her words were a peace offering to Rose, encouraging her to continue.

"It was more than that. As you all shared your magic with me to face Aterra, how he shared his was different."

"I'd say so." His words entered her mind as they spoke of his magic. Like talking about him called his voice to her.

"You did connect quite quickly to his magic," Carter added.

Rose nodded, remembering when they tested the connection at the Suden training grounds. "With each of you, I had to find and open the connection point." She shook her head, unable to hide her smile. "Luc's magic was just kind of...there. Like it was waiting for me."

She thought of his words, the ones that had pulled them from fake relationship to real partners... *"It's been real for a while, Rose; I've just been waiting for you to catch up."* She swallowed thickly. Luc always let her find their connections in her own time—no matter how sure of them he was. Like he knew she'd never accept them otherwise. Now, she'd never let go of her love for him.

"Our paths are bound—by that choice to love each other."

He chose her, too. She'd never tire of hearing it.

"I'll never tire of telling you."

Coughing, she tried to clear her throat of emotion as she continued. Talking to him this way was going to take some getting used to.

She focused once again on the others and the breakfast conversation. "When I finished his weapon, our magics connected like we were sharing power..." Rose coughed again, feeling the familiar heat in her cheeks as she thought about precisely what they'd been doing. More than just their magic had come together in her workshop.

"He spoke to me, or his magic did, before and after he left during our battle with Aterra. Now that I've acknowledged our bond, we can speak to each other through our minds, though I'm still figuring that out." She paused, wetting her lips, giving herself a moment to continue. "Since he's been gone, I've gone into the heart of my magic to try to find our connection. It took me a while because it was different than before he left. His magic... seems to *be* the foundation of my lake there. I think he's a part of me now."

JILLIAN WITT

Heat flared in her chest again. *"It's a permanent fixture, I'm afraid."*

She smiled at his words. "The more I say it, the more solid it feels," she finished, meeting each of their gazes, accentuating the surety quietly growing within her.

"When I returned from searching for Zrak, I could feel the difference in how your magics connected. And according to your timeline, that was even before the connection fully cemented," Arie said. "To be fair, I tried to bring it up before we returned to the Lake of the Gods, but I think Luc knew you weren't ready to confront it yet. Then, before he made his stupid sacrifice, I spoke with him." Aurora moved her hand to cover Arie's as he continued. "I asked him if he knew what he was doing. I guessed what he would do once he picked up his sword. Instead of worrying about his plan, his only reply was to tell me that the two of you were bound. He wasn't sure you'd acknowledge it and might need someone to reassure you that it was real."

Rose was on the knife's edge between swooning over his assurance in their unprecedented bond and wanting to throttle him for not sharing his certainty with her.

Arie must have seen as much in her face. "Were you ready to hear that before you faced Aterra under the mountain?"

"I might have been if I knew he was going to be a self-sacrificing idiot, and we wouldn't get to talk about it later!" Her hands clenched into fists under the table.

"Selfishly, I didn't want to tell you. I wanted you to know on your own—but have the reassurance you needed when you thought it impossible."

"I know," she replied. She hoped the clench of her teeth came through. His reasons were good ones. She wouldn't have wanted to hear it from anyone else... *"I'm glad I found it this way."*

"But..."

"I don't know," she said, and meant it. She didn't know what she wanted. Maybe she just wanted him here. *"I just wish you'd been with me. That we'd found the bond together."*

"I am with you," he said with an unshakeable certainty. *"And it wouldn't be possible if we hadn't found it together. Acknowledging it, what it meant, what was possible. That had to be our own."*

She shook her head. Just hearing his voice in her head was its own reassurance. Being able to debate how she felt and what he had considered its own remedy. She was greedy for more of his words. They'd been apart too long.

"Do we know what being bound means?" Carter asked calmly, pulling Rose from her conversation.

He was officially Rose's favorite. She smiled and looked at Aurora. Her earlier comment indicated she might know more about bound fae than the others. "Did you know other bound pairs? Do you know what this means for us?"

"Conceptually, it's your magic's perfect match in another. You know better than others, Rose, all that is encompassed in the heart of a fae's magic. Your greatest truths, deepest desires, and the things you hold dear are all there. Being bound is to find another whose magic is your match—whose magic compliments everything you are," Aurora said. "More than conceptually, though, there have been so few bound fae. And none between fae courts." Aurora nodded at Juliette, acknowledging her skepticism. "I don't think it's because it's impossible though," she said hesitantly. "I think it has more to do with how the courts have operated for the last five hundred years. With how the courts have held themselves apart, there has been little opportunity for fae from different courts to spend time together, let alone develop this kind of connection."

"Unfortunately, that's fair criticism," Juliette said.

"I can think of a pair from the first generation of fae after creation," Aurora said. "Marissa and Alma. They were both of the Norden court. They could indeed communicate without words. They could also share magic. I couldn't say if the way they shared magic differed from what you all do as Compass Points, but I'd assume, based on your explanation, Rose, that it was closer to your description. A more permanent residence of their magic within each other."

"There was also a pair in the Osten court, under the second Osten Point. We have a record of the wordless communication— even without passing secrets on the wind. We don't have anything about how their magic connected though." Juliette shrugged. "That obviously doesn't preclude it. They're very rare, and from what I know, the pairs don't always like talking about the connection."

"True," Aurora added. "It's a very private thing to share so much of yourself with another. Think about how much you learn about someone when you make them a weapon and then multiply that by an order of magnitude."

"Fair." Rose nodded. "So, you don't think I'm losing it for believing Luc and I are bound?"

"We might still think you're losing it," Arie answered without missing a beat. "But I do think you're bound. I agree with Carter." The Vesten Point beamed at his patron's praise. "If something is impossible, we should expect you and Luc to make it so."

CHAPTER NINETEEN

The group finished breakfast and relocated to the Norden library. Aurora sat in the plush chair, and Arie sprawled across the couch. Carter and Juliette stood by the bookshelves, though Juliette's gaze lingered on the Compass Point table. The books Aaron brought were spread out and left open to key entries.

"Getting a head start?" Juliette asked. Rose followed them in and walked to the table, flipping through one of the books.

"Aaron brought them. I only read a few passages with him, but they make it clear that you were both right to suspect the stories about the Lady of the Veil," Rose said, glancing at Carter and Juliette.

"How so?" Carter asked.

"They are journals from villagers in Marcil—it was maybe the only village to have documents preserved from before the Flood. They indicate the governor's daughter had some kind of interaction with Cassandra. It might even be what helped preserve part of the village."

"What kind of interaction?" Carter asked.

"That is very much up for debate." Rose gestured to the stack of journals. "The entries I read said a bargain was made. Aurora and Arie seem to think it more malicious."

Carter looked like he had many more questions, but Arie interrupted, asking, "Aaron didn't want to stay and help?"

Rose looked at the others. "I think he's hesitant to be around us all working together. And nervous to know what we're doing. With Luc gone, the Suden will ask him questions. He said he's a terrible liar, so the less he knows, the better." Rose shrugged. "Though he did say he would continue searching through the Suden archives and for the governor's daughter's account."

"Trust me, everyone is still confused about us working together," Juliette said.

Carter nodded. "My advisors accused me of illicit relationships with you both." He blushed, the words had come out before he'd thought them through.

Rose smiled. That, at least, meant he was comfortable with them, even if his advisors didn't care for it.

"Honestly, it's to be expected," Juliette added. "Changing how the entire political structure of Compass Lake works will take time." She glanced at Rose, who had opened her mouth to respond. "I'm not saying it's impossible, and I'm not saying I won't support the effort. I am saying we still have a bit of a time-sensitive mission here. The mist plague may have paused, but we don't know if Zrak has complete control of when it's deployed or if anyone else is pulling his strings. And we still don't know how or if we can wake those impacted. We need to end this. And we need to get Luc back." She added the last part offhandedly.

Rose crossed her arms over her chest. "Agreed. So, what's next?"

"Well, it doesn't make sense to go beyond the veil again until we have something concrete to say to the Lady since we know she'll be waiting for us," Carter said. "Maybe we should dig into these texts to see if they give us anything to work with."

Aurora coughed slightly, drawing Rose's attention. The way her eyes lit up when Rose's gaze met hers told Rose it was feigned.

The morning had been so full she had already forgotten the boon Aurora had shared with her.

"What if it's not necessarily the case that Cassandra will be waiting for us when we arrive? What if we can enter the realm undetected?" she asked, fingering the dagger in her belt and pulling it into her palm. "What if the Norden artifact does more than we realized?" She held the handle firmly.

"What did you learn, Rose?" Arie asked, a small smile curling his lip.

"Our problem was that the Lady of the Veil knew we were there before we'd even had a chance to look around. What if we could go beyond the veil but not have to deal with the Lady or her cats as soon as we arrived?"

"If possible, it would be faster if you explained how," Carter said.

"Fine." She flipped the dagger in her hand. She used her wind to safely land the tip between her fingers—a game she remembered Luc playing with his magic while they chased Aterra around the continent. "The dagger doesn't only enhance Norden magic, it can help the bearer go unnoticed." She flipped the blade again, palming the handle.

"*That could work.*" As if thinking of his magic had brought forth his voice.

"How?" Carter reiterated.

Rose gestured to Aurora to see if she wanted to share. "By all means, Rose. It's yours now."

Rose flipped the dagger again. This time, allowing it to pierce her finger as it slid into place between her thumb and pointer. As soon as her blood touched the blade she saw magic ripple through the room. Concentric circles surged from where she stood and from other locations in the library as if decoys were already set up. Then, the raindrops of magic Aurora described started to fall. It was dozens of raindrops pouring into the room at once. They hit the ripples, creating more of their own, further obscuring Rose's position.

She smirked as the others looked around the room for her. Juliette turned toward the window facing the lake. Carter glanced toward the fireplace, and Arie slowly turned as he sought her out. He shifted into his black bird form when he couldn't find her and flew to the fireplace to perch. His head swiveled back and forth. Each of their senses appeared to indicate Rose was elsewhere in the room. Aurora stared straight at Rose, who hadn't moved from her place by the table. The goddess gave her an approving smile.

"So much trust built, and you still knew they wouldn't believe you. You needed to show them." The others turned back to the table where Rose still stood—the location where Aurora's words were addressed. Rose felt the ripples and drops dissipate, and Carter and Juliette's eyes widened ever so slightly to see her standing in the original location, the dagger still poised between her fingers.

"Well, that might do it," Carter said, stepping forward from his place against the bookshelf to reach for the knife. "May I?" he asked.

"Sure." Rose handed it over, unsure what Carter could do with it but willing to let him try. He sniffed it. Some may have laughed at the gesture, but Rose's nose was so attuned to magic scents that she knew what he was doing. It made her pause to wonder if his shifter nature strengthened his magical scent detection.

"It doesn't smell like you," Carter said. "But when you used it, we could sense your power throughout the room." His cheeks flushed. "Clearly, in places you were not present. This is strong magic."

"That's the idea exactly," Aurora said. "And it's not so much the strength of power as honing the magic used into the perfect weapon. Wherever the blade goes, the ripples and drops will mask the origin." Aurora looked a little smug. Rose decided she deserved it.

"There is a reason the best weapons-makers on the continent are Norden," Aurora said, her gaze seeking Rose. "My people have my innate understanding of the balance between blade and magic."

Rose lifted her chin. The words felt like Aurora was again claiming Rose as her own. Her family had always instilled that she was Norden—no matter her extra magic. The deep, hidden part of Rose that let what the elders had said bother her preened. She was where she was supposed to be. Her unique mix of magic had helped them get this far.

"Can the dagger's magic cover more than just the Norden Point?" Carter asked. He was the obvious requirement to shepherd Rose on this journey beyond the veil. If only the dagger's wielder was covered, they wouldn't be better off than they'd been during their first attempt.

"Why don't you two test it out?" Aurora said with a gleam in her eye.

"I'm game if you are," Rose said.

"What do you need from me?" Carter asked.

Rose tilted her head to the side, thinking. She wasn't quite sure. Aurora's gaze was still heavy on her. The goddess seemed to sense Rose's hesitancy in asking for help. Rose smiled gently at Aurora but shook her head. She appreciated the offer, but if everything went according to plan, Aurora wouldn't be with them beyond the veil. They would be on their own to figure this out. They might as well see what they could do together without the goddess's assistance.

"Give me a second," Rose said, closing her eyes. She needed to feel the magic of the blade a bit more. Even from the brief test, it was clear how the magic shielded her origin point. The question was whether it would shield two points and for how long. Her weapons-master magic pushed against the blade. She rarely had cause to evaluate the magic of a blade already forged. It was similar to how she tried to understand the heart of a wielder before forging a weapon for them. Before fully wielding the dagger, she needed to understand the core of its power.

The blade was solid and well-made. Not that she doubted her

     JILLIAN WITT

patron goddess. Her magic slipped along the knife's edge, coalescing at the tip. Though a dagger, she could tell this weapon was created for defense. As Aurora had alluded, she had asked her first Norden Point to trail Aterra on the continent. The magic was to keep him safe as he carried out his patron's request. Her situation was slightly different but the same at the heart.

The gods still needed the Compass Points to clean up their mess. Rose just wouldn't be doing it alone. She needed the blade to offer the same protection to the Vesten Point. Heat flared from the blade at her evaluation. As if it knew she questioned its ability. This was good. The blade's heat almost felt like the Vesten fire. She opened her eyes and glanced at Aurora, who smiled wickedly.

Maybe it did feel like Vesten fire.

"I think we should give this a try," Rose said. If some of Arie's fire was already within the blade, Rose was sure it would strive to protect the Vesten Point as easily as the Norden. She turned to face Carter. "I'm not sure what to expect, but that's why we're testing it here." Rose shrugged. "I'll activate it, and then the others will tell us if they can see us."

"Seems simple enough," Carter said.

Rose poked her finger with the tip of the dagger. The moment her blood coated the blade, she felt the magic activate. Ripples cascaded, and water drops fell. The magic covered her and her movements—she could feel its shield. It didn't feel like it covered the Vesten Point beside her though.

Turning to face Carter, she saw the magic didn't spread over him the same way. He was still visible, though she wasn't sure he would disappear to her eyes. It was more likely those covered by the blade's magic would be able to see each other. Something about this was off. The waves and ripples didn't disguise the location where Carter stood. They didn't seem to notice him at all. She knew she'd failed when Carter's gaze roamed the room.

"Carter, can you see me?" Rose asked. His gaze snapped back to where she stood. He could hear her, but he couldn't see her.

"We can see Carter," Arie drawled. He had returned to his human form and sprawled across the couch again.

Rose let the dagger's magic fall and ran her fingers through her hair. "It didn't naturally spread to him." Her gaze roamed to Aurora as she spoke. She didn't ask a question—yet.

She stared again at the dagger. A drop of her blood still covered the blade's tip... Of course. "Carter, I think it needs your blood, too, if we expect it to cover you."

Carter tilted his head in a very Arie-like gesture. "What do you mean?"

"If I'm not mistaken, it's another form of blood magic." Rose's gaze met Juliette's. "It seems all the gods dabbled with it, no matter what the humans on the continent thought." Juliette tipped her chin in acknowledgment. Rose knew she'd been self-conscious about the ritual she performed to strengthen the Osten court. But the more they learned of the gods, the more she saw the line that separated their innate elemental magic and the blood magic considered less than was blurred at best.

"When I offer my blood, I'm asking for protection from the blade," she said once again, turning to Carter. "If you also want the dagger's protection, you must offer your blood to receive it."

"That makes sense," Carter said, slowly taking the dagger as Rose offered it. He poked his index finger, similar to what Rose had done. She repeated the gesture with him—immediately feeling the difference in the magic.

The ripples formed an oval shape around them. Carter was within the protective shield of the magic this time. She wanted to test it a bit more. Tugging his arm, she moved them toward the fireplace. Juliette's eyes narrowed as she tried to find them in the room. Arie sat up, appearing to do the same. When he couldn't see them, he shifted. Rose knew she'd made a mistake. She'd dragged Carter to the exact spot on the fireplace Arie had previously perched in his bird form. The bird's wings brushed Carter's head before they could relocate. Arie flapped again, this time in delight as he realized what he had done.

          JILLIAN WITT

"*I found you!*" he said for everyone in the room to hear. "*I win!*"

Rose released the blade's magic. "This isn't a winning game, Arie," she said. "Either we all win with Carter and I sneaking into Cassandra's realm unnoticed, or we both get captured by the Lady of the Veil."

Rose's thoughts strayed to Luc. "*Will I be able to find you?*" Her thoughts then shifted to her compass that spun in circles.

Picking up on her thoughts, Luc replied. "*I think your compass will work once we're in the same realm, but if not, I can guide you.*"

As if sensing where her thoughts had turned, Arie landed on her shoulder. "*I'm sure he's fine.*"

"He is," she said with certainty. They were bound—if he were hurt, or worse, she would feel it.

She nodded and looked at Carter as he released the blade's magic. "Again?" she asked.

CHAPTER TWENTY

Rose and Carter spent the next few hours testing the dagger's ability to shield them both. It was more challenging than anticipated. The blade's magic did not hide their voices, and two people moving together required coordination. Though Rose would travel with a veil cat and not the Vesten Point, practicing this way was even more difficult. It may have helped stop their voices from carrying but being able to signal directions between veil cat and fae made for slow movement.

Plus, the longer they were under the dagger's protection, the more visible they became.

"If we're going to use it this long, we'll need to provide multiple offerings." Rose shrugged as they let the magic fall from their latest test.

Carter nodded after shifting back to his fae form. "You'll have to help with additional offerings when I'm in my veil cat form."

Rose didn't like that. She'd have to randomly poke his cat form with the blade to retrieve more blood. Conceptually, she knew it was still Carter in there, and he wouldn't attack her, but she'd been taught a healthy respect for wild animals.

"At least we won't be separating," Carter offered. They briefly discussed if they could accomplish more by splitting up when they arrived. The blade allowed them some distance, but it was evident, with the multiple offerings required, that distance couldn't last for long. And if the compass worked beyond the veil, it could only guide them to what one of them desired. Rose needed to find Luc, retrieve him, and try to understand Zrak's place beyond the veil—in that order.

While there were infinite ways for it to go wrong, Rose held higher hopes for this trip than the last. They would at least have time to get their bearings and explore.

"You two ready to take a break?" Juliette asked, looking up from her seat at the Compass Points table. She'd started reading the books Aaron had brought them in earnest while Rose and Carter practiced. Aurora also sat with her, reading while watching Rose and Carter's tests.

"I think we're ready to try crossing." Rose clapped her hands together. She was not looking forward to the trek back down the stairs in Osten house and the caves. But she'd do it all—as often as necessary—to find Luc and bring him back.

"I'd do the same for you; it's just, this time, I'm a bit tied up."

Rose had tried desperately not to focus on Luc's situation beyond the veil. He knew she was coming for him, and he'd tell her more as she got closer. His words now bubbled so many questions to her mind.

"I'm fine," he reinforced her thoughts. *"I'll tell you everything when you're beyond the veil. Communicating will be easier when we're in the same realm."*

She nodded to herself at his words, then turned to Juliette. "Can you take us back to the caverns?"

"I think there might be a faster way for you and Carter," Arie said from where he lounged, in human form again, across the wingback chair.

"What?" Rose asked as all three of the Compass Points gazes narrowed on the Vesten god.

"That is if you don't want to try talking to Zrak." Arie

shrugged. "I'd recommend crossing beyond the veil on Vesten property."

"Arie, explain yourself," Rose said, glancing at Carter, who looked equally bewildered. There was no way the Vesten Point knew there was a way to cross beyond the veil on his property. Rose spoke again when it was clear that Carter couldn't find the words. "We don't know of a place to cross at Vesten house."

"Don't look at me like that," Arie said, pointing to himself. "I wouldn't be able to cross there, but I believe the tree where my coin was buried will get you where you need to go if you have a veil cat to take you."

Carter finally found his voice. "If it won't work for you, how do you know it will work for us?"

"I'm a god," Arie said simply.

Aurora rolled her eyes at his statement. "What Arie means to say is that the tree was planted due to the negotiation between Cassandra and us. She insisted on its location."

Carter's eyes went wide. "The Lady of the Veil chose the placement of the willow tree?"

Aurora nodded and continued. "It's the only way we knew something had happened. She accused us of vast mismanagement of the continent and said it impacted her realm. She demanded something for our crimes against her." Aurora had the good grace to look ashamed. "We were, of course, guilty of the mismanagement, but we were unaware of any crimes against her." Aurora flipped through a few more pages in the journal. "As I said before Carter and Juliette arrived, I don't think these journals offer the full perspective."

Juliette and Aurora shared all they had read. They detailed what Rose had only skimmed and Aaron had only hinted at: the village's desperation, use of blood magic, and a deal with the Lady of the Veil. The village healer's journal spoke of another woman with Celeste regularly—Andie—though Andie didn't appear to have a journal in the stack Aaron had provided.

"Our sins were generally those of negligence, not plotted

destruction," Arie added. "But Aurora's right. Zrak was the one who talked to her and decided on the tree as recompense," he said, clearing his throat.

"Mind you, the fae courts were not established then," Aurora added. "It was quite a surprise to us when we realized this was the same location where we set the Compass Points' seats of power." She shrugged as if trying to convince herself it wasn't all that odd. "This is a place of its own unique magic. It's why we selected it. Cassandra must have felt that much as well."

"You are right to be suspicious," Juliette said oddly reassuring the Norden goddess. "This place does have magic, but how could she know how important it would become or how it would grow with time? It seems more likely that she knew something about the future of this place."

"That's not possible, is it?" Rose asked.

"I thought we decided this morning we shouldn't hold ourselves to assumed conventions of what is possible. Bound fae from two different courts, for example, shouldn't be possible." Juliette spread out her hands. "But here we are."

As if summoned by her words, Luc chuckled in her head. *"She's got you there."*

Rose pressed forward. "Okay, so Carter and I will go to Vesten property and try to cross at the willow tree." She looked at the others. "What will you three do?" Rose added as she moved her hand to her hip.

"I think we've read everything we can here," Juliette said. "I hope Aaron finds Celeste's journal. Maybe she'll have a slightly more detailed understanding of what happened."

"He should have an update for us tonight," Rose replied.

"As long as you don't mind missing it, Rose, I'd like to try to talk to Zrak," Arie said. He looked to the Osten Point with a question. "Would you take us to the caves where you commune with him?"

Juliette glanced at Rose, who shrugged in confirmation. "I can do that though I'll warn you to temper your expectations."

"He owes answers," Arie said.

Aurora cut off any further discussion. "We can meet back here this evening to continue reading and discuss our attempts. Zrak may not come, but we must try. He will have more relevant information than even these journals if he chooses to share it." She sighed.

"We have no idea what he did to ensure he could stay beyond the veil," Arie added. "Or how that is connected to his Nebulus spreading the mist plague. Just as you and Carter were discovered immediately, it's safe to assume Zrak was also."

"He seems resourceful," Carter said. "Maybe he charmed her?"

Arie snorted. "Zrak is many things, but a charmer he is not."

"Agreed," Juliette added with a scoff. Rose wondered again at the Osten Point's interactions with her patron god over the years of her rule.

Aurora sighed. "I agree. I just don't think we can rule anything out. He's been able to send the mist plague, and he's been able to commune with you." Aurora gestured to Juliette. "He seems free to do many things beyond the veil. Rose has carefully avoided the topic, but I assume Luc and Aterra are not so at liberty. What has Zrak done to earn his freedom? Especially when we know Cassandra's perspective on intruders to her land."

Arie's brow furrowed. "There's only one way to find out." He shifted into his black bird form and flew out of the room.

TRYING to call the Osten god would be its own burden. Rose didn't envy the others as she and Carter left Norden house and walked to the Burning Garden. The last time she was here was the night before the Compass Points went after Aterra. She shook her head, remembering when they thought the Suden god was their biggest problem. Even before that, when they thought the mist plague was a symptom of a single problem with the balance on the continent.

They were well past that now.

What Aurora and Arie were saying, what Juliette was hinting at, was that all of this was bigger than one god seeking to disrupt the balance. If this tree's presence predated the Flood, what other problems were further entangled with the continent's history?

It was fitting, then, to begin to see how all of the pieces wove together. Zrak paid penance for the greed of the gods. He bargained with Cassandra, the Lady of the Veil, to exist there. Aterra continued with his selfish ways, unconcerned with Zrak's sacrifice. It was almost like Zrak knew Aterra would do it. At least, he'd prepared accordingly, convincing the Lady of the Veil to allow his Nebulus to alert the continent's leaders of Aterra's disturbance.

It fit too neatly to be coincidental. And Cassandra negotiating to have this tree planted on Vesten property, hundreds of years before the fae courts were created? That was the icing on the cake. Rose agreed with Juliette. Someone knew these pieces would fall into place eventually. Did Cassandra have some gift of foresight as she ruled over the spirits beyond the veil?

Rose hoped not, as they were about to, once again, circumvent her hospitality. Suppose she had another way of knowing when visitors arrived—some sight? Rose wasn't sure Aurora's dagger would protect them.

She shrugged. They would try regardless. Fleeing last time had worked, and hopefully, it remained an option on this second venture.

They walked through the garden. Only blooms of oranges, reds, and yellows were allowed in the Vesten garden. Each flower was chosen to represent the Vesten's element. It made the entire garden appear aflame when it was in bloom.

Rose marveled at the tribute to the Vesten court. What would she do with the Norden property now that it was hers? She'd always loved living in the caretaker's house as a child, but her father had made it clear they couldn't truly customize the property.

It wasn't theirs.

Now it was, and she would make the changes her father always dreamed of. He loved greenery. He always said he'd love to grow ivy everywhere, even on the house. It was a small way to honor her family when this was all over.

Rose envied the way Luc had made Suden house his. It was a stark contrast to how she currently felt about Norden house. Admittedly, she had her own history with the place she needed to overcome, but Suden house felt like a family home the moment she walked into it.

She could admit she wanted that same feeling in Norden house. Her stomach churned. It wouldn't be a family home without him—without her bound partner. She didn't even care if they forever held two households, calling Norden and Suden houses their own. It was inconvenient but workable. If that was their biggest challenge after saving the continent, she would take it.

"We'll make it feel like home, Rose," he whispered. She wondered how many of her thoughts he could hear. Did he know of the future she dreamed of for them?

"I dream of it, too. I'll do anything to make it happen," he whispered into her mind.

She took a deep breath. They would have plenty of time to figure this out when she got him back.

As they approached the familiar weeping willow, Rose steeled her spine and readied herself for the next part of the journey. They would find Luc on this trip if everything went according to plan.

Carter parted the long, wispy branches of the ancient tree, and they walked under the canopy. The ground was still disturbed at the trunk where Rose had dug up the Burning Coin at Arie's command. They had done a terrible job covering their tracks. Rose saw Carter's hand slip into his pocket, likely touching that same coin. Giving him

JILLIAN WITT

the Vesten god's artifact was a game changer in their relationship and journey. This wouldn't have been possible if the coin hadn't successfully helped unlock some of the unique abilities of his veil cat form.

"Ready?" Carter's voice broke into her thoughts.

"That's it? We're here, and you know what to do?" Rose put her hand on her hip as she asked the question.

"Kind of." Carter shrugged. "I hadn't been back in the garden since we returned. I like to think I would have felt the tug of magic at this tree if I had been. I have to assume that having the coin, having this new connection to Cassandra's realm, would have made the magic here more recognizable."

"Do you know how it will work? Or is it best if I don't know, like last time?" she said as she elbowed him.

"Less is more on this trip. I'm not positive what will happen, so it's best not to set any expectations."

Rose gave him a heavy dose of side-eye.

"I know with complete certainty that we will be able to cross," he said with a finality she believed. She was less reassured as he tilted his head from side to side, seeming to take the tree in from all angles.

"Fine." She brushed away her concern with her hand. "You got us there and back last time. I trust you to do it again."

He nodded. "I'm going to shift now. The same rules apply. You have to hold on to me. And this time, don't let go once we make it across. Holding on to my fur will ensure we stay close, to let the blade's magic do its thing." He coughed. "And to let you replenish its magic if necessary."

"Are you giving me permission to stab you?" she asked.

"I was hoping for a gentle poke, but don't worry about hurting me. The magic is more important than a little scratch."

She gave him a wary glance but agreed. "It probably makes sense to enable the dagger's magic now, right?" They wanted to have the magic active before they arrived in the Lady's domain.

"Yes. Once I shift, it should only take a few moments for us to cross. It's better to do it now. Who knows where exactly the border is that alerts the Lady to arrivals."

Rose pulled Aurora's dagger from her belt and slit the tip of her finger, letting her blood drip onto the blade. Carter did the same. She felt the magic as soon as her blood touched the weapon. Turning to check that Carter was also covered, a veil cat prowled where the Vesten Point had stood. The magic rippled around them both, the water droplets obscuring their origin point. She stepped forward, the magic moving with them, and latched her fingers into the scruff of fur at the cat's neck.

"Ready when you are," she said since Carter could no longer speak to her. Unsure what to expect, she was slightly surprised when the veil cat growled loudly. She searched the area, thinking he was signaling danger. His growl pierced the silent garden again, and a yelp slipped out of her mouth as the old tree before them shifted.

She blinked, trying to make sense of what she saw. The branches swayed, and the trunk widened. Her eyes were fixed on the tree as it grew. It cracked loudly. Rose's head snapped up, thinking a branch was falling on them. Instead, the trunk hollowed out at the center, the bark disappearing. It created a dark passageway straight through the center of the tree. The willow's canopy hid this mysterious passageway from the view of any passersby.

Her grip tightened on the veil cat beside her. She had a sinking feeling about where they were headed. Carter stalked forward, and she matched his pace. They stood at the precipice of the dark passageway. It was large enough for them to walk into. If the tunnel were straight, it should simply take them through to the other side of the tree trunk, but Rose knew that wouldn't be the case. The darkness was unending.

"You want to go through that, don't you?" Rose asked wryly.

The veil cat dipped its head and continued their forward progress. With their first step into the passageway—Rose realized what this was.

JILLIAN WITT

Her connection to Carter's magic.

The way she was able to connect with his power source as a Compass Point to share magic—it had been through a tree just like this one. The way the magic of the Compass Points worked together held more answers than she had realized.

Carter hadn't known about this tree's magic until today. Sure, it was an essential feature in the Vesten garden, but until today, it had been just a tree. She had watched the surprise cross his face in Norden library as Arie revealed a passage beyond the veil on his property. So, the real question was, what did it mean about Carter's magic that it chose this tree, this pathway, to represent it?

Rose had no answers. They had already known Carter could see spirits and that his magic was connected to the land beyond the veil, especially with his shifter form. This felt like more. She shook her head, refocusing on the goals of this trip. She was determined to save Luc and, hopefully, the continent.

A shiver raked her spine as they crossed beyond the veil. She thought of Cassandra demanding this tree be planted, Zrak and his Nebulus, and Aterra and his plan to make a Suden Point. How many other players had stakes in this game of which they were unaware?

CHAPTER TWENTY-ONE

There was a moment as they crossed when the already active magic of Aurora's dagger flared to life around them. The ripples spread, the drops fell—and icy water soaked her clothes. The splash into the river was an unwelcome surprise. Rose swept her arms as she searched the river for Carter. He was swimming to the riverbank in his fae form.

A deep cold pulsed in her bones as the river rushed against her. Though they'd entered from a different location, the river appeared to be the same.

Hauling herself onto the riverbank next to Carter, Rose let her breathing return to normal. "That is not a welcoming entrance," Rose said.

"Some would say it's quite unwelcoming," Carter said wryly. "It's like she doesn't want any visitors to make it into her realm. I'm shifting back. I want to be able to get us out of here at a moment's notice," he said. She didn't have time to reply before a veil cat sat beside her.

Rose used her magic to squeeze water drops off both of them. Then she squinted to try to confirm if the magic of Aurora's dagger was still working. It wasn't as easily seen here as in the

Norden library, but peering hard enough, Rose could see the ripples fanning out and the droplets around them obscuring their location.

The river might be the same but the bank was different than last time. They were still in a forest, but there was a structure in the distance she didn't recognize. Rose pulled her compass from under her tunic and looked down. Her heart skipped a beat as the needle stopped its endless spinning. Having a direction to follow, she tugged gently on Carter's scruff.

"*Luc?*" She sent the thought out, hoping they could speak freely now that they were closer.

"*Come here often?*" His voice slipped into her head with all the tact his shameless pickup line deserved.

"*I'm glad you're in such good spirits. It looks like we have a bit of a walk—it's time you tell me everything.*"

Luc sighed. "*We're in her castle dungeon.*"

Rose's heart was in her throat instantly. "*We?*"

"*Aterra and I. She found us as soon as we arrived, just like what happened with you and Carter. I'll tell you the details later.*"

Rose looked around again. The sizeable structure could certainly be a castle. Rose bet this was their destination. It would be a few hours' walk.

"Carter, can you carry me for a bit?" It was an awkward question, but she wouldn't ask if they had other options.

The veil cat nodded.

"*I think you have time to show me now,*" she pressed. They'd danced around the details of this connection. She wanted to test it —to see what they could do. If she went into the heart of her magic, could his mind shadow reach her? "*Can you show me?*"

Luc's mind shadow was a gift few Suden had. He'd shown her scenes before. This seemed like the next step, since she could feel his magic on her skin in the lake. Could he show her his arrival through their connection, which usually required physical touch?

"*We can try.*" She could the slight furrow of his brow as he spoke the words. As soon as she settled on Carter's back and dove into the heart of her magic, Luc's washed over. Rose felt herself fall into Luc's memory just as she had in Loch.

D**ARKNESS SURROUNDED HER**.

It was a darkness so complete Rose wondered if she'd ever see the light of day again. Lifting her hands, she felt for...something... anything as she wandered in the darkness. Nothing was available to touch, so Rose continued to meander. With her, she dragged a heavy weight, one that seemed to be struggling to free itself from her hold.

The path was unclear. Rose turned left and right, trying to find her way. Nothing guided her. She might be lost in this expanse forever.

Something pulled below her sternum—a heat flared that Rose was all too familiar with. It tugged her in the direction opposite of where she was headed. She sighed deeply and nodded to herself, continuing opposite the tug.

Rose landed with a splash. Icy water enveloped her before she could organize her thoughts. She moved her arms, treading water as she looked around. The river was, unfortunately, familiar at this point. She'd fallen into it enough times to realize it must be the entry point for all those passing beyond the veil. Pushing one hand through her hair, she noted it was black and much shorter than her own.

She was in Luc's memory. That made her Luc for the time being.

If this was his entry beyond the veil, then where was...

Aterra was swimming toward the shore next to her. He appeared fully recovered from the stab of the Suden ring. Thinking of the ring, Rose didn't see it on Luc's finger. He must have had to remove it to pierce Aterra the way he did. Rose felt Luc's arms move as he started swimming after the earth god.

         JILLIAN WITT

The pair pulled themselves up on shore. Aterra glared at Luc.

"What do you think that accomplished, boy?" Aterra growled. "All you did was delay the inevitable."

Luc's mouth opened to respond, but no words came out, his gaze lifting over Aterra's shoulder to a new threat. Rose barely had to process what she was seeing. It was all too familiar from her journey beyond the veil.

A host of veil cats surrounded them.

"I thought they were extinct," Aterra whispered as he turned to face the new threat. If possible, these veil cats looked even less inviting than the ones that had greeted her and Carter. Aterra and Luc both got to their feet slowly.

"Did you have a plan from here, boy?" Aterra taunted.

Luc didn't have to respond for Rose to know he did not. His one goal had been to get Aterra to a location where he couldn't continue to cause chaos on the continent. The rest, she was sure, he planned to figure out as he went.

"I don't mean you any harm," Luc's voice came from the body she inhabited. "He's the one disrupting everything." Luc shrugged in Aterra's general direction.

"They're animals. They can't understand you," Aterra growled. He took a few steps to the right, away from Luc, like he would try to run. The veil cats refused to allow the visitors beyond their reach, snapping and snarling as they held a half-circle around the pair.

Aterra looked over his shoulder. Only the icy river was behind them. He could jump back in, but odds were, the veil cats would be waiting for him wherever he emerged. His teeth clenched as he realized he'd have to fight past the beasts.

He hesitated. For the first time, she wondered how familiar Aterra was with the Lady of the Veil. Given Aterra's penchant for destruction, attacking a host of veil cats with his earth magic didn't seem like a tough decision for him. Rose watched his brow furrow, and his fingers clenched into fists as he considered his options. Unfortunately, it looked like he had none.

Pebbles danced on the ground as the earth began to shake. Aterra shook the meadow in a pattern that tried to move the veil cats into a huddle to his left. Rose understood his plan. If he could move the pack left, he could split the earth around them and create an escape route.

The fact that he didn't open the earth beneath himself and slip through it made Rose wonder if that wasn't an option in this realm. Rose had no concept of what was possible with each of their magics and what was not.

Herding the veil cats with the earth shakes seemed to be working. They clumped together just to the left of Aterra. The pathway was opening for the earth god to split the ground. Just as it was coming together, an avalanche of power rolled into the meadow.

The same roaring of magic that had tried to trap Rose—had forced her to choose to flee—she felt it now. Lady Cassandra rode in on a powerful horse. Unlike Rose and Carter's visit, Luc and Aterra had nowhere to go. Roots shot from the ground to wrap around Luc and Aterra's limbs.

Luc's hands raised in surrender as the roots held him in place. Aterra seemed to realize he was running out of time. The veil cats weren't far enough away for him to make a clean exit, but he no longer cared. He split the earth, causing one of the beasts to slide into the crack he created.

Cassandra's roots reached to catch the veil cat, pulling it back to its pack. The already rolling thunder of her power echoed across the clearing. As she came more clearly into view, a blinding light erupted from where she rode.

The crack Aterra started filled with roots—a thick spider web he could not penetrate—pulling the earth back together. They wrapped themselves around Aterra just as quickly, freezing him in place.

"Will I never be free of the continent's disasters?" Cassandra said as she dismounted. Rose felt even more justified in her decision to flee on her and Carter's first trip, seeing what their fate

 JILLIAN WITT

would have been. The Lady of the Veil was terrifying. If those on the continent thought Luc's power was immense, she couldn't imagine what they would think of this ruler. There was a fire in her gaze as she stared down Aterra. "How dare you attack one of my own in my realm?"

Aterra said nothing. Some of the magic thick in the air around them started dissipating, and Aterra's mouth opened as the roots peeled away just enough to let him speak. Aterra pointed at Luc. "He is the one who disturbs your peace. Not me."

"So like a god of the continent," Cassandra purred. "It's never your fault, is it?"

Aterra opened his mouth to speak again, but Cassandra's roots reemerged to hold it shut.

"Let me guess," she said, her gaze turning to Luc. "He was poised to ruin the continent?"

Zrak stepped into view, responding before Luc could say anything. "Well, you are so well-adept at preventing ruin."

She ignored Zrak, her gaze locked on Luc. "You. What makes you think my realm is the place to bring your problems?"

Luc sucked in a breath like he wasn't quite sure how Cassandra knew the details of his situation so fully. He recovered quickly. "I apologize, Lady. I didn't know what else to do."

"Well, that's honest, at least." She pushed her hair back over her shoulder. "How did you even make it through?"

Luc shook his head. "I'm not sure..." She felt him hesitate like he didn't know how much to say.

As she opened her mouth to speak again, Zrak cut in. "His bound partner is on the continent... I'd guess he used all his strength to move away from her—from that connection. The opposite direction of that pull would lead him here," he said smoothly.

Rose was stunned. How did Zrak know that she and Luc were bound? They had only just found out themselves, and there had been no Nebulus on the continent since Luc realized.

"I wasn't asking you, Zrak," she said coldly. Her gaze raked over both Luc and Aterra in evaluation. If Rose had to guess, Cassandra appeared to find them both wanting. She noted the lingering gaze on Aterra's hand in his pocket.

"Interesting, isn't it?" she continued. "Not quite what you led me to believe." Her teeth clenched around the words. They were said with such quiet anger. Rose wasn't sure they were meant for anyone but the Lost God.

"I haven't failed yet," Zrak replied. "Why are you here?" Zrak asked Luc. He appeared to be ignoring Aterra entirely.

"They are my prisoners, Zrak," Cassandra growled. "You overstep. I did not give you leave to question them."

At the word prisoner, the veil cats' behavior shifted. While calmed by her presence, they quickly returned to the fierce guardians encountered on arrival. It gave Rose pause as if maybe the veil cats understood more than Aterra gave them credit for.

"Moving right to prisoners?" Zrak said, looking at Cassandra. "You don't even want to know if he'll work for you?"

Cassandra glared at Luc. "He's not the one I need. He's worse off than you were when you arrived."

"Ah, but you let me work for you," he said. Rose sensed this conversation wasn't for Zrak's benefit.

"You know you had to offer me more than simply your service," Cassandra hissed. "And so far, you've failed to deliver on your other promises." The look she gave him was pure rage.

"But the steps are in motion," Zrak said, his lip curving into a smile.

Cassandra nodded begrudgingly. "Let's return to the castle."

She suspected Aterra couldn't reach for his magic, or he definitely would have. The veil cats ushered Luc and Aterra forward, the roots licking at their feet with every step, showing their willingness to rebind the duo at a moment's notice. Rose could only assume they were headed to the castle she was currently en route to. Rose's head spun as she considered Zrak's words. He knew more than should be possible. He'd offered them information

   JILLIAN WITT

they needed through this conversation, that he did more than work for Cassandra to remain beyond the veil during his exile. Something about a promise he would deliver on... It was almost like he knew Rose would see it.

ROSE SLID from Carter's back as she returned from the memory. Their invisibility followed them as they moved, but Rose took a moment to replenish the few drops of blood on the dagger's tip. Carter growled as she poked him.

"There is a lot to unpack there," Rose said.

Luc's laugh was a balm to her soul. *"Where do you want to start?"*

"We've never had trouble crossing," Rose told Luc through the bond as she thought about everything else she'd seen in the memory.

"I don't know how he knows, but Zrak was right. I felt the pull of your magic and went in the opposite direction. The space between realms is kind of terrifying."

Rose agreed. *"It seems Zrak knows a lot he shouldn't, right?"*

"Yes, it's become increasingly clear he promised Cassandra that something would happen. I don't know what it is or how he plans to fulfill his promise."

Rose longed to see his face as he spoke. The worry lines on his sharp features. The crooked brow when he challenged her and his hand dragging down his face when he wasn't sure how to proceed. This ability to communicate was one she was thankful for, but she wanted more.

"Do you know how she's holding Aterra?" Rose asked.

"No, I don't understand the magic here well. I can tell Aterra's power doesn't work the same as it did on the continent. I can even feel it's somewhat diminished. But I can't understand the magic of this realm."

Rose looked down at Carter as he let out a low rumble, catching her attention. They were nearing the city gates. She pulled out her compass again to check the direction. It indicated continuing into the city, straight towards the center.

The castle there was large, taking up her entire view as they approached. Rose could make out a wooden drawbridge at the center of the town that led over a small body of water to the castle proper. The building was made of dark stone, and multiple towers stuck in the air, creating an imposing skyline.

Rose hoped their invisibility held. She pricked her finger again out of habit and poked Carter's leg to replenish the magic. She let her conversation with Luc quiet. It was reassuring enough to know she could contact him when she wanted. Now, she needed to focus on getting to him.

"A little convenient, isn't it?" Rose said before they had to stop speaking. "The connection from the Vesten property to beyond the veil leads directly to Cassandra's doorstep?"

Carter looked up at her, suspicion evident in his feline eyes.

"I'm not the one that did it!" Rose said defensively. "I'm just saying it's suspicious."

The veil cat accepted that, and they continued walking. She had time for one more question before they entered the gate and needed to be silent. "What do you think we're about to see?" Rose asked. Everyone here should be spirits. Rose wondered if they would be visible to her. Again, she asked Carter the last part out loud, knowing he couldn't answer. He gave another low rumble as they walked into the city.

It was like any city on the continent. Homes lined the main pathway to the center of town. She chanced another whisper to Carter as she said, "Do spirits need homes?"

Carter looked at her with a glare that only a feline could produce.

Apparently, it was time for her to stop talking. She tugged his fur a little harder than necessary as they entered the village. The compass pointed straight toward the castle.

Rose couldn't help but search her surroundings as they walked. This was her sneak peek into the afterlife, and while, hopefully, she and Luc had a long time before they arrived here, her curiosity was getting the best of her.

She tugged on Carter's scruff to slow down when she finally saw someone. They looked...human—a woman carrying food. Rose noted eggs, bread, cheese, and other similar staples that one would purchase in a market on the continent. An odd light drew her eyes to the woman. The only unique feature was a glowing, fuzzy outline surrounding her. Was this the delineation of a spirit? Cassandra and her veil cats did not have such a glow when they saw them on their last visit.

Carter's steps continued, pulling her forward. As they moved deeper into the settlement, Rose found more of the same. They were...people. People of all ages filled this village, going about their daily tasks. Some shopped, some had clothing for washing, others appeared on an afternoon stroll.

This was the afterlife? It appeared so...normal.

Everyone they passed seemed peaceful. Maybe it wasn't bad, just a little mundane to Rose's imagination. One thing didn't add up though. There was nowhere near enough of them. When spirits came here, shouldn't they exist indefinitely? This village should overflow with over five hundred years of the continent's past inhabitants. How many other settlements existed? She was spiraling with questions. They were only a distraction as they got closer to the village center and the drawbridge that led to the castle. Her curiosity about the afterlife could wait. She was here for Luc.

Her gaze caught on an oddly familiar-looking face crossing the drawbridge. She couldn't have claimed to know his features by heart, but having so recently seen him in Luc's memory, she knew him immediately—Zrak.

He was tall and broad. His dark brown hair stood in contrast to his white skin. He strode across the bridge with purpose.

Rose must have thought something to Luc before she even acknowledged the shift in her plan herself.

"I'm not going anywhere, Rose. Follow him while you can. Please be careful."

Rose nodded to herself in response, though she knew Luc couldn't see it. She needed to know what Zrak's plans were.

JILLIAN WITT

CHAPTER TWENTY-TWO

Zrak's steps slowed as he entered the castle. Rose was thankful since she was still holding fast to a veil cat, and there were many more people to weave through. They maneuvered around others crossing the bridge with business in the castle and followed the Osten god down a hallway. Rose still had her compass out when it shifted direction. She looked up, the arrow pointing to a doorway across from where they stood. Luc told her to go—they needed to know what Zrak was up to. Decision made, Carter narrowly avoided running into a guard in the staircase as Rose turned them sharply in the opposite direction.

Zrak was heading to one of the towers.

Rose would take this chance. If Zrak was here, he couldn't be speaking to the others. He must still be ignoring them. The more information she had, the more she knew Zrak was at the heart of what was happening beyond the veil. They needed to know what he knew.

They were approaching their third guard post station since entering. Rose's eyes narrowed as she watched the guard wave Zrak through without discussion or question. It only left her with more questions. Who was Zrak to these people?

Juliette had prepared them for Zrak to have freedom of movement beyond the veil. He was able to meet her regularly for the ritual. It starkly contrasted the greeting Luc and Aterra received. What did Zrak know that Cassandra wanted so badly?

Unfortunately, it mattered to Rose because their overarching plan was to reinstate Zrak on the continent instead of Aterra. Whatever Zrak had done by controlling the mist plague was misguided, but it at least seemed to alert the Compass Points to the imbalance around them.

The results were devastating for the villages—their residents were still sleeping. But Rose held out hope that the mist plague could be reversed. She held out hope that Tara and other villagers could be awoken.

A part of her feared more lives would have been lost without the direct warning the mist plague brought. From the villagers' journals, Rose knew the first warning signs before the Flood had been less forgiving than Zrak's plague. Famine and disease had spread, and people had died before natural disasters took the continent.

They would fix it. She shoved down the thoughts of her mentee, Tara, and the residents of the continent who needed her as she slowed her pace. Zrak reached a door at the top of the winding stone staircase. He didn't walk right into this one. He knocked.

Rose and Carter in his veil cat form shared a glance and inched as close to him as they dared. Following Zrak into this room would be tricky if he closed the door behind him. She pricked her finger and Carter's paw again for good measure. Aurora's dagger gave her no reason to think it would stop work-ing, but Rose was nervous, already suspecting who was behind this door.

The magic wasn't as suffocating as the first time they'd entered the realm unwelcome, but its power was still palpable. Cassandra, the Lady of the Veil, opened the door wide. A glimpse over her shoulder showed a room lined with overflowing bookshelves and a large wooden desk as the central piece of furniture. Rose could see a chaise in one corner. She wondered how often Cassandra used it. The Lady didn't appear to be one who took moments of respite. She was all business as she acknowledged Zrak's presence, leaving the door open for him and walking back to her desk.

This was it. They had to try to enter the room. Rose grabbed Carter's scruff and readied to move as Zrak stepped inside. He grasped the door to close it. There wouldn't be enough time for the two of them to enter.

Then, Zrak looked down at his tunic. Something on the chest must have caught his eye. He wiped at something on the fabric that Rose couldn't see. She didn't question it. These extra seconds were what they needed. As Zrak brushed away the non-existent speck, Rose and Carter slipped into Cassandra's study. Zrak gently closed the door behind them.

With her heart rate elevated, Rose went straight to the chaise. It looked just the right length to catch her if she fell onto it, and she wanted to. Instead, she took a silent breath and positioned them in the out-of-the-way corner to watch Zrak and Cassandra's meeting. It seemed a regular occurrence if the guards' reactions to Zrak were any indication. Rose hoped they were about to learn the agenda.

"Avoiding your Osten Point again?" Cassandra drawled as she sat back in the plush chair. She lounged, putting her feet up on the corner of her desk, and Zrak took one of the less ornate seats for visitors.

Zrak made a non-committal noise of acknowledgement.

"You're right to assume the others will be with her now," Cassandra continued, oblivious to Zrak's discomfort. "The Compass Points worked together enough to send Aterra here. They'll all be with her if she's back at Compass Lake and calling you."

"Are you avoiding your friend Arctos, then?" The conversation in the room pulled her focus. Rose rubbed her sternum as she listened to Cassandra needle the Lost God about his peers on the continent.

"Who I'm avoiding isn't your concern, Cassandra," Zrak said as he rubbed his temple. His hair was in disarray. He must have run his hands through it already. Rose could tell Zrak didn't have the carefree persona Arie did. Nor did he portray the direct strength she was beginning to associate with Aurora. The god pulled his hands from his face, placing them in his lap where he attempted to hold them still. Instead, they rubbed together silently as Cassandra continued to speak. Zrak seemed stressed.

"You can't just stop your duties. You may avoid them, but you still must complete your work for me," Cassandra pressed. Her feet fell back to the floor, and she leaned forward.

"I'm aware," Zrak replied, his teeth clenched and a note of exhaustion in his voice.

"Just because you don't have your own reasons to send your Nebulus anymore doesn't mean you can let the spirits linger."

"Like I said, I'm aware." Zrak took the deepest breath Rose had ever seen. He seemed at his limit, but Rose had no idea why.

"Well, then act like it," Cassandra snapped. "You must fulfill this duty until another takes it over."

The words were too vague to make sense to Rose. Clearly, they meant something to Zrak.

His head snapped up. "Don't doubt me now, Lady. It's been hundreds of years. It's a little late to lose faith." His smile held no warmth.

"I know better than anyone that it's been hundreds of years," she hissed. "Don't patronize me." She stood from her seat and placed her palms on the desk. "You came to me. You agreed to my terms and will continue your work until they are fulfilled."

"The fate of the continent—" Zrak started.

"I don't care about your plans," she said, her arms folding over her chest. "All you've done is cost me."

Zrak sighed deeply again. "I understand your position," he replied. "It hasn't changed."

    JILLIAN WITT

"Fine. Go. Do your job." She waved a hand in dismissal.

Zrak shook his head as he stood slowly and moved toward the door. Rose's heartbeat accelerated again. They had been lucky on the entry. Rose couldn't help but think they wouldn't have the same opportunity for the exit. She tucked her fingers back in the scruff of Carter's neck, readying them to dash through the opening. There was another door behind Cassandra's desk, but it was also closed. And it looked like it was heading in the wrong direction. To make it back down the tower, they needed to make it out the door with the Lost God.

Zrak pulled open the door. He held it wide and turned back to Cassandra.

Rose and Carter didn't waste this second boon. They slipped out the door in front of Zrak and waited on the staircase to follow him back down.

"You should know, I'm leaving as soon as he arrives. That was the extent of our bargain."

They couldn't hear Cassandra's reply, but the way Zrak slammed the door behind him left no question on the terms of his exit.

THEY USED Zrak's movements as a shield to get back down the tower staircase and past two guard posts. Zrak and Cassandra's meeting at least clarified Zrak's work. His Nebulus guided spirits beyond the veil. It also appeared Cassandra was well aware he was letting them take other liberties while on the continent. The additional part of their deal was still a mystery, but by the way both their tempers flared, Rose knew it held weight.

She just didn't know why.

Feeling like she'd received all she would from this unexpected detour, Rose pricked her and Carter again for a little additional cover while they followed the compass to Luc.

Zrak, for his part, walked away wordlessly. Rose tracked his path as he moved out of sight. She wasn't sure what she expected. It's not like he would look over his shoulder and wink at her. No matter how convenient some of his actions today had made their travels, he didn't know they were present. There was no way for him to know. Not even Arie could see them when they were under the blade's protection.

Rose glanced at the compass in her hand and looked across the hall to the opening descending into the castle's depths. Tugging on Carter's nape, Rose directed them to the downward spiral. If Luc was somewhere in a dungeon below, she would find him.

It got darker and damper as they descended the next spiral staircase. The stone floor was uneven. Stray pieces of rock peppered their path, requiring them to mind their feet. They may be invisible, but the sound of their footfalls, or any debris they might kick, wouldn't be.

Torchlight lit the hallway, casting dancing shadows in the warm glow. Carter looked up at her, his yellow-green eyes piercing in the dim light. She couldn't decipher what he was trying to communicate as they approached another guard post. This one would be a tight squeeze.

It was the only way forward, and the compass also wanted them to proceed.

"We're coming," she sent through the bond to him. Something in her magic told her they were close, his magic a siren song, and she couldn't help but move closer. When they had been on the continent together, her magic always felt a pull toward the Suden Point's. The moment she entered a room, her magic knew if he was present. He'd indicated it was the same for him. Even the way he crossed between realms, leveraging the pull of her magic as the opposite direction he should take.

"About time, love," he said. She could feel the wry smile in his voice.

"You'll pay for that comment," she whispered aloud instead of through her mind.

　　　JILLIAN WITT

Carter glared at her through yellow-green eyes, and her hand shot up to cover her mouth. Rose shrugged. They were still far enough from the guard post. He didn't blink as he held her stare. So, she mimed tightly pinching her lips together in promise no more words would escape.

The veil cat did not look amused.

With no other option, they squeezed past the guard post. The two guards stood strictly at attention as if they'd recently been chastised for slacking off on duty and were now trying to make up for it. Rose and Carter slipped through single file.

Their journey through the dark hallway continued for another few minutes before splitting in two directions. Rose peered down both paths. The compass pointed left. As they kept walking, a row of cells came into view. They lined the hallway on both sides, but her eyes were immediately drawn to the shock of black hair under a familiar hood and cloak.

Her magic circled him immediately, drawing his gaze in her direction before she could even send him a thought.

"Learn some new tricks while I've been gone?" His voice in her head was playful. She checked the daggers magic, drops still fell— the invisibility still worked—he must feel her as she had felt him.

The clear view of his face made her heart sink. It couldn't have been more than a week that he'd been here, but he looked exhausted. His exposed skin was dirty and bruised. She wanted to scream. She wanted to throw her arms around him and sink into the warmth she knew she'd find—even in this cold, damp place.

Carter gave a warning rumble as they crept forward slowly. She couldn't do any of those things. Another familiar head of black hair was in the neighboring cell. If they revealed themselves, Aterra would not let them leave unhindered.

"I have all kinds of new talents," she said playfully as her heart raced, thinking through how she'd get him out.

"I never doubted." This close, his words were like a whisper against her skin, speaking to her from the very heart of her magic. Rose couldn't fight the feeling that he could see her, no matter her

invisibility. It had her sliding the dagger against the pad of her finger again, replenishing the magic. Confident she was still invisible, she looked up and found his gaze waiting for hers.

His brown eyes held every word she needed to hear from him, even the ones he'd already said. He was sorry. He wished he had more time to explain. He loved her. He would do this all over again because he knew she needed it of him and would never ask.

Any lingering anger she'd been trying to hold onto slipped away.

"*You left me little choice,*" she replied. "*I needed to compete with the realm-crossing power of a demigod.*"

His low chuckle was more than she could bear. The need to touch him, overwhelming. She couldn't hide the twitch of her lip into a smile—nor did she want to. This. This was familiar, even as everything changed around them.

His dark brown eyes left hers, scanning the area. They flicked to the guard post behind her, evaluating their options. "*I'll spend the rest of our existence making it up to you.*" His words were a promise she had no doubt he'd deliver on.

Rose tried and failed to hold her lips into a thin line as she replied. "*I am holding you to that.*"

Luc's gaze never landed on Carter. She was relieved to know their shield held, and he could only see her due to their bond.

"*Carter is here with me as a veil cat, too.*"

She wasn't sure how to explain this to Carter. He looked up at her, awaiting their next move. "*Do you know how we can open the cell? If we can get you out, Carter can get us back to the continent.*"

"*I'm not sure. The guards you passed have keys, but Aterra won't let us leave quietly.*" Luc glared at the god a few cells down: his father.

"*Aurora's dagger is responsible for this new trick—our invisibility. If I can poke you with it, we might be able to get out unseen.*"

"*So, you still feel a need to stab me?*" he teased.

Rose smiled even though he couldn't see it. "*Only a little.*"

"*We will need to be quick. Aterra will alert the guards if he sees me disappear. He's not exactly thrilled with the situation I've put us in."*

"Well, he can get in line. I have first dibs on emotionally exploding all over you for this...after I get you home."

He couldn't hold back his grin this time. *"As you wish."*

Carter nudged her leg. His patience was wearing thin. Even if Aterra would react, she couldn't leave without trying to get Luc. His cell was at the beginning of the row. Formulating a plan, she started to play it through.

Sending her wind forward to work the lock, just as she'd seen Juliette do at Osten house, she watched for the guards or Aterra to notice. The click sounded, but Rose didn't pull the door open. She would need to wait for the right moment.

Somehow, she knew she could extend the magic of Aurora's blade to him. He didn't have the Vesten fire she'd felt in the blade, but the longer she stood and stared at him, the deeper she felt the strength of their connection. Aurora's dagger would cover him simply because her magic was intertwined with his.

He was right, though, his disappearance would be a problem if it was noticed.

Sighing, she moved as close as she dared. There was no way they were leaving without trying something.

The bars of Luc's cell were a whisper from her body. With a final glance at Aterra, still facing the opposite direction, she pricked her finger again on Aurora's dagger and closed her eyes. Her magic sprawled out, encircling Luc again. She reached the dagger through the bars so Luc could do the same. The shield stretched and rebounded, bringing him into the shield when his blood touched the blade.

She breathed a little easier the moment the ripple of Norden protection snapped into place. The drops of magic fell around them, ensuring protection from magical detection and visibility.

"I have you," she sent through the bond.

"I never doubted," he said again.

She rolled her eyes at him. *"Now I have to open the door."* She chanced a glance at Aterra. *"He's going to notice."*

Luc shrugged. *"He can't get out himself. He's tried."*

Either way, they had little choice, and this was as good a plan as any. Her wind rushed forward, opening the cell door as quietly as possible. Aterra still faced the opposite direction, but who knew when he would turn? Her luck ran out as she swung the door open.

"What do we have here?" Aterra's drawl echoed through the cells as he turned to face them. "A jailbreak?" Aterra's voice rose, drawing the guards' attention down the hall.

Rose already hated this god with every fiber of her being because of what he had done to Luc and the continent. Her wind and water magic raged like a storm on the seas inside her—desperately wanting to fight him for everything he'd done and everything he was still doing.

"You'll want to get back here!" Aterra yelled. "The prisoner is escaping."

Rose grabbed Luc's hand and tugged him deeper into the protective shield with her and Carter. "Get us out of here, Carter," she whispered.

Carter's yellow-green eyes met hers with such panic that she knew something was wrong. He tugged her forward, leading her back down the hallway from which they'd arrived. Unfortunately, this meant they were running toward the approaching guards.

He couldn't explain but wanted them to leave the dungeon cells before transporting them back across planes. A chill ran down Rose's spine.

Could he not transport them from here?

Rose cursed under her breath. Even invisible, they would never escape without being caught by one of the approaching guards. The hallway was too narrow. She wanted to scream as the guards neared. It wouldn't help. Instead, she kept a tight grip on Luc and Carter as they positioned themselves to try to slip past.

"They're invisible! Spread out!" Aterra yelled.

Rose clenched her teeth. The guards listened to the god, fanning out and covering the already small breadth of the hall.

"Get out of here, Rose. I can wait a little while longer." Luc's words flooded her senses as she tried to make a new plan. She hated everything the words implied.

She squeezed Luc's hand tighter. *"I can't lose you again,"* she all but screamed through the bond.

"You're not losing me. You'll never be able to be rid of me." His words distracted her enough that he slipped his hand from hers, his magic pushing her shield away.

The guards collapsed on him, allowing Carter to drag Rose past. She froze, staring at Luc. Tears welled as she realized it was too late to get back to him; the guards were already roughly ushering him back into his cell.

Carter tugged harder—forward—turning briefly to show his teeth. She glared right back at him as the sound of Luc's cell shutting echoed through her bones.

She knew Luc was right—once again making the decision she never would—but her heart broke nevertheless as she left him behind.

CHAPTER TWENTY-THREE

Carter sprinted down the hallway and up the stone steps. Rose didn't stop to question. She kept pace with him as he ran, keeping her fingers intertwined in the scruff of his neck so he could return them to the continent as soon as possible. Rose had a million questions. Clearly, he couldn't take them back from the castle dungeon—or he would have. But did he know where to go now to make the jump?

They tore through the main castle entryway, narrowly avoiding everyone they passed. Carter barely paused as they turned the corner and made for the drawbridge. Rose huffed out a breath and kept running. Turning, she didn't see anyone pursuing them. The guards must have been distracted enough by Luc's appearance.

The knot in her stomach twisted and bottomed out. She couldn't believe she'd left him.

Carter's constant pull at least kept her from breaking down. If she and Carter were caught, she couldn't try again. She flexed her fingers, not gripping Carter as they ran. Her hand had threaded in Luc's. She'd thought she'd never let him go again.

Yet here she was, fleeing without him.

Her fury burned with a singular focus on Aterra. The Suden god was the bane of her existence.

As soon as their feet crossed the bridge exiting the castle, Rose felt the tug of Carter's magic. She wound her fingers tighter into his fur, bracing herself to fall through realms. No matter how good she was with portals, this was different. She wasn't sure she'd ever get used to the feeling. Especially after seeing Luc and Aterra wander, lost between realms, she had no desire to try this without Carter's inherent expertise.

A sharp tug thrummed behind her breastbone. Her magic was as loath to leave Luc again as she was.

"I chose this." His whispered words were in her head. He must have been slotted back into his cell.

"I could have fought harder to hold onto you," were her last words to him as she fell between realms.

She landed with an 'umph.'

Rose pushed up on her arms and stretched her neck from her prone position on the ground. This felt familiar. It was cold, hard, and damp—not all that different from the castle dungeon they had just left. She looked up. Carter stood above her in fae form, smirking.

"You don't seem to be getting better at that," he said dryly.

"Glad that leaving Luc there is funny to you," she huffed as she stood.

His smirk flattened. "I'm sorry, Rose. I should have found a way to tell you I couldn't take us back from within the castle." His gaze didn't meet hers as he kicked a rock on the ground.

"Why? What happened?" she asked.

"Cassandra must have some protection directly around the castle. The entire realm has magic encircling it so that all new visitors end up in the river." He shrugged. "Exiting isn't as heavily monitored, it seems, but it still has restrictions."

"You can feel that?" Rose pressed. She had felt the Lady's presence when they were near her but not otherwise.

"Oh, yes," Carter replied. "Her magic's presence is...strong.

At least to my senses." He scratched the back of his neck as he finished—like maybe he thought he'd said too much.

Rose was intrigued by the conversation. She let herself focus on it rather than the anger welling in her chest at leaving Luc again. Theoretically, she should have the strongest sense for the magic of others based on her weapons master talents. For Carter to feel Cassandra's magic so keenly, something else must be at play. She turned her head in consideration. Her gaze skimmed the tunnel hallway in which they found themselves. Distracted from her thoughts on magic, she started to walk. This tunnel was too familiar.

"Do you know where we landed?" she asked Carter, her mind already having its own suspicions as to the answer.

Carter didn't get to respond as she heard a familiar voice at the end of the tunnel. The hallway widened into a stone amphitheater.

"And what exactly do you believe you are owed?" The voice was tense. Even more so than when they had last left it—slamming the door closed on Cassandra's reply.

Zrak was speaking.

His voice echoed in a way she remembered from her evaluation of Juliette's magic. They were in the caves where Juliette completed her ritual. The others must have finally been successful in their call to Zrak. Rose was shocked.

"Zrak," Arie's usually carefree voice sounded almost hurt. Rose hated Zrak just a little for making him sound that way. "She's just asking for a little clarity on the situation. We all are."

Roes shared a glance with Carter. He gave her a silent nod and followed her into the more open room. They stayed behind the stalactites at the entrance, not ready to make themselves known. Personally, Rose would rather hear what Zrak had to say for himself. What they had overheard—she needed more time to think about it.

"Why didn't you tell us you would be beyond the veil?"

Aurora asked. Her tone also held a hint of disappointment, but not hurt like Arie's.

Rose and Carter peered around from the rock they hid behind. Juliette, Aurora, and Arie stood in the center of the room. They faced a circle of light on the wall. Though it had remained a solid stone surface when Carter dragged Rose through it yesterday, it now held a shadow—an outline—of Zrak.

"I don't have time to chat," Zrak said, sounding bored. "I can't be found here." His voice was cold, unfeeling, as he replied. "I have completed the ritual, as Lady Osten can attest. Now, I must go."

That made no sense. Cassandra knew he met with the Osten Point—she knew he was avoiding Arie and Aurora. Rose couldn't see Arie's face but saw his shoulders sag at the Lost God's words. She couldn't take it. Balling her hands into fists at her sides, she stepped out from behind the rock. "Why are you lying to them, Zrak?" She put a fist on her hip. "Lady Cassandra knows of your meetings with the Osten Point. This isn't about keeping them a secret. Why don't you tell us the truth?"

She swore the shadow looked upward like the Lost God was asking for patience from some higher being. Good. Let him realize there was no one there to help him. They'd all felt that way enough because of his actions.

"Rose? Where did you come from?" Arie asked, turning to face her. Then he wiped his hand at the words as if removing them from the space. "Never mind that. What are you saying?"

"We saw Zrak speaking with Lady Cassandra," she said. "Not only is he free to do as he wishes beyond the veil, but she's aware of the ritual he performs with the Osten Point. I want what you've been asking for—for him to explain what is going on."

Arie, Aurora, and Juliette returned their focus to the shadow of a god ringed in light on the cave wall.

"You have no idea what you're talking about, Norden Point." His words were terse, but at least he knew who she was. "You will have to trust I know what I'm doing." His words echoed through the room as he disappeared from the circle. The light left with him, and the room fell into darkness.

ARIE's and Carter's hands each held a ball of flame as the cavern returned to view. They floated the balls of fire around the room, bringing back the eerie purple glow of Rose's first visit to this cavern.

"What was that, Rose?" Arie asked, not unkindly.

"We saw him, Arie. We saw him talking to Lady Cassandra." She shared a glance with Carter and charged on. "He's no prisoner there. He had free rein of her castle, and though their relationship seemed strained, Zrak certainly wasn't under lock and key like Aterra and Luc." A swell of emotion overtook Rose as she spoke. Luc's magic filled the space that was his, but she hadn't heard his voice again since leaving Cassandra's realm.

She rubbed her chest, hoping to somehow activate the connection.

"You saw them all?" Arie's head tilted to the side, looking so much like the reactions of the black bird form she was familiar with.

"Yes." Rose coughed. She had only seconds to process leaving Luc. They'd been so close...She cleared the thickness in her throat with a cough. One glance at Carter said he wasn't buying her attempt to cover her devastation. She shook her head at him. Now was still not the time for it.

"We couldn't get Luc out without being captured ourselves. But before we found him, we observed a meeting between Zrak and Cassandra."

"What did they say?" Arie pressed.

"Cassandra taunted him about having to confront you and Aurora. She said he'd avoided meeting with Juliette since realizing you and Aurora knew where he was." Rose looked to Juliette. "I

     JILLIAN WITT

assume he pushed the power-sharing ceremony timeline to its limits, and he finally had to show up?"

Juliette nodded, her lips pressed flat, clearly unhappy at Rose's words. "I've never been on truly good terms with Zrak, given everything he cost the Osten people, but I've never considered him an enemy either." She clasped her hands together. "Do you think he's working against us?" Then, a little quieter, "Is bringing him back worse than having Aterra here?"

"We need three gods on the continent as the minimum requirement for balance, right?" Carter asked.

Aurora nodded. "That was the goal."

"I know I'm repeating myself." Arie's gaze shot to Rose. His eyes held a plea for understanding. "I just don't think Zrak is capable of working against us."

Rose felt for her friend. It was hard to think differently of someone he'd been fond of for more years than she could even consider counting. She was reassured when she noticed Aurora grasping his hand. She felt a little stronger in her reply though she delivered it with care. "You admitted that you might not know the Lost God as well as you thought."

"I did." He canted his head again. "But there are parts of him that can't be misconstrued. His respect for the balance is absolute. Everything he's done, everything he did at the creation of the fae, was to preserve the balance, even at great personal cost." Arie sighed and rubbed his temples.

"Not even hundreds of years beyond the veil could have changed his perspective on balance. We can spend time arguing whether his ends will justify his means"—he sighed loudly—"but I still believe he wants the same thing we do."

"And what is that, exactly?" Juliette asked. "Are we still aligned on our goals?"

Juliette now seemed suspicious of all the gods. While Rose trusted Arie, she knew none of the other Compass Points had any reason to. Honestly, she was surprised they'd made it this far without more pushback on Arie and Aurora's involvement. Juliette's gaze found Rose's. To her relief, it didn't appear that her suspicion was directed at herself or Carter. For once, the Compass Points knew they were on the same page.

"We want to bring balance back to the continent," Aurora said, spreading her arms wide in exasperation. "Just like all of you."

"And we think the best chance for balance is with Zrak on the continent instead of Aterra." Arie held Rose's gaze as his following words landed. "Even Luc believed that. He believed it so thoroughly he put his own life on the line."

Rose glared at Arie. His words struck a chord within her. "Don't tell me what Luc believed, Arie. I'm well aware," she snapped. She closed her eyes, this time feeling the thrum of magic in her chest. Taking her own deep breath, she let her emotions settle while her magic quietly strained for her bound partner.

"He's not wrong," Luc's voice broke into her thoughts as if her longing summoned him.

"I know that," she snapped. *"He just didn't need to be such an ass about it."*

She felt his sinful smile through the bond. She shook her head as she clung to their connection. The other Compass Points needed her reassurance. Regardless of her internal turmoil, she fell back into the position of leader and rallier, a position she'd struggled with since Luc's departure. This conversation proved she couldn't afford to lapse in her role. The group needed her to pull them together. They required her unwavering belief that they were all on the same side.

She tucked her chin, reassuring herself first and foremost. Her words would be authentic, or she would not say them. Arie was aware of his own bias. He was trying to rectify what he knew of his friend and what he was hearing from him. This wasn't blind faith that Arie had in Zrak. It was a calculation of his overall end goal. She respected that.

"I think Arie is right about Zrak." She met Carter and Juliette's gazes. "I know I just called Zrak out on his words—his

    JILLIAN WITT

misrepresentation of how things are beyond the veil—but his prior actions still show a desire for balance."

"Past behavior is not a promise of future," Juliette said. "You know that."

Rose did, and she agreed. But Zrak's actions—his behavior—weren't small gestures. "Zrak went to great lengths to point out Aterra's interference. I know he wounded the Osten by sacrificing himself, but he also found a way to patch the problem he created." She shrugged. "He does seem to have a plan." She shook her head. "Even if he refuses to share it with us. Ultimately, though, questionable actions with an aligned end goal are still better than Aterra's blatant disregard for the balance and intention to throw the continent into chaos and natural disaster."

Carter and Juliette nodded as they took in Rose's words. Carter ran his hand through his shaggy hair like he would say something else. She gave him a moment, but he shook his head, dropping whatever topic he would have broached.

"I don't think we'll get any more information today." Rose considered. That final word had given her pause. They were so deep in the caverns. They'd spent so much time beyond the veil. "Is it...still today?" she asked.

"Yes, it should be," Juliette replied. "Though we'll lose more of the day by the time we return through the caves."

Rose turned to glance down the hallway she and Carter had come through. The prospect of the wind crossing and the staircase's mental challenge was disheartening at best. She knew Juliette had an uncommon strength, but thinking about how often she took on these obstacles—for love of her people—had Rose in awe.

At this point in the day Rose didn't even care for the walk through the cavern tunnels. She was exhausted, emotionally and physically. Her bad mood wouldn't help anyone though. They were all fraying. She held an arm before her, gesturing for Juliette, their guide, to lead them. "Shall we, then?"

CHAPTER TWENTY-FOUR

It would be too soon if Rose ever had to face the staircase again. Its ability to prey on her worst fears was one she didn't care to relive as she walked back to Norden house. Her failure to bring Luc home—her fear she'd never bring him back—was a decadent feast for the staircase today. Without Arie kicking her leg, she would have taken up permanent residence there.

"Rose?" Arie's voice called from behind her. He and Aurora walked more slowly, hands intertwined but in the same direction. "I'm sorry to interrupt whatever spiral you're in..."

He didn't sound sorry. His voice sounded chipper. It held too much energy for the end of a too-eventful day.

He continued. "I do need to clarify... We're following you because we plan to stay at Norden house." Rose heard him grunt but didn't turn around. She assumed Aurora had elbowed him in the stomach.

Rose laughed and turned to face them. "Did you elbow him for his presumption?" Rose asked Aurora.

Her blue eyes danced with delight. "It's polite to ask first," she replied.

Rose smiled. "Hopefully, you'll be a good influence on his manners," she said wryly. "But yes, sorry. My head is elsewhere. You're both welcome at Norden house. You can have your choice of the open rooms."

"Thank you," Aurora said more formally than Arie could ever pull off. "We know it's a bit of an imposition, but we'd rather stay close to continue to help."

"I assure you, it's no problem," she said. "I give Arie a hard time, but he knows he's family and welcome in whatever home I have." Rose continued her walk, leaving the two of them to chat a little ways behind her while her mind wandered over the day's events.

Arie caught up with her as she opened the door to Norden house. "Where were you just now?"

She gave him a sad smile. Of everything she had to plan, her mind kept returning to the fears the staircase preyed on. "Just thinking about how my fears seem to keep coming to life."

Arie seemed to know exactly what she was referring to, even if her thoughts were muddled. "You did the right thing leaving him today," Arie replied. "In fact, I'd bet it wasn't even your decision to leave him. Luc would have given himself up as soon as he realized you couldn't all make it out."

Rose rolled her eyes at the god's presumption. He was right, of course, but she didn't need to give him the satisfaction of a response.

"Welcome home," Walter greeted them in the entryway.

"Good evening," Rose said. "Do you mind helping these two find a room in the house?"

"Of course." He turned to the god and goddess. "Please, follow me."

"Let me know if you need anything, but you're welcome to anything you find," Rose called as Walter led them away.

Rose knew she wouldn't find sleep until she tried to connect with Luc again. He may have told her to go. He may have sacrificed himself—again. But now that she'd acknowledged their connection, she wanted desperately to see if they could connect more fully within the heart of her magic.

She wanted to let him in completely. Slipping into her room, Rose was ready to push her and Luc's bond further than she had before.

Physical exhaustion threatened to overtake her as soon as she was under the covers. Her mind was far from rest though. It took almost no thought as she closed her eyes, leaving her body still in bed while the rest of her fell into the heart of her magic.

It was only this morning she'd acknowledged aloud they were bound. That acknowledgment had strengthened the mental bond between them. She was sure it would have done the same for this connection through their magic. Desperately, she needed reassurance that he was okay.

The gentle breeze across her lake drew her attention; the trees circling it swayed in the same wind. It was peaceful here, whether Luc would meet her or not.

But she knew he would.

She dove into the refreshing waters, this time knowing exactly what she was searching for. Her arms stretched as she swam, her fingers itching to get closer to the lakebed—to see the black stone she was certain spiderwebbed through it. A moment later, she reached the bottom. Her eyes lit as the black swirl became visible in the water's movement. Rose pushed the sand away, and the material became even more apparent.

This wasn't the tunnel she'd entered when their magic merged. What was a spiderweb of stone streaking across the lakebed yesterday was now large stone slabs replacing the sandy bottom of her lake at every opportunity.

Her hand reached again for the onyx stone. The familiar magic pulse around her. At this point, she could not determine whether the feeling came from her chest or the lake itself.

"We're bound," she said to the stone. That nagging thought—the worry she was being ridiculous, was no longer present. Some part of her knew the words were magic. Her acknowledgment and acceptance strengthened the connection.

His low chuckle sounded through her very bones. It brought her body to life in a way she couldn't explain—didn't want to explain. She just wanted to feel.

"I think we're past that." His voice was a purr through her thoughts. *"I'm yours, and you're mine. Our paths are bound."*

"I'm sorry... I left you," Rose said, the words tightening her throat as they spilled out. If this was all she got of him, she would use it to at least speak her heart. With the thought, something shifted in the lake. The stone came alive as it expanded deeper into the lakebed. It took over every inch of land, magic pulsing with each new slice it claimed.

She let it.

Rose wanted the stone to take more. She wanted no distance between herself and Luc. Every additional section of onyx brought a frenzied beat in her chest. She dared not hope for what she really wanted—this place to be theirs, a place they could connect, no matter what separated them.

The stone agreed. The water swirled with more force as the onyx base of her lake expanded. Rose desperately wanted an open connection to not just Luc's magic but to the male himself. She didn't know if whatever the stone was doing would accomplish her aim, but she felt sure it understood what she wanted.

She wanted Luc here—with her.

The more she tested their connection, the surer she was of her plan. When she was here, she could smell and feel his magic—why not the fae himself? The realm had a physicality to it she didn't understand, but she planned to leverage.

Her eyes lit as the stone cracked in a way that only a Suden could provoke. The base of her lake didn't fall into a tunnel of Luc's magic but parted to open for something more tangible. Familiar black tendrils of power swirled up through the opening first, holding the water in place. Rose didn't have to think twice as she cast her own magic toward the opening. Ensuring he would have separation from the water to breathe when he came through —and she *knew* he would come through.

She didn't have to wait much longer as fingers crested the edge of the split. The tendrils of magic tossed Luc into the heart of Rose's magic.

His face looked strained at the effort. But it cleared quickly, his gaze seeking and holding hers. His mouth opened, and a wicked smile crossed his face as he realized he could breathe beneath the water.

"Your magic missed me," he said.

She didn't deny it. Her magic accepted and protected him as soon as he crossed the threshold.

He moved slowly toward her underwater. Hesitance stilted his movements. With his decision this afternoon, he seemed unsure of his reception.

"I was a little nervous that wouldn't work—that you wouldn't want me here." The exhaustion was still evident on his face, but his eyes were alert and focused on her.

She didn't make him wait. Holding his hand today as they ran through the castle dungeon wasn't enough. She needed to feel him. Her water pushed her forward. He caught her without hesitation, solid around her, relief apparent in the sag of his shoulders as his arms encircled her. The rightness of the moment was more than she could verbalize.

"I always want you here, you self-sacrificing idiot. I want my bound partner with me always." Her hands roamed his skin, absorbing the physical connection she'd longed for.

"Say it again," he replied, pulling away slightly to see her face. Pure satisfaction lit up his every feature.

She leaned forward to whisper in his ear, her legs wrapped around him of their own volition. "We're bound."

His low chuckle danced along her skin, shooting straight to her core as she finally—finally—had hold of him. She wasn't letting go. Her magic pushed the water away from them enough to lean close to his neck and bury her nose against it. Pine and cinnamon rushed her senses. The scent was a part of him, and she'd missed its constant presence as much as she'd missed the fae himself. Her mouth wasn't far behind her nose as she dragged her lips along the edge of his jaw.

"Are you going to lick me again?" he asked. "I always knew that was a good sign for us," his voice held a smile that warmed her thoroughly, even as they were soaking wet beneath the water.

She pushed back slightly so she could pound her fists on his chest, but her legs wouldn't let him go. "No, I'm going to kill you. Why did you do that?" She was angry at herself for not being able to enjoy this. He was solid, and he was here. Why did her brain spiral toward...everything else?

Luc didn't try to stop her fists as they pushed against his solid chest. "I know your magic won't strain at this," Luc said, gesturing that they were still at the bottom of the lake, "but do you want to have this conversation somewhere else?"

"Can you leave the water?" Rose asked. She wasn't sure of the rules, and she wouldn't risk him being sucked back into his magic. She'd rather they have the conversation right here.

"I can go anywhere you let me, Rose," he said cautiously. "It's always been your choice."

She tugged him to the surface, her magic ushering them where she wanted them and drying them as they moved. They fell onto the small beach beside her lake, surrounded by trees. It felt remarkably similar to the woods where they first fought at the Lake of the Gods.

Rose lay on her back. She propped herself up on her elbows to see where Luc had landed. He had crashed onto shore on his hands and knees—maybe that was intentional from her magic.

He breathed deeply like he'd been starved for air, though she knew that wasn't the case.

"Rosewood and vanilla," he crooned as he crawled toward her—the scent of Rose's magic. "I've dreamed of its scent every day I've been gone."

Rose's heartbeat spiked with every inch he moved forward. The curve of his lip tilted impossibly higher as he tracked her reaction. "I told you I'd spend the rest of our existence making it up to you." He hovered above her now. "I might as well start now."

She could feel his weight settle over her as he lowered himself. The rightness of their bodies sliding against each other had her head falling back and her breathing uneven.

"I knew I had to get to you," he whispered, his hand sliding down the side of her face. "Your look this afternoon..." He let his head hang. "I knew you'd blame yourself for not bringing me back. I had to find a way to make sure you understood, to make sure you knew that I would throw myself into the unknown time and time again for you. That," he said pointedly, "is my choice."

Need drove her forward. She reached up, wrapping her hand around his neck and pulling his lips to meet hers. Their magic flared around them with this physical connection. She tilted her head to improve her angle and nipped his lip with her teeth. Luc matched her eagerly. His tongue slid against hers as he gave more than he received.

She lost track of time—of the list of things they should discuss—there was only both of them here on the shore of her lake, exploring with hands and teeth and tongues.

"I need," Rose started. Her words were breathy. She could not complete her thought process as Luc's lips moved to her skin.

He growled low. "Tell me," he urged. "Tell me what you need." His words sounded like those of a desperate male. He licked her neck as he moved down her body to her chest. "Name it, and it's yours," he said, his voice reverent as his mouth found her breast over her nightshirt. The material didn't slow him down, his tongue swirling her through the fabric.

Rose arched into him as he pinched his teeth around the peaked tip, dancing the line of pain and pleasure. His mouth moved back to hers to catch her moans like they were a prize he could devour. His fingers quested down her body, eager to map every dip and curve.

She couldn't respond to his question. He was everywhere—all at once—and somehow, she wanted more. Eagerly, they removed the barriers of their clothing. She was writhing, begging for more before his lips even hit her thigh. "I need you, Luc."

"You have every part of me," he said, looking up through hooded eyes, his mouth inches away from where she wanted him.

"That's not—" She didn't finish the sentence as his tongue slid against her center. Words failed her, and her body arched impossibly further into him. Luc's hands caught her hips to hold them steady as his tongue slid against her again.

"Luc..." She couldn't complete a sentence, but she needed his name on her lips like she needed her next breath. He sucked on her clit, and she let out a strangled cry, her pleasure building as his tongue licked and swirled. He was a male starved in the wilderness —finally allowed to feast.

Catching her breath was not an option. His fingers slid inside her as his tongue continued to lap up her pleasure. Heat built in her core, and her love for this fae swirled in her chest. She couldn't hold back—nor did she want to. A wave crashed inside her as she found her release.

His mouth covered hers in another scorching kiss, and she tasted herself on his lips. It was a heady feeling to know Luc was hers—that his need for her matched hers for him.

She reached for his hard length between them, stroking from base to tip. His eyes rolled back, and his hips rocked forward into her touch. She needed more—she needed everything.

Luc sensed her need as she lined him up at her entrance. She pulled his mouth down into another scorching kiss as he slid in, giving her the connection she'd so desperately missed.

Her hips raised to take him deeper. His slow strokes were

maddening, but he relished her need. Each steady thrust had her head spinning, their magics coalescing, and her body demanding more. His lips slid against her throat as he buried his face along the side of her neck. "We're bound," was his low murmur against her skin. A reverent refrain of their connection echoed by the movement of their bodies and their magic. She cupped his face and brought his mouth back to hers, their tongues tangling in another searching kiss.

A small spark built to a burning flame inside her. "For the rest of our existence," she said.

"For the rest of our existence," he replied, following her over the cliff of release.

Rose lost track of time as they lay in each other's arms. She hadn't fully realized how much she needed a physical connection with him. Discovering they were bound, only to be separated, had to be the reason for the ache she'd felt when he left.

"This feels right," she said.

She felt his face twitch, and though she couldn't see it, she was sure a satisfied smirk danced there.

"We'll have many more nights like this, Rose," he whispered into her hair.

He was right. She wouldn't accept otherwise—wouldn't give up on bringing him home—no matter the obstacles.

"I should go," he said, planting a kiss on top of her head.

She pushed up on her arms to look down at him. Something in his voice set alarms off in her head. "What is it?"

He sighed and ran his fingers through his hair. "I think Aterra is starting to notice when I connect with you. When I'm physically here, my body is unnaturally still there."

"How do you know Aterra's noticing? Don't you look asleep there?" she pressed.

"He seems closer and closer to my cell each time I return from the connection."

"What do you think he's planning?" she asked. It never sat well with her that Aterra was in a cell the same as Luc. Although godly powers seemed different beyond the veil, she was sure Aterra wouldn't accept defeat so easily.

"I'm not sure yet. I'll let you know as soon as I have an idea. For now, I just need to be careful."

She nodded as he pressed another lingering kiss to her lips and slipped back into the lake.

CHAPTER TWENTY-FIVE

Still exhausted but floating on the high of seeing Luc, Rose greeted the Compass Points early the following day. They needed to decide what to do next. With Zrak's unwillingness to help and Luc locked up right next to Aterra, Rose feared that avoiding Cassandra was no longer an option.

They needed more information about what had happened to the Lady of the Veil and her realm based on human desperation. It was clear from the journals that Celeste did something, but what it was and its impacts were still a mystery.

Aaron had left a note last night. He must have arrived before they returned from the Osten caves. Unfortunately, he didn't leave any books, which led Rose to believe he only had bad news. The Compass Points walked together to Suden house to see what he'd learned.

They took the route through Compass Lake Village, which would lead them around Vesten property to get to Suden house mainly because Rose wanted pastries from the village for their walk.

Rose tried to let her mind wander away from their current predicament. It would be helpful if Aaron found more texts that explained the strain between Cassandra and the continent, but what would they do next if he didn't?

The walk would help clear their heads and provide fresh perspectives.

They needed to get Luc back. They could try sneaking in again, but she feared they'd encounter the same issue unless they devised a plan to distract Aterra. Her magic throbbed at the thought. She couldn't leave Luc...again.

It might break her.

While Zrak was being unhelpful, he did seem to have a way to leave the realm. In their overheard conversation, he said he would leave as soon as 'he came.' This was hard to plan against since they didn't know who he was, but Zrak had proved adept at planning this far. She hoped he could take care of himself. Rose shook her head. She needed to focus on something—*anything*—else.

"I'm not sure we thought this through," Carter said as they entered the village. His voice was no more than a whisper. Rose looked around, and a hush had fallen over the market. Ah, right, this was their first public outing together at Compass Lake—and the Suden Point was missing.

Enough of the Norden villagers had seen them together when Rose took the Norden Point position, and everyone had seen them leave together to go on their undisclosed mission. Gossip circulated the market now—some Rose could nearly hear on the wind, it was so enthusiastically spoken. The way villagers stopped what they were doing to stare. It spoke to the fact that a group of Compass Points hadn't entered the village together in a long time.

"Do we acknowledge it?" Rose asked, feeling self-conscious.

Juliette steepled her fingers and made brief eye contact with each of them. "No, this is the new normal we want. We proceed as if nothing has changed. Give them time to adjust, but we shouldn't make it seem like this is an anomaly."

Rose's throat unexpectedly choked up at Juliette's words. She couldn't entirely fight the swell of emotion at the matter-of-fact way she spoke them.

This. This was what she'd been working so hard for.

This was what she wouldn't stop fighting for.

This was the leadership she wanted for the continent when everything was over. The leadership their people and the continent deserved.

Unfortunately, Juliette seemed to notice her response.

"Don't get soft on me now, Rose. You're the one insisting on this path."

Rose nodded and swallowed thickly. She pushed herself to focus on the tactical action their visit required. "Here's the bakery." She gestured to her favorite store in the market.

Juliette gave a reassuring smile as Carter opened the door.

"Can I help...." The baker's voice trailed off as he realized who entered. Rose smothered a giggle. The same baker, a Suden, had been in a state when she and Luc had walked into his shop weeks ago. It seemed he was just as rattled by the rest of the Compass Points as he was by the Suden leader. He coughed and tried again. "Can I help you?"

Carter took the lead. "Can we have an assortment of pastries?" Carter pointed to a few of the ones in the tray.

The baker gave up on words and worked quickly to wrap up the requested items. As with Luc, the baker seemed to need to ask something. "Any progress on the mist plague while you were traveling the continent?"

Juliette nodded. "We're working together to find a solution. We believe we've halted the plague for now, and our focus remains on bringing back those impacted."

"All of you, together, are working on it?" the baker stuttered. "Even the Suden Point?" His eyes searched the market behind them, looking for Luc.

"The Suden Point is well aligned with our efforts," Carter said. Rose was about to open her mouth to add reassurance when the shop door opened behind them. Rose's mouth curved into a smile as Aaron walked in.

Not only was it fortuitous timing since they were on their way to visit him, but also because he was the one person who could reassure the baker about their progress.

"Rose." Aaron smiled warmly at her before noticing the other two Compass Points. "Looks like we had the same idea," he added, shying away from the larger conversation.

"Aaron." Rose stepped toward him, begging him with her eyes to go along with her—to trust her just a little bit more.

He seemed to sense the request in her gaze and nodded, a Luc-like smirk crossing his features.

"We were just explaining to the baker that the Suden Point is working with us to return those impacted by the mist plague to their former state." She smiled sweetly at him.

"Ah, yes, Christopher." Aaron stepped around the group and toward the counter to shake the baker's hand more familiarly. "Luc is whole-heartedly supporting these three. May I also get an assortment of pastries? Extra chocolate ones for the boys, please."

"If that's true, where is he?" the baker asked, his brows raising.

"Christopher, you know it's not the Suden Point's job to declare his whereabouts to everyone. Trust that he is doing what needs to be done to help restore those impacted by the plague." Aaron's words were so genuine. Rose was glad she'd told him more than he needed to know about Luc's current whereabouts.

"If you say so," the baker replied skeptically, passing a box to Carter and setting to work on Aaron's. He seemed to have Aaron's order ready as he quickly handed him another box from behind the counter.

"Have a good day." Aaron waved to Christopher as he left with the Compass Points. They stood together momentarily, moving just out of earshot of other shoppers.

"Thank you, Aaron," Juliette said. "The timing was perfect."

Aaron nodded. "I'm surprised you're all out together like this."

"It's our new normal." Rose beamed. "But really, thanks again. We were actually on our way to see you. We received your note last night."

"I'm sorry, Rose. I couldn't find anything else at Suden house, but I think I know where they are." His gaze shifted around the market as he spoke.

"Where's that?" Carter asked.

Aaron glanced between the other two Compass Points and must have decided speaking plainly in front of them was acceptable. "My father has always had a collection of pre-Flood texts with details to magically improve farming. Of course, they were humans using blood magic to tend the soil, but he always said it was the foundation, the origins of the Suden's earth magic as we know it. Any I can't find here must be with him."

"Really?" Carter's voice raised in pitch, too excited by half. Rose shot him a glare as he continued too quickly. "What does your father do?"

"He's an agricultural researcher. He works in programs that try to pair human farmers with fae who can support them with various techniques."

"No wonder Luc was so passionate about funding that program," Juliette quipped.

Aaron's reply was sharper than Rose had heard from him. "He cared so much because he knew it was our duty as fae. It was your duty as leaders of this continent to protect the balance, and supporting farmers in these efforts is a huge part of ensuring we have food for everyone."

Juliette lifted her hands in peace. "Apologies, Aaron. I meant nothing by it. It sounds like you both had a strong example of the benefit of these programs and how they help the communities."

Aaron bristled but let it go. "I think they may still be at my father's house in Loch."

"Your father lives in Loch?" Rose was startled. They were there recently, and she couldn't believe Luc wouldn't have stopped to see his stepfather.

"Yes, but he's not often home. He spends most of his time traveling to human communities to teach. The texts are there because he still uses them occasionally to reinforce specific tech-

niques with humans. He also tends to carry journals of humans
wielding magic when he travels. For the humans more reluctant to
accept his help, he tries to show them another human's
perspective."

That made sense. Rose was impressed by the lengths Aaron's
father went to in order to reassure humans about magic use.

"I'll have to go get them. It might be a long trip if he has any
of them with him in the field."

Rose's shoulders fell. So much for taking her mind off their
current problems. She couldn't wait days to try to get to Luc
again. Not having a plan wasn't exactly a strength of hers. None
of this was Aaron's fault though. "We understand, Aaron. But we
would appreciate them as soon as possible."

Aaron nodded.

Rose perked up momentarily, realizing she had a way to speed
up Aaron's trip. "Actually, when will you leave? I can get you
some help for your search."

Aaron looked skeptical. "I can leave today."

"Okay, I'll meet you back at the Suden stables. I have to
retrieve someone from Norden house."

It was clear Aaron disapproved of this plan. Likely because he
knew the others at Norden house currently were gods. He
nodded anyway and left the village with his pastry box.

"Are you sending Arie with him?" Carter asked, a bit of a
smile surprisingly present on his face. "He will not like being
treated as a messenger bird."

"Oh, stop," Rose said, gently pushing Carter's shoulder. "I'm
just going to present him with an opportunity to help resolve the
problems on this continent that he did nothing to prevent."

"Harsh," Juliette responded with a wicked chuckle as they
returned to Norden house.

CHAPTER TWENTY-SIX

"I am not your messenger!" Arie's reply was predictable when Rose told him about his new assignment. It might have gone better if she'd asked him to go instead of telling him they had decided he'd go, but Rose enjoyed pushing his buttons.

She couldn't hold back her laugh as she replied. "I know, Arie." She put a hand on his arm. She'd found him once again in the kitchen when they returned. "It would help us a lot if you could work with Aaron on this. We need to know Celeste's side of the story." Annabeth hadn't even been angry when Rose offered some of the pastries from the market. The cook seemed happy enough to see the house full again, her eyes lighting at the group of Compass Points and gods parading around her space.

"It could take Aaron weeks on his own. You could do it in days."

His metaphorical feathers smoothed out at her words. "Fine, if you think I can help that much."

Rose nodded. "He'll be leaving shortly. It'd be great if you could either go straight to the house or wherever his father is to see if he has the book with him. Then you can bring it back to Aaron however far he's made it on the trail behind you."

Arie looked at Aurora. "I'll be fine here, my love. We can be separated for a few days."

He looked like he wanted to disagree, but Aurora arched a brow as if daring him to voice it. He didn't.

"Everything okay in there?" Juliette asked from the dining room. Rose had let her and Carter start rereading the texts while she, Aurora, and Arie worked in the kitchen.

"We're just about done. Tell Carter to clear away his stacks of books for now," Rose called back. Arie and Annabeth had teamed up to make eggs and sausage when he saw the Compass Points returning. The warmed pastries were a nice bonus. Now, if they could just heat them briefly without letting it burn. Toasted was delicious. Burned was a travesty.

"Watch this like a hawk, Arie," she said as she left to set the table. "If it burns, it's your fault." She swore she saw his body shake like it wanted to ruffle its feathers at her words. The flying would be good for him. He acted like he missed spending time in his favorite form.

Rose walked into the dining room with a stack of plates. Carter had not heeded her warning. She put the plates down and started stacking Carter's books until he finally looked up. "Rose! That's not how any of ..." He was appalled that she'd ruined his organization, but he finally seemed to realize a meal was happening around him, and he was in the way. He shook his head. "I'm sorry, I'll get them." He quickly stacked his books as if trying to move the pile before anyone else could disrupt his arrangement.

The table was set, the meal was ready, and Rose's steps quickened as she returned to the kitchen to see Arie cursing and pulling the pan of pastries off the fire with his fingers.

"I told you to watch it!"

"I got distracted with the sausage. You knew I'd get distracted."

Rose smothered a laugh with her hand. Annabeth shook her head as she went about other meal preparations. The tray wasn't ruined but perfectly toasted. Arie caught it just in time.

This felt nice. The Compass Points, Arie, and Aurora. Yes, they were set back in coming up with their next plan. But being with the people here reminded her of why she was doing this. She liked working with them. She liked *them*. She wanted more of this future—she just needed Luc in it, too. Together, they could bring balance to the continent.

Her magic thrummed in her chest as she thought of the missing piece of her heart. She *needed* Luc. Though still a revelation that she could connect with him on such a level in the heart of her magic, it wasn't the same as bringing him home. She wanted him here.

Being with the Compass Points and gods gave her hope for a future however. Hope for the continent they were fighting to preserve.

"You smelled like pine and cinnamon again this morning," Aaron said as he walked out of Suden house. Rose flushed. She had no doubt why. Luc's magic had been wrapped tightly around her when they'd met the night before. She wanted to explain the bond to Aaron but felt it was Luc's news to share. Just thinking Luc's name brought his voice to her head. After their physical connection last night, even communicating across realms seemed easier.

"You should tell him," Luc said.

"It's your news," she hedged. *"He'd want to hear it from you."*

"Where is he going?" Luc asked.

Rose filled him in on the next steps of their plan while Aaron readied his horse.

Luc sighed. *"In an ideal world, I'd love to tell him, but I need him to do something for me, and the request won't make sense unless you explain."*

Rose was intrigued, so she didn't fight him. "Luc and I are bound."

          JILLIAN WITT

Aaron dropped his pack as he worked to secure it to his horse. It hit the ground with a slight squish.

"That's not possible," he said.

Luc laughed. *"Figures that would be his first response."*

Arie, in bird form, chose that moment to land on her shoulder. He projected his speech for both Rose and Aaron to hear. *"Rose is very good at making things possible that shouldn't be."* She swore he winked at her, though it was challenging to confirm as a bird. *"I'm Arctos, by the way. You can call me Arie. You must be Aaron."*

Luc couldn't hold the laugh from his voice. *"This is a lot for my brother."*

Rose agreed as Aaron looked up to the sky, likely contemplating if he wanted to continue the conversation with someone who was clearly—in his mind—delusional. Now, one of the gods of the continent was introducing himself.

Rose watched Aaron take a few deep breaths before returning his gaze to the pair. "It's nice to meet you, Lord Arc...ie." Rose saw his mouth trip over the informality of the god's nickname. At least Luc had told his brother Lord Arctos traveled with them. He wasn't nearly as shocked by the talking bird as he should be.

Aaron nodded, guessing Rose's thoughts. "He might have mentioned a shapeshifting god before he left."

"For the safety of the continent, of course, in case I didn't return..." Luc said

"Honestly, it's one less thing I have to convince you of," Rose said. "Arie will travel with you to retrieve the book. You can pick wherever you think will be farther away and send him there to search. Then he can bring it back to you on the road."

Aaron nodded. He bent to pick up his pack and finished securing it as he looked at Rose again. "Why did you tell me you were bound? It's not something you'd share without reason."

Rose smiled. "In a perfect world, I would have let Luc share with you in his own way." She sighed. "I told you because I can speak with him—even while he's beyond the veil. He wanted me to tell you because he has something else to ask of you on your trip."

Aaron's face gave nothing away as she spoke. Not disbelief. Not surprise. It was as if she'd shocked all emotion from his expression.

Luc spoke into her mind again, laying out his request. He was still worried about Aterra's plan—how Aterra might use him. Rose wasn't surprised he'd come up with a countermeasure. As Rose passed on Luc's request, Aaron's eyes widened.

"*What are you two up to, Rose?*" Arie asked only into her mind.

Rose shook her head in response to Arie while Aaron seemed to weigh a decision. She couldn't answer him now. This was too important. She had to ensure Aaron believed this was from Luc.

"You're asking a lot," he said, his eyes pinching as he glared at Rose. He rubbed his brow in indecision. "You smell like him, but...can I test you?"

"*Oh, this will be good,*" Luc said. "*Bring it on.*"

"He says yes." She sighed. He sounded far too excited about it.

"Where did we spend our time when he got kicked out of school?"

Luc scoffed. "*What an easy one. The tree out back.*"

Rose repeated his words, and Aaron's eyes widened impossibly further.

"Who was faster in a footrace?" Aaron asked, narrowing his eyes as if this one would get her.

"*Oh, this is how he will get me to admit it? Fine, if that's what it takes. Father always beat us both.*"

Rose passed on Luc's answer.

Aaron rubbed the back of his neck, considering. He only would have admitted that to prove a point. Rose didn't say a word. Aaron was working through it all on his own. The less she tried to convince him, the better.

"Fine. I'll do it. But I want to talk to Luc again when I return, before we do anything that can't be undone."

     JILLIAN WITT

Rose beamed. "That sounds fair." She also didn't quite understand the why of it yet. But if Luc felt he needed backup, she wanted to ensure he had the flexibility to shift his plans. If he believed Aterra was still scheming, even in their imprisonment, she didn't want Luc stuck with whatever Aterra sprung on him.

"So, do you want to send me to your father?" Arie said, reinserting himself into the conversation. *"I should go wherever is farther away. Since I can fly faster than you can move."*

Aaron nodded. "Yes." Aaron pulled a map from his bag and pointed to an area with few settlements farther south than Loch. "He said he was working in this area. Find the largest farms or farming communities, and he'll be there. Usually in the center of everything."

Arie nodded. *"Try to keep yourself out of trouble, Rose."*

"I wrote my father a note you can give him." He sifted through his pack to find a rolled-up piece of paper and handed it to Arie.

Arie clutched the piece of paper in his claw, and then he was off, wings flapping, taking him away from Compass Lake.

"Thanks for doing this," Rose said as Aaron mounted his horse. "I know you don't desire to be away from your family."

Aaron nodded in acknowledgment. "You're all doing so much. It's the least I can do to help." He coughed into his hand as if deciding whether to say his next thought. "I know you don't need me to say it, but I believe you."

"I don't need it," Rose said with a smile, "but it doesn't hurt to hear."

"Welcome to the family, Rose. We can celebrate more formally when you get Luc back."

CHAPTER TWENTY-SEVEN

Rose took a needed moment to herself as she returned to Norden grounds. She agonized over their next steps. Was she just supposed to wait for Arie and Aaron? Or try again? The invisibility Aurora's dagger offered had given them free rein, but so long as Luc and Aterra remained in cells next to each other, Rose didn't see another attempt going differently—not that she would stop trying if that were her only option.

Rose felt untethered. Before becoming a Compass Point, Rose found her center in forging. Her skills had come so far, especially on their recent trek around the continent. She'd evaluated not one but three Compass Points. Each one's magic was complex and wholly unique. As she walked Norden property, her fingers twitched for her forging hammer.

The Norden forge was hers. She hadn't been there since she'd returned, avoiding it like she had avoided the cottage. It, too, was a place so filled with memories of her family. Confronting those memories seemed like a small matter in the face of...everything else. But if Rose had learned one thing from evaluating the Compass Point's magic, it was that small things carried heavy weight. Ignoring them, especially thorny emotional areas, might be more convenient, but it could ultimately impact her magic.

Juliette had been a prime example of that on their trip. Luc proved this point many times during his childhood.

Rose would take the time she'd been granted to at least face the memories.

"I'll confront them with you if you want me to." Luc's voice slid into her mind. She hadn't realized she'd reached out to him, but she wasn't surprised. Her thoughts were scattered.

She appreciated the company. Not just anyone could be with her for this, she wanted it to be him. Sharing memories of her past with him was the only way to move forward.

The forge was just how she remembered it. The building that housed it was far enough away from the cottage that it didn't burn down with the fire that took her family. Tools hung neatly on the wall by the prominent forge, just like how Mom had always organized them. Finished weapons were on the opposite wall. A thin layer of dust covered the work tables. Rose suspected no one used the forge regularly. Mom had been training her to take over. With both of them out of the picture, it would have taken the Norden Point time to find a new weapons-master with the appropriate talents. Rose was sure it hadn't been high on Aterra's priority list.

She pulled a blade off the in-progress shelf. It was better than starting from scratch, but not by much. The blade was dull, but at least the shape was there. She lit the fire and waited for it to heat the old-fashioned way—without magical intervention. Her gaze roamed the room as the heat built. Part of her just needed to be here. To remember being here with Mom.

"Tell me about her," Luc said.

Rose didn't have his power to share memories, but she described some of her favorite moments here, the corner of her lip twitching as she told him about the first time she admitted she had stronger water magic than Aiden. The look on her mother's face was priceless. First—the complete acknowledgment that she was correct. Then, the quiet conversation about why she might not want to say that directly in front of Aiden's parents. Now that

Rose thought about the scene, she could see the smile on Mom's face. She was always proud when Rose owned her talents.

"Mom was a talented weapons master, and she knew it," Rose said.

"Sounds like someone else I know," he replied.

Everything Rose knew, she learned from her mom. She could only imagine what else she could have learned if they'd had more time. As Luc's words teased her, she wondered what her mom would have thought of him.

She was sure her family would've accepted Luc, just as they'd accepted Aiden. They never treated Aiden differently because of who his father was. In fact, they treated him like another member of the family. She coughed as she fought back tears, thinking again of the sticky feelings surrounding Aiden. Like she'd told herself under Mount Bury—she didn't think they ever would have become friends again, but she hadn't wished him dead.

No, her family wouldn't have wanted her to bear the burden of his death. Even if Luc had done it for her, she would have carried a weight all the same. Rose smiled to herself. She was confident Dad would have liked Luc; every protective instinct that her dad suppressed, Luc's magic owned—with flair.

My magic does have flair, doesn't it?" he said as she sent him her stream of thoughts.

Grandpa would have taken some time to warm up to the Suden Point. He would have thought his motives suspicious—as Rose had herself. Eventually, Luc would have worn him down.

"Just like I wore you down," he said.

She smiled at the thought. A smile at a memory or idea of her family was an accomplishment on its own. But Rose realized she was just getting started.

The fire finally heated, and Rose took her position before the Norden forge. She didn't wait long for the metal to heat. This was more about the repetition of the familiar motions for her. She wasn't truly looking to make a weapon.

Scenes from her childhood ran through her mind with each

swing of the hammer. She shared them all with Luc, describing in detail what she remembered. Her thoughts were in opposition to the fears she faced on the Osten house stairs. In every scene—every memory—she was surrounded by family. Even when she was with Aiden—her family was never far. Mom always watched from the workshop window. Or Grandpa tended the garden while they played on the property. Rose's childhood was everything she could have wanted.

She was just forced to grow up too fast at the end.

Luc's power wasn't present the same way it was in the heart of her magic, but she felt it clench in her chest, trying to wrap itself around her as she shared her thoughts and memories.

Rose swung the hammer. She would always wish for more time with her family. But she accepted that Aterra's attack put her on the path to make her the fae she was today—a fae she was proud to be. Rose was honored to lead the Norden people. She had big plans for them and the other courts as soon as she got them out of their current mess. There was no doubt in her mind that they would find their way past the mist plague. The Compass Points would bring balance back to the continent.

"You'll be the best leader this continent has ever seen."

She wondered at that. Luc's people respected him, but as she'd seen during their time in Loch, they still feared him. He was a leader who would do anything for his people, but he couldn't force them to move past what they thought they knew. While she wasn't sure she agreed with Luc's plan—the errand he sent his brother on—she supported him nevertheless.

A few more swings had Rose wiping her brow with the back of her hand. This was perfect. She felt a connection to her family. A connection to the life they had given her and the life she wanted to give to those on the continent under her care. Most of all, she felt an impossibly deeper connection to Luc, sharing this space with him. He'd never replace her family, but a spot in her heart was his all the same.

Her swings grew in intensity as she accepted the thoughts.

This property was hers. She would fear no corner of it. Thoughts of the family she'd lost wouldn't keep her from enjoying the places she loved being with them.

Her arm came to a rest at her side. The hammer was heavy in her hand. It felt right. Her gaze roamed the forge. She wouldn't let it remain unused for so long again.

WALTER GREETED her when she returned to the house. "I wondered if we could speak for a moment," he said formally.

Something was on his mind yesterday that he hadn't quite been comfortable enough to share. Rose hoped he was ready now. "Of course. Will you join me for dinner?" She gestured toward the dining room.

His hesitation was all Rose needed to reframe the offer. "Or we could grab something from the kitchen and sit in the library?"

"That would be preferable," he said. The formal dining room was imposing even to Rose.

Annabeth was happy to oblige, sending them off with slices of roast meat and fresh vegetables. The table in the library was filled with books, but Carter had neatly stacked them at least. Rose shifted a few aside, clearing space for her and Walter. His fingers skimmed the chair as if considering whether to sit. Rose did, hoping it would comfort him.

"I didn't mean to overhear, but the elders...well, *ex*-elders were gossiping about you in the village." He coughed then looked up at her, finally making eye contact. "Is it true you have both wind and water magic?"

Rose smiled softly. She wasn't surprised the elders had shared the information, nor did she care. "It is." She waited for him to continue.

"And you were—you are—Norden Point with both elements?" He didn't sound like he doubted her. Instead, his voice was filled with what she could only place as hope.

"I am," she said. "Not even the elders could deny me—though they would have liked to."

Walter smiled at that. "It was right that you dismissed them, especially after what they let Aiden do. They needed to be held accountable for their actions."

"Thank you," Rose said, appreciating his acknowledgment.

"I have a daughter," he said.

Rose nodded at this. She hadn't seen the female, but it wasn't uncommon for fae to have children. Walter had the ageless perfection of the fae, but she knew he'd been in this position for many years. He was likely the same age as her parents would have been.

"Her mother is Vesten." Worry lines creased Walter's face, and now she knew why. The same weight had marked her mother's features, though Rose had been too young to realize it then.

"I'm sure you never thought you'd say those words to a Compass Point," Rose said, acknowledging what they both were thinking.

He chuckled, but his mood started to lighten. "I did not imagine it, no."

Rose waited to catch his eye again, ensuring she had his full attention for what she said next. "She has nothing to fear—from myself or any of the Compass Points," Rose said firmly. "Juliette, Carter, and Luc all know about my magic. They accept me for it and agree the practices of our predecessors were more than detrimental."

Walter let out a shaky breath.

Rose couldn't imagine how Walter lived in the center of fae society. Rose's wind magic seemed to come from somewhere in past generations. Her mother and father had both been Norden. But Walter... His current partner, or at least the mother of his child, was of another court. How often did they see each other or gather as a family unit? "You don't need to fear being seen together. I don't know your situation, nor do I need to, but I assure you, Luc and I will pave the way for couples of different courts."

"*You should tell him.*" Luc's voice was in her head. She must have sent him the last part of the conversation without realizing it.

She agreed. "In fact, Luc and I..." She cleared her throat. "We're bound."

Walter's thick brows raised, his eyes widening in shock. "But—"

"Believe me, I'm aware of the impossibility." She smiled. "It doesn't change what we are. I share it with you so you know our support isn't going anywhere. We'll demand the change at Compass Lake and on the continent."

Walter put his head in his hands like this was all too much for him—it probably was. Rose still heard the words he spoke though. "I knew you would be good for this place. I knew it the moment you stepped onto Norden soil."

"I'm glad to hear it," she said, swallowing thickly around her own emotion. "I look forward to working with you and the Norden to make this a court that represents us all."

He nodded, finally sitting down to start his meal.

"I'd love to meet your daughter if you ever want to bring her by the house," Rose said.

"She'd love that. She's been obsessed with you since she over-heard the elders in the market." He chewed thoughtfully. "Do you think we can bring more of the Norden by to meet you?" he asked. "Most don't agree with Meg and Catherine, but that hasn't stopped them from sharing their thoughts...on you." He took a sip of his water. "It could benefit the Norden to hear things from you more directly."

"That's a great idea. I'm ashamed I didn't think of it myself," she said.

"I won't pry, but it does seem you've been a bit busy since you returned. The rumors of the Luc Suden Point missing make your behavior a little clearer. I'm sure he works with you, but if he's not here, that must mean you're trying to get to your bound partner—wherever he is."

Rose gave him a soft smile. She wouldn't undercut what

Aaron had told the Suden court. "We are all doing everything we can to right the wrongs on the continent."

That was enough for Walter. He said he'd gather some of the Norden tomorrow, and they spoke of his family and life at Compass Lake as they shared a meal. Layers of stress peeled off Walter with every word. And their conversation gave Rose no small amount of hope—she could bring change to the courts simply by being herself.

CHAPTER TWENTY-EIGHT

Rose had exhausted herself in the forge yesterday. Though their mind connection became more accessible with each conversation, she didn't search for Luc at her lake of power again. She wouldn't let him put himself in more danger than he was already in.

It was only day two of waiting, and Rose was restless. This would be even more challenging than she thought. She took a walk, this time heading east toward Osten house.

Once again, she was at the door, probably too early for a Compass Points meeting. To her annoyance, it was Lela who greeted her. The Osten Point's protege hadn't joined them since her last trip through Osten house. Rose assumed it was because she was left with the more mundane tasks of ensuring the court continued running as required.

"It's too early to see the Osten Point," was Lela's gruff response.

"Lela." Rose tried to put on a smile. "We've been through this already. She said I had an open invitation. We were both there. We both heard it."

Lela's features pinched like she was trying to determine if she had to follow this line of reasoning. And possibly how much trouble she'd be in if she didn't.

"Can we discuss what you find so off-putting about me?" Rose asked. Not for the first time, she wondered what it would be like to have someone so ready to bully others on her behalf. Lela's dedication to Juliette was unparalleled—that much was clear.

"It's my job to protect the Osten Point," Lela said as if it were the most obvious thing in the world.

"Isn't it actually the Osten Point's job to protect you? You're the future of the court," Rose pointed out.

Lela tilted her head like she couldn't determine if Rose was mocking her. "I don't trust your intentions either way." That much was unsurprising, but she wasn't sure how to fix it. Lela had been in the room when she and Juliette had discussed their goals.

"I intend to return those impacted by the mist plague and bring balance to the continent. I also plan to get my bound partner back from his stupid decision to throw himself into another realm." Rose was building up steam now. "I doubt you'd fault me for that." She smiled sweetly. "I want to ensure the Compass Points will never be fractured like they were before me. And that"—Rose paused for emphasis—"is exactly why you and I need to work out whatever this is. Juliette won't be Osten Point forever. And I won't have all my work to unify the Compass Points dissolve because you don't trust my intentions. Ask me whatever you need to, challenge whatever decisions of mine don't make sense. But don't stew on an opinion you haven't tried to test."

Lela's spine straightened as she held the door between herself and Rose. It looked like Rose's words had landed. Her features didn't entirely give away which direction she was leaning. Rose was ready for an onslaught of questions or challenges. Maybe Lela had them stored up. Or would she snap back in anger at Rose's confrontation?

"She's right, Lela," Juliette's smooth voice carried down the hall. Rose tilted her head around the door to see the Osten Point gliding toward them. "You're certainly entitled to be wary of the other Compass Points—I'd be hypocritical to say you shouldn't be—but you should challenge Rose directly with your questions. Test how honest she'll be with you. It will surprise you." Juliette's lip curled into a smirk.

Lela opened the door wider, allowing Rose to enter as Juliette approached. Rose nodded to Juliette and Lela as she stepped inside.

"What brings you here so early again?" Juliette asked as she led Rose to the plush sitting room she was growing familiar with.

"I don't know what to do to be useful while we wait for Aaron and Arie to return, so I wondered if we could talk about Zrak." Rose shrugged as she took a seat on the green velvet chair.

Juliette requested food from someone in the hallway before she took a seat herself.

"Lela, do you want to join us?" Juliette called toward the doorway where her protege stood guard. "Maybe you can ask some of your questions while Rose asks hers."

Lela's eyes widened, surprised to be asked to join the leaders, but she didn't hesitate. "Yes, of course," she said as she sat beside Juliette on the couch.

"What did you want to know about Zrak?" Lela asked cautiously, testing her ability to question the Norden Point.

"I guess I want to know if Juliette trusts him," Rose said. "It's clear the gods want to. Luc even seemed inclined to believe Zrak's intentions support the greater good of the continent." Rose sighed. "I wanted the opinion of the one who has dealt with him most consistently over the past few hundred years."

Juliette set her cup on the low table between them. She sat back in her chair and crossed her legs as she worked through Rose's question. "Whether I trust Zrak is a complicated question." She sighed as she glanced at Lela. "Zrak has put our people in a terrible position. No matter his intention or the necessity, that was the result. It's not something I take lightly, and it's not something I've ever been able to get him to acknowledge fully."

"How often do you talk to him?" Rose asked.

"Not very. We've had a few conversations over the hundred years I've been doing this ritual." She paused. "That's the other thing. He's not open about...anything. He still believes he's a god and I'm the Osten Point, and this distance between us can't be crossed. But if anyone understands the bind he's in, shouldn't it be me?"

"He could be embarrassed that you must help him at all," Lela said quietly.

"It is a valid idea. And definitely a reason that an ageless god would act so childish, even if it is literally all his doing." Juliette ran her fingers through her hair. "I'm angry at him all the time for this. I have been since I found out what the Osten Point had to do to preserve the court's magic." She looked at Lela again. "But I don't want to pass that anger on to you. If I have anger, my predecessor was filled with rage. She'd had to see more directly what the Lost God's choices had done and how the first Osten Point had been weakened."

"It's understandable to be angry about what his choices cost you," Rose said.

"Yes, but I don't want it to be the focus of the Osten court. It has been for so long—but we are more than the weakness he created." Juliette nodded at Lela. "We can do better than the legacy he left us with." Juliette coughed. "But that wasn't your question, was it? Do I trust him?" She shrugged her shoulders. "I don't think he meant the harm that he caused. I'm not even sure he realized the harm he caused at first."

"Isn't that worse?" Rose asked.

Juliette smiled. "Some might think so, but this is one piece of information I did pick up from Zrak over the years. Cassandra's control over her borders is more absolute than he realized when he first went to her for help. He didn't know how much his power and his ability to provide balance to the Osten people would be impacted by existing beyond the veil. He knew his ability to affect the continent would be hindered—which was his overall plan. The full result of where he existed was a much more complete removal than he anticipated."

"He was able to find a way to send the mist plague," Rose pointed out.

"Yes, but as we learned, that has to do with the bargain he struck with Cassandra. She needed someone to shepherd spirits—his Nebulus were her best option." She sighed. "I'm sure Zrak took advantage of that task to send the mist plague and to refuel the Osten fae connection, but from what you've said, Cassandra was aware of both."

"I don't think you're reassuring me." Rose laughed without any real mirth.

"I'm not sure I mean to," Juliette said. "I told you it was complicated. He has specific plans in mind, and he doesn't see fit to share them. The only reason I don't hate him is that I'm not sure what other choice he had." She paused again, her expression thoughtful. "Even now, I don't think he has another choice. There is much more going on beyond the veil than we understand. I know you hate waiting, but our plan is sound. Without further understanding of what sins Cassandra holds against the gods, it would be unwise to confront her."

"I'm going crazy, yes," Rose said. "But I also agreed to give Aaron a chance to find Celeste's journal. I can talk to Luc, so I at least know he's okay." Rose took a deep breath and put her hands on her knees. "I'm committed to our third attempt beyond the veil to be more fruitful."

"Look at you, coming to terms with waiting." Juliette's smile didn't meet her eyes. It was clear she didn't wish this on anyone. She took another sip of her tea. "I believe that Zrak is on our side. My hesitation is that he is willing to pay any cost to meet his ends, even one he doesn't have to bear directly. *That*," she emphasized, "makes him dangerous."

NEXT ON THE list of things to occupy Rose was exercising her water magic. She had a little time before Walter was supposed to bring the Norden he'd spoken of last night to the house. Until then, she hadn't much cause to let her magic play with the waters of Compass Lake since her return. It unfurled in waves now as she hit the Norden property line.

While chasing Aterra, Rose had spent so much time with her wind. She prioritized it in her attempt to connect with Juliette. It was also the first time she'd been able to use her wind without guilt—having been taught to hide it as a child. Her thoughts strayed to Walter's daughter. She had likely grown up just like Rose. It was Rose's mission that she wouldn't need to continue that way.

The magical waters of Compass Lake called to her. All those times she couldn't swim in the Lake of the Gods, she made up for now, diving into the water as she had when she was a child. Her power spread throughout the lake, touching every shore. It put on a display to rival the one she'd done at the Solstice Ball, but she didn't watch. Rose floated in the comfort Compass Lake provided. She was too relaxed, stretching her magic, to notice a crowd had gathered on the beach.

As recognition hit, Rose got out of the water. It was the group of Norden she and Walter had discussed. She recognized many of the faces from when she'd claimed the Norden seat. Meg and Catherine stood with the group, but Rose couldn't tell if they considered themselves part of it.

"Welcome," Rose said. Walter appeared next to her, handing her a towel. She thanked him but dried herself with a flick of her magic and then addressed the group. "I'm glad to see so many Norden faces. Walter thought it would be beneficial for us to meet as a court." She spared a glance at Meg and Catherine. "And for you to have the opportunity to ask me questions directly."

"Your magic—it was a thing to behold in Compass Lake. We

haven't seen a Norden's power exercised as such in a long time," Walter said.

Rose nodded. "I admit, it felt great to do," she said, addressing the crowd again.

"Is it true you have wind magic, too?" someone asked.

Meg's face lit up like she was expecting trouble and delighting in it. Rose wanted to roll her eyes at the elder. It was no accident that she'd told Meg and Catherine about her mixed lineage. She had wanted everyone to know. The fact that they didn't understand that was another representation of how little the ex-elders understood Rose. "It is," Rose said without hesitation. "I have both wind and water magic, but as Samuel attested, I have claimed the Norden Point seat."

"How is that possible?" a woman in the front row asked.

"The courts were never meant to be as separated as we've allowed them to become," Rose said. "The gods created the courts in hope of us working together. It's not a surprise that our magics might also eventually blend. I don't want another generation of fae to believe there is anything wrong with having the magic of multiple courts or of having human ancestry."

"Why are you able to be so frivolous with your magic?" Meg asked, referring to her display on Compass Lake. Her voice was low, almost a hiss in its exasperation. The crowd was hanging on Rose's every word as she spoke of the future she strived for. Of course, Meg would want to choose a different topic of discussion. "Shouldn't you be saving the continent with the Compass Points?" she asked snidely.

Rose searched the faces of the others gathered. They didn't appear to hold as much anger as Meg's tone indicated, but they did look interested in the response.

"I see the same question in the eyes of many gathered. So, I will share my response though I caution against your tone. You are a member of the court like all others gathered here. We should show each other the respect we wish to receive."

　　JILLIAN WITT

Meg lifted her chin, her pride continuing to get the better of her.

Rose focused on the rest of the group, those who looked genuinely interested in what Rose was doing as Norden Point. "When the Compass Points left the lake together, we went to stop the mist plague. No new villages have been attacked since we returned."

"Not all the Compass Points returned," Meg said snidely, cutting Rose off.

"Now you care about the Suden Point?" Rose asked, unable to rein in the shock in her tone. Meg and Catherine had been appalled by Rose's relationship with him. The fact that they now questioned where he was—as if they cared whether he came back alive—was rich.

The pair glanced at each other. A few in the crowd laughed awkwardly. Many had witnessed Rose and Luc's relationship. It seemed not everyone was as opposed as the ex-elders would have Rose believe. "I want to assure everyone that our goal is to stop the mist plague and restore those impacted to their former state. The Compass Points still work together to secure that future. We need a resource that Aaron went to help us find—that will help us make our next move—"

Rose cut herself off as a large black bird appeared, flying over Norden house. Rose's heart felt lighter as she noted a large wrapped package in his claws.

"Need any help down there?" Arie asked as he flew straight toward Norden house and the window Rose had left open.

Rose shook her head and hoped he could see it.

"Well, get in here and read your book. It's heavy, but I stopped to talk to Aaron on the way back, and he said this is the one you want—and it's even better than he expected."

"In fact, it seems our resource has just arrived," Rose said. I must return to my work, but please spread the word. We'll start open court sessions in Norden house next week. I'd love to hear from more of you, and I'm eager to share my own ideas."

Walter spoke up again. "I'm happy to organize such an event."

"Thank you, Walter. That would be perfect."

Meg and Catherine glared, but it was clear Rose had won over the majority of the crowd. The rest, Rose knew, would take time. But she would continue to show up and prove herself to them.

CHAPTER TWENTY-NINE

Arie was already in human form in the library with Aurora when Rose entered the house. They were hunched over the table, the book laid out before them.

"This is Celeste's journal?"

"It is...but it looks like it's more than that," Aurora said.

"What do you mean?"

"These are two different writers," Aurora said, pointing to various entries in the journal. Her eyes skimmed the pages as she kept speaking. "All the other journals spoke of the governor's daughter, Celeste, but...I think there were two daughters."

"How could we have missed that?" Rose asked.

"I'm not sure it's us so much as the villagers. Even in this entry—Andie notes the villagers follow Cee—that must be Celeste."

"So, who is Andie?" Rose asked, though the pounding of her heart told her she already suspected the answer. But it couldn't be —could it?

Arie pulled out the chair on his opposite side. "Your questions aren't going to speed this up. Sit down and read with us."

*

"We can take the excess," Cee said.

Cee and Andie, each in veil cat form, faced off. The rest of the pack growled around them.

"Look at it, Celeste. Really look at it," Andie said, gesturing with her nose toward the lake. She rarely used her sister's full name, but Andie needed her to understand. This wasn't the solution to their problems. This only created another problem. *"There may have been excess at one point, but there isn't now."*

Cee glared, her teeth showing. *"Don't condescend, Cassandra. I can use your full name, too. The cats said more spirits than normal were crossing. We can take some of what's here, and it will refill shortly."* Her tail swished frenetically. *"A small shift in balance here could be recovered. Our village—our continent—needs this."*

Andie wasn't sure she agreed. An answer was rooted somewhere in the ground beneath her feet. Andie inherently knew her sister was wrong. A small shift in balance was all it would take to tip the scales, to leave this land beyond the veil in the same ruin as the continent.

It was telling that Cee stared only at Andie. She no longer looked to the veil cats for approval. Somehow, Cee understood the veil cats would listen to Andie's decision.

"Andie." Cee returned to the pet name she used for her sister.

The weight of her name on her sister's lips. The desperation in her gaze when Andie met it. This was more than she could bear. The knot in her throat grew heavy like the weight of this decision.

She'd let someone down either way.

Even if Andie believed it wouldn't ruin the land beyond the veil, using magic from the lake—even the excess—would require sacrificing spirits. This still didn't sit well with Andie. She couldn't imagine spirits going without a choice. But did the humans on the continent have any choice in what was happening to them? They were victims of whatever the gods had or hadn't done. They didn't deserve the level of devastation they received.

They deserved to live.

Before Andie could see where the thought took her, Cee was moving.

"They need it," Cee said as she flung herself into the lake.

A chorus of growls echoed. Celeste, still in veil cat form, joined the spirits. Andie's stomach plummeted. She heard herself growling along with the pack. Celeste must have cut her paw while walking because Andie felt the blood magic spring to life within the Lake of Spirits.

"What are you doing, Cee?" Andie screamed through the connection in their minds.

"I'm going to feed our people! What do you think?"

"You're doing to these people the same thing the gods did to us!"

Andie knew it was too late, but she tried reasoning with her sister anyway. The water in the lake of the spirits swirled and rose. It seemed to know it was readying to move. Andie had no idea how this worked, but her moments of indecision slipped through her fingers like beads of sand.

She didn't stop her sister.

Whether a conscious decision or not, Andie allowed Cee to do this—to take this magic. She'd analyze the hesitation endlessly for the rest of her time beyond the veil.

The lake water rose higher, spilling over the shore, the spirits with it. Cee's intention must've been clear because the hole between worlds opened above the lake's surface. The water tunneled through it in the blink of an eye.

Andie was running before she realized what she was doing. She leaped through the hole and followed the spiraling tunnel of water and spirits as it traveled back to the continent. Andie wasn't sure Cee could navigate the space on her own. Something in the lake's magic must have powered her as the swirling water rolled through the void and dropped onto the continent.

The water and spirits flowed through the darkness between

realms, the path between them remaining open. Cee landed in her human form. Andie could see a large gash on her hand, still fresh with blood. Her sister pressed on it as she called forth more magic. They landed in the woods outside the village. The water continued to swirl, a storm of its own, and Celeste was its center. Her goal was simple—Andie could feel her intention—save the village. She no longer just wanted magic to fuel food growth. Now that she knew the extent of the corruption on the continent, she wanted a way to save her people from it.

Andie's paws barely hit the ground when a net was thrown over her. A growl tore through her as she thrashed against the trapping. She recognized Garth and a few villagers who helped Cee regularly, trying to hold it down. They shouldn't be here. How much had Cee told them before they followed the second spirit? Andie snarled again, but they all froze in place as the magic shifted—with Cee's growing intention, there was a larger need for power.

Something beyond the veil pulled at Andie. It felt like her spirit was ripped from her body.

This had been her fear—her hesitation—before Cee took the choice from her. The way Celeste pulled now, it was more than excess. Every spirit at rest in the lake cried out to Andie as whatever Celeste had planned emptied the lake.

The lake shifted to a stream as it came through the space between worlds and swirled around the village borders. A soft glow wrapped around the circling water, building higher and higher. Screams followed the flow. Andie could no longer tell if they were from the spirits or the villagers. No one knew what was happening. It was unlikely Cee knew what she was doing. Andie only knew that the land beyond the veil was crying out to her, the scream more devastating than anything she'd ever heard from the continent. The water crested, and the earth shook as the spirits spiraled toward the crop fields. The plants grew before her eyes, and magic from the spirits continued to flow. Andie didn't think it would ever end. She was going to be sick.

The magic appeared able to cycle itself. It wasn't a single crop growth being produced but an unending cycle of growth and renewal. This was more than feeding the village. It was a wall of protection from whatever the gods subjected them to.

The water rushed around the village border, protecting it. It rose like a dome to surround the borders. Cee separated the village from the continent. The wind swirled through the water as an icy blast, almost freezing. Finally, fire followed the wind and water, creating a sizzling barrier of steam rising around the city.

Andie had no doubt this would work.

The elements continued to swirl and rise. The magic sustaining the interaction started to wane. The combination of elements covered the village. Andie knew: It would keep the inhabitants safe.

Andie thrashed beneath the net, still captured by Garth and the others. She didn't think too hard about it as it tore beneath her claws. Freeing herself to save her realm was as natural as her next breath. She had only seconds to get back—to do what needed to be done. The weight of her realm's pending collapse was heavy on her shoulders. She landed in the realm beyond the veil in human form, a jagged rock in her hand as she cut long and deep on her arm, offering everything she had to the realm.

She hadn't stopped her sister.

Celeste had taken everything.

The lake bed was nearly empty, so few spirits remained. It was Andie's fault this was happening. It was her fault the realm was at risk. Her intention was clear. She'd do anything—give anything—to fix it.

CASSANDRA, Lady of the Veil, landed in a crouch outside of the human village of Marcil.

The governor and some villagers waited closer to the new, magically erected wall.

There was no sign of Celeste.

Cassandra hadn't felt her sister's presence beyond the veil—but it had only been a few days since the Lake of Spirits had been stolen. Celeste may never recover from the power she wielded. Cassandra wasn't sure she felt anything one way or the other.

"Andie?" The governor's use of her pet name was all she needed to hear.

"Eric," she replied.

His head tilted as if surprised by the greeting.

"I'm no longer who I was. Celeste's actions have consequences you can't even begin to understand. I should take back everything that was stolen and leave this village to the fate the gods have in store for the continent."

Her father's eyes widened in surprise. "We hoped you were returning to us."

"Hope is not a strategy," Cassandra replied, pulling the sword from its sheath at her hip. "When I last arrived on the continent, these villagers"—her gaze lingered on Garth over her father's shoulder, and she gestured with her weapon—"tried to trap me. I know Celeste told you more about the spirits and veil cats than she let on." Cassandra's sigh was deep. It was unclear if Celeste had known the implications of her actions. Cassandra wasn't sure what to believe. It was another knot in her chest where all her feelings about her sister should be.

The reasons didn't matter.

The damage had been done.

"Veil cats will no longer travel between realms. I keep telling myself this isn't your fault. You are reacting to the situation the gods put you in, but every time I think about the devastation you have wrought...I have a hard time remembering that."

"Cassandra," her father tried.

"Please don't." Cassandra shook her head. "You've made your choices, and I've made mine. Celeste knew what her actions would cost me. She took them anyway." Cassandra lifted her chin. "Now, we must each play the parts we chose."

"And what part is that?" her father asked.

"You may call me the Lady of the Veil. I rule the next phase of human existence, and I will not take kindly to any interruption of a spirit's journey to my realm."

Her father swallowed.

"Remember,"—she pointed again with her sword—"each of you will end up in my realm someday. Any actions you take against helpless spirits will be paid back tenfold."

This was why she was here. These villagers were the only ones who knew about the magic of the spirits. She needed to ensure the information didn't spread. Spirits needed to remain protected on their journey. The wide-eyed villagers, her father included, seemed to understand her threat. All would be residents of the veil at some point.

It was inescapable.

"I see we understand each other." Cassandra didn't wait for the villagers to finish nodding. As their heads dipped in understanding, the Lady of the Veil returned to her realm.

CHAPTER THIRTY

"That makes a lot of sense, actually." Luc's voice broke through the stillness in Rose's head after reading the journal entry that used Andie's full name.

Her suspicions had been confirmed. The how was more devastating than she could have imagined.

"*Which part?*" she asked. The entire thing made perfect sense. It wrapped all the pieces they had together in a nice, neat bow. Rose didn't have siblings, she couldn't even begin to imagine Cassandra's heartbreak. She'd suspected Celeste had done something terrible, but this surpassed her expectations. Celeste and Andie's—Cassandra's—journal was part research, part confession.

Cassandra had been human once.

Her entries stopped after waking up beyond the veil with a host of veil cats surrounding her and calling her one of their own. What followed was wholly different. A confession of a woman responsible for the lives of many and deciding their care was worth the existence of others—was worth the price of her sister's human life. It took Rose longer than she cared to accept who Andie was—what Andie would become based on Celeste's actions.

Taking it all? Desperation could drive one to reckless actions. She knew that. But this seemed particularly careless.

The gods' carelessness had driven Cassandra's twin sister to a level of desperation Rose couldn't comprehend. To steal her sister's decision from her—to force her to a life beyond the veil. No wonder Cassandra didn't take kindly to visitors.

"The Suden only have these journals because they were encased within a protected area on the continent, even after the Flood. It took a lot of earth magic to...excavate them," he replied.

The fortress Celeste built around her village with the magic from the spirits she stole would have been the only thing protecting the text. No wonder so few remain. How could Arie and Aurora not have known this had happened? She shook her head, realizing this was further proof of their negligence.

Her gaze raised to meet Arie's. Seated next to her, he looked a little sad, but not like he wanted her pity. Next to him, Aurora's shoulders fell as she finished the last passage.

Arie coughed. "Well," he started, "I guess we know why Cassandra dislikes us so much."

Rose searched his features. Regret and remorse were plain to see, but something like fear etched the lines of his face. Her mind called forth their conversation over breakfast. She didn't know all he'd done—and he wasn't sure he wanted her to. This was part of that history, she guessed.

He feared her reaction.

She meant what she'd said. He was different now. The way he carefully considered her reaction showed it. A god so separated from the continent, incapable of noticing his people in need, or this level of blood magic enacted—he was nowhere in the god before her.

"That's generous phrasing, Arie." Rose smirked, reassuring him in the only way she knew how. The situation wasn't funny. Rose couldn't imagine the weight that led to Celeste's actions. She seemed to understand what her decisions would cost but was more than willing to let her sister pay the price.

Rose nodded at Arie in reassurance as she teased him. He smiled softly in return.

The god had plenty of faults, but he wasn't the same as the callous god not even described on the page because he was so remote. He hadn't let Rose be alone on this continent. He'd supported her when she had no one else. She respected that he was trying to do better.

Cassandra though... This didn't help their dealings with Cassandra, but at least it made them make more sense.

"What would emptying that lake of spirits have done to the realm beyond the veil?" Rose asked, already fearing the answer.

Arie and Aurora's gazes met in silent conference. It was one of shared guilt. "It would not have been good," Arie said.

Aurora flipped through more pages in the journal. "We obviously don't have Cassandra's perspective after the act. It appears she visited her father once after the lake was emptied, but wasn't in a sharing mood." Aurora closed the book for now.

Rose nodded. She knew blood magic could be powerful, but what Celeste described was more than power. It was an explosion of hope and desperation. Her words indicated it combined all four of the god's elements to protect a single village. Rose hadn't heard of anything like it. Though, looking at the god's faces in this room, the shock still plain in their features as they read, it was clear it was a well-kept secret from all.

"*We didn't intend to keep it a secret,*" Luc said. "*I don't think I've read all of this—I'm not sure we knew that blood magic and spirits saved the village.*"

Rose believed him. Without a connection to the realm beyond the veil, the information in the journals added little value other than the earth magic farming techniques the Suden fae had pulled from the pages. "*I know. I also don't know what anyone would have done with the information up to this point.*"

"Cassandra had to have given herself to the land to save it. It must have been another twist on a blood magic offering like her sister describes, with the land soaking up Cassandra's blood when they visited together." Neither sister had been in a particularly good situation, but reading Celeste's account, she knew the consequences of her decisions—she made them anyway.

"I agree with that," Arie started, pulling Rose's focus. "I assume, on some level, she would have had to offer her entire human life. I'm not sure what Cassandra is, but I assure you, she's no longer human."

"Would that have been enough to save the realm?"

Arie shrugged. "I don't know. I think the fact that it still exists proves she figured it out. Whatever price she had to pay, she paid it."

"At least the reasons she hates you are becoming clear," Rose said wryly.

"This does bring back the question of why she let Zrak stay," Luc added. He was right. It wasn't just dislike Rose could sense between Cassandra and the Osten god.

"He promised her someone would come. Someone who could help."

"Whatever she did could still be some kind of temporary solution. She could be holding her realm together through sheer force of will; she seems capable. The important part is that Zrak promised her some kind of relief. She is waiting for…something."

"Zrak seems to do that a lot." Rose let the words sit in her mind. How could he always gain others' confidence in his plans and ideas? He must have built enough credibility with Arie and Aurora over the years that, eventually, he'd been correct enough times for them to believe him. But how was he always right? So many things about the Osten god didn't add up. He might be on their side, but his secrets seemed more abundant than gusts of wind across Compass Lake in the autumn.

"The realm doesn't seem ruined," Rose stated the obvious as she stood. It reminded her of Zrak's words from Luc's memory.

"You're so well adept at preventing ruin."

Her fingers opened and closed into fists at her side, itching to be interlocked with Luc's as she thought. His voice in her head was a balm. It soothed her nerves to have him there—but his physical presence was a grounding force—one she desperately missed. If Cassandra's fix was only temporary, had she held it in place for over five hundred years on her own?

"I know," Aurora said, her forehead scrunching with thought. "I knew she was powerful, but this is something else." Rose watched as Arie's hand rested gently on Aurora's lower back as she thought.

"It makes sense, at least, why she closed her borders," Arie said. "If Celeste's villagers tried to capture a veil cat, likely to help with the collection of spirits for magical energy...that was another level of betrayal for Cassandra."

"Especially given that Cassandra was the veil cat in that case." Rose didn't discount the connection between Cassandra and her cats. "Do you think they helped her?"

If Cassandra tying herself to the land wasn't enough, maybe the veil cats had also done so. Celeste's journal didn't focus much on the cats other than to say they had already considered Cassandra their leader before Celeste emptied the lake.

Rose was afraid she knew part of the answer. It was the only logical one, given everything they knew about balance in a realm and what it required. Zrak wanted to leave, but he was filling the role of shepherding spirits beyond the veil now. A veil cat, or veil cat shifter, was most adept at this role. The only question was, why not let her host of veil cats take over again? And if, as Rose suspected, she waited for a veil cat shifter from the continent, what did Cassandra need from the shifter, and how long could she afford to hold out for one?

"Do you know what you're doing?" Rose tried again as she and Carter entered the Burning Garden on Vesten Property. She may be frustrated, but she took the time to appreciate the orange, red, and yellow blooms. After Carter had read the new journal entries, his mind was made up. Like Rose, he believed Cassandra needed a veil cat shifter from the continent.

Carter gave her the glare her comment deserved and closed the metal garden gate behind them.

It was a fair reaction. Rose's interpretation was the same as his, but she didn't agree with him walking up to Cassandra to tell her what he was and offering his services in exchange for Luc and Zrak. Rose shook her head as she followed him to the willow tree.

They hadn't been able to change his mind. He was set on traveling beyond the veil and walking right up to Cassandra.

"What if she takes the whole fight-first approach again?"

"We agreed. If that happens, I'll shift. It should catch her attention." Carter ran his hand through his shaggy brown hair. "I felt the onslaught of magic last time as much—maybe more— than you did. I know what she's capable of, but I'm sure of what she needs." He sighed heavily. "You are, too. We've been over this. I need you to trust me."

Rose sighed. "I do, Carter. I hope you know that. I just don't want you to feel an undue burden here. We might agree she needs a veil cat shifter for something, but that doesn't mean it has to be you. It doesn't mean you revealing yourself is the way to find out what she needs one for is for either."

Carter's answering sigh was heavier than Rose's. He was right. They had been through this before—at length in the Norden library. After their initial discussion, Arie flew to Osten and Vesten houses to retrieve the Compass Points. Everyone agreed with Rose's conclusion. Zrak was waiting for a veil cat shifter to take his place, shepherding spirits beyond the veil. Rose suspected Cassandra needed the shifter for more than just Zrak's replacement though.

"It's my turn to shoulder something for the continent. Juliette has been sustaining her people for hundreds of years. You unmasked an imposter within the Compass Points and tracked down a rogue god. I haven't had anything to give yet. This is my thing. I get to decide how it unfolds."

Rose understood that sentiment. It was the same way she felt when they were trying to learn how their magic worked together. Evaluation of power and weapons-making were her things. She'd felt the weight of the continent on her shoulder as she'd tried to find a way for them all to work together.

"Just know you don't have to do it alone," Rose said. It was the one piece of advice she could offer.

They may still not know what Cassandra needed a veil cat shifter for—but they were confident she needed one. Rose didn't understand Cassandra's magic nearly as well as Carter did, but even she could tell the veil cats had a unique connection to the Lady of the Veil. It made even more sense knowing Cassandra could also shift into one of them. But Rose feared what Cassandra needed of him.

None of them were asking Carter to be their bargaining chip. He had kept his shifter form a secret for his entire life. They wouldn't force him to share now, especially since none of them knew what the Lady of the Veil would ask of him. As he stomped through the garden, his determination clear in the direction of his path towards the willow tree, Rose knew she wouldn't change his mind.

Rose feared the Lady of the Veil might already know Carter's secret. She had some experience with the way another's magic called to her. In her case, Luc's magic called to hers as much as her magic called to his. Cassandra may be more aware of Carter's unique magic than they were willing to admit.

Carter, of course, argued it didn't matter. He said if anything, it meant she wouldn't try to attack them upon their arrival. Rose let out a sigh as she walked.

"You can't stop him." Luc's words through their connection were unhelpful but true.

"Oh, I know that," she mentally whined. She couldn't stop him—nor would she if she could, as Luc had reminded her of his actions under Mount Bury. It was his choice. No matter how much she wished she could bear the burden, she had already

proved they were stronger together. That meant she had to let each of them shoulder their share of the weight they carried.

No, Rose wouldn't stop him. She just wished they had more information. Based on the events detailed in the sisters' journals, the only one with the information they sought was The Lady of the Veil herself.

"You know this is the right move." Yes, she knew that, but that didn't mean she had to be happy about it. Luc's words weren't as reassuring as he thought they were.

"I heard that."

Rose could almost hear the smirk in his tone. It gave her a brief moment of comfort before jumping into the unknown—again.

"Are you there, Rose?" Carter's voice broke through her thoughts and silent conversation with Luc. Carter's head was cocked. It must not be the first time he'd tried to get her attention.

"Sorry, what did you say?"

"I was just asking if you're ready. We're here." He gestured to the tree as he parted the curtain of willow branches, and they walked under its canopy.

The tree looked normal now. The last time they came, a crack appeared in the trunk at the veil cat's growl. Rose hadn't given it a second thought as to whether the tunnel that opened had remained so. Apparently, it had closed.

"I'm ready if you're ready," Rose said.

Carter glared at her again and then shifted into his veil cat form. He raised his paw to let her poke him with Aurora's blade—covering the tip with drops of his blood. His growl shook the land. She wrapped her fingers into the scruff of his neck, a now familiar practice, as the tree cracked and the tunnel opened.

As if in retaliation for her last comment, he didn't give her a moment to adjust her grip before he was off and running at the tree. They plunged together into darkness, sending Rose and Carter beyond the veil again.

CHAPTER THIRTY-ONE

The space between realms was just as dark as she remembered. Given Luc's memory, she looked from side to side as Carter dragged her through. There were no paths, no markers that she could discern. He knew how to lead them all the same.

As they moved through the darkness, Rose tried to feel for anything she could anchor to—magically or otherwise. Luc had seemed so lost in his memory. There had been no light, no path, no way to even know which direction was forward. Her hand gripped tightly to Carter's scruff, and he pulled her along. Rose was confident she'd have no means of crossing without him.

The space's emptiness was all-consuming. She let her magic roam as they moved, evaluating the power of this in-between space.

Nothing.

There was nothing here to evaluate.

Rose pricked her own finger with Aurora's blade as they traveled. The plan was to talk to Cassandra, but they might as well start with the upper hand. She felt the magic of the realm shift as they crossed beyond the veil. Her muscles involuntarily tightened, readying to splash into the icy river.

Preparation didn't help as her body hit the water. Pins and needles struck her exposed limbs as the frigid water swallowed her. It was somehow colder than she remembered. Not that it would stop the Norden Point from swimming to the shore on the other side.

She flopped on the bank next to the veil cat that was Carter. The sensation of the frigid water, mixed with the magic of Aurora's dagger, was not something she would get used to. The water magic swept out in broad circles around them, the continuous, raindrop-like plops distorting their location. She took a deep breath and rolled over to check in with him. His feline form's yellow-green eyes blinked steadily back at her, waiting for her to pull herself together.

"Alright...let's go," she said.

"*Aren't you the leader of the fae court known to wield water?*" Luc's sass was warmth flooding through her veins.

"*The cold is distracting,*" she replied as she stood and used said magic to wring the water from her clothes. "*I actually don't think I can stop myself from hitting the river when we land. It's like a required entry point into the realm.*"

"*But you could...keep the water off you as you swim across?*" He chuckled as the words sank below her skin. She could. But she'd like to see him think quickly when the bone-chilling water wrapped around him. She let the sentiment dance back to him, silencing a retort. Then, she focused on the Vesten Point and their next steps.

"So, find her in the castle and make ourselves known?" Rose asked as they walked. The river dumped them in the same location as last time. The familiar city was visible in the distance. They had a walk ahead, but it would be the same as their previous visit. The veil cat growled at her in acknowledgment. She didn't bother with the compass. Until they were more permanently reunited, it would continue to lead her to Luc.

"Since we know you can't jump us back to the continent from inside the castle, do you have to stay in veil cat form when we get there?" It was more convenient to be able to speak with him, even if they were supposed to stay silent while under the protection of the dagger. They would be exposing their presence soon enough. They might as well strategize.

"I also think I'll want to be able to speak for myself," Carter said, brushing off his clothes with his hands. He'd seamlessly shifted to his fae form.

Rose had expected he'd shift at some point. She was too cautious about his current plan for him to allow her to speak on his behalf.

"It will be more impactful leverage if I can show her the shift when we present ourselves. We might as well see how she reacts to the change," he said with a shrug.

"You're not leverage, Carter," Rose replied. The look he shot her was sympathetic but seemed to label her naive. She didn't have a chance to argue with him further as they arrived at the city gate and needed to stop talking if they wanted to remain unseen.

The city was much the same. Villagers seemed all too human as they went about their daily tasks. Knowing what she did now, she wondered how full the city should be. Were more spirits supposed to be here but had been taken by the river's currents? How full was the Veil Lake now?

Rose pricked her and Carter's fingers again as she let her mind wander. They knew where to go this time. Invisible, they went straight across the drawbridge and into the castle proper. Their best bet was to talk to Cassandra alone. They hoped to find her in the same study Zrak had found her in. This meant they scaled the same staircase they had followed Zrak up on their last visit.

The invisibility of Aurora's dagger shielded them as they found the stone spiral staircase and slid past the guards standing at the bottom. They made their way up to the large, heavy door. This was where they would have to make themselves known. There was no opening this door and hoping no one noticed. If Cassandra were inside, she'd be alerted to their arrival as soon as they opened it.

Rose and Carter shared a final glance. Carter took the lead as he moved closer to the door. This was his show, as he kept reminding her. He reached for the handle and twisted.

If Carter was set on this, Rose was determined to be there with him. She readied for the worst as he opened the door to Cassandra's study.

"WHAT DO WE HAVE HERE?" Cassandra's voice was all brisk efficiency. If she was surprised to see the door to her private study open without anyone visible, she didn't show it.

Rose figured it took a lot to shake Cassandra, given everything she now knew the Lady to have dealt with in ruling her realm. This land beyond the veil was so dependent on others—a refuge for spirits once their time on the continent was done—she was forever reacting to their actions.

At Carter's nod, Rose let the water magic of Aurora's blade wash away. The pair became visible as they entered the study.

"That's a neat trick," Cassandra mused, her gaze falling momentarily to Rose. "It explains something I hadn't quite worked out yet about the Suden Point's mysterious escape."

"She did not believe I escaped on my own. It was a humbling conversation," Luc added through their bond.

She wanted to laugh, but now was not the time. They had Cassandra's attention—well, Rose watched as Cassandra's brief focus on her faded... It swept toward the Vesten Point like a magnet. This supported Rose's belief that whatever Carter felt about Cassandra's magic, she must also feel about his.

Rose stretched her fingers and balled them back into fists. She might as well start this with their requests, and let Carter negotiate with whatever he was willing. "We're here for the Suden Point," she said, laying their cards on the table.

The slight nod of Cassandra's head was the only acknowledgment she'd heard Rose's words. Her gaze remained fixed on Carter.

"And why should I give him to you?" Cassandra asked. Her gaze finally bothered to turn to Rose.

"You do not need him here." She was unable to help herself. A pit opened in her stomach as she saw Cassandra's gaze return to Carter. This was getting uncomfortable, but Carter didn't seem ready to enter the conversation yet. He stood tall and unflinching against the Lady of the Veil's stare. His shaggy brown hair fell in waves around his face. His eyes held the yellow-green shine usually reserved for when he was in his veil cat form.

Rose was sure Cassandra noticed.

"You know nothing about what I need, Norden Point. Having him here suits my current purposes," Cassandra said.

Well, that was concerning. Rose had hoped Luc was an unfortunate bystander in this game. There was no way Cassandra actually needed him. He was a demigod of the continent—his magic should be impacted at least half as much as Aterra's had been. He couldn't be useful to her.

Then again, what did Rose know about what Cassandra needed to heal her realm?

"What good is having the Suden Point here? And two gods?" Carter spoke. "We know you're aware the balance on the continent is in shambles. We know it continues to impact your realm. Work with us to fix it."

Rose was impressed by how boldly Carter spoke to the Lady of the Veil. His words held a confidence that was usually overlooked because of his quiet demeanor and unwillingness to make eye contact. Carter had a strength all his own.

Growing up a veil cat shifter could not have been an easy thing. Hiding what he was—what he could do—for so long had shaped him. She felt a kinship with him over this, as it was similar to the way she'd had to hide her wind magic. It renewed her focus that, as one of the fae leaders, she didn't want future generations to carry the burden of hiding a part of themselves.

"The continent's business is not mine," Cassandra said, pushing her long white-blonde hair over her shoulder. She stood and moved around her desk, perching on the front corner, her eyes focused solely on Carter. "Your gods have done nothing but take. I should take something from the continent in return." As she crossed her arms over her chest, a fire shone in the Lady's eyes. It wasn't a flame like the Vesten's, but a rage Rose understood too well. The actions and inactions of the gods had caused catastrophe even in this realm. Cassandra would continue to do what it took to hold this place together.

Carter bristled. Even in his fae form, Rose could tell this was the equivalent of his hackles rising. "It's easy to blame. We could do the same. None of the Compass Points caused this mess," he replied. His fingers balled into fists at his side. "We're trying to make it right."

Cassandra's answering laugh was low. The sound was one more appropriate for a bed chamber than a study. Rose suddenly felt out of place in this negotiation, though she couldn't quite understand why.

"That remains to be seen," Cassandra replied. "The Suden Point dropped into my realm with your baggage, like it was a dumping ground for things that harm the continent." That fire flared in her eyes again. "I can't keep cleaning up your messes."

"Well, she might have me there." Luc's thoughts slipped into Rose's mind. Yes, Cassandra's words were valid, but they ignored the intent. The Compass Points were blind to the history between this realm and the continent. They were simply stuck in a no-win situation.

"How could you have known? We only knew Zrak had done it. It didn't seem unreasonable to...trade one god for another," Rose replied.

Carter shook his head. "We didn't mean it like that, and I think you know it." He raised his hands, gesturing to the realm around them. "This place isn't so mysterious. It's an independent realm, to be sure, but its existence is necessarily tied to the continent. You should want to help us."

Cassandra's lips twitched in barely masked amusement. "My realm is a mystery to most, Vesten Point. You'd be wise to remember that, lest you give too much away."

Rose was more than convinced the Lady of the Veil knew to whom she spoke. The how of it and what she wanted from him were the current mysteries. "We hoped you'd be reasonable," Rose said, trying and failing to break the tension between the Lady of the Veil and the Vesten Point. "Already, you harbored one god. We hoped to make a trade."

"Reasonable? Was it reasonable that the gods of the continent ignored my warnings? Was it reasonable the Osten god inserted himself into my realm with false ho—" Cassandra cut herself off, shaking her head. "It doesn't matter. What matters is my realm and the continent remain separate."

Carter gave Cassandra a doubtful look. "Lying to yourself won't fix it." He paused. "Give us back the Suden Point. Keep Aterra here and let Zrak return with us. We'll restore balance to the continent. It will start to right whatever is wrong with this place." Carter's hands gestured back toward the city.

Cassandra pushed herself from her seat on the desk and stood. "What makes you think something is wrong with this place?"

Carter didn't get to answer as the door opened again, and Zrak walked in.

The Lady of the Veil's glare would have withered a lesser man. The Osten god barely acknowledged it as he strolled unconcernedly into the room. He sat on the chaise lounge, lying back and putting up his feet.

"You're not needed here—you may return to being lost, Zrak," Cassandra said through clenched teeth.

"And miss the fun? I don't think so." A smirk curved the Lost God's mouth. "Please, continue. The least you could do is let me see the fruits of my labor." His hand flicked as if to usher on the conversation he'd interrupted.

Cassandra rolled her eyes. "You overvalue your talents," she said coolly.

"And you overplay your hand," Zrak replied just as quickly, a hint of challenge in his voice.

Rose tended to agree with Zrak. Whatever their discussion, the fact that Cassandra let Zrak barge into the room and remain told her all she needed to know. Zrak's talents, whatever they were, were important—important enough to allow his irreverence.

Cassandra appeared to make an effort to ignore him and focused again on the Vesten Point. "What will you give me for the Suden Point?"

Rose wanted to answer. She wanted to say they would give anything to get the Suden Point back. She held her tongue. Carter said nothing as he leveled his gaze at the Lady of the Veil.

"*Carter knows what he's doing.*" Luc's reassurance distracted her long enough for Cassandra to continue speaking.

"Too long, the realm beyond the veil has been considered an afterthought. Too long, we've been forgotten and lost." She gestured to Zrak. "I want only what I was promised for harboring him for hundreds of years."

"And that is..." Rose couldn't stop the thought. They had their own assumptions, but she might as well ask if they were being direct. She let the statement hang, waiting for Zrak or Cassandra to fill it in.

Carter swallowed thickly, and Rose knew his next words before they left his mouth. "Me," he said, his voice barely a whisper. His yellow-green gaze darted back and forth between Cassandra and Zrak. "She was promised me."

CHAPTER THIRTY-TWO

"So he says," Cassandra replied as her gaze slid to Zrak. Rose still didn't understand how, but the meaning was clear. Zrak had come to Cassandra with more than the offer to shepherd spirits beyond the veil. He'd come with knowledge of another veil cat shifter that would find his way into her realm.

What interested Rose now was that Cassandra, for all her intensity towards Carter, spoke as if she didn't believe he was... whatever was promised.

"You don't believe it?" Rose couldn't help but ask. She assumed Cassandra meant that Carter was a veil cat shifter, but as the words came out, she realized she had no idea what 'it' was. Maybe it wasn't just the shifted form he took, but something else about him that had been promised to the Lady of the Veil. Rose held her breath as she waited for a reply.

"I've not had the best luck dealing with those from the continent," she replied slowly.

Rose could only imagine the pain she buried in that statement. Those from the continent who betrayed her were her own blood—her twin.

"Why don't you tell me what you were promised then," Carter said calmly. "We can clear this up now."

Cassandra's eyes flashed in surprise. She must be too used to dealing with Zrak and his half-answers. Rose had barely dealt with him and was already fed up with his secrets. She could imagine that hundreds of years of his behavior would be grating. Hopefully, Carter's directness would be a reprieve.

"If you have to ask, you aren't the solution," she said with a dismissive wave.

Heat filled the room. It took Rose a moment to realize it was Carter. His flame must have flared with his discomfort. His face didn't change, and the temperature eased as he leashed his power.

"Glad I'm not the only one who has that issue," Luc said through the bond. The situation in Cassandra's study was too tense to laugh. She'd never seen Carter lose control before. She barely saw him emote.

"For being the one in need, you're not doing yourself any favors," Carter said when he finally collected himself. "I'm saying I want to help. Regardless of what you were promised." He shot a glare at Zrak. "Tell me what you need."

Cassandra's eyes widened, surprise and hesitation warring across her features. It was a shame that kind of offer appeared so foreign to Cassandra. It had to be lonely ruling this realm on her own. The gods of the continent, for all their faults, at least had partners in their existence. Cassandra was alone. Given the circumstances of her origin, she'd had little choice in taking ownership of the realm. Yet one mistake, one misstep, could cost her realm and those she protected.

A chill ran up Rose's spine at the lingering standoff between Carter and Cassandra. *"I feel like we shouldn't be watching this,"* Rose couldn't help but send through the bond.

"I'd be happy to entertain you while they sort it out," Luc purred.

Heat rushed through her body at his tone. Cassandra couldn't hold off Carter's persistence forever. They had to be close to knowing if Cassandra would free Luc.

"What makes you think I need something?" Cassandra finally said, breaking the standoff. She also took a moment to glare at Zrak before continuing.

"We've read your journals," Carter said. "We know what your sister took. We don't know what you did to prevent the catastrophe her actions set off, but I know it made you what you are today."

"Well, they have you there," Zrak said, sitting up from the lounge chair, like the conversation was finally getting interesting. He dipped his chin in Cassandra's direction.

Rose would not want to be on the receiving end of the look Cassandra returned. It was clear from all the interactions she'd seen that Zrak and Cassandra weren't friendly, but it was becoming more apparent by the moment that whatever grace he'd been granted was wearing thin.

"Why I let you stay will always be a mystery," Cassandra said through clenched teeth.

"My information has proved to be exactly as valuable as I said it would." Zrak was the most composed of all of them. He seemed uninvested in the conversation even though he was clearly the orchestrator behind it.

Rose wracked her brain to put the pieces together. Both Zrak and Cassandra intimated that Zrak had known Carter would come. As much as Rose wanted to focus on how that was possible, she knew they still hadn't covered what exactly Cassandra needed Carter for.

"Fine," Cassandra said, her hand moving to her hip. "If you've read the journals, you know the spirits could benefit from a shepherd."

Carter nodded. "Isn't that what he is doing for you now?" The Vesten Point gestured to Zrak.

Cassandra rolled her eyes. "Allegedly, though I question the use of his Nebulus daily." She looked like she meant it as she tilted her head, considering.

"Then why use them? Tell me what exactly he promised you," Carter urged. He took a step toward her. Rose had never seen him enter someone's space before. His frame wasn't bulky, but he positioned himself to ensure he was all she saw.

He understood Cassandra in a way she couldn't grasp. Rose didn't know if it had to do with the pull of magic he felt in this realm, but her gaze tracked his movement. Solely focused on Carter, she began to speak.

"I needed something to prevent the ruin you assumed was imminent after Cee—Celeste's actions." Cassandra looked down at her hands clasped before her and Rose wondered how long it'd been since she'd thought of her sister fondly or called her by her childhood nickname. "Keep in mind, I don't blame her. I blame him." She gestured at Zrak, that fire still evident in her gaze. "And the other gods of your continent."

Rose wasn't sure she believed that entirely, but she was sure that's what Cassandra wanted to believe, so she let it go.

"Understood," Carter whispered.

"Zrak's Nebulus did what they could for the spirits. They help them beyond the veil but can't help them cross the river like the veil cats could before"—she paused—"before they stopped."

"But you needed to refill the lake anyway, right?" Carter pressed.

"I needed the realm's balance to return," she replied. Rose didn't miss that she didn't answer his question. Carter appeared to catch it as well.

"I will happily shepherd spirits beyond the veil," Carter said. "I will help them cross the river into your realm."

Cassandra met his eyes. More surprisingly, the Vesten Point held her stare as she asked, "Why?" Her eyebrow raised at his offer.

"The pull of this land is strong. Its magic calls to me. Whether

I have a reason to be here or not, I know I'll be back. You know that—you know what I am." He held her gaze again, and her chin dipped in the barest motion of acknowledgment. "I want to help."

Cassandra's mouth opened and closed. For the first time, she seemed unsure what to say. Carter pressed his advantage. He shifted into his veil cat form. A growl rumbled through his lean frame as he fell to all fours.

Rose noted the tilt of his head as he circled the Lady of the Veil. His tail flicked, getting dangerously close to Cassandra's leg. Whatever Carter was doing, he was still speaking to her. The way her eyes widened, and the knuckles of her fists whitened as her grip intensified told Rose all she needed to know. Cassandra sucked in a breath as Carter's tail swept across her leggings. Even this brief touch was more than Rose had seen him offer anyone.

"I guess we're not the only ones with a connection," she said through the bond.

"Our connection defies reason, Rose. It's outside of anything that's ever been known. Clearly, Cassandra can communicate with all her veil cats. Whatever they have isn't unique." She wanted to laugh at how offended Luc seemed by the comparison; she hadn't had a chance to tell him about the mind connection the pack of cats was capable of.

She wasn't willing to say whatever was happening with Cassandra and Carter wasn't unique. Carter still barely made eye contact with Rose, even with the trust they'd built. Every one of the Vesten Point's secrets had been pulled from him through circumstance. He had fought it most of the way. Yet he seemed intent on prying Cassandra's secrets free. His determination to do so appeared to overtake the Lady's insistence that she didn't need anything.

"Fine," Cassandra said, pushing her hair back again. "You can shepherd spirits. That's all I require."

"For now," Carter said.

Rose turned to see Carter had shifted back into his fae form. Once again, he held Cassandra's gaze as he responded.

"Wonderful," Zrak said. The sound of his hands clapping together before him broke the standoff in the room, pulling all eyes to him. "If that's settled." He looked at Carter. "I could use a ride back to the continent."

"Excuse me?" Carter turned to the Lost God.

"You want to bring me back to the continent, do you not? If I'm not mistaken, the balance requires three gods in place. You currently only have two." The god's voice was so even. Rose couldn't begin to imagine what was going through his mind. "I need you, a veil cat shifter, to help me cross back over."

Carter shook his head in confusion. "Can't your Nebulus take you?"

Zrak rolled his eyes. "I can only call on them when the Osten Point has strengthened me. As you might have guessed, she's not speaking to me at the moment."

"I can't imagine why," Rose said, straightening as she realized the words had slipped out.

"Oops," she said to Luc.

"He deserves it," Luc replied. *"Did he leave this conversation without explaining how he knew Carter would come?"*

"We will absolutely be finishing that conversation," Rose replied. She wondered if Cassandra had told Carter anything about Zrak in their weird, private conversation. Carter would tell them what they needed to know when they left the realm.

"You can't leave before deciding what to do about Aterra," Cassandra said. She looked at Rose. "The veil isn't your dumping ground. I won't have another god of the continent holed up here for hundreds of years. I regretted having this one"—she gestured to Zrak—"no matter what he promis—"

She didn't finish her sentence, her words cut off as the ground shook beneath the castle. The items on Cassandra's desk shook and slipped to the floor. Rose felt the movement for what it was: earth magic.

"What is happening?" she asked, pushing her fear through the

bond to Luc. No one but him and Aterra could cause this kind of disturbance.

"I need a moment," was Luc's strangled reply.

Rose couldn't handle that. She tore from the study to the shouts of those around her. Rose made it down the stairs and back to the main level. She heard Carter calling but didn't stop. It was clear Zrak and Cassandra were with him, too. She couldn't be bothered to slow down for them. She headed for the staircase that led to the cells where Luc and Aterra were being kept. Rose charged past all number of guards.

No one stopped her.

The disturbance must have shaken loose more than she realized this low within the castle for them to be so distracted. Or possibly, Cassandra, in trailing after her, waved off her guards and let Rose charge through. She wouldn't push the bond again. If Luc needed a moment, she would give it to him. Even if Aterra wasn't at his full strength in this realm, he was still the Suden god. If he'd found a way to use some of his power, Luc would need to remain focused to challenge him.

Rose ran down the hall until the way was blocked. She stopped at the path she'd taken initially to get to Luc in their escape attempt. It was caved in.

She could use her elements to try to blast through the rock. Cassandra, Zrak, and Carter finally caught up with her as she decided how to navigate this.

"Do you know what is happening?" Rose asked Cassandra.

"I can feel that Aterra tested my cells. He must have decided they were weak enough to try."

"About that," Luc's voice broke through. *"She's right."* He sounded exhausted.

"Luc says you're correct. What would have happened?" Rose asked.

"I collapsed the tunnel to stop his escape," Luc replied. *"That should hold him for the time being. He used all of his energy to fight*

the roots and get out of the cell. He doesn't have his full power here. Something about the realm doesn't agree with him."

Rose repeated the words to the group.

"He no longer has the wild magic supporting him," Zrak said coolly, as if he'd been offended by its participation the entire time.

"It's more than that," Carter replied, looking at Cassandra. The Lady of the Veil didn't meet his gaze as she stared into the pile of rubble.

"I have regained a hold on him," Cassandra said.

Rose could only picture the roots reaching from the ground to wrap around him. She was too worried to pry into whatever was happening between the goddess and the shifter. She repeated Cassandra's words to Luc.

"I knocked him out with the cave-in. Her roots are moving him back to where he was previously held." He sighed, and Rose could hear his exhaustion in the sound. *"Even if Cassandra let me leave right now, I can't return with you."* He let his desire and anguish flow through their bond. He wanted to be back on the continent as much as she wanted him there, but this wasn't over. *"She may have him again now—but it's temporary. She was right before: We need a long-term solution for Aterra."*

Rose knew he was correct. It just broke her heart again to know they were so close to returning with him, only to have this physical divide between them.

"How long can you both hold him?" Rose asked.

"Her cell leashed him for days—if I'm vigilant in helping, we should be able to last a bit longer."

"Any ideas on what to do with him?" she asked.

"We need somewhere more permanent to put him—somewhere he can't continue to cause harm," Luc said.

The gods were the ones to decide the solution to the balance, which was to hold three gods on the continent and banish one. Where else could they banish a god?

Rose met Cassandra's gaze. "Luc will remain here and help hold Aterra while we return to the continent and finalize a plan.

You know what he is to me. Know that is your insurance policy. We will be back as fast as we can."

Cassandra nodded, and Carter led her and Zrak out of the castle. They were a somber group. Rose was unwilling to celebrate that they had accomplished part of their goal. Even though Zrak returned, they still had to figure out what to do with Aterra.

They traveled through the void between realms, back to the continent. Rose looked around at the nothing in every direction. She let the darkness close in, her feelings mirroring the space as she, once again, left Luc in the realm beyond the veil.

CHAPTER THIRTY-THREE

"You still have to explain!" Rose called. They had fallen through the void and landed back at Compass Lake. Rose was still picking herself up off the ground when Zrak started to leave.

In no realm could he just walk away. Carter agreed, growling still in veil cat form, herding Zrak away from the willow's branches. She shook herself as she caught up to him. This god might be more trouble than he was worth, but he had answers they needed. Cassandra was happy to be rid of him. That didn't give her a lot of hope for his usefulness.

Zrak's face was impassive as he replied. "You'll do what is needed to retrieve him, I'm sure." He picked an invisible piece of lint from his shirt as he continued. "Everything is going according to plan." His reply wasn't cocky, but it was sure.

"Aterra trying to escape was part of the plan?" she hissed, her hand moving to her hip.

"Those details aren't always evident in the bigger picture." He didn't look at her as he spoke, proof that he knew his answer was as useless as it sounded.

"Whose plan is this, Zrak?" Carter asked, having returned to his fae form. "You haven't shared yours. How do we know we have the same goals?"

The directness Carter had started with Cassandra was overflowing to the Osten god. Rose was right there with him though. None of their questions had been answered so far as Zrak was concerned. They were still operating on the idea that he was the lesser of two evils.

Zrak turned to him, appraising the Vesten Point in a new light. "You don't."

Rose tried to count to ten to calm herself. She was failing miserably. She agreed with Zrak's initial statement. She would retrieve Luc, but that wasn't the question. "What are we going to do with Aterra?" she asked. "If you have a plan, does it include solving that god-sized problem? Does it still hold that we need three gods to balance the continent? What about a demigod?" She decided to launch a stream of questions at Zrak and see if he'd answer any of them since all other attempts to reason with him had been unsuccessful.

They had reappeared in the Burning Garden, within the shelter of the willow tree they traveled through. Zrak gave no further reply as he stood there. His unhelpfulness was maddening, but Rose was pretty sure he knew it.

"What was your plan, Zrak? If things are still going according to it, then it's time we knew." She gave Zrak one last opportunity to share this himself.

His lips pressed into a firm line.

"Fine. I can start guessing." Rose had a list for Zrak. She wasn't sure how they would help with Aterra, but she knew she needed to get Zrak talking if they were to solve anything. And time was of the essence. Even with Luc helping to hold Aterra, it was only a matter of time before he slipped his leash again. He'd found some weakness in Cassandra's magic, and Rose was sure he'd continue to exploit it.

She started thinking through everything she knew out loud. "You somehow knew what Carter was." She scratched her head.

　　　　JILLIAN WITT

"You knew before he was born what he would be." It was a state-ment, not a question. Cassandra and Zrak had made this deal five hundred years ago. Carter couldn't be much older than Luc. Somehow, Zrak knew another veil cat shifter would be on the continent, and he knew Carter was him when he arrived.

"Yes," he said, though he offered no additional information.

Rose turned to Carter. "Did she tell you why she needed you?" Rose didn't think the Lost God would be much more help on this front. Though she wasn't positive, they could leverage this to help with Aterra. Even if they could—would Carter let them?

"Not really," he replied. "She at least acknowledged that she did need me. But she was intent on what she said aloud—I would only shepherd spirits to start." He ran a hand through his shaggy hair, damp with sweat from the movement between realms.

"What does she need from him?" Rose challenged Zrak again.

The Osten god was unphased as he replied. "That's for her to tell him."

A low growl rumbled from Carter's chest. Rose turned to look at the Vesten Point. He was still in fae form, but the noise emanating from him was all feline.

"Yes," Zrak said too casually. "He's becoming more aligned with his shift. The more he lets the magic of Cassandra's realm in, the more the three parts of his magic will unite."

Rose's attention whipped back to the god. "I don't know what to do with you." She waved her hands in exasperation. "You're coming with us." She wanted to walk right up to him and grab his ear, yanking him by it back to Norden house like the petulant god-child he was. Let Aurora, Arie, and Juliette deal with him. He was their friend and patron—allegedly.

He looked down his nose at her. "You can't force me to. You're down a Compass Point," Zrak replied. There was plenty of arrogance in the statement.

Rose saw red. Just as she was about to explode, an unlikely voice of reason broke through the tree branches.

"Do they need to hold you?" She'd never been so happy to

hear Arie's voice aloud before. Her shoulders wanted to sag in relief as Aurora and Arie parted the tree branches and let themselves in.

"Would you make the Compass Points' existence harder than we have already?" Aurora asked, not unkindly.

The dynamic changed instantly.

Zrak's easy confidence—his carefree stance—was gone. He appeared far too still. Rose wondered if he was even breathing. "Arctos." His head turned. "Aurora." His gaze returned to Arie as he said, "I can explain."

"That's what I've been telling Rose," Arie replied. "But you seem to be bringing my defense of you into question." Arie let Aurora's hand slip from its place in the crook of his arm. She let him go as he closed the distance between himself and Zrak. "Please, Zrak." Rose wasn't sure she'd ever heard Arie speak so softly—so kindly. His tone was gentle, and Rose feared his heart would break if Zrak turned out to be the villain of this story. "Tell me I haven't been lying to her."

"There's so much you don't know," Zrak's words were quiet, but exhaustion thrummed through each one of them.

Rose couldn't take it anymore. She couldn't take what Zrak's words might do to Arie. "Why don't you explain it? Arie said you like plans. You seem to be the puppet master of our lives at the moment. We deserve to know what you do."

Zrak's sigh was dramatic. Rose wanted to roll her eyes but held the motion to see if the Lost God would finally reveal his secrets. For everything to fit into place, he had to know things before they happened.

From Arie's memories, it was clear Zrak had suspected Aterra wouldn't change his behavior. He seemed sure that one of the gods, though he never named who, would continue to throw the continent into chaos. Did he also know how to stop him?

Zrak had to know that another veil cat shifter would come before he went to Cassandra seeking sanctuary.

    JILLIAN WITT

Finally, he had to know that something would drive the Compass Points beyond the veil. He had to know they'd eventually come for something. Need on the continent would be so great that the realm beyond the veil would be the only sanctuary. Or, in their case, the only place strong enough to hold the Suden god.

Her magic thrummed in her chest. The bond with Luc pulsed as she considered the only available option—magic.

"Can Zrak see the future?"

"It's the only thing that makes sense," Luc's voice echoed in her mind. She could feel him considering the thoughts she was already processing, putting into words the things she hadn't yet been able to. *"I don't think it's...see though."*

Of course, the Osten could hear secrets on the wind. Rose's experience was that secrets traveled on the wind when they were particularly potent—when strong emotions were attached. She didn't know if they had to be in progress when they were carried.

The pulse of Luc's magic was strong as she completed the thought. He seemed to agree. There was nothing left to do but test her theory.

"You can hear secrets on the wind," Rose said, not as a question but as a statement.

Arie's head swiveled toward her. It tilted to the side in his traditional bird-like movement. "That's always been his power," Arie said carefully. Not having fully put together what Rose had only guessed.

"The secrets he hears"—she looked at Carter—"they're not just in the present."

Now, she had Carter's attention. His gaze pinched as he worked out what Rose was saying.

"He knew my secret before I existed. It's what he went to Cassandra with," Carter said. "He knew a secret from hundreds of years...in the future."

Zrak's lack of response to her accusations was its own confirmation.

"Zrak?" Arie echoed. "Is that true?" The hurt in his voice was too much for Rose. She wanted to throttle the Lost God for the pain he was causing Arie, a friend who trusted him—who believed in him against all odds.

"Yes," Zrak replied, defeat coating the single word reply.

"Secrets from…" Arie repeated the words, trying to make sense of them. "Secrets from the future?" He was in Zrak's face now. His finger pushed into Zrak's broad chest. "You didn't think that was important to tell us before we started down this path five hundred years ago?"

Zrak sighed again.

"No! You don't get to sigh at me like this is exhausting," Arie said. "How much did you know? How sure were you? How much information did you have before you bet all of our futures—the continent's future—on these secrets?"

Arie pushed Zrak back with both hands. "Get out of my sight. I can't even look at you." He shook his head as he paced in a circle. He pointed at Zrak. "But answer their questions first." He waved his hand like he was flapping a wing. "They're cleaning up our mess and deserve to at least know everything we do." Arie couldn't be stopped now. He appeared to be unraveling before them, talking to himself. "I guess it's not things all of us know, is it? It's things only you know."

He ran his fingers through his hair. Rose agreed with the sentiment but was relieved to finally have some of this out in the open. Seeing her friend's world come crashing down brought her no joy. Arie held Zrak on a pedestal for hundreds of years. It was heartbreaking to watch his realization: the Osten god was as flawed as he was.

"I made the best decisions I could with the information I had," Zrak said, straightening his spine.

"You made decisions for us!" Arie said, fire rimming his eyes. The temperature in the burning garden elevated as Arie's temper rose.

"I had to go with what I knew!" Zrak roared back. "I didn't know what telling you would change."

"Oh, please," Arie yelled. "You could have at least tried to talk to me!"

Zrak's shoulders sagged. He appeared to be losing steam. "I couldn't, Arie. The secrets are never clear. They are simple scenes, simple words. I had to put the pieces together about the speakers." He sighed again. "While I only heard Aterra's plans for power, I couldn't be sure he acted alone." His gaze flicked to Aurora.

Her eyes narrowed at him like she didn't appreciate the implication. She didn't interrupt though. She sensed Zrak needed to make his case to Arie alone.

"I heard you with the Norden Point, but I never heard enough to determine if you knew of Aterra's actions. You were so guarded with her."

Rose couldn't disagree there. She and Arie had lived together for a decade without either admitting what they were. Rose, the rightful Norden leader, and Arie, the Vesten god.

"What about my Vesten Point?" Arie baited him. *Don't you think I deserved to know your plans for him?*

"Now he's yours?" Zrak laughed darkly. "I heard the Vesten Point's secrets. One of them being that he feared his patron had no use for him!"

Arie's gaze finally left Zrak's, fixing on Carter. His face seemed to soften momentarily in regret. Then he shook his head, the flame of his anger overtaking any gentler emotions. "He didn't need me. Rose did...no thanks to you," he added.

"You could never imagine the responsibility. The weight of knowing these secrets. Of piecing together the paths we could take, but knowing there was only one chance of preventing another natural disaster."

Arie pulled his hand down his face. "We might have if you'd shared it with us. But I guess we'll never see how that could have turned out." He turned to walk away. Aurora took his hand, but before they left, she had her own words for Zrak.

"Do what they want, Zrak. Don't make us get involved further. You've meddled to get us to this point. Let them finish this. Tell them everything you know. They don't deserve what we've left for them."

　　　　JILLIAN WITT

CHAPTER THIRTY-FOUR

Zrak didn't put up a fight as the Compass Points led him back to Norden house. Arie had been angry, yes, but Rose suspected it was his final disappointment that moved Zrak. The straight-backed, stoic god was gone. In his place was the Lost God, who appeared to finally reflect the name.

Carter went to get Juliette since he was the fastest. Rose hoped Carter would catch her up on the walk to Norden house. Juliette had more reasons than most to be upset with Zrak. Learning he had kept another power of the Osten a secret might push her over the edge. And that didn't begin to contemplate if she would inherit the power with Zrak's return to the continent.

"I don't know what else you want from me," Zrak said as he looked out the front window over Compass Lake. His back was to Rose. She was the only one in the room with him. Arie and Aurora made noises as they moved around the house, but so far, they had refused to enter the library. Aurora must be trying to calm Arie down. Rose hoped Aurora won him over soon. They both needed to join them when the Compass Points returned. No matter Arie's anger or disappointment, he should still hear what Zrak had to say.

"We just need the information you have," Rose said. "What

are we supposed to do with Aterra? We can't hold him indefinitely." Rose ran her hand through her hair and tied it back as she spoke. She had more questions than she realized. They still had a lot of ground to cover.

"You mean your bound partner can't hold him indefinitely," Zrak said as he gestured across the lake to Suden house.

"I wonder how our relationship is relevant in your grand plan," she replied sarcastically.

"That, Rose, was one of the most fascinating secrets I've heard in my existence. It gave me hope that the idea of the Compass Points might work." Zrak lit up just a little as he spoke. It was the most genuine he had sounded yet. Rose decided to try to leverage it.

"One set of bound fae put you on this path?" She waved her hands around them. "This plan to mess with all of our lives?"

"Not just one set. *The* set," he said enthusiastically. He was like an explorer recounting his discovery. "The Norden Point and Suden Point. Not only from different courts but the rightful leaders of each." He finally turned from the window, and his gaze narrowed as he focused on her. "It seems so normal to you, given how your relationship with the Suden Point evolved—but I assure you, it is anything but."

"My and Luc's relationship is our business—not yours. I'll not have some god claiming credit for us." Rose didn't want to think of how many secrets Zrak knew. How many must have come his way from the present and future in order to build his plan. She was unwilling to be considered a feather in his cap.

"You miss my point. I freely admit your relationship was and is outside of my control." He crossed his arms over his chest. "Just imagine you had all these options to right the imbalance of the continent. Some involve untold devastation, others bickering leaders, and still others violence and loss." He sighed. "Bickering leaders was the best choice I had—but knowing that one day the leaders of the Norden and Suden courts would defy convention

          JILLIAN WITT

and fight for what they knew they had, enough to save the continent? It made my choice simple."

"And you know what Luc is?" Rose asked. They hadn't dwelt on it, but her mind kept circling the fact that Luc was a demigod. She felt his presence in her mind as Zrak responded.

"It would have been risky, loosing a demigod onto the continent, any way you look at it. But knowing the demigod was the bound partner of the Norden Point made things clearer."

"How so?" Rose pressed. She knew this would be the answer to what they sought with Aterra. She just wasn't sure she was going to like it.

"I'll do whatever is needed, Rose. You know that."

"That is exactly what we won't be doing," Rose shot back. *"We'll see what this god knows. What he thinks you can do. And we'll discuss our options."*

Rose could feel Luc's smirk through the bond. *"Of course, love,"* he teased her, but she didn't care. The sound of the word *love* on his lips, even through their bond, was enough to send shivers through her body. She took a deep breath. He would not be the self-sacrificing idiot again.

"That—"

"If you tell me that is for me to find out, I will drown you in Compass Lake," Rose said. Her water magic was stirring before she could decide if the threat was a real one.

Zrak held his hands up in surrender, though she noted the twitch of his lip as he did. This was not funny. Zrak was less than helpful to them in everything they tried. What good was hearing secrets of the future if he did nothing with them? She supposed that wasn't right. He thought he was doing something. He just wouldn't share the information with those who needed it.

"If Luc is a demigod...he has to at least be able to counteract Aterra's greed and provide balance within the Suden." She paused, considering. They didn't want to repeat Zrak's mistakes. Whatever they did with Aterra, they didn't want to leave the

Suden's magic diluted. "That would position him as a god, though, not the Suden Point."

"*It's a good thing I prefer Mr. Norden Point now.*"

Rose couldn't hold back her smirk even though they contemplated more change for the continent. The Suden Point test was still a mystery to her—she was sure she would learn more soon. She set the thought aside.

None of this mattered unless they knew what to do with Aterra. "It still doesn't answer where to put him." She bit the inside of her lip as she thought. The concept of a demigod still spinning through her thoughts gave her an idea. Luc was half-god and half-fae—he was something in between. If his existence could help the balance, Rose wondered if she could use a similar solution to solve where to put Aterra.

Cassandra didn't want her realm to be a dumping ground for the continent. And to preserve the balance, Aterra couldn't be on the continent. Could they store him in between the two? She thought of the darkness she and Carter fell through when they crossed beyond the veil, the memory Luc shared with her and the inability to find the way through the darkness without Carter's shifter-provided talent.

They had crossed beyond the veil from multiple places, but each crossing felt the same to her. They bore the same darkness and unmarked paths, and yet they led to different locations in Cassandra's realm. She knew they were distinct to Carter. He never faltered as he guided them through. With Zrak's return, Rose could assume the Osten Point wouldn't need to return to the caves. That pathway might no longer be necessary.

"*It would require both myself and Cassandra to lend strength to hold him there,*" Luc warned.

"*Yes, but it shouldn't require so much from either of you,*" she speculated. Aterra's inability to navigate the expanse would be its own trap.

"*We would need Carter to talk to Cassandra again...but it's possible,*"

     JILLIAN WITT

"It's the only plan we have."

She wouldn't let this solution take Luc from her. Although Zrak claimed this was the best path, the costs were still high. And they were far from out of the woods on the chaos Zrak wrought. Her thoughts returned to her young friend Tara, the only human in Bury who had relentlessly pursued a friendship with her—now taken by the mist plague. She still lay in the barn they used to train in. How many other paths that Zrak had imagined included the mist plague?

"Can you at least heal those impacted by your mist?" Rose asked, her voice turned bitter. If Zrak wasn't going to help them with Aterra, he could at least clean up his mess here on the continent.

Zrak's lips pressed into a thin line. He didn't respond.

That seemed like a bad sign. "It's your plague. Can't you just"—she waved her hands around—"undo it?"

"I know what you're thinking, Rose."

Could he read minds, too?

He shook his head. "No, that's not a talent I have," he replied as if answering her unspoken question. "Your thoughts are written plainly on your face."

"Fine. What am I thinking then?" she challenged.

"The mist plague is bad—yes. But the other options were worse. I gather you've at least started understanding what Celeste and Cassandra's generation went through on the continent. The mist plague was my way of preventing that from recurring."

Rose opened her mouth, ready to press him again on fixing it, when Juliette and Carter arrived. Juliette surveyed the room, her eyes locking on the Osten god. Rose could see in the stiffness of Juliette's movements that she was holding back her reaction. Wind swirled around her ankles as the Osten Point fought for composure; Rose wasn't quite sure what feelings were being represented.

Was Juliette glad to finally have her god on the continent? To be free from the ritual she'd been shackled to for her entire tenure? Or had Carter filled her in, and this again was her rage at her god's involvement, similar to when Rose and Luc first shared that they suspected the mist plague was Zrak's doing? They must have been outside the library for a few moments because Juliette pressed Zrak on a point earlier in their conversation.

"Answer at least one of her questions, Zrak. Do you need Osten support to remove the mist plague? Rose and I will be happy to oblige. We should remove it from the continent immediately."

Zrak finally turned. His gaze locked with Juliette's—a fire dancing between them that Rose couldn't comprehend. "It's not that simple."

"Nothing ever is with you," she replied.

"Lady Osten," he started.

"No." She held her hand up to stop him. "Don't. I'm sure my words will echo what I have been told Lord Arctos has already said to you, so I'll be brief. You had every opportunity to share whatever it was you were doing. You made decision after decision that impacted our lives. My life. My people's lives. And yet you didn't see fit to discuss them with me or any of my predecessors." She paused to catch her breath. "This ends now. The Compass Points will finish it. We need what information you have—that is all. We want nothing else from you."

Rose hadn't seen a lot of emotion on Zrak's face since she and Carter had returned with him. But whatever had been there vacated with Juliette's words. It was as if Zrak had prepared himself to disappoint Arie and Aurora—he had understood the cost—but for whatever reason, he seemed ill-prepared for this dressing down from the Osten Point.

"The Nebulus cannot undo what they have done," he said. "As with everything else, the Compass Points must remove it."

"Like we haven't done enough..." Juliette sighed, exasperation and exhaustion coating her voice.

Rose felt the weight of it in her bones. Juliette was tired. Justifiably. A pit opened in Rose's stomach as she considered what this meant. They had the power to wake those impacted the entire time? Her hand went to cover her mouth as it hung open. She had tried her own magic, of course, but once they'd learned how to join their powers, she hadn't thought about using it for anything other than holding Aterra.

"You have," Zrak replied to Juliette. "But the continent is asking you to give a little more."

"The continent? Or you?" Juliette challenged.

"My Nebulus caused their sleep. I won't further explain my reasons. You know it was the only way I had to bring all of you together. To correct it—to awaken those impacted—is similar to holding a god in check." He looked knowingly at Rose. "I understand you learned how to harness that ability amongst yourselves."

"We could have removed it the entire time?" Rose couldn't believe it was something so simple. Her mind raced as she thought about correcting the problem now. Her heart plummeted in her chest again. They couldn't fix this until they had Luc back. The problem of Aterra still eluded them.

"Not quite," Zrak said, halting her thoughts in their tracks. "It's not only the power to hold a god you need, but a sacrifice— like the sacrifice made to right the original imbalance."

The Compass Points looked at each other slowly, sure they misunderstood him somehow. A sacrifice—like Zrak was supposed to have done? How would they merge their powers to wake those sleeping if one of them had to sacrifice their existence? Their haunted looks must have alerted Zrak to their confusion.

Zrak coughed. "No, sorry," he said, wiping his hands in the air as if to erase his words. "Not the exact same. Just a sacrifice from each Compass Point—something important to each court."

Rose tilted her head. What had Juliette said? Nothing was ever easy with him.

"What's the sacrifice exactly?" Carter asked.

"That is for you to decide." It seemed his favorite refrain. "As you said, you four—the Suden Point included—will be the ones to clean this up. You'll have to give something of worth or power as an offering to restore the balance."

"Gods dammit, Zrak!" Juliette lost her internal struggle. "Why have you left us in this position?" Pages flipped in the open books on the table. The curtains in the window where Zrak stood blew in a gust. Juliette was losing her grip on her magic.

"Would you believe me if I told you this was the best possible outcome?" He sighed and rubbed his brow. He had to know that wasn't enough. "Every other option I had left the continent destroyed."

		JILLIAN WITT

CHAPTER THIRTY-FIVE

Rose wasn't sure what to make of Zrak. As much as she found him insufferably frustrating, he seemed to genuinely care about the outcome for the continent.

The idea Rose and Luc had started to shape needed to solidify before they acted. They needed one more conversation with everyone before proceeding. Rose wouldn't risk not bringing Luc home again.

She left Juliette and Carter to harass Zrak and searched for Arie. He was pacing in the hallway as if he'd been trying to decide whether to enter the room.

"Are you going to come in?" she asked, closing the door to the Norden library behind her.

Arie's eyes narrowed. "Is he still there?"

Rose laughed. "Where do you think he would have gone?" She turned back to look at the closed door. "You can hear him in there."

"I don't know. Who knows anything about him?" Arie's voice started to rise.

"I know you're angry with him, but maybe you should cut him some slack." She glanced at the library door again.

Arie's eyes widened. "Why?"

"We're all guilty of trying to solve this thing on our own. You, by protecting me and ultimately guiding me back to Compass Lake. Me, thinking I had to find out how the Compass Points would hold Aterra. Luc, taking Aterra off the continent…" She sighed. "We've all had plans." She shrugged. "Zrak's plan may have more information than some of ours did, but the only certain thing is our plans don't work when we don't share them with each other." She ran a hand through her hair. "I only figured out how the Compass Points could work together when I explained what I was doing. It was difficult for me to give everyone all of the facts. Just like it was difficult for you to share who you were, and that was after only ten years." She looked at her friend, making sure he heard her. "Zrak has been making his own plans for as long as the continent has existed. He's not used to explaining himself or sharing information. His habit will be harder to break."

"If he were anyone else, I'd agree with you. But Zrak…" He sighed. "He was supposed to be the best of us, planning for the future we all wanted for the continent." Arie ran a hand through his hair.

"Don't you think this might be you putting him on a bit of a pedestal?" Rose asked quietly. "Why did you believe that of him but not yourself? He's no more infallible than you are. In fact, he's made many of the same mistakes you have." She laughed.

Arie glared like he didn't find her comment all that amusing. His lips formed a tight line. He looked like he would respond to her jab—something about being a god and never making mistakes. It was only weeks ago he'd apologized to her for not sharing his secrets. He had acknowledged when they spoke after her first battle with Aterra that he'd made a bad call. They were all guilty of trying to make plans and solve the problem independently. "You might have a point," he mumbled.

"Of course I do. I'm the Norden Point," Rose said, mocking Arie's usual phrase.

"Do you know what you'll do with Aterra?" he asked. "That's

the only reason I contemplated going back in there." He gestured toward the library. His brow was furrowed, and he looked worried. Rose never saw him seriously show concern over her actions. Arie, like Luc, seemed to think her capable of anything.

"I think so," she said. "Come back to the library. Let's talk it through."

"You think so?" his voice rose again, but this was a more familiar exasperation. "You're going to lure me back into the library with a half-baked plan?" he asked. "And we still haven't discussed how you will balance Luc's power in his position as Suden Point when he returns to the continent."

She nodded. "I know, Arie."

Arie raised his brows. "You're far too calm about this. Threatening the Suden Point's return should have had you cursing us all." He tilted his head.

Rose shrugged. The balance of her and Luc's idea made sense. Yes, she still needed to talk to Carter, but given what he'd just done in offering his services to Cassandra, Rose didn't think he'd object to their ask. "I'm finishing this the only way that has worked for me, Arie. I want to work with and use the trust I've built with my fellow Compass Points."

"You saw what my trust in Zrak got me—got all of us," Arie said flatly.

"Arie," Rose put her hand on his shoulder. "I'm telling you this because it's an exact mirror of your situation, yet you seem too consumed by your own anger to see it."

Arie's head tilted again in a birdlike gesture. "I'm not that dense, Rose. I see it. I just disagree with you. I want you to learn from my mistakes, not replicate them."

Rose smiled. "I hate that Zrak made you feel this way. I even hate Zrak sometimes. He is completely unhelpful and infuriating. But I also think he's telling the truth. He picked the best path available to him. He shared what information he could. Things he was unsure about, he kept to himself."

"That doesn't justify..."

"It got us to where we are today. We haven't succeeded yet, but we are so close." She could feel the plea in her own voice, like she willed her words to be true.

"We are close, Rose. We just need to push a little harder," Luc said, his voice attempting to provide the comfort his touch normally would in these situations. She longed for him to be there with her, convincing Arie to release his anger.

"I know you don't like that we have to clean up your mess, but that was always going to be the reality of the situation. Zrak's plans only came to be after the gods had already made a mess of things." She locked eyes with her best friend. "It was never going to be you who fixed this, Arie."

"I didn't want it to have to be you," he whispered.

"I didn't particularly want to do it, either," she said with a wicked smile. "But"—she raised her arms in an exaggerated shrug —"this is our path."

"I'm sorry," he said, water rimming his eyes.

"I know." She reached out, squeezing his shoulder. "Now, let's go finalize things with the others."

He scrunched his features like he was ruffling his feathers, then walked into the library. Aurora must not have been far, following quickly after. The pair sat on the couch as far from Zrak as possible. Arie refused to meet the god's gaze as he spoke.

"So, all three of you are going back?" Arie asked, looking at the Compass Points. "Can someone please tell me what the plan is with Aterra? I feel like you all don't understand the enormity of the problem."

Arie wasn't wrong. It was a problem over five hundred years old: where to banish a god. But Rose thought the half-in, half-out idea held merit. Carter did, too, as they started discussing. He had no problem further bartering with Cassandra. The gleam in his eye told Rose he might be a little too eager to work with the Lady of the Veil.

They were interrupted by a knock on the library door. Rose

stood to answer it. Aaron stood before her, and she beamed at him. "You made it."

"Walter sent us to you. I hope that's alright," Aaron replied.

"Of course." Her gaze slid over his shoulder to the fae standing behind him—a male who appeared to convey both being thoroughly put out and slightly scared in the way his green eyes darted between Aaron and Rose. The male was shorter than Aaron and had brown skin. Rose was glad to see Aaron had succeeded in tracking him down. "You must be Darren. Welcome to Compass Lake."

Darren nodded at her. "Not to be rude, but do you know why I'm here?" His words had no bite. A nervous energy hung in the air around him.

"This is your fault," she said through the bond to Luc.

Luc laughed softly. *"Trust me, he was more put out by me knocking a kid over by accident when I first met him. He'll be fine."*

Rose remembered everything Luc had said about Darren when they were in Loch. This male was a powerful Suden, one who made Luc question what the continent would look like if Aterra hadn't plotted to birth a demigod. She could feel why. Her weapons-master magic stretched toward the new arrival. It was eager to test him.

"Come in, and we can try to explain," Rose said, stepping aside to let him and Aaron pass as she reined in her magic.

Aaron appeared to realize he would be required to shepherd Darren through whatever came next. His movements were stilted as he turned to Rose with a whisper, "How many of them are here?"

Rose's smile was devious. "Two other Compass Points and three gods."

Darren faltered in his step, overhearing her words. He halted before crossing the threshold. "Did you say...gods?"

Based on Luc's overview of his frank conversation with Darren in Loch, Rose was sure he didn't care about the Compass

Points. He'd been irreverent at best to Luc. It appeared the gods were another matter. She nodded. "Will that be a problem?"

"I didn't have much choice about joining Aaron here." He slapped Aaron's back familiarly, though they must have only been traveling together a few days. Desperation on the continent must form strong bonds. "So, I'm guessing I don't have much choice in this next step either."

Rose smiled. Luc had been right about this fae.

"I told you," he said. She could feel his smugness through the bond. She ignored his gloating and glanced at Aaron.

"Have you been to Suden house yet?" she asked.

Aaron tensed. "Not yet. I wanted to give Luc one more chance to change his mind."

Darren glanced between them, suspicion in his eyes.

"Does he know?" Rose asked. She was sure she knew the answer, and now she was just teasing Darren, the same way Darren had picked on Luc in their first conversation.

"Who knew you would be so ruthless in your revenge for this perceived slight against me." Luc laughed through the bond.

"He does not," Aaron said. He studied her momentarily in the entryway. Rose had a feeling Aaron could sense she was talking to his brother. The way he tilted his head and sniffed the air made her laugh nervously.

"You really need to stop doing that," she said.

"You're communicating with him, aren't you?" Aaron asked.

Darren gave up on understanding their conversation and crossed his arms over his chest while waiting to be filled in. He tapped his foot loudly to hurry them along.

She smiled. "I am."

"And he doesn't want to change his mind?" Aaron asked.

"Change his mind about what?" Darren tried.

Rose ignored him as she heard the reply from Luc she expected. "He does not."

Aaron shrugged and gestured them forward. "You might as well go in the library and learn for yourself," he said to Darren.

Rose ushered them into the room. "You all know Luc's brother, Aaron." A round of hellos and acknowledgement greeted him. "And this is Darren. He's the Suden Luc requested to join us."

Darren tried another question as he took a seat. "Where is the Suden Point, if I may ask?"

"He's beyond the veil," Rose stated matter-of-factly. She would start telling him what he needed to know now that they were all assembled. "It's a long story, but he went and took Aterra with him to work towards restoring balance on the continent."

"Is he...dead?" Darren asked cautiously. She saw his mind working through the conversation he'd overheard between Rose and Aaron in the hallway.

"No," she replied.

"And how do you know that he wanted me here then? If he's beyond the veil but not dead?" Darren's questions were quite reasonable. He'd shown calm in the face of a lack of understanding. He sought facts before calling them all crazy and walking out.

"He's my bound partner. Our connection allows me to speak to him."

"I see," was Darren's reply. She was sure he had more questions about that statement, but he looked around the room and seemed to decide that if no one else was objecting, he wouldn't either. "Do..." Rose could see his mind working, but he could not put the pieces together. "Do you need my help to retrieve him?"

Rose smiled. "We do."

"So, you're all going back? The new guy, too?" Arie asked again, bringing the conversation back to the beginning.

"We're all going back, and we'd like Darren to join us," Rose said.

Darren looked around the room and pointed at his own chest. Confusion was evident on his face. "What do you need me for?"

"This is going to be fun," Luc said, his voice giddy through the bond, like he was excited to play puppet master for this part of their plan.

CHAPTER THIRTY-SIX

"Everything good?" Rose greeted Aaron and Darren a few hours later as they approached the willow tree inside the burning garden. Darren had a dazed look on his face, which, though Rose felt for him, she could only take as a good sign.

They'd agreed on their plan and split up to make final arrangements. It was now late afternoon as the Compass Points readied to cross beyond the veil again. Rose had been task-free after adjourning from the library, so she'd stopped by the bakery in Compass Lake Village to get everyone sustenance before their trip.

"All good," Aaron said, squeezing Darren's shoulder. "He's still adjusting."

Darren's eyes flashed red, a traditional sign that Suden emotions were high. Rose handed out chocolate pastries with the best half-apology face she could muster. Darren was really only doing what was always meant to be his calling.

He nodded in thanks as he accepted the food.

"You'll fit in fine," she said, welcoming Darren. "Any questions before we go?"

"The plan is clear," he said and took a bite. He swallowed. "All of the life choices that brought me to this point are in question, but the plan is clear." He glanced at her and shrugged. "I doubt you can help me with that."

Rose smiled. Working with Darren would be a pleasure.

"Here we go," Rose said as Juliette and Carter arrived. She handed them each pastries as they walked toward the willow tree.

"Everyone good?" Carter asked, glancing around. A chorus of nods was their response. Carter finished his food in two bites and decided everyone else could eat as quickly as he had. He seemed eager to get beyond the veil, shifting into his veil cat form.

Darren took a step back from the Vesten Point. They'd told him what to expect, but seeing the large feline was a different experience than hearing about one. Carter's growl sent the willow tree shaking. By now, Rose was familiar with how the dark tunnel opened, but her attention was on Darren, who, having just pulled his gaze from his first veil cat sighting, turned to see a giant willow tree split and open a tunnel into darkness. He rubbed the back of his neck, likely continuing to question his life choices.

Rose guided Darren and Juliette to Carter, showing them how best to hold onto each other or the scruff of Carter's neck. He allowed them all a moment to position themselves, and then he was off.

This time, Rose counted. One, two, three. How long did it take them to pass through this void, even with Carter's expertise? The space was vast—the darkness unending in all directions. Though Carter knew the way and easily led them, she could feel Juliette's hand tighten in hers. Darren's fingers accidentally bumped hers as he gripped a little more tightly onto Carter's scruff. To these other fae with immense magic, this space was terrifying. Rose felt for her own magic. Whatever dampened the god's power beyond the veil may or may not be at play here—she didn't think it mattered. The overwhelming nothing of the void meant there wasn't anything for their elements to manipulate. She loosed a breath. Gripping Carter's fur a little tighter herself, she nodded. Their plan would work.

Rose hadn't adequately prepared everyone for the plunge they took upon entering the realm beyond the veil. The river rushed around them as Darren shouted curses, and they all began swimming towards the shore. As Luc had teased her last time, Rose used her water magic to usher everyone across the river after the initial splash.

"A little warning might have helped," Darren said as he pulled himself onto the bank.

"It only would have made you nervous," Rose replied.

Darren glared as Juliette sent her wind rushing around them to dry their clothes. The city was before them in no time. Rose barely glanced at the familiar backdrop. What had first been the mysteries of the afterlife unfolding was now just another marker on her path to retrieve Luc and finally end this. The way to the drawbridge was familiar, and it was unsurprising that Cassandra leaned against the castle wall. They hadn't sheltered their arrival. She waited with a host of veil cats prowling at her feet and her arms folded over her chest.

"Do you have a plan for this rogue god now?" Her cats paused their pacing, tilting their heads as if to listen for the Compass Points' explanation.

Carter approached her, and she rolled her eyes. The cats growled. She unhooked her arms and began massaging her temples. She glared at Rose this time instead of Carter. "No matter how earnest the Vesten Point is in helping me, this realm isn't a dumping ground. I won't just hold Aterra here for you, and you can't send him"—she pointed at Carter—"to plead your case."

Rose wanted to laugh but knew Carter needed space to speak with Cassandra directly again. "He's not pleading my case," Rose said. "He's the one who wanted to work with you. I suggest you talk to him about our plan."

Cassandra's brow rose—intrigued. The veil cat on her left sat back on its haunches, its tail flicking back and forth, keeping time as the seconds passed.

"You're right. We do need your help," Carter said. He wasn't

     JILLIAN WITT

saying anything Cassandra didn't already know, but his words seemed to soften something in Cassandra's stance. "But we don't want to dump the responsibility on you. We want a partnership. Help us hold him. Let us save our continent."

"What does that entail?" she asked. "If not here, where will you put—" Her words were cut off as Carter took another step forward. The clowder of veil cats were in attack positions within seconds—hackles raised, and a rumbling chorus of growls echoed across the bridge. "They sense what you are," she said as her arms unfolded and scratched the head of the animal closest to her.

"It's not a secret here." Carter smirked, taking another step forward. "We want to hold him in the space between realms."

"That is questionable at best," Cassandra said. None of the animals took their eyes off the Vesten Point, nor did they move to attack. It was clear they were waiting for some kind of signal from Cassandra. "What about the balance?"

"We've got that taken care of," Rose said. Cassandra's gaze raked over Juliette and Darren, likely sensing the strength in them both. She already knew what Luc was. She could put together the pieces of their plan as quickly as they had.

"It might work..." she started, "but there's no guarantee." She hesitated.

Carter held her gaze and pressed. "Help us do this. I know you haven't asked, but think of it as insurance that I'll do more than shepherd spirits. I'll help you save your realm."

Cassandra's eyes hadn't left Carter. She almost seemed like she hadn't quite heard what he'd said. Or, possibly, she'd heard it but hadn't fully processed the words.

"You don't know what you're offering," she whispered.

"I know enough," Carter said. "You cared more for your realm sooner than the gods of the continent. This realm didn't have to be yours—it could have fallen after Celeste's actions. You took responsibility anyway." He sighed. "I can feel it—what you did."

"That's enough," Cassandra said, cutting him off.

Rose opened and closed her mouth, unsure what she was witnessing.

Carter glared at her in an odd standoff. He didn't continue whatever he was going to say, and he didn't shift so they could have a more private conversation. "I'd bet it's why Aterra could even attempt what he just did," Carter hissed through gritted teeth.

Rose knew what he was doing. He was respecting whatever boundary she'd put in place. He wasn't saying anything more of what he knew about her magic, but he'd use an example they all knew about—Aterra's attempted escape—to prove his point.

"I know the balance here needs to be corrected as much as that of the continent," he said. "What you did was risky!" The volume of his voice rose, and he shook his head.

Cassandra, still standing behind him, sucked in a breath. "It was necessary."

He sighed deeply. "I don't doubt it," he replied. "I just want to help you fix it."

"But you require payment?" She lifted a brow skeptically. "You will only help me if I help you?"

Carter sighed. "That's not what I mean." He held up a hand to stop her retort. "Though I know it's how it sounded." He ran his fingers through his hair. "Our problem is the same. The continent's imbalance affects this realm. We've been through this. We're trying to clean up the mess left for us, but we can't do it alone." He gestured to her. "Neither can you clean up the mess the gods' and Celeste's actions wrought on your land." His gaze finally met hers, and Rose saw the hint of a smile. "Think of it as us helping each other."

Cassandra pushed off the wall. "Fine. I'll do it. But you must know I can't do it alone." She eyed Carter skeptically.

Rose didn't miss Carter's smirk. One she was sure she'd never seen from him before. It was all charm and aimed directly at the Lady of the Veil. "I am at your service," he said.

Cassandra couldn't know what she was getting herself into

          JILLIAN WITT

but replied again anyway. "Fine." She nodded, and though Rose didn't understand the bargain that had just been struck, the light in Carter's eyes told her that he did—and he had won.

"You'll be able to cross back to the continent from the cell," Cassandra said as they walked down to the castle's lower level. "Once you secure him for movement, I'll open the wards momentarily."

Carter nodded as they walked. This instruction was mostly for him anyway. Their ability to cross back to the continent from within the castle had been restricted. This, too, was something Cassandra controlled. No matter what Carter hinted about her magic failing and letting Aterra slip from his cell, Cassandra was still a formidable ruler.

That was a problem for another day. She glanced at Carter and Cassandra, who were still speaking softly as they walked briskly through the castle. The way things were going, it would be Carter's problem to solve.

The tunnel leading to the cells was still collapsed. She guessed that was a good sign since the ones most qualified to move it were on the other side. Rose glared at the mess. It held the biggest problem they needed to solve but also separated her from Luc.

"I can move it. We just need to be ready when I do," Luc said through the bond when she asked him.

She looked at the others before giving Luc the go-ahead to clear the way. They were ready to act quickly once it was done. Aterra was already getting desperate. His brute force attempt to break free of Cassandra's cell was evidence of that. This would be his last chance to try something if they were successful. Luc was already on edge—he suspected his father had more tricks up his sleeve.

Rose tended to agree with him. Aterra had plotted for hundreds of years. His son disagreeing with his plan and not participating willingly was something he would have anticipated. She agreed with Luc's caution, and glancing at Darren, she knew they'd done everything they could to prepare for Aterra's strike.

"*Ready when you are,*" Rose said to Luc.

The collapsed tunnel that blocked their way started to shake and break apart. Luc wasn't just moving the rock. He was decimating it. Anything he didn't know where to put, he crumbled into dust.

The hallway opened. Rose could see Aterra in a cell, with Luc sitting against the wall on the other side. Luc stood as he poured more magic into removing the collapsed tunnel barrier. Aterra's magic flared as the rock shook. The god hadn't had much time to recuperate, but rocks rumbled and fell as his magic overtook the space, trying to interrupt Luc's work. He might be unable to tunnel out of the castle, but that didn't mean his magic was useless here.

Cassandra glanced at Carter, and he nodded. Whatever their communication, Aterra sprang free from his cell afterward.

Now freed, he cracked the ground and sent waves of stone toward the hall they'd entered through. Pieces of earth slid from beneath them and lifted as he attempted to disrupt the incoming party. Juliette's wind pushed to break the stone down into smaller pieces. Rose let her work without calling on their joined power. She kept her gaze locked on Aterra.

"*Rose, look out!*" Luc sent through the bond.

Only as Luc feared for Rose did his attention slip from his father. The Suden god must have been waiting for it. The group had barely dealt with the rock onslaught when Aterra revealed his true attack. Rose noticed too late the familiar glint of onyx and gold on Aterra's finger.

Luc rolled his eyes at his own stupidity, but he was already in Aterra's grasp. The pointed tip of the ring struck Luc's neck before his magic could react.

"LUC!" Rose couldn't stop the scream that ripped through her as the needle pierced his skin.

Luc gave her a lazy smile as if Aterra's trying to overwrite his will and make him compliant wasn't a problem. With the needle sunk into Luc's neck, Aterra had everything he needed.

Aterra's grin was all teeth as the Suden magic of the ring lashed out into Luc.

Rose tried to tell herself they'd done everything they could. They'd prepared for every outcome. Luc had survived being struck by this once before. Aterra had survived when Luc struck him with the same magic.

The breath left Rose's lungs as Luc's body shook, absorbing the power. He took another step to get away from his father but crumpled to the ground.

"This place has its own magic—more than the continent," Aterra said. "I have the artifact and the Suden Point's blood and…" They all watched as Luc stood again. A blank sheen covered his dark brown eyes, making Rose deeply uncomfortable as Aterra finished speaking. "Now I have his will."

Luc nodded and said, "Take what you need, Father."

CHAPTER THIRTY-SEVEN

Aterra's brow creased, his confusion evident as he pulled harder on Luc's magic to get the power boost he'd plotted for. With every moment that passed, he tried to dig deeper into the magic. His confusion was understandable. Rose had seen how easily the power flowed when the process worked, as the Compass Points had tested between Arie and Carter.

Aterra had done everything right. As he said—he had the artifact, he was in a place of great magic, and he'd stolen the will and blood from Luc.

The problem was—Luc was no longer Suden Point.

Rose used Aterra's momentary confusion to ready the Compass Points' magic. She dove into her lake of power. The connections to Carter and Juliette were easy to find. The tree trunk tunnel that mirrored the passage on Vesten property, and the windswept doorway that mirrored the entrance to the portal at Osten house.

What would this new connection look like?

She stood on the shore of her lake and looked for something new. Luc was still connected to her through her lakebed. That onyx presence wasn't going anywhere—it was a part of her now. Even in his crumpled state, as he fought off the magic of the Suden ring, his power was sure and steady beneath the waters.

This connection point would be like Carter's and Juliette's, outside of the water, on the shore. Only now, searching for a new one, did she realize how intimate it was that even Luc's initial connection, the tunnel, was in her water—the very heart of her magic.

She should have known from the beginning that their connection was something different. Maybe she did.

"We were always something different. Something the continent wasn't ready for—but what it needed nonetheless." She smiled as Luc's voice pierced her thoughts. He must be waking.

The earth shook beneath her feet. When she looked up, a hole appeared past the southern shoreline.

Rose ran to it. It was deep, and she couldn't see a bottom. She hoped this harkened back to Darren's feelings about the hole in Loch, and wasn't a way to tear through the heart of her magic. She smiled to herself—her connection point with Darren, would start with his perception of Luc. She peered into the hole and sent her magic gently into it, requesting whatever he was willing to offer.

Darren's magic shook the ground in acceptance. They were ready.

Rose released the breath she'd been holding as she left the heart of her magic, and Luc returned to himself. The slight curl of his lip into her favorite smirk was its own kind of reward. He pushed himself up.

"He's all yours, love," Luc said.

Aterra shook his head as he noted the tilt of Luc's head, a signal he was mentally communicating with Rose. He clenched his teeth together as he finally realized something hadn't gone his way.

"What did you do?" He glared at Rose like this was all her

fault. She shrugged, unbothered, though unwilling to waste Aterra's momentary confusion.

Rose ignited the connections to the Compass Points. She reached into the heart of her power and pulled their magic together. Water, wind, fire, and earth magic rushed through her, meeting in a central stream of magic directly pointed at the Suden god.

They'd done this in the cavern below Mount Bury. They'd held a god but had nowhere to put him. Luc had made a decision for them by taking Aterra here—beyond the veil. Rose respected his decision. It was the best they had at the time. But Cassandra was right. The veil wasn't a dumping ground for the continent. The realms were connected, as Carter had argued. Both realms needed to be balanced for everyone to thrive on the continent and in their afterlife.

That worked for Rose. They had a new plan for Aterra. He wanted to strengthen his own power. He tried to rule whatever land he occupied. They would give him no land to occupy, making it impossible for him to plot. They would put him in a space where no one resided.

The idea had come to Rose slowly. Although her and Carter's journey proved the space between realms was vaster than it appeared, the shared memory of Luc's journey gave her the initial spark. The space between the continent and beyond the veil wasn't easily traveled by any party.

Rose thought again of Zrak's words about her and Luc's relationship being the key to his choices. It was, in more ways than she could truly understand. Luc had thrown himself into the void without knowing how to cross beyond the veil. He didn't have the innate skill that Carter's veil cat did in understanding the paths between realms. No, it was Luc's connection to Rose that drove him forward. He knew where his bound partner was, and though she knew what it cost him from the memory he shared, he knew to cross; he had to walk away from her.

He had to walk through the emptiness.

He had to cross the expanse of nothing.

Rose was glad he did because it was the perfect place to store a god who strove to be all-powerful. He could be all-powerful over the nothing between realms.

Rose glanced at Carter as the combined power of the Compass Points poured forth, pushing against the deflection Aterra attempted.

"What did you do?" Aterra roared. His magic pushed against theirs, but Rose understood it better this time. She also understood that this place wasn't helping him like the wild magic at the Lake of the Gods had. "Why didn't the power transfer work?" Aterra growled, his head swiveling from side to side as he assessed the threat of the Compass Points.

He moved again, reaching for Luc with the ring but finding himself held in place. His power flared, and the dungeon quaked with his rage. Stones crumbled, and loose rocks scattered, but this was far from the power he'd displayed beneath the Lake of the Gods. Aterra's power had limits here. It would have limits where he was being taken as well. The space between worlds had no earth to manipulate. His element would be meaningless there.

Rose pushed the stream of magic within her even harder as Aterra reached for Luc again. Even if it was pointless, she couldn't stand the thought of this father who'd abandoned him trying to further abuse his connection.

"Are you going to tell him? Or should I?" Rose asked through the bond.

"Consider it one of the first gifts I'll give you," he said. *"The first in a long line of ways I'll make this up to you."* She smiled as he teased her. As much as she had enjoyed him on his knees, crawling to her in the heart of her magic, there was no ledger between them.

"One doesn't preclude the other," he said, hearing her thoughts and winking at her across the room.

"It won't work," she shouted at Aterra. A smile grew as she

said the words that would bring his plan crumbling to the ground. "He's no longer the Suden Point."

"What do you mean? Of course, he's the Suden Point! He's the most powerful Suden on the continent! I made sure of it!" Aterra roared. The ground shook beneath him as his magic struggled against Rose's hold.

"But I'm no longer on the continent," Luc said with his wicked smile. "And I felt it was a dereliction of duty not to have a Suden Point in my absence. I wanted to ensure we had a leader incorruptible by your plans, a leader who would do what needed to be done for the Suden people and the continent." Luc gestured to Darren, who held his gaze briefly, accepting his words with his own nod—his own acknowledgement of what he would do.

"Ready Carter?" Rose asked. Aterra may be weaker here, but sweat still dripped down her brow as she channeled the magic of the Compass Points to hold him.

He stalked closer to Aterra but didn't shift. Rose would lose his power through the connection as soon as he did. They needed Aterra to be immobile, and they would only have seconds to make this work.

Luc seemed to realize what she needed. While the Compass Points' hold leashed Aterra, he yanked the ring off his father's finger. "I'll be taking this back." He didn't hesitate, repeating the motions from under Mount Bury. With the ring on his finger, he stabbed Aterra with the already outstretched point. The same point Aterra had tried to use against him.

Aterra froze momentarily.

Carter growled as he fell to all fours in his veil cat form.

The magic around them changed as Cassandra allowed Carter the freedom to move within the castle walls.

Carter wrapped his mouth around Aterra's leg, and Luc grabbed Carter's scruff. For a brief moment, Carter's yellow-green eyes searched the room as if looking for the best path to cross. He stared at the cave wall next to the cell. His gaze pierced the stone.

     JILLIAN WITT

Then he jumped, the passage to the continent opening before them as it had above the river and out on the plains. The veil cat didn't hesitate, pulling the Suden god and demigod along with him.

The hole didn't close, but they were running out of time. Luc's move to stun Aterra would only buy them so long.

Seconds that felt like hours later, Carter returned—alone. Luc was placed in the Osten caves, and Cassandra was here. Together, they would close off this passageway between realms, sealing Aterra's fate. Rose remembered Cassandra's words: "*You must know I can't do it alone,*" she'd told Carter. The Vesten Point seemed ready to do whatever he'd bargained for as he stalked to Cassandra's side in his animal form.

The Lady of the Veil's hand went to his scruff. Instead of jumping into the passage, Rose felt a pull of magic.

Cassandra had said she couldn't do it alone. Carter had said he was at her service. As the magic flowed in the castle dungeon, Rose knew he offered himself to bolster whatever magic Cassandra needed. Power flowed between them. Rose had only ever seen this much power exchanged when the Compass Points merged their magic. She swallowed and hoped Carter knew what he was doing.

She was familiar enough with Carter's magic that she felt it heating the room as Cassandra pulled so hard his element took over. The cyclical nature of flame and shift had never been more evident to Rose than in this moment. Carter's power flared hot like his element and cooled like a spirit falling into the icy river surrounding these lands. His magic twisted with whatever Cassandra's power was, and it seemed to both burn and freeze the hole between realms as it started to seal.

Aterra roared as he awoke from the ring's strike in the darkness. She heard his yells but didn't feel his earth magic at all— there was nothing to use against them where he was. The pathway through the wall Carter had opened continued to seal with the combination of his and Cassandra's magic.

"I've closed it here. He won't be able to get through," Luc said through the bond.

"He's done it," Rose said, alerting Cassandra and Carter.

Cassandra's fingers dug impossibly further into Carter's scruff as she requested more magic. The veil cat growled, setting off a chorus of noise from the pack of veil cats standing guard around the Lady. With this final pull on the connection between Cassandra and Carter, the pathway sealed.

They had done it.

Carter shifted back into his fae form. He looked as if he would reach for Cassandra momentarily—his hand outstretched—but it gently fell to his side as he looked at the mark on the wall their magic had created.

Even though it had only been the two of them, and Luc on the other side, the symbol on the wall looked strangely like a compass. It was a circle with locks over the four cardinal direction points.

Rose wanted to believe it would hold. More than anything, she wanted to see what Luc had done on the other side.

"I'll be back," Carter told Cassandra, realizing the group needed him to leave.

"Take care of your people first," she said, looking resigned. "I still have time, and if things aren't settled on the continent, we won't settle them here."

He turned to her and nodded. Rose might be over-reading, but she would say a lot was communicated in a single nod. Carter wouldn't spare more words to try to convince her of his intention. He would prove it to her by returning.

A cool mask once again slid over Cassandra's face. "You should go back the standard way, head to the fields outside the city," she said. She sounded tired and a little wistful as she let them go. The Lady of the Veil had dug deep into Carter's magic. Rose wondered what she had found.

"We should get back," he said to Rose, Juliette, and Darren.

 JILLIAN WITT

"Let's see what damage the Suden Point did to my caves," Juliette said.

"Not really the Suden Point anymore," Darren pointed out.

Juliette laughed. It sounded good on her. Juliette had carried more weight than the rest of them through this ordeal. Her connection with Zrak was something she had to work to sustain. Rose couldn't imagine what Juliette would feel to truly be free of the ritual. "You've got me there," she said as they left the castle.

CHAPTER THIRTY-EIGHT

For the first time, Rose landed gracefully in the Osten caves. She had barely stood when fingers intertwined with hers.

Luc.

She gripped back tightly, pulling him into a desperate embrace. Her lips pressed to his, a promise that she would never let him go again if she could get away with it. His returning kiss was just as bold, his tongue sweeping into her mouth as he cupped her face in his hands. The touch of his skin on hers was electric, a power she was only beginning to understand—one she'd spend the rest of their existence studying.

Someone coughed behind them. She broke from Luc and searched the cavern in which Juliette had paid so much. Rose hoped this would be the last time the Osten Point had to visit these caves. Juliette smirked at her, as if she, too, was finally starting to believe it was over. Of course, Juliette and Carter had landed gracefully. Only Darren, still unused to the travel, ended up on his hands and knees.

Luc's hand slid back into hers, unruffled by their interruption, and led them to where Darren pulled himself off the ground.

Luc let his other hand reach for Darren's. "Thank you. I know that took a lot of trust."

Darren tilted his head. "I couldn't say no to the Suden Point."

Luc let go of Rose's hand only long enough to slide the gold ring with the onyx stone off his finger. He laughed as he reclaimed her hand and dropped the ring into Darren's open palm. "I hope you don't expect that to be the way it works for everyone. I assure you," he said, looking around the room at the Compass Points, "they had no problem saying no to me...frequently."

Darren smirked as he stood, wiping the dust off his pants. "That was not pleasant."

"I don't want to tell you how many trips it took before I was able to land on my feet," Rose replied.

"Well, hopefully, that was our last one," Darren quipped.

"Speak for yourself," Carter said back in his fae form.

Rose glared at him. "How dangerous is the task you're helping her with?"

Carter directed his attention to the wall, the first location he and Rose used to journey beyond the veil together. "I don't know for sure. But I know she can't do it without me. I also know it's the right thing to do. Our continent and her realm are connected."

Rose pulled her hand down her face in a very 'Luc' gesture. She agreed with him, but part of her wished it was a burden she could have carried.

"This matches the other side," Carter said, pointing at the circle on the wall. He floated fireballs around them to light up the room, giving the cave that eerie purple glow.

Luc smiled at her and kissed her cheek. "You won't get him to say he shouldn't have done it," he said. Carter released a breath like he appreciated Luc's intercession. Rose was far from letting this go, but whatever it was, it was done. The best she could do now was make sure Carter knew she'd help him when he needed it.

"He did what he had to do. Just like I did by taking Aterra

beyond the Veil in the first place." Luc shrugged. "Thank you," he said, his gaze resting on Carter.

Carter nodded but didn't make eye contact.

"Do we think this will work?" Darren asked.

"Dear old Dad hasn't come bursting through yet," Luc hedged. A mischievous gleam danced in the corner of his eye. "Trust me, he would have if he could. You couldn't see it, but without Carter—without a veil cat to show the way through— the space between worlds is challenging to navigate. I'm amazed he and I made it through the first time."

Juliette tipped her chin up in thought. "I can't believe you gave up the Suden Point seat," she said, leveling her gaze at Luc. "How do you know that part won't backfire now that you're back on the continent?"

Darren's face squinted in thought. Maybe he hoped this was a temporary position.

"As Rose said, we needed to rethink our definition of balance. When the gods first corrected their mistakes, they left three on the continent with the four compass points. But the scales have changed based on their actions and Aterra's." He sighed. "We didn't want another situation like yours and Zrak's."

"You think you can bridge the power gap with Aterra in between realms?"

Luc nodded. "And when I met Darren in Loch... I can't explain it, but I knew I wasn't meant to be Suden Point." He gestured to Darren. "If another Suden of my generation had that kind of power—I couldn't remain in the position."

"So, this is what rebalance looks like?" Juliette asked. "Three gods and a demigod on the continent, four Compass Points, and the rogue god held between realms?" Her gaze slid to Carter. "Oh...and a Compass Point inextricably linked with the Lady of the Veil."

"I think so." He shrugged. "The Veil and our continent were already linked. Even if Cassandra had let us leave Aterra there, and I was not needed to hold this space between realms closed, I don't think a demigod could remain a Compass Point—it might be less significant in the face of some of our problems, but it's an imbalance of its own."

Rose agreed.

"I didn't want to bother Aaron since I knew he was already handling a lot, but we don't have to worry about the Suden test for power being invalidated now that you're back?" Carter asked.

Luc waved his hand. "No, it's irreversible. A past Suden can't reclaim power, even if something happens to the current Suden Point before the next is found." He smiled at Darren. "The job is all yours."

Carter, no longer concerned their plan would fall apart, was ready to move them along. The Suden god was held safely in the space between.

"Let's get going. We may have removed the problem of Aterra, but we need to make the sacrifices and remove the mist plague."

"Oh, you're going to love this," Rose said, squeezing Luc's hand and looking back at Darren. They hadn't had the pleasure of the Osten caves yet.

"The way you say that," Darren said, "leads me to doubt very much that I will love this."

Rose smirked.

"Here's hoping this is the last time any of us have to come down here for a long, long while," Juliette said as she led them out into the ridge.

"THAT WAS TERRIBLE," Darren said. "You did that regularly to commune with the Lost God? No wonder you hate him."

Rose wasn't sure hate was the right word for Juliette's feelings about Zrak. From her brief understanding, it was much more complicated than that, but Juliette only nodded as Lela greeted them in the hallway at Osten house.

"Success?" she asked, looking among the Compass Points.

"Best we can hope for," Carter replied as he left the house.

"You should come with us, Lela," Juliette said. "We need to perform a sacrifice before we can heal the continent from the mist plague."

Lela's eyes widened at the opportunity, and she was quick to drop whatever she'd been doing and follow the continent's leaders.

The group gathered on the beach in front of Norden house. Some unspoken understanding led them there. This was where they met to do the annual lake refilling ritual. This was where they would unite to sacrifice, to heal the continent.

Arie, Aurora, and Zrak walked out as the group readied themselves on the beach.

"Success?" Zrak asked, echoing Lela's words.

"With Aterra, yes," Rose replied. She gave Carter a little side-eye to see if he'd say anything about his commitments beyond the veil. He didn't, and Zrak didn't press.

"Now we must heal the continent and take care of the people we steward," Juliette said.

"Making the sacrifice here should be as good a place as any," Zrak said, walking to the shoreline. "Do you each know what you'll give?"

The Compass Points looked amongst themselves. Rose saw Darren eye the ring Luc had given him. They hadn't discussed the details of the sacrifice. Zrak had shared that information before he arrived. She had an inkling that they were all on the same page. "Something that means a lot to us and our people? Something powerful?"

Zrak nodded. Darren looked at the ring again, and she knew they had the same idea. The gods had gifted these artifacts to the Compass Points at the creation, but each of the current leaders was where they were despite the god's meddling—not because of it. It was time for the Compass Points to stand on their own.

"I'll sacrifice Aurora's dagger." Rose looked at the goddess as she said it. She was lucky because she'd still have the compass, even after the dagger was gone.

"I'll sacrifice Aterra's ring," Darren said, holding up his prize. "It's done enough damage from what I've learned." He spared a glance at Luc as if he still wasn't sure this was his decision to make now that Luc was back.

Luc wrapped his arms around Rose and rested his chin on her shoulder as he said, "All you, Darren. I'm Mr. Norden Point now."

"Exactly as I knew he would be," Arie said.

Rose snorted but leaned back into Luc's embrace.

Juliette pulled at the necklace that always hung around her neck, hidden beneath her dress. The vial with Zrak's blood. "I guess I don't need this anymore." Her gaze narrowed as she looked at Zrak, who nodded.

"It's still powerful," Rose said, adding what she feared Juliette wouldn't, especially with her patron present. "And it still means something to the Osten people. Even if they never know exactly how much you sacrificed to keep them safe."

Rose turned her glare at Zrak, who coughed into his fist. She noted Lela's critical gaze tracking the conversation and nodded in acknowledgment of what Rose said on Juliette's behalf. The glare Lela lobbed at Zrak was one Rose never wished to be on the receiving end of.

"I would do anything for the Osten," Juliette said. "It was my commitment to myself as Osten Point that I would ensure the required sacrifice ended with me." She smiled softly at Lela, whose stare was still fixed on Zrak. The familiar catlike grin crossed Juliette's face as she looked at Rose. "I wouldn't have been able to do it alone."

Those words meant much to Rose. They held everything Juliette wasn't saying. Everything Juliette was attributing to Rose in this journey, even if she resisted Rose's actions at first.

"It wasn't me," Rose said. "We all had to work together to get to this point. I was just ready to shake up the Compass Points."

All eyes swung to Carter, anticipating his sacrifice. The Vesten Point loved the Burning Coin more than words could describe, and they all knew it. Receiving the coin was what had changed his relationship with Rose. It was also what had unlocked his ability to access the unique gifts of the veil cat. Rose was sure he would be nervous to be without it. What if he could no longer access those gifts? What if he couldn't fulfill his promise to the Lady of the Veil?

"Believe it or not, I am confident I can access my veil cat gifts without the coin," Carter said as if reading Rose's thoughts. "I like having the coin as a reminder though. A reminder of what we were all like before you brought us together." He shrugged. "It gives me a goal, something I don't want to let happen again."

Rose nodded. "We won't let you forget that," she said. "And it makes the coin an even more important sacrifice."

Carter nodded, pulling the coin from his pocket.

"Alright, if everyone has their sacrifice, we should start a fire," Zrak said, his head turning to Arie. "Will you do us the honors?"

Arie glanced at Zrak and nodded. They must have had a conversation while Rose and the others were gone. Arie was no longer openly hostile to Zrak. It was progress, but any change to their relationship would take time. Arie tossed a few sticks together on the beach—for optics, she was sure—then set them ablaze. Rose didn't have to ask what came next.

"Will the magical items burn?" Rose asked. "Not that I'm doubting your flame, Lord of Fire," she teased.

"Oh, they'll burn," Arie said.

Carter moved toward the fire first. With no ceremony, he tossed the coin into the center of the flame. Rose followed, throwing the dagger in right after Carter. Darren gave the ring a longing glance and did the same. Juliette paused.

"It's been such a weight on me for so long. I don't know what I am without it." Her words were a whisper. A conversation meant for only Rose and Lela to hear.

Rose nudged her gently with her hip. "You're the leader of the

Osten fae. The one who saw them through an ordeal they were generally unaware of. One who carried all of their burdens and the burdens of your predecessors with grace and determination." She paused. "You're kind of a badass, in case you didn't know."

Lela beamed at Rose's words. Juliette's eyes lit up as they met Rose's. "Oh, I'm well aware," she purred. She took a final deep breath and tossed the vial into the fire.

The flame that followed with Arie's help was stronger and hotter than anything Rose had ever felt. She had to take a step back from the blaze. It burned and burned, and Rose could see the magic of the items released into the atmosphere.

Finally, she glanced at Zrak. "Do we have to do anything else?"

Zrak's gaze appeared to track the release of the magic as well. His eyes only moved to hers when she felt a pop and a wave of magic cascade from the fire in all directions. Her hair blew back from the gust of the magic's release.

"That should do it," he said.

CHAPTER THIRTY-NINE

Despite the sacrifices, the Compass Points had to travel together to heal the continent. No matter Rose's personal preferences, she knew the others were right when they suggested going to the northeastern cities, where the mist plague first originated. They all had things to do at Compass Lake, a new continent they wanted to work towards, but all of their magic would be required to pull those impacted from their slumber.

Rose ached to get to Bury, thinking of Tara lying in the barn outside of town, but she respected their decision.

Luc traveled with them, his horse never far from Rose's, their new wordless communication a source of constant annoyance to their travel party. Darren had asked Luc to help announce his position as Suden Point, but Rose knew Luc wouldn't have so easily been parted from her even without Darren's request.

"We will stop in Bury on the way back," Carter said days into their ride. They had taken a seldom-used eastern path out of the mountain range that held Compass Lake, then took a northern road in the valley on the continent's eastern side. They thought they had a good idea of everywhere the mist plague had struck. Zrak had outlined his targets on a map for them before they left.

They would need to go northeast. Then, they could follow the Nebulus's path southwest. It would be a long trip. The fae leaders would need to spend weeks circling the continent, but this was their priority.

They were almost to the village of Eris. Rose could see the mist hanging around it as they rode. "We'll have to see if we can move it from the outside," she said. She hadn't had time to make a weapon for Darren though she would eventually.

"Let's give it a try," Carter hedged.

The Compass Points hopped off their horses outside the gates. It was easy now for Rose to make the internal connections of their magic. In a matter of moments, she was at her internal lake, the power of the Compass Points flowing through her. She focused on Eris. This wasn't holding a god, but it was shifting a god's power. She let the stream of their combined elements flow from her. It acted as a strong gust of wind, sweeping the mist away from the village.

"That was easy," Rose said, watching the mist dissipate under their magic's pressure.

"Let's go see if it worked," Juliette said more cautiously.

"These are the spirits I'm most worried about," Carter added. "I'm not sure all of them will be able to find their way back to their bodies after having been separated for so long." He'd explained to them that the longer the bodies lay in the endless sleep, the more likely it was their spirits left them. Carter was still convinced they weren't dead. The spirits weren't trying to cross beyond the veil. They simply ventured while the physical body slept.

Rose nodded. This first village taken was one Aurora had initially noticed. The reason the remaining gods had come together and taken the test Zrak had laid out for them under Mount Bury. Rose was trying to do the math; that must have been three hundred years ago.

The mist plague rapidly increased in its presence once Aterra took the Norden Point seat through Aiden, but its origin point, the few villages hit in the first few hundred years, might be more challenging to correct than most.

"I can see some," he said as they entered the village gates. "They haven't all returned to their bodies," he mumbled quietly. Plenty of other villagers seemed to have immediately awoken and began to approach the Compass Points.

Rose and Luc surveyed the village and the approaching residents hand in hand. The questions started immediately as the people woke.

"What happened?"

"Is it over?"

"Who are you?"

These villagers had been asleep so long, they wouldn't even recognize the names of the Compass Points. Rose let Juliette speak first. She wasn't Osten Point when this village fell, but she had the most history of the Compass Points to offer them.

"We're here to help. We know this has to be incredibly confusing for so many of you. We are the Compass Points. You are likely only familiar with our predecessors." Juliette offered introductions and then took a breath. "I don't know how much you realize, but it's been hundreds of years since the mist plague took Eris."

Rose watched the crowd of villagers and noted a sea of nods at Juliette's words.

"Why do some of us still sleep?" someone asked. The crowd made noises of agreement at the question.

Carter glanced around. Rose knew enough to realize he was watching the spirits' movement. He looked at Rose, who shrugged. She knew what he would do. It would cause more questions, but if he was comfortable, the rest would be, too.

A moment later, Carter had shifted, and a veil cat stood before them. Juliette raised her voice and continued explaining things as Carter worked. Rose watched him growl at the sky. Her confidence in his abilities told her he was directing spirits back to their bodies, but those in the village didn't know that as they began to shrink back in fear.

"What is he?" someone yelled.

"That's no animal I've ever seen," another said.

"He's helping." Rose held out her hands in a gesture of peace. "Some of the spirits need help getting back to their bodies. The Vesten Point can shift into a veil cat. He can guide the spirits."

"I thought they were extinct!" someone shouted in the crowd.

More villagers woke with Carter's gentle growls. Until finally, everyone stood.

"We're rare but not extinct," Carter said standing before them again as a fae male. "You'll see more of me in that form, so please don't fear it."

The villagers looked on with hesitation. Rose thought that was fair. They had thrown a lot at these people in a very short time. As the remaining villagers woke and joined the group, the joy increased, and suspicion dimmed.

Action was how they would win this village's trust. They would be Compass Points who proved willing to do what they said.

Luc's hand slipped into Rose's as they walked through the village. He squeezed their interlocked fingers, and she smiled at him. He'd only been back for days, and they were on the road again, but she would never get used to the hum of her magic when they touched.

His magic thrummed in appreciation of her reaction and wrapped around the two of them. Their display may be visible to some villagers, but most were too concerned for their loved ones to notice the bound pair's flirtation. And Rose wasn't hiding that they were bound. She would continue her tenure as Norden Point the same way she'd started it—with as much honesty as she could. In the session Walter had organized with the Norden before Rose left Compass Lake, she told them about her and Luc. The continent's people needed to know relationships like hers and Luc's weren't impossible. Bound partners might be rare, but love between members of differing fae courts was something she intended to highlight.

While the others couldn't see their magic, they could smell it. Darren rolled his eyes in feigned exasperation as they walked the streets. "You two are the worst."

Rose didn't blame him, though he teased. It was unfortunate that their first few weeks together as bound partners were on the road with the Compass Points. Her desire for Luc was all-consuming—his need to touch her after their separation seemed to match her own.

"They deserve it," Juliette said with a wink. "They worked hard for this."

Rose agreed.

The Compass Points and Luc visited five other villages in the northeast in this manner. Slowly, they traveled west over the mountains. Rose's breath started to race at the familiar peak in the distance—Mount Bury—where so much of this began with the gods of this continent. More important to her story, it was the home she and Arie had created for ten years while hiding from Aiden and Compass Lake.

Rose had tried not to focus too much on Tara her almost apprentice—her friend. The young girl had seen Rose for what she was: not fae, but a talented weapons master. Most villagers only believed Rose to be a shop assistant. They never considered her the one to make and use the weapons herself. Tara had, and she begged Rose to train her as the mist plague worsened.

Tara had been so worried something would happen. And, of course, the worst had. Rose hadn't been in the village with her weapons when the mist hit, and she carried heavy guilt for leaving Tara defenseless.

She couldn't decide if she was excited or nervous to see Tara again. More than anything, whether Tara also blamed her, Rose needed to know that she was okay and had risen from her endless sleep.

Luc's magic wrapped around Rose as they rode. Her mind ran in circles of anxious thoughts. Her bound partner didn't say anything; his words wouldn't help. She knew she had to face whatever was at the Lake of the Gods, but his magic held her body steady while her thoughts scattered.

They made their way up the familiar mountain path. The west side of the crater was the part that held the village. The eastern side was so wild that there wasn't a direct path up. They had to go around the mountain to climb it on horseback. Rose bit her nails as they finished the ascent.

The Compass Points dismounted outside the village. Luc reached for her hand and squeezed before she started her work. Her heart thrummed in her chest. It was all she needed from him, and he knew it. He would be there for her no matter what happened in Bury. While not a solution to her concerns, it was a reassurance all the same.

Using their joined magic got easier each time she made the connections. Their power worked together effortlessly to push away the mist. Rose breathed as it swept away from the place she'd called home for so long. Taking Luc's outstretched hand, they entered the village as its occupants awoke.

Word spread through those who woke that the Compass Points were here. Though mainly human, this village considered Aurora its patron goddess. Rose hadn't thought there was much reason behind villages claiming patrons. She thought it had to do with location on the continent and that, generally, more Norden fae lived in the North. Now that Rose knew the history of the lake and that Aurora had created it, the designation was all the more fitting.

It made sense then, that this village was particularly interested in the new Norden Point.

Whispers followed them as they walked. Word had even spread that the Norden Point was a powerful weapons-master.

Rose received a few surprised gasps as those who knew her made the connection.

"Rose, you're the Norden Point?" The youngest of the Dawson family approached her. The young girl had been helping her family sell vegetables across the market aisle from Rose for years.

"Hi, Samantha," Rose said. "Yes, I am."

The girl's eyes went wide—and impossibly wider as they focused on Luc standing beside her. It seemed she recognized the ex-Suden Point. That was funny in itself. Rose had chosen Bury as a place to hide because the people seemed so far removed from Compass Lake politics. Rose had been so removed herself that she hadn't recognized Luc when he'd first arrived. But the Dawson family traveled more than most in the village to sell their vegetables at other markets.

"It's okay, Sam," Rose tried. "He's with me." She winked, and the girl relaxed a little. "Is everyone..." Rose coughed a little over the word. "Is everyone awake in the village? Carter, the Vesten Point, can help if anyone didn't wake up on their own." Rose couldn't imagine anyone here needed that level of help, but she asked anyway. This village had only been impacted for weeks instead of hundreds of years like Eris. Rose couldn't believe it had only been six weeks since the mist struck her island home—since this journey had started for her.

Luc squeezed her hand to return her attention to the girl before them.

The girl beamed. "We all woke up. I haven't seen anyone still sleeping. We're all meeting in the square now, though, to make sure."

Rose nodded. She'd expect nothing less from these villagers. They would do a full roll call and ensure everyone was accounted for. Rose's breath caught when the girl kept going.

"I've heard people asking about you," the girl said quietly. "The villagers realized we didn't know where you lived."

Some organ constricted in Rose's chest at the words. She

never truly considered herself among the Bury villagers—but the villagers counted her among their number. Luc's hand slipped into hers again and squeezed, a grounding gesture.

"I think Tara is searching..." The girl's words were cut off by a voice yelling Rose's name across the town square.

"Rose! Roooossse!"

Rose sucked in a breath and pushed her fingers tighter into Luc's solid grip. Her nails dug into his knuckles as her nerves overtook her. Tara's dirty blonde hair bounced in a ponytail as she ran. The pendant she always wore, a mark of her devotion to the goddess Aurora, bounced against her sternum as she sprinted through the square. Rose wasn't sure what to do. A part of her wanted to expect a hug. She imagined Tara throwing herself into Rose's open arms. But another part of her was sure she was about to face Tara's disappointment and anger for leaving her to this fate. Rose held her breath, unable to prepare for either option.

"Open your arms, you idiot. I'm not stopping!" Tara yelled as her feet carried her nearer.

Rose did as she was told, and the young girl threw herself into the Norden Point's open arms. Before Rose could overthink it, her arms collapsed around Tara, and she squeezed tightly. The number of times she'd assumed the worst, the number of times she thought Tara would no longer want a place in her life because her training failed when she needed it most—all her worries slipped away as Rose breathed in the girl's scent. This wasn't a magical scent. Tara was human, but it was the smell of fresh air and long days. It was a scent that reminded Rose of the home she and Arie had made. As she set Tara down and straightened herself, it finally occurred to her that it was a home she no longer claimed as her own. Luc's hand touched the small of her back as if reading her thoughts—maybe he was. She'd kept the link between them open more and more on their trip, addicted to the connection.

"I'm so sor—" Rose started, but Tara held up a hand to stop her.

"I knew you'd start with something stupid. The mist plague

came, Rose. You had prepared me the best you could. I've heard a lot in the short time since I woke. If the rumors are true, it seems you could have stopped it, so I won't say you couldn't, but you didn't know! And look at me! I'm fine. And you're fine."

Tara glanced over Rose's shoulder at Luc, his palm lightly pressed on Rose's hip. The weight of it was a reassurance Rose craved, but the placement was undoubtedly intimate to Tara's eyes.

"More than fine, it appears," Tara said with the most unsubtle wink Rose had ever seen.

Rose laughed loudly. "I am Tara. But are you okay? Was it painful being taken by the mist plague?" She'd been a little afraid to ask, but Rose needed to hear the answer.

Tara smiled. "It was like taking a nap. My body didn't know it was taking longer than it should. I awoke feeling refreshed. Although, I was instantly terrified to learn no one could find you."

"I'm sorry, Tara. I should have left a note of some kind for you. It's not an excuse, but Luc can attest I wasn't in the best state of mind when we left."

Luc nodded. Tara took that as permission to give Luc her full attention. Her posture held no fear like that of the Dawson girl. "What are you to her?"

Rose coughed.

Luc glanced at Rose, unsure if he should answer or let Rose handle it. She shrugged. "She asked you, not me," Rose replied playfully.

"Rose is my bound partner," he replied.

Tara may be human, but she understood the significance of the statement. "I didn't think..." She glanced at Rose, unsure how to finish the question.

"You seem like you know Rose well enough to understand that if she wants something, she will find a way to get it." Luc's smile was pure pride as he finished the thought, and it had Rose itching to reach for him again.

Tara nodded as if in complete agreement with his assessment of Rose's determination. She tilted her head. "You're also the scary Suden Point?" she asked, her gaze narrowed as she sized him up.

"I was." A smile curved his lip. He pointed back at Darren. "He's Suden Point now. You can decide if he can live up to the scary image."

Tara scrunched her nose like she'd already decided Darren didn't deserve the title, though she seemed to accept that Luc was no longer Suden Point quickly enough. "Do you still have magic? Can you protect her?" Tara asked.

The earth rumbled beneath his feet as he replied. "I will bury anyone who tries to harm her so deep within the earth they'll forget the sun existed." Then he shrugged. "However, I think you'll find she has her own defenses."

Tara nodded as if he had provided the correct answer in the test she was giving him. Rose and Tara had never spoken about her magic, but Rose had always suspected Tara knew more than she let on.

"It's not just water magic, is it?" Tara asked, looking at Rose.

She shook her head.

"I always knew there was so much more to you than we all saw," Tara said, though she seemed to be speaking to herself. She refocused on Rose. "Will you live at Compass Lake now?"

Rose couldn't speak as emotion tightened her chest, so she nodded. She coughed as she tried to spit out the question she hoped to ask. Tara was an orphan in the village. She lived at the temple. But she was undoubtedly human, and Compass Lake was predominantly fae. It was on her long list of changes to make. To offer more opportunity for fae and humans to live together, even in the center of fae politics at Compass Lake. She'd make space for humans the same way she would for fae with multiple elements. As with Walter's daughter, she needed them to feel safe and included to come out of hiding.

These were all on the list of changes she'd bring to the continent, but they wouldn't happen overnight. She wanted Tara with her, not just to help make the change but to be a part of the family she was building. But she had to know it wouldn't be easy. Rose tried to pour all of this into a rambling explanation.

Tara looked between Rose and Luc, trying to decide if there was a question in everything Rose had spewed.

"I think she's asking if you want to come live with us there," Luc said when Rose's grip on his hand tightened in a desperate plea. Rose nodded.

Tara's eyes widened, and she flung her arms around Rose's neck again. "Yes!"

     JILLIAN WITT

CHAPTER FORTY

Getting settled into their new life at Compass Lake was everything Rose had dreamed of—everything Rose had fought for.

"Are you going to help Darren at all?" Aaron asked as he, Andrew, Luc, and Rose sat on the beach at Norden house. His question was directed at Luc, but his eyes were fixed on his three boys playing in the water. Tara was with them, splashing at David, setting off a battle cry from the others coming to his defense.

"My goal is to stay out of his way." Luc shrugged. "It's bad enough that I'm still here." He scooted his chair closer to Rose and slid his arm around her. "But that can't be helped. I won't undermine his authority by offering suggestions."

"What if I want your suggestions?" Darren's voice carried across the yard as he joined them on Norden beach.

Rose gave the Suden Point a nod. She would let Luc sort this out. As much as he was no longer the Suden Point, these were his people—and his family. He was still very much Suden and needed to find his place with them.

"You know I'm happy to help you, Darren. It was never my intention to dump everything on you with no support. I just figured Aaron would do a better job than I could in getting you acclimated to everything, and it would be less contentious to have his help since you decided to keep him on your staff."

"And promote me," Aaron added. "Something my brother never thought to do." His words were cheeky, his smile wide as he delivered the barb.

Luc had dismissed the Suden elders as advisors when he took the position of Suden Point. Darren didn't try to reinstate them, but he was building a new set of advisors, with Aaron as the first. He had put out calls to the rest of the Suden population to nominate two others from various cities and villages across the continent.

"See," Luc responded with delight. "You don't need me. I'd only weigh you down with poor decisions."

Darren glared at Aaron. "We would welcome your input. I already told Rose this in the last Compass Points meeting, but we'd also like to help you with the school you're building."

Luc nodded. He had picked up his own project now that he was no longer leading the Suden fae. He had agreed with Rose, suspecting there were many more fae with multiple magic lines in the population. Beyond that, even more half-fae were being actively ignored by the courts at Compass Lake. He proposed to build a school to bring any of the magically inclined, even humans who practiced forms of blood magic, together to learn how to use their power safely—since the traditional court schools hadn't educated those who didn't fall into the strict definition of their element.

Rose and the other Compass Points had already begun changing that, but she knew Luc was right—it should be up to the individuals if they wanted to train with a specific court or in a place more catered to their abilities. Housing the school in Compass Lake Village ensured the courts were actively engaging with the community. Even Carter, Juliette, Darren, and herself needed to learn more about the types of magic on the continent to better understand how to support those who wielded them.

If anyone knew how to harness unruly magic, it was Luc. He

     JILLIAN WITT

was also working with his stepfather to teach the classes. After reading the twins' journal, it occurred to them that he must have been working with humans using blood magic for years.

"Hi, Juliette!" Tara's yell drew Rose's attention to the eastern border of her land. Juliette was walking over with Zrak and Lela. They looked tense, but the Osten leader couldn't let go of her anger at her Lost God overnight. Rose understood it; really, she did. No matter his knowledge, he had put his people in a terrible situation. Rose just hoped the anger wouldn't pass down to the next Osten ruler—selfishly hoping the Compass Points could find peace with the gods. The pinched glare Lela sent Zrak's way told Rose she wished for something that might not be possible. She waved at the trio as they approached.

"Are Arie and Aurora here?" Zrak asked.

Rose glanced around to see if Arie in his bird form had snuck up on her. "I think they're still over at Vesten house." As she said the words, she saw the tell-tale black bird flying over the lake and Aurora and Carter's shapes walking the western edge of her property. "Looks like they're headed here as well."

Rose marveled at the collection of fae and gods so naturally assembling on her beach. It was as unheard of for the Compass Points to collect like this as it would be for the gods to join them. But Rose found she was in no rush to have the gods leave. They weren't interfering with the Compass Points' rule of the continent. They were helping in a way that Rose imagined they originally intended the relationships between Compass Point and patron to work.

Even though Zrak faced reluctance from the Osten Point and her successor, he worked with them regularly to test the Osten magic now that he was no longer...lost. Rose could feel her wind strengthen just by his presence on the continent. She couldn't imagine what it was like for Juliette. Rose hadn't asked, but she suspected the strongest among them, like Juliette, would start gathering secrets on the wind from more than just the present.

Aurora spent time in the forge with Rose. It was sometimes

forgotten that Aurora was the master-maker of the gods. There was a reason she'd been chosen to make the compass that decided Zrak's fate. She spent as much time as they could spare working in the forge, teaching Rose what she knew. She even taught Tara when she could—regular weapons-making, not magical. But Rose didn't miss the gleam in Tara's eye when Luc talked of the human magic wielders his stepfather was reaching out to. She and Luc would have to speak with Tara about her options sooner rather than later.

"Lost in your thoughts again, Rose?" Arie appeared in bird form on her shoulder and spoke aloud. She'd accept him in whatever form he chose, but it made her happy to know the form he'd lived in for most of their ten years together was a preference, not simply something he used to hide who he was.

"I'm just enjoying how far we've come," Rose said.

"We still have a long way to go," Carter replied as he and Aurora arrived on the beach.

"Agreed. But we've got a solid foundation to lead us." Luc said. His magic wrapped around Rose as he spoke—a feeling that would never get old.

Rose didn't want to be a downer but couldn't help the questions that bubbled to her mind at Carter's approach.

He shook his head fondly at her. He already knew what she would ask. "It will be fine, Rose. I'll take care of it." He looked so confident that Rose could only trust him. "She wanted me to settle things on the continent before assisting her." He coughed at the word assist. Rose was sure she was missing something, but Carter had been tight-lipped about any further communication he'd had with the Lady of the Veil. It was his business, but Rose couldn't help but worry about him.

"Arie!" Tara called as she and the boys came up the beach from the water. "You said you'd show me how to make that pasta tonight. Annabeth said I could be in charge of dinner and the boys are getting hungry. Are you ready to start?"

Arie nodded and shifted into his fae form. "I am at your

disposal, tiny weapons-master." He followed her and the boys up the hill to Norden house.

"We had better go supervise," Aaron said, standing with Andrew.

"You're welcome to stay for whatever they're making," Rose told the group. "I volunteer Arie and Tara to cook for all of us." She smiled.

"Is that part of your official duty as Norden Point?" Luc laughed.

"I think it might be," she replied.

There was a chorus of nods, and everyone was headed up the hill to Norden house, leaving Rose and Luc alone on the beach gathering the cups and refreshment plates they had been using. Rose stacked the dishes in a neat pile to carry up before walking into the circle of Luc's arms.

"Is it everything you thought it would be?" she asked him.

"More," he replied and kissed her forehead.

"It's only been weeks since the mist cleared, and already, more progress has been made than the entire decade prior." He squeezed her tightly. "You're amazing."

She tilted her head to look up at him. "I'm only as strong as the partner who holds me up."

He chuckled. "I choose to believe you because it's good for my delicate ego." He bent and caught her lips in a scorching kiss. She met it—tongues sliding against each other, seamlessly picking up an exploration that would never be complete. The spark between them only grew the more they were together. Luc's hands skimmed her cheek—her neck. His fingers tangled in her hair.

"This continent is lucky to have you," he whispered as they parted. "As am I."

She nipped his lip. "I know," she replied with a wink.

He grinned as they shared breaths.

"Are you love birds coming?" Aaron called from the balcony.

Luc swatted a wave at his brother. "We'll get there when we get there," he called back.

"I love you," Rose whispered to him.

His mouth caught hers again. His answer was in the move of his lips across her skin. "I'm glad, because our paths are bound for this existence and the next." He smiled as they linked hands and walked up the hill to Norden house.

EPILOGUE

I t had been months since Rose had thought of the terrible staircase in Osten house. With the mist plague victims restored, Luc's magic school project, and her duties to the Norden and the Compass Points, Rose was rarely alone.

Sitting on the balcony of her and Luc's bedroom, reading, was a welcome moment of peace. Compass Lake was at its most beautiful as the sun was rising. A soft fog coated the lake that, in another time, could have been much more worrisome. But the mist plague was gone, the continent was restored, and the Compass Points did their best to bring forth the future they all dreamed of.

The pine and cinnamon scent hit her before she saw him. Luc groggily stumbled onto the balcony and took a seat next to her on the giant daybed. It had been her one furniture purchase since becoming Norden Point. It was wide enough for them both to sprawl out, and the hours they spent relaxing here at the start and end of each day were some of her favorites.

"Did the heroine get her happily ever after?" Luc asked as he snuggled beside Rose, throwing an arm across her waist and pulling her close. His magic wrapped around them. It was never far from Rose since they'd been reunited.

"I think she did," Rose said with a smile, setting her book on the table. She rolled into Luc's warmth.

"I knew she would," he said, pressing a kiss to her neck.

"It was a little sketchy in the middle there," Rose said. She could feel the exhale of a soft laugh against her skin as he journeyed lower.

Her lips parted as his mouth covered her nipple over her shirt. His hand, in no hurry at all, slipped under her sleep clothes and explored her skin, traveling toward her other breast.

"I'll admit I think she deserves the happily ever after she got."

Luc's hand cupped her breast under her shirt, kneading it as he replied, "Oh, she deserves so much more." Then he took her nipple between his teeth.

She hissed in pleasure, her body awakening at his touch.

The hand working her breast dropped lower, teasing the band of her undergarments until Rose was begging him to remove them.

"I guess our heroine doesn't like to wait," he laughed.

"Or maybe she's waited long enough," Rose replied. She didn't have time to enjoy their banter as he removed the final obstacle between them, granting him full access to her center.

She gasped as he explored her heat. His fingers swirled and slid. Her body arched to him—her bound partner. It had been months, and this bond between them was still a daily exploration. She would never grow tired of it.

Neither will I, he spoke to her through the bond.

The heat, the pleasure already building in her body, built with his words. Their bond heightened their intimacy in ways she didn't know possible. He was inside her in more than just the physical sense when they were together. She couldn't get enough of him.

I assure you, it's a mutual obsession, he said as he slipped another finger inside her.

She bit his shoulder to cover her moan. Though no one could

see them on the balcony, they weren't exactly in the privacy of their bedroom.

"Do you want me to stop?" he asked. The silk and sin in his voice told her he already knew the answer.

A growl slipped through her lips as she replied, "Don't you dare."

His chuckle was low as his weight slid further down her body. Her body buzzed in anticipation as his mouth came to rest inches from where his fingers worked. His breath on her core had her bowing further into his touch. As her body lifted of its own accord, he granted her the friction she sought.

The first lap of his tongue had her fingers tangling into his hair as she reached to pull him closer.

His laugh was sinful again as he resisted. "Don't rush me," he said as his tongue lapped again in a long, smooth stroke.

Something like a whine slipped from Rose's lips as his tongue and fingers worked her together. She could feel his lips curve into a smile as her body responded to his every move. He took pride in learning her every reaction.

Heat built rapidly. Her fingers in his hair didn't have to pull him closer. He devoured her with a single-minded focus. She couldn't process how much she loved him—how obsessed she was with their bond—how much she believed she had her own happily ever after, just like the heroine in her romance novel.

Then, all her thoughts scattered.

Luc didn't stop. His fingers and tongue wrung every drop of pleasure as she rode the wave of her release.

She felt boneless as he crawled back up her body, rolling over next to her. Her hands reached for him, cupping his face and pulling him into a scorching kiss. The taste of him, mixed with her own, already had heat building again in her core. She rolled on top of him as their tongues twisted together.

"My turn," she said through the bond, their mouths otherwise distracted. Her hands explored his naked torso. The defini-

tion of his muscles had her wanting to lick him. She settled for pressing kisses and nips on her path down his body, removing his undergarments as she sought her prize.

His length sprang free, and her hand explored, working from root to tip. Her tongue swirled the head in a tease that had Luc hissing before she took him in her mouth. The steel and silk of him mixed with the pine and cinnamon that was always present. She hummed as her tongue swirled, her mouth working to bring him as much pleasure as he'd brought her.

Her hand at his base worked in tandem with her mouth. He twitched and hissed again in pleasure. His reaction to her was its own high. She met his gaze; the adoration in his was more than she deserved.

"It will never be enough," he said into her mind, then his lips curled into a wicked smirk.

Then he was moving, lifting, and flipping them, sheathing himself inside her. A moan escaped as her body, more than ready, welcomed him. They moved together, each anticipating the other's wants before they could articulate. It was a language they would practice for the rest of their existence.

"Luc," she whispered as his mouth sought hers, their tongues sliding together in an exploration that never stopped. Her fingers scratched his scalp, and his pace quickened, both building toward their shared goal. Everything they'd been through had brought them this. She wouldn't change it for anything. Luc's lips captured Rose's moan as she reached her peak. He thrust through her pleasure before finding his own. The couple collapsed into each other's arms in their shared bliss.

Luc kissed her again. He opened his mouth to speak when a growl echoed across the lake.

Rose knew that growl. She'd heard it many times. It wasn't an alert of danger—well, not for the continent, at least.

"I guess he finally decided it was time," she said.

The echo of the growl quieted, but Rose could picture the

willow tree as it separated and took shape into the crossing Carter would use to return to the Lady of the Veil.

For updates on new books and more, join my newsletter:
https://jillianwitt.com/subscribe

ABOUT THE AUTHOR

Jillian Witt reads more romantic fantasy than is strictly necessary and writes books she would love to read. Her stories unleash powerful women into fantasy worlds, usually turn enemies into lovers, and always offer an escape from reality.

When not reading or writing, she's enjoying all four seasons in Michigan with her partner and their dog, Loki.

instagram.com/mythandmagicbookclub
tiktok.com/@mythandmagicbookclub

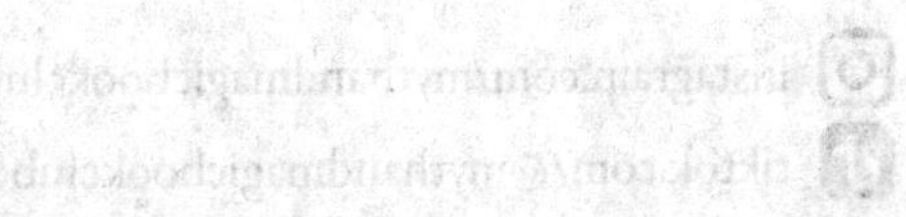

ALSO BY JILLIAN WITT

For a full list of Jillian's books, please go to www.jillianwitt.com/books,
or use the QR code below:

ACKNOWLEDGMENTS

I can't believe we're here! It felt like a lot to finish one book, let alone a trilogy. I'm thankful to all the readers who have joined Rose and Luc on this journey.

Thank you to Ian and, of course, our dog Loki. Our family walks remain my favorite place to brainstorm.

Rebecca, Kate, Isla, and Josh, you all continue to make my book baby better, and I forever appreciate your thoughtful feedback.

Rose and Luc's story may be complete, but it sure seems like Carter and Cassandra have an adventure out there waiting to be told.